CW01096279

Miss Bryson Heads For A Fall

The Eclectic Earl's, Volume 1

celeste de sales

Published by celeste de sales, 2024.

MISS BRYSON HEADS FOR A FALL

First edition. August 30, 2024.

ISBN: 979-8227975393

Written by celeste de sales.

To my lovely daughter, Emili whose unfailing support, constant nagging, and sly but pointed comments about sloth, not only induced me to finish this book but also exacerbated my ulcer. Thank you.

in all seriousness I wish to thank the many people who prodded, coaxed, and encouraged me to finish this book. There are too many to mention. :)

Chapter 1

April 1815, London

A Pride truly does go before a fall. Pride—and a pair of satin slippers on a freshly polished salon floor.

Flat on her back and disoriented, Miss Emma Bryson stared at the white painted ceiling of an elegant Mayfair townhouse. What the deuce happened? One moment she was reveling in the adoration of an audience enthralled by her singing, and the next she was laid out like a rag doll on a cold parquet floor. Her pride bruised. Her gown crumpled. And one question tumbling through her mind.

Had her fall ruined her chance to fulfill the deathbed promise she made to her mother to sing for the Queen?

The sound of rushing feet penetrated Emma's thoughts, and she lifted her head. Good heavens, the whole room was racing toward her, bearing down on her like dogs after a fox. She had not been this mortified since she had fled the altar, leaving a church full of wedding guests and a confused Hamish McIntosh behind. She had run then. She could run now.

Emma shot upward and a wave of dizziness crashed through her, and she collapsed back.

Perhaps not.

She needed a straight, unhindered way out of the salon. Emma clamped her eyes shut and prayed. Dear God, please clear a path for me.

"Clear a path, please," a deep masculine voice said, "and give the lady some air."

Emma gasped. Never had she received such a direct answer from above. The request for air an inspired touch.

"Are you hurt?" The voice hovered over her.

"No, I don't believe so."

"Are you certain? No bruises? No broken bones?" A shoe scuffed near her head, and a whiff of sandalwood intoxicated her. He must be close. But just how close? Emma opened her eyes. That close. Closer than any gentleman had ever dared. Even Hamish.

She squirmed backward, discomposure at his nearness replaced by fascination at his attire. Fashionable and stylish. A study in masculine elegance. Smooth black leather shoes, sheer white silk stockings, black satin breeches, a dark kerseymere coat, a neckcloth. A starched, flawlessly tied, snow-white neckcloth. Blindingly white. Emma shaded her eyes.

"Is something amiss?" he asked, amused.

"What? No, I..." Oh, dear. He had caught her staring. "I was admiring your neckcloth. It's exquisite. And extraordinarily white."

"The fields of Islington."

"I'm sorry?"

"Fields outside London. My valet insists on drying them there to avoid the soot."

"Oh," she said, but his look of expectancy demanded a more thorough response. "He must take his duties quite seriously."

"He does."

"You're lucky to have him."

"I am." He settled lower onto his haunches, and a shaft of dark wavy hair fell onto his forehead. "Now that we've established my good fortune in my valet, perhaps we can move on to a more immediate concern, Miss Bryson," he said. "Your unfortunate fall."

Heat crept across Emma's face, and she picked at the folds of her skirt. "Yes, well, I'm not sure how that happened."

"Alas, some things must remain a mystery. Though no reason for you to remain on a hard floor." He smiled, showing a line of even white teeth. "Shall we get you up?"

Emma nodded, and within moments, he had her to her feet and settled on a velvet-cushioned chair. Less horizontal and more composed, she dared a glance around the salon. To her amazement, the pale blue and white painted walls still charmed. Hundreds of wax candles still set the room ablaze. Vases overflowing with wisteria and roses, peonies and lilies, still reminded Emma of a lush garden.

A lush garden transformed into a cage by an encroaching mob.

"Good heavens," she blurted. "Must they gawk so?"

"Don't worry. They'll get bored soon enough."

"Do you think so?"

"Trust me. I know so."

The hint of cynicism in his voice impelled Emma to study him more closely. Upright and vertical, he was more handsome than she first thought. Tall and broad-shouldered. The sharp planes of his face softened by a hint of silver at the temples. An unexpected dash of elegance that prompted a lingering nod of approval from Emma.

"Does your neck hurt?"

"No." She smiled. "Why do you ask?"

"Your head keeps bobbing up and down."

Oh, dear. Caught again. She coughed and rubbed her neck. "You know, now that you mention it, I might've wrenched it a bit."

"The doctor will know what to do. Amelia is sending for him now."

"Amelia?"

"Lady Heyer."

"Of course." Her hostess, the wife of the Earl of Pembroke. And the highest-ranking lady willing to take a chance on an unknown singer.

If only she would hurry.

The mob did not seem to be anywhere near growing bored. They gawked and leered, as if Emma were an exotic animal at the Tower of London. Emma twisted her amber pendant in nervousness. The gold chain shimmered and caught the gentleman's eye. He stared hard at it, and a frown formed on his brow, surprising Emma. "Is something the matter?"

"No, nothing." His frown vanished, replaced by an easy smile. "Nothing except my atrocious manners. Allow me to introduce myself." He impressed Emma with a graceful bow. "Lord Blackbourne, at your service."

"Yes, yes, Blackbourne, thank you." Lady Heyer's soft agitated voice interrupted the introduction, and she swirled into view. "I see my brother has helped you, Miss Bryson," she said, "as I knew he would."

Her brother? Impossible. They looked nothing alike. He, dark and imposing like a block of granite, and she, light and fair and delicate as sea foam.

"I've sent for the doctor." She clasped Emma's hands in her own pale ones. "I'm only sorry I had to."

"Not as sorry as I, my lady." Emma's self-deprecation garnered a smile from Blackbourne, who said, "It shall all be forgotten by tomorrow, Miss Bryson. No one will remember a thing."

"Oh, yes, no one has any reason to," Lady Heyer said. "No one except—" She stopped, and her blue eyes grew large and round and apologetic while Emma's heart raced.

No one except who? Who, who, who?

"No one except... Mr. Claimore."

An icy dread filled Emma. Mr. Stanley Claimore. She had forgotten. Forgotten Lady Heyer had invited the well-known critic at Emma's request. Forgotten he had promised to write a review on her debut. Forgotten it would be published in the morning broadsheets.

By tomorrow, all of London will know of her fall. Worse, Prince George would. The one person she had spent the last six weeks trying to meet. The one person she needed to impress. The one person who could invite her to sing for his mother, Queen Charlotte.

Determination swelled in Emma. Mr. Claimore must not publish his review. She must stop him.

"I must go." Emma jumped up and darted forward and barreled straight into the rock-hard form of Lord Blackbourne. She reared back, but his arms swept around her and pulled her against his chest—tight against his chest. Emma gasped. Now much closer to a gentleman than she had ever been.

"My dear Miss Bryson," Blackbourne said as pulled her, if possible, even closer. "I'm afraid I can't allow you to go anywhere."

EMMA STOOD BY THE fireplace, her cheeks as hot as if a fire burned in the grate. Lord Blackbourne had allowed her to go somewhere. To a second-floor bedchamber of the Heyer townhouse. Pushed her to it. The imprint of his hand still burned against the small of her back.

"I believe you'll be more comfortable being examined in here, Miss Bryson," Lady Heyer said in a calm, friendly tone meant to soothe Emma. "Much more privacy."

"And much less gawking." Lord Blackbourne smiled at Emma. She did not return it.

"Thank you both," she said and headed for the door. "But I really must be—"

The door swung open, and a rotund gentleman lumbered into the room.

"There you are, Doctor Hamilton," Lady Heyer said. "Thank you for coming so quickly."

Quickly? Emma shot a glance at the mantel clock. It had been almost an hour since her fall.

6

"Always happy to be of service, Lady Heyer." Hamilton peered inquiringly at Emma. "Is this the patient?"

"It is, Doctor," Emma said. "And as you can see, I'm perfectly fine." She twirled around for effect.

"Be careful, my dear," he said with a laugh. "I understand you already took one tumble."

Heat mounted Emma's cheeks. "An accident, Doctor. I'm certain it won't happen again."

"Let's make certain no harm has come from the first one." He waved a hand at the settee. "Please, have a seat."

There was no getting out of it. Emma swallowed her irritation and sat, tense, and poised to flee as soon as he finished. His leisurely retrieval of a wooden stethoscope from his bag indicated it would not be soon. Finally, he sat beside her and lifted the stethoscope. "May I?"

Emma nodded and allowed him to place the stethoscope against her chest. He listened for a long moment, stepped back, and mumbled, "Mmmm, hmm."

"There, you see, Doctor—"

"Hold on," he said. "I'm not quite finished." He peered into one of Emma's eyes.

"My father was a doctor."

"Was he?" He peered into the other eye.

"Yes, in our village in Scotland." He lifted her arm up and down. "And I accompanied him quite often."

He lifted her other arm. "You must've been a great help."

"Yes, but more to the point, I know how an exam should go, and how quickly." She jerked her legs up and down like a marionette, forcing Hamilton to move back. "See?" she said. "Perfectly fine."

He placed his stethoscope back into his bag. "You do not appear to have come to any harm."

"Thank you." Emma jumped up. "Now if everyone is satisfied..." She started for the door.

"What of your neck, Miss Bryson?" Blackbourne asked, and she stopped, her hand on the doorknob. "My neck, my lord?"

"You mentioned something about injuring it."

"Oh, right, yes, I did... but..."

"An injury to the neck can be quite serious," Hamilton said.

Emma turned around and said, "It's perfectly fine, Doctor, I assure you." Her protest fell on deaf ears.

"You must allow me to make that determination. I'm certain your father would agree."

The late Dr. Cameron would agree—if she had injured it and not just been caught staring at Lord Blackbourne. She glared at that gentleman. Blast his brilliant neckcloth and the delightful silver at the temples.

"Please," he said, "have a seat."

Emma sighed and returned to the couch.

"Thank you. Now, how does this feel?" He tilted her head from side to side.

"No pain whatsoever."

"And this?" He gently moved her head up and down.

"I can touch my head to the floor if you wish, Doctor."

"No reason for that, my dear." He laughed and sat back. "There doesn't appear to be anything wrong."

"Thank you." She stood.

"Still," he said, tugging Emma back onto the settee. "I think it prudent you rest. Stay in bed for a day or so, just to be certain. One can't be too careful."

"I promise to go straight to bed as soon as I get home."

And after she stopped Mr. Claimore.

"Home? Where would that be? Surely not all the way to Scotland?"

"I'm staying with my Uncle Carstead in Grosvenor Square. Not far at all."

"A good half a mile, my dear. Much too far to be rocked about in a carriage." He turned to Lady Heyer. "Wouldn't you agree, your ladyship?"

"Yes. Much too far." She smiled at Emma. "You must stay with me, Miss Bryson, until you're well."

Emma blinked. Surely, they weren't going to insist she stay the night. How ridiculous.

"I'll come back tomorrow afternoon, Miss Bryson, to check on you." Hamilton picked up his bag and strode to the door. "Good evening, all."

"I hope this room is amenable, Miss Bryson." Lady Heyer gave Emma a smile.

"No, it isn't," Emma blurted. "Not at all."

"No? The green bedchamber is just down the hall, though not as large—"

"I beg your pardon, this room is lovely, but I meant I can't stay. I must leave. Now. This very moment."

"You heard Hamilton," Blackbourne said. "It's too risky for you to go anywhere."

"There's far more risk to me if Mr. Claimore publishes his review."

He studied her. "I see."

He could not possibly see.

"You're afraid of what he might write."

Fine. He might see a little. She tilted her chin. "Yes."

"Then allow me to put your mind at ease," he said. "He wrote your review long before he even heard you sing. The only thing he need add are incidentals, such as the style of your jewelry." He surprised Emma by staring at her necklace again. "And the color of your gown." He squinted. "Pink with purple flowers? A rather bold choice."

"Thank you," Emma said, unsure if he approved. She smoothed the folds of her gown. Not that his opinion mattered.

"The only real decision he need make is whether to describe your voice as brilliant or superior."

"Or whether I fell forwards or backwards," Emma countered. "Or both at once."

"I suppose that's a possibility."

"More than a possibility, my lord. It'll be the first thing he mentions."

"Whilst I know nothing stings harder than injured pride, Miss Bryson."

"Hardly a matter of pride." Emma bristled. "If I don't stop him, he'll ruin any chance of my singing for..." She stopped. Telling them she must stop Claimore was one thing, telling them of her deathbed promise quite another. "For others."

"I'm afraid it's too late."

"Not if I stop Mr. Claimore."

"You misunderstand me," Blackbourne said. "By now, the type has been set and the newspapers even printed."

"That quickly?" she asked. "Are you certain?"

"Trust me, I've a bit of experience with the press."

She knew that to be true. She had read his name in the broadsheets every day since she had been in London. What parties he had attended. What parties he planned to attend. No detail was too small to mention. Even the particularities of his wardrobe seemed to be of great interest to the press.

"So, you see, you must stay. If not for your own sake, then for mine."

"Yours?"

"I mean my reputation, of course, and Lady Heyer's for her hospitality." He smiled. "It'd be ruined if we were not seen to take care of someone injured in our home."

There had been no injury, except to her pride. Would it matter if she left now? She had no idea where Claimore lived or worked, and if Lord Blackbourne was right about the newspapers having already been printed, it would be a waste of time. No, she must stay the night and hope that Claimore's review wasn't as humiliating as she feared.

BLACKBOURNE LISTENED with half an ear to the bustle below his bedchamber window. The morning clatter usually engendered a strong desire to flee back to his country estate. Not so today. He barely noticed it. His mind pleasantly occupied by a smooth oval face and a pair of large expressive eyes.

Miss Bryson certainly was fetching.

Her unexpected bolt into his arms had confirmed his suspicions of a trim curvaceous body hiding beneath the demure gown, and when she had reared back, instinct—and habit—took over. He pulled her to his chest, determined to keep her upright and uninjured.

His gallantry had gone... unappreciated.

Surprise had flamed in those dark amber eyes and a deep blush suffused her cheeks, followed by a parade of other emotions. Anger, dismay, pride. Every emotion except the one Blackbourne usually saw when he held a lady—desire. He chuckled. Hardly a mystery why. They were standing amidst strangers in a crowded ballroom, after all.

There was a mystery, though. The necklace dangling from her slim throat. An exquisite, gold-plated chain. "None like it in all of England," according to the jeweler—and the very one Blackbourne had given his mistress.

"Do you remember the chain I purchased for Lady Wallingford, Simms?"

His valet helped Blackbourne into a linen shirt. "The one you bade me pick up, so you'd not miss a sparring match at Fives Court?"

"That's the one." Blackbourne slipped on the shirt and tucked it into his pantaloons. "The strangest thing. I'm positive I saw it hanging from Miss Bryson's throat last night."

"That is odd. Perhaps you're mistaken, and the chain is merely similar in design?"

"Thirty is hardly an age for one to lose one's eyesight." He laughed and pulled his braces atop his shoulders. "It's the same one. Albeit with another jewel attached to it."

Another mystery. Why replace the sizable diamond that had originally hung on the chain with a paltry amber one? One reason came to mind. Miss Bryson had sold it.

"I take it you are wondering how Miss Bryson acquired it?"

"I admit to being curious."

"And your curiosity has led you to think she's associated with a certain ring of thieves you're working with Bow Street to apprehend?"

"You know me too well."

"Since you were a little boy." A brief smile appeared on Simms's lined face, then disappeared.

"Has Lady Wallingford mentioned it's missing?"

"No, but I've rarely seen her since I gave it to her two weeks ago." Their relationship being casual in nature, as befitted two adults uninterested in marriage.

"There's only one thing to do." Simms attached a starched collar to Blackbourne's shirt. "You must ask her about it."

"What? And risk my life?" Blackbourne stepped back in mock horror. "My dear Simms, my asking Lady Wallingford how her gold chain came to be around the neck of another lady would compel her to inquire how I got close enough to the lady to recognize it. You may comprehend the danger."

"An exaggeration, I believe."

"Trust me. More dangerous than a duel," Blackbourne said with a laugh. "Though a duel would serve the purpose..."

"I'm not following, sir." Simms handed Blackbourne a bright white neckcloth.

"A ruse, Simms. One that requires a minor injury."

"Like a shoulder grazed by a bullet?"

"Precisely." Blackbourne turned to the mirror and quickly knotted the neckcloth into a perfect *waterfall*. "After which I'll send a note to Lady Wallingford telling her of my injury, causing her to rush to my side, where I, made insensible by pain, cry out, oh, by the way, whatever happened to that gold chain I gave you?"

"Now I see. You're hoping an injury will induce her to answer your question without asking any pesky ones of her own," Simms said. "Such as the name of the lady whom you think has stolen her necklace."

"Precisely."

Blackbourne knew Francesca would confront the singer, and he could not allow that to happen. Not when he was finally close to capturing the thieves who'd stolen Amelia's prized emerald bracelet.

"I'm afraid I must disappoint you, my lord." Simms slipped a gray-and-white striped waistcoat over Blackbourne's shoulders. "Your diary does not include a duel this morning."

"Pity." Blackbourne buttoned the waistcoat. "I don't suppose you'd shoot me?"

"I, sir?" Simms removed a blue topcoat from the wardrobe.

"Why not? You've handled my Manton pistols many times."

"The ability to clean a pistol doesn't ensure one's ability to shoot it—or one's master." He tugged the snug coat over Blackbourne's shoulders.

"You leave me no choice," Blackbourne said with an exaggerated sigh. "I must come up with another solution."

"I've every confidence in you." He held out Blackbourne's hat and gloves.

Blackbourne was not as confident. He placed the beaver atop his head and walked to the door. He must come up with another solution—and soon. Miss Bryson appeared poised to bolt—and not back into his arms—delightful as that would be. It had taken all the charm he possessed to convince her to stay at Amelia's. A novel situation. He usually had trouble convincing a lady to leave. Which led to another mystery.

Which did Miss Bryson think a bad review from Claimore would affect the most? Her singing career or her career as a thief?

EMMA WHIRLED AWAY FROM the bedchamber window and away from the din and noise below. Having lived her whole life in a tiny country village, she was unused to the morning commotion and the turbulence stirring in her breast.

She had barely slept. How could she after such a catastrophe? Her evening ruined. Her debut ruined. Even her scheme to stop Claimore ruined, thwarted, by the unwanted interference of Lord Blackbourne. Unwanted and shocking. Holding her against his chest? Tight against his chest? What sort of gentleman did that? Her cheeks burned at the memory.

His reaction had been less... animated.

Only a slight widening of his eyes. Gray eyes, deep and rich as muted silver, and lit with a devilish gleam. Perhaps not a devilish gleam. That might have been her imagination. In fairness, he had seemed concerned for her safety. Just not her feelings. Otherwise, he would never have kept her from finding Claimore.

Instead, she had stayed and fretted all night about the review. Emma stared hard at the bedchamber door. Where the deuce was her maid, Jo, who had come with her from Scotland and had returned with the footman the night before, bringing Emma's trunk? What Emma wanted now was for her to bring the newspaper.

The door swung open, and her maid lumbered in, carrying a tray and a newspaper tucked under her arm.

"Finally, Jo, you've come."

"Aye." The older woman strode briskly across the room, as fit and trim as a girl half her age. She placed the tray on the table next to the bed. "An' I've brought ye a wee bit to eat too."

Emma ignored the warm buttered scones and steaming cup of chocolate and snatched up the paper. "I'm much too nervous to eat anything."

"Not even a wee bit of marzipan?"

"Marzipan?" Emma lowered the paper. "Perhaps one piece wouldn't hurt." She popped a piece of the almond confection into her mouth and returned to the paper and rifled through it. Who cared about Napoleon's whereabouts? Or about a ship leaving for the penal colonies? Where the devil was the review? "Here it is, Jo."

Jo stopped gathering up Emma's discarded clothes. "Go on then, lass, and read it aloud."

Emma took a big breath and started, "*Though Miss B—n's astonishing voice traveled higher and farther than a carrier pigeon, alas, it did so without that bird's talent for a safe landing. As her last note soared to the heavens, her body tumbled to the floor, compelling the gallant Lord B—e to dash forth, and sweep the stumbling songstress into his arms.*"

Dear God. It was worse than she imagined.

"What's the matter, lass?"

"Lord Blackbourne got it all wrong. Mr. Claimore said nothing of my gown or my jewels. He called me a stumbling songstress and—"

"Ye did stumble, lass."

"Thank you, Jo."

"Fell flat on your backside."

"I remember."

"In front of God and everybody."

"The point is," Emma interrupted, "Mr. Claimore compared my voice, my splendid voice, to a pigeon."

Jo shrugged. "I like pigeons."

"Aye, but who wants to hear one sing? Certainly not Queen Charlotte." Emma threw the paper onto the settee and flounced down beside it. Hot tears stung her eyes. "No one else will ask me to sing now, Jo. Certainly, no one of note." No one who could introduce her to Prince George. She made a self-pitying sniffle, and Jo shuffled over and handed her a handkerchief. A knock sounded on the door, and Emma said, "Send them away, Jo. I don't wish to see anybody. I'm much too depressed."

Jo opened the door a crack. "Miss Bryson doesn't want to see—"

"She'll see me." A tall angular woman darted into the room, her skirts flaring out, wide and green, like the wings of a parrot.

"Aunt?" Emma straightened. "What are you doing here?"

"Visiting my injured niece." She swooped low and pecked Emma on the cheek, the ostrich feathers topping her bonnet, tickling Emma's cheeks.

"Of course, thank you." Emma glanced at the door. "But where is Lady Heyer?"

"She isn't home at the moment."

"Why didn't you wait downstairs in the salon? Like a proper visitor?" Emma knew why. Sheer nosiness. Katherine "Kat" Carstead would never miss an opportunity to inspect an elegant Mayfair townhouse.

"You come down with an injured neck? I dare say Lady Heyer would be appalled." Kat ran a finger across the mahogany escritoire. "No, my dear, you must stay in this delightful bedchamber until you're completely healed." She glanced around the room, and Emma knew she was memorizing every detail to recreate in her own home. A task easily accomplished thanks to her wealthy tradesman husband. "Even if it takes weeks."

"It won't even take a day, I promise you," Emma said and laughed. "My neck isn't injured."

Kat turned around. "Didn't Lady Heyer say so in her note?"

"I might've told a bit of a plumper. I needed an excuse. Lord Blackbourne had caught me staring at him. Twice."

"Oh, my dear. A lady should never stare." Kat settled next to Emma on the settee. "If one must stare—and one can't help but stare at Lord Blackbourne—one should be discreet and do so only from a distance or from behind one's fan."

"I'm afraid it didn't occur to me to open mine, splayed out on the floor as I was."

"Ah, yes. Your fall. I am sorry it happened." She peered closely at Emma, her black eyes, so much like Emma's father, filled with concern. "Were you injured at all?"

"Just my pride."

"We all suffer from that now and again," she said brightly. "But see how well everything has turned out."

"I'm sorry?"

Kat picked up the newspaper. "Claimore's review."

"Now all of London knows you've captured the attention of gallant Lord Blackbourne."

"Gallant? Ha!" Emma said. "He held me against his chest, Kat. *Tight* against his chest. What sort of gentleman does that?"

"Why a sporting gentleman." She crowed with laughter. "He's a Corinthian, you know. Boxing, racing, fencing, he excels at them all. I dare say he couldn't help but hold you tight."

"It's not whether he could have," Emma said, "but whether he should have."

Kat blinked. "But you might've toppled over again if he hadn't," she said. "I for one should never complain about being held by such a handsome gentleman."

"Handsome? Do you think so?"

"An Adonis come to life. The firm strong jaw. The gray eyes. The dark wavy hair. The silver at the temples." She sighed.

Emma shrugged. "I suppose he's handsome enough but no more so than Hamish."

"Hamish?" Kat squawked and shot off the settee and flew to the door, opened it, scanned the hallway, shut the door, whirled around, and pushed her back against it.

"Good God, what's the matter?" Emma said, alarmed. "Is someone out there?"

"Luckily for you, no." She returned to the couch. "You must never ever mention that name aloud again."

"Why not?"

"My dear niece, if it were ever discovered you'd left a man at the altar—that you're a jilt—your chance to marry the Earl of Blackbourne would be ruined."

Emma stopped. Froze. Her whole body immobilized by her aunt's daft proclamation. Marry Lord Blackbourne? Suddenly the despair, the misery, the sheer wretchedness that had threatened to overwhelm her disappeared, vanished like a puff of smoke, and she burst out laughing. "Oh, thank you, Kat. I needed something to pull me out of the doldrums and your absurd notion did the trick."

"I'm happy to have been of service, but I didn't say it to be humorous."

"It's a wee early to have had some champagne, even for you." Emma laughed again.

"I'm not foxed, either."

"Then you must be mad. As contrary to the fanciful and, dare I say, slanderous claims of Mr. Claimore, I can assure you Lord Blackbourne has not fallen in love with me."

"Who said anything about love?" Kat settled back onto the sofa, composed and unruffled, as if she hadn't uttered the most shocking thing in the world.

Emma joined her on the couch. "What other reason could there be?"

"English gentlemen marry for all sorts of reasons. Money, land, titles." She gave Emma an arch look. "To beget an heir."

"As you know I can provide none of those," Emma said and cleared her throat. "Except, perhaps, the last one."

"As it happens, he isn't after any of those but something far more important to a gentleman." She sat forward and grinned. "To win a bet."

"Are you saying Lord Blackbourne wagered on his own marriage?"

"Rumor has it he placed a large wager at White's that he'd marry before the end of the Season."

"How large?"

"A thousand pounds."

Emma gasped. She could live comfortably off that for a decade. "What if he doesn't win?"

"He pays the thousand pounds. Gentlemen always pay their gambling debts. It's a matter of honor. In this case, though, it's a moot point." Kat straightened. "Lord Blackbourne has never lost at anything in his life."

Nothing? Not a wager? A curricle race? A duel? Hold on. Did he duel? Of course, he dueled. He's a gentleman. All gentlemen dueled.

At least every gentleman in the novels she devoured like marzipan did. Emma asked, "Not even a duel?"

"One would be foolhardy to meet him in the fields of Islington."

"Where laundry is hung?"

"Yes. And duels to the death."

Good heavens, the shocking revelations just kept on coming. "My goodness, Kat, has Lord Blackbourne actually killed someone?"

"Well, I can't say for certain, but I've no doubt he could. I told you. He's a Corinthian, a sporting gentleman, and an excellent whip. Why, he can direct his cattle, all four bays at once, with the mere tips of his fingers." She gazed off into the distance. "His long supple masculine fingers."

Emma stared at the same far wall and recalled his long supple masculine fingers in the small of her back. A knock interrupted her reverie. "May I come in, Miss Bryson?" Lady Heyer asked, and Emma jumped up and opened the door. Lady Heyer entered, wearing her bonnet and pelisse, and holding a handful of calling cards. "I was told we had a visitor." She cast a pleasant but curious glance at Mrs. Carstead.

"This is my aunt, Mrs. Carstead," Emma said. "She's been quite worried about me."

Kat curtsied. "Yes, please forgive the intrusion, my lady."

"No intrusion. I'm only sorry I wasn't here to greet you." Lady Heyer turned her attention to Emma. "I'm afraid I've bad news, Miss Bryson. Hamilton won't be able to come today. He's gone to attend a birth. Those can be so unpredictable." She placed a hand over her abdomen. "One never knows when a baby will choose to come."

"My eldest was stubborn that way," Kat said. "Came a full week after she was expected. It was like she was hiding or something."

"It's fine, Lady Heyer." Emma attempted to stop Kat's embarrassing and forward behavior. "There's no reason I can't return home now."

"I'm not sure I agree, Miss Bryson." Lady Heyer's eyebrows drew together.

"Neither do I, your ladyship," Kat said. "In fact, I think—"

"What if Hamilton came to my uncle's house tomorrow?" Emma said quickly. "Would that be agreeable?"

"I suppose that could be arranged," Lady Heyer said. "Would you be so kind as to give me your address again, Mrs. Carstead?"

"7 Grosvenor Square. On the corner. There's a large, lovely garden on the side designed by Mr. Repton, himself. One could hardly miss it."

"I'm sure," she said, and Emma wondered at Lady Heyer's composure. Kat could be so trying. "But to ensure Hamilton doesn't, could you please write it down?" She took a card from the dozens in her hand.

Mrs. Carstead took the card and her eyes widened as she quickly wrote the address. "Thank you, my lady."

"You're welcome." Lady Heyer glanced at the card and a frown formed on her brow. She tucked the card away. "I'll make arrangements for your trunk to be returned, Miss Bryson."

"Thank you, your ladyship," Emma said. "You've been most kind."

The moment Lady Heyer left the bedchamber, Kat grabbed Emma by the arm. "Come along my dear. We must hurry. We've a lot to do."

"I can't leave this minute. My trunk must be—"

"Your maid can take care of it." She pushed Emma toward the door.

"Why the hurry? A moment ago, you insisted I couldn't leave. Now you're all but dragging me out." Emma planted her feet. "It has something to do with the card you wrote the address on, doesn't it?"

"I don't know what you're talking about."

"Fustian. You and Lady Heyer both reacted strangely to it. Who sent it?" Emma crossed her arms. "I shan't go anywhere until you tell me."

"Lord Hefton. He's invited Lady Heyer to a masquerade at the Royal Saloon tonight."

"What does that have to do with us?"

"Not us in particular, but Elizabeth," Kat said. "He's the gentleman I wish her to marry."

Emma laughed to cover her shock. "I thought she had an understanding with a soldier."

"Lieutenant Gibson?" Kat snorted. "He's nothing compared to the lord of one of London's greatest estates."

"That's lovely but what makes you think he and Elizabeth would suit?"

"Simple. She has a dowry of 30,000 pounds, and he's lost all his money at the gaming tables."

"Good God. He's a gamester?"

She shrugged. "It's probably why he's going to the Saloon. All sorts of games are played there. It's a cesspool of ruffians and roues, gamesters and blackguards."

"Yet you wish to take your eldest daughter, who is barely out of the schoolroom, there?"

"Oh, heavens, Mr. Carstead would never allow her to go. She could be kidnapped or worse."

"You read far too many gothic novels." Emma said as she laughed. "But I agree she is too young to go to such a place."

"But you're not." Kat gave Emma a sly look. "As long as you're properly chaperoned, of course."

"Well, I'm not going."

"You must, Emma. How else am I to meet Lord Hefton?"

"It's not as if I can introduce you. He's hardly a friend of mine."

"Lady Heyer is."

22

"No, she isn't, and even if she were, I'd never presume upon her in such a manner," Emma said. "Besides, she might not be going. She doesn't strike me as someone who'd wish to keep such low company as you claim frequents the Royal Saloon."

"Half the *ton* is there most evenings. Lord Byron and even the Prince Regent."

Emma straightened. "Prince George goes to the Royal Saloon?"

"Yes, on occasion."

Emma's mind whirled. Would tonight be such an occasion? Would he come to the Royal Saloon, and more importantly, could she get his attention? She must at least try. It might be her only chance.

"I've changed my mind, Kat." Emma fingered her amber pendant. "I would love to go to the Royal Saloon this evening."

BLACKBOURNE HANDED the butler his hat and gloves and wandered into the Wallingford parlor, his footsteps muffled by the plush Aubusson carpet. A Waterford vase atop the mantel caught his eye. One of a pair, if he remembered, and he should. He'd bought them. He'd seen them in a shop window set amongst lesser glassware. Slim, long, and delicate, they had reminded him of Francesca.

An image of Miss Bryson arose in Blackbourne's mind. A Waterford vase she was not. Small, sturdy, and curvaceous, she reminded him of the rare Ravenscroft glass he had locked up at Blackbourne House. He smiled. A small sturdy tumbler.

"My goodness, what an interesting smile. I wonder what has caused it." Francesca's soft feminine voice floated from the doorway and Blackbourne turned.

"Thoughts of you, of course." His gaze roved over her. "They hardly do you justice. You look ravishing."

"Thank you, my love." She joined him, and a heady floral aroma enveloped Blackbourne. Night Jasmine—her favorite perfume. She ran a finger down his cheek. "It's been far too long since I've seen you."

"It's unfortunate your uncle's illness has kept you so occupied. Is he doing any better?" Blackbourne led Francesca to the couch and pulled her down beside him.

"Yes, he's almost recovered, I think. Though not soon enough."

"No?"

"It seems I missed a most entertaining evening." She waved to the *Morning Gazette*, lying open on a chair. "How embarrassing for the poor girl. But you were very gallant." She slanted a look at him, her lids half closed. "Sweeping her into your arms."

"It was the proper thing to do."

"Quite proper but also quite dangerous." He raised his brow, and she continued, "If you aren't careful, darling, the poor thing might fall in love with you."

Blackbourne chuckled. Miss Bryson's reaction to his attentions had been anything but lover-like. "You know I've no interest in the tendres of young ladies. I prefer the love of a more... experienced lady."

"Do you?" Her lips curved into a sultry knowing smile and a strange thought struck Blackbourne. Had she ever blushed around him like Miss Bryson? He shook his head. What the deuce did he care? He'd left such nonsense behind him after his wife's betrayal.

He ignored the tightness in his chest that thoughts of Clarissa still engendered and returned to the business at hand. He cleared his throat and, having caught Francesca's attention, lifted the flap of his topcoat pocket, and slowly removed a gold-plated chain bracelet.

"How beautiful," Francesca breathed, and pleasure suffused her cheeks.

"It is, isn't it?" He clasped it around her wrist. "You were so enchanted by the necklace I gave you I thought I'd surprise you with a matching bracelet."

The first part of his ruse.

"You needn't explain." She laughed and twisted her arm to admire it from all angles. "I'd have accepted your delightful gift whether it matched or not."

Now for the second part.

"Funny you should say that as there was a bit of a disagreement between the jeweler and I about it. I'm certain they're an exact match, but he insisted they were made by two different goldsmiths."

"One should never argue with a jeweler, my love," she said. "Imagine the poor gems one might get in retaliation."

"True, and I would've been happy to let it go, but you know Hefty..."

"What does Lord Hefton have to do with it?"

"He was there and overheard us. He said the only way to resolve the controversy was to see the bracelet and necklace together. My cousin has always been exceedingly sensible."

"Quite sensible, if one must prove—oh, I see." She stopped. "You made a wager with the jeweler?"

"Written in the book at White's and everything."

"You do make the oddest wagers."

The oddest one of all hung in the air between them. Blackbourne's wager to marry. They had never discussed it. He couldn't discuss it, even with her. The scheme he and Bow Street had worked out depended upon everyone believing he was on the marriage mart. Besides, he knew she was no more interested in marriage than he was.

"I told him we'd meet at Gunter's this afternoon." He stood. "You can wear your necklace and bracelet."

"Wear that beautiful, elegant chain with this day gown? It'd look ridiculous."

"Then bring the jewelry in your reticule."

"Are you mad?" She stood and walked to the mantel, her back to Blackbourne. "What if I lose them?"

Her unwillingness to accommodate him surprised Blackbourne. "If it makes you feel better, I'll carry them in my pocket," he said. "Then if something happens all the blame shall be mine."

She seemed inordinately interested in the vase. "I'm not sure..."

"Come now. It's Gunter's. You love their ices." He joined her at the fireplace and slipped his arms around her slim waist. "What is your favorite? Lemon? Orange?"

"You should know its raspberry," she said with a hint of reproach.

"A raspberry ice it is, then."

He trailed kisses down her throat, and Francesca sighed against him. "How can I resist that?" she said and took his hand and led him to her bedchamber. Blackbourne leaned against the door jamb and waited as Francesca walked to her rosewood jewelry box.

"I wonder," she said over her shoulder, "If I should demand more than a raspberry ice for helping you win this wager?"

"I promise you two."

"I'll hold you to it. Ah, here it is." She held up a gray velvet case. "The means for you to win another wag—oh, my God."

Blackbourne straightened. "What's the matter?"

"My necklace." Francesca turned wide blue eyes on him. "It's gone."

"Gone?"

"Yes, Philip, gone." Her voice rose in alarm. "Here, see for yourself." She shoved the case into his hands. Blackbourne gave it a cursory glance. He knew the chain wasn't there—and he knew who had it.

"I don't understand," Francesca said. "This is where it's kept."

"Let's not panic," Blackbourne said. "When did you wear it last?"

She thought for a moment. "Sir Thomas Mayfield's birthday party. Last Wednesday. I took my uncle, remember?"

Blackbourne's mind whirled. Had Miss Bryson sung at that party? He'd check Briggs's report when he got home. "Are you certain you still had it on when you returned?"

"Yes."

"Is anything else missing?"

Francesca quickly checked her jewelry box. "No. Nothing else," she said. "Just the necklace."

It must've been stolen from the birthday party. A private party. Just like the rest. Had Miss Bryson sung at any of these other parties? He must reread Briggs's report. Still, a servant could've done it. Blackbourne turned back to Francesca and said, "Who has access to your bedchamber?"

"Besides you?" She joked, then gasped. "You think someone stole it from my room?"

"We know this was the last place you remember having it."

"I suppose Fairfax, but you can't think she stole it?"

Blackbourne remained silent. Bow Street had suspected that maids or footmen or even a housekeeper like Mrs. Fairfax could be abetting these thieves.

"Impossible. She's been with me for ages."

"One can know someone, even live with them, and still be fooled." Clarissa had proven that during their short, disastrous marriage.

"I don't believe it. She'd never do such a reprehensible thing. She loves me like her own child. She's been more of a mother to me than my own."

"Your trust is commendable, my love, but not, I hope, misplaced."

"It isn't. I'm certain she didn't steal it."

"You sound as if you know who did."

"How would I? Though if I ever do find him..."

"He? It might be a woman."

"A lady thief? How intriguing," she said. "What makes you think so?"

"A hunch."

He had more than a hunch. He had a suspect. A singer with a golden voice and a golden chain dangling from her beautiful throat. Miss Bryson's deep blush when he held her screamed innocent village girl, but Blackbourne knew better. He had been fooled by an innocent act before. Besides, Emma Bryson wasn't that innocent. She had jilted a man at the altar, after all.

EMMA LIFTED A WHITE-and-pink spangled mask to her eyes and stared into the mirror. Any misgivings she had about her impulsive decision to go to the Royal Saloon had disappeared as soon as she learned there would be a masquerade. How delightful! Except for a few daytime outings to Hyde Park, Emma had done nothing exciting except sing since her arrival in London.

The *clop* of horses' hooves down the street drew Emma to the bedchamber window. She pushed aside the brocade curtains and stared out into the darkness. Newly installed gas lamps—a point of pride for Mr. Carstead—cast a pale glow upon the street. Suddenly, a man stepped from the shadows, and Emma stepped back, her heart pounding. Wait. Was it Malcolm? She glanced back out, and he waved and pointed to her aunt's side garden. Oh, heavens. He would not dare.

Emma rushed to the side window and pushed it open. Malcolm was already on the branch outside her window grinning, as if it were the most natural thing in the world for a grown man to be sitting on a branch outside a second-story bedchamber window. "My dear

Malcolm!" Emma said and held the curtain aside so he could slip in. "What are you thinking of taking such a risk?"

"I can still climb a tree, lass," he said and slipped his lanky body into the room with ease. "Even with this."

He held up his right hand, and Emma stared at the gnarled broken fingers—the result of a carriage accident and the poor ministrations of a drunk English surgeon—with compassion. "I didn't mean... I meant the risk of you being seen climbing through my bedchamber window."

"I did so many times as a lad."

"Aye, but we're not children anymore, and there were no gas lamps outside my cottage and—"

"And you weren't staying with a dragon of an aunt?" He laughed. "That's the thing, lass. She'd never have allowed me to see you, it being so late."

Emma agreed Kat would not have allowed it. Her adherence to propriety was circumstantial at best, except where Elizabeth was concerned. And that young lady had taken an inordinate interest in Malcolm the one time he had come for a visit—much to her mother's chagrin.

"I'm not sure I should allow it," Emma said. "It isn't proper."

"My presence in your bedchamber has never been a problem before. Why the sudden reserve?" He tilted Emma's chin upward with his finger. "Don't you trust me, lass?"

"More than anyone, Malcolm. You know that."

"Aye, I do. It's how I knew you'd open the window." He flashed a cocky grin that made Emma laugh. He was incorrigible.

"I'm sorry ye fell, lass." His voice held a depth of sincerity one expected from a beloved childhood companion.

"Thank you, Malcolm," she said. "It wouldn't bother me as much if only I could've stopped Mr. Claimore from printing his review," she said with a sigh. "I did try, but Lord Blackbourne stopped me."

"Did he?" His eyelids lowered. "How?"

"He wouldn't let me leave. He held me against..." She paused, loath to share Blackbourne's impertinence of holding her against his chest, tight against his chest, with Malcolm. "He held me against my will. He insisted I needed to see a doctor first."

"I'd have insisted on the same thing," he said, then gave her a sly grin. "Quite the gallant."

"Ha! Try gamester. Did you know he wagered a thousand pounds that he'd be married by the end of the Season?"

"Aye, I heard about it, and I'm not surprised. Like most English gentlemen, he has more blunt than sense."

"He didn't strike me as being foolish." Arrogant, self-confident, and even charming but not foolish. "There must be another reason."

"Attention? Vanity? The wager has certainly brought out dozens of mamas eager to throw their daughters at Blackbourne's head. Any place he is you'll find a bevy of young unmarried ladies decked out in their finest gowns and jewels. As if he needs their dowries," he said, and Emma detected a hint of bitterness.

"Is that why his name appears in the broadsheets every day? To attract a wife?"

"Aye," Malcolm said. "I'm not surprised Claimore wrote more of him than of your fall."

"Mr. Claimore shouldn't have written about either," Emma snapped. "He should've written only about my singing."

"Ah, now the truth comes out." Malcolm grinned. "It isn't so much that Blackbourne played the gallant but that he overshadowed you. Outshone you. Admit it, lass—your pride has been hurt."

"Don't be ridiculous." She turned away, annoyed his playful barb had hit its mark. "You're the one who said I needed a stellar review, and I should've got it. I sang beautifully, Malcolm. Claimore should have said so."

"He said your voice was astonishing."

"He compared me to a pigeon."

"A compliment, my love. I've been told it was a pigeon who first brought news of Napoleon's defeat at Waterloo just last month. Flew all the way from France with the happy news. Surely such a comparison portends happy news for you too."

"All of London now knows of my fall, Malcolm. That is not happy news."

"Many ladies would consider Blackbourne insisting you stay with his sister as happy news."

"Not if they—hold on. How did you know he insisted? I said nothing about it in my note."

"Broadsheets aren't the only means of spreading gossip, love. Servants do just as well."

"Thank heaven, I returned to my aunt's house. To have stayed longer would have courted even more ridiculous chatter," Emma said, irritated. "Now I wonder if I shouldn't just go all the way home."

"Back to Scotland? Don't be ridiculous."

"Why not? I could always come back next Season." Emma warmed to the idea. "By then, my fall and even my jilt would be forgotten."

"Next Season would be too late."

"Too late for what? I've set no timetable on fulfilling my promise."

"I might not be here to help you."

"Where else would you be?"

He didn't respond. "It isn't like you to turn tail and run, Emma," he said, setting her back up.

"I'm not running anywhere," she said. "In fact, I'm even going out this evening."

"That's the spirit. Where?"

"The saloon."

His dark head jerked up. "The Royal Saloon?"

"Yes. Is something the matter?"

"It isn't a place I'd expect Mrs. Carstead to take a young unmarried lady."

His straightlaced and prudish manner—and the strong mischaracterization of her aunt—amused Emma. "I'm two and twenty. Hardly a schoolgirl."

"Yet you still hide your valuables under your pillow like one." He lifted her satin pillow from her bed to reveal her velvet bag of jewels.

She shrugged. "I like knowing where my treasures are."

"As long as the maids don't know either."

"My dear Malcolm," she said with a shake of her head. "You're so distrustful."

"And you, lass, aren't nearly enough. The Royal Saloon is dangerous for one so gullible."

"I promised my Aunt Carstead I'd go, and besides, it might be my last chance to meet Prince George. I understand he occasionally comes to the Royal Saloon, and I plan to meet him."

Incredulity covered Malcolm's features. "How? Do you plan to just walk up to him and introduce yourself?"

"I don't know. I haven't thought that far ahead."

"If he is there, he'll be spending his time in one of the boudoirs."

"Boudoirs?"

"Tents set up for... private engagements."

"Oh. I see." Emma said, and heat mounted her cheeks. "I suppose I'll just have to get his attention before then."

"You shan't have a problem doing so wearing such a... daring ensemble, lass. I doubt any other lady there will be as colorful as you."

A tap sounded on the door. "Mrs. Carstead is waiting for you in the salon, Miss Bryson."

Emma's heart pounded. She hissed, "You must hide," and pushed him toward the bed. He remained bolted to the floor, his arms crossed. "I'll not hide from an English servant like a lad in leading strings."

"Oh, Malcolm, please. I can't risk us being caught in here alone. My jilt would be nothing compared to it."

"Don't worry, love, I promise to marry you."

"For heaven's sake, Malcolm, neither of us wants to get trapped into marriage."

A shadow crossed his features before he grinned. "You're right, lass," he said. "I'll not get trapped into marrying you, nor will I get trapped under a bed. I'll leave the same way I came in." He returned to the window. He grabbed a branch and swung his body onto it. The branch shuddered and groaned under his weight, and Emma shuddered too. "Malcolm, please be careful."

He grinned. "You know I always land on my feet." He shimmied down the tree, waved, and disappeared into the darkness.

Emma shut the window. Before last evening she could have said the same. But now? What if she fell tonight? She shrugged off the thought. Her fall had been nothing but a cruel twist of fate. It'd not happen again, and even if it did, who'd know? She would be perfectly safe hidden behind her mask.

THE BEDCHAMBER DOOR swung open, and Simms rushed in, carrying a pair of Hoby boots.

"It's usually you waiting upon me, Simms," Blackbourne said, putting aside the paper. "I finished shaving nearly a quarter of an hour ago."

"I know, my lord, and I'm sorry, but I couldn't let you be seen tonight without giving your boots a fresh coat of polish. My newest blacking." He placed them by Blackbourne's chair. "They shine like a mirror."

"Indeed, they do." Blackbourne glanced at the boots. "One can even see his reflection."

"Thank you." Simms puffed up a bit.

Blackbourne chuckled. "Not every gentleman wishes to see it."

"Only those who don't like what they see."

The remark surprised Blackbourne, and he stared closer at his boot. An indifferent, cynical, and even hardened visage stared back. Good God. Was that him?

"Is something amiss, my lord?"

"Not at all." He straightened. His reflection was surely distorted by the curve of the boot. "I was just thinking this excessive fastidiousness, even for you, only means one thing. You're losing your wager."

"Not quite, but it's a close thing." Simms pulled a linen shirt from the wardrobe and gave it to Blackbourne. "You were only mentioned twice in today's newspapers."

"I'd think two points in one day would be sufficient." Blackbourne tucked in his shirt and pulled up his braces.

"Not when Mr. Brummell got three."

"One would've thought a cut direct from Prince George would've toppled the Beau from his throne as the arbiter of fashion by now."

"Not when his valet behaves as if it never happened."

"A tactic he learned from his master." Blackbourne laughed. "Don't despair. The Season isn't over yet. You've still time to beat Robinson and the other valets in the... what's the name of your club?"

"The Gentleman's Gentleman Club, and I fully expect to win the ten pounds, my lord." Simms handed Blackbourne his fob watch. "Though I'm dreading our weekly luncheon tomorrow at the King's Head. Robinson insists upon bringing the papers and reading them aloud after we've eaten. He never misses an opportunity to brag. Last week he rattled on about the splendor of Mr. Brummell's topcoat, as if he were a mother discussing her favorite child."

"I daresay these boots should take him down a notch or two."

"Alas, there's no guarantee their magnificence will be written about in the morning papers."

"Then he must hear about them from his master."

"How so, my lord?"

"Brummell spends much of his time at the Saloon. If he's there tonight, I'll ensure he sees them. Even if I must place my foot upon a table like a barbarian."

"I knew I could rely on you, sir." Simms removed a snuffbox and a black satin mask from the wardrobe.

"What's that?"

"Your silver snuffbox." He held it up. "A favorite I believe."

"In your other hand." Blackbourne said quietly but firmly.

"Oh, this. I assumed you knew." Simms placed the mask on the bed, removed a cloth from his pocket, and buffed the snuffbox. "The festivities tonight include a masquerade."

"I'm rather surprised Lady Heyer invited me. She must know my feelings on the matter."

Simms stopped buffing and said in a steady voice, "Forgive me for saying so, my lord, but why would she?"

True. How would Amelia know he loathed masquerades—or why? She'd been fast asleep on the other side of Blackbourne House when he and his wife had returned from that last, disastrous one, eight years before. Simms had been awake though, waiting to assist Blackbourne, and had heard everything; Clarissa's screaming fit, her lies, her betrayal. The tightness in his chest returned. "You know my reasons."

"I do."

"You might've said something."

"I beg your pardon, but I got so busy. The boots..."

They both knew his failure to mention the masquerade had nothing to do with his rivalry with Robinson. For months he had been pushing Blackbourne to let go of the past in a manner only a long-serving and trusted servant could. He even believed Simms's wager was only made to facilitate Blackbourne's continued appearance in Society.

"Besides," Simms said, "I knew you wouldn't refuse to escort Lady Heyer. She relies on you, quite rightly, whilst her husband the earl is serving on the Continent."

"She would've understood." He knew she only went to keep an eye on their cousin, Hefty, not for any pleasure of her own.

"What of Lady Wallingford?" He handed Blackbourne the snuffbox. "Would she understand you missing an opportunity to capture the thieves who stole her necklace?"

"The thieves I'm searching for won't be at the Saloon."

"But Miss Bryson will be."

Blackbourne went still. "Are you certain?"

"Gossip from the servants' hall travels higher and farther than a carrier pigeon."

How interesting. Had she—and the band of thieves—decided to forgo their usual venues to strike at the masquerade? Many of the *ton* would be there. All dressed up in their finery and jewels. As enticing and lucrative to thieves as any ball or rout—with the added benefit of having a mask to hide behind.

"There we have it, my lord. Three ladies who, for varied reasons, require your attendance at this masquerade," Simms said. "For my part, and discounting your feelings on the matter, I can't see how you can get out of it."

Blackbourne smiled, amused suddenly that he did not want to. He had planned to visit Miss Bryson tomorrow, to interrogate her, but why wait? It'd be easier and less obvious to do so over a glass of

Bucelas, the Royal Saloon's famous Portuguese wine, instead of under the calculating eye of Mrs. Carstead.

A strange sense of—what exactly? Curiosity? Intrigue? Excitement?—coursed through Blackbourne. It'd been a long time since he'd pursued a lady. He grimaced. He wasn't pursuing a lady. He was pursuing a thief.

Of course, he could not let his valet know he had capitulated so easily. "I beg to differ, Simms. One could get out of going if one were injured."

"You appear in perfect health, my lord."

"A situation easily rectified if you'd but retrieve my pistol from the top drawer of my bureau and shoot me."

"I must decline, my lord." Simms removed a black topcoat from the wardrobe and held it open. "You know what a poor shot I am."

"What if I promise to stand perfectly still?" Blackbourne struggled into the tight-fitting coat. "It shan't be too difficult. You've just immobilized my arms."

"An exaggeration, my lord, it's a perfect fit." Simms ran a brush down the coat. "But thoughtful of you to offer."

"You've served me well through the years. It's the least I could do."

"Thank you. It's been an honor."

"Yet not such an honor that you'll shoot me?"

"I'm afraid not."

"Really, Simms, if a gentleman can't rely on his valet to get him out of going somewhere he doesn't care to be by shooting him, I'm not sure what he can rely on him for."

"He can rely on him to ensure that when the gentleman arrives at such a place, he's exquisitely dressed."

"In that case, you've quite outdone yourself." Blackbourne checked his frame in the mirror. "I expect to be three points ahead tomorrow."

"Thank you, my lord. Now sally forth and find Miss Bryson." Simms held out the satin mask toward Blackbourne. "The mystery of the gold necklace depends upon it. The recovery of Lady Heyer's stolen bracelet depends upon it. The very capture of the thieves terrorizing the defenseless, helpless, frightened ladies of the *ton* depends upon it."

"Just so, Simms, but you don't fool me." Blackbourne ignored the mask and walked to the door. "You only wish me to go in the hope of Brummell seeing my boots."

CHAPTER 2

Emma did not know which was worse, the sweat trickling between her shoulder blades or the enervating lack of air. She snapped open her lace brisé fan. Was the Saloon always like this? Hot and loud and teeming with people?

"What's the matter my dear?" Kat asked.

"I did not expect such a crush."

"It's delightful, isn't it?"

"Hot and miserable, more like."

"Your uncle shall return soon with our refreshments."

"It must be as hot as the desert inside those tents." Emma stared curiously at one of the boudoirs Malcolm had warned her about.

"I would love to be inside," Kat said. "Just to see who's in there."

Emma laughed. "How would we even know? Everyone is wearing a mask." In her excitement at realizing her face would be concealed, it had not occurred to her that everyone else's would be too. "If Prince George were to walk by this very instant, I'd not even know it's him."

"Don't worry, you'll hear him." Kat smirked. "His corset creaks louder than the mast of a ship whenever he moves."

"Prince George wears a corset? I don't believe it."

"Why not? He's hardly the trim handsome man he was in his youth." Kat leaned close and said in a conspiratorial tone, "I'm told many gentlemen of the *ton* do."

"Even Lord Blackbourne?" Emma asked without thought.

"You'd know better than I."

"I beg your pardon?"

"He held you against his chest, didn't he? *Tight* against his chest. Surely, you could feel a corset after—"

"Lower your voice," Emma said with a panicked glance around. "What if he's here?"

"There he is."

"Oh, heavens. I knew it." Emma ducked behind Kat. "Do you think he saw us?"

"I would hope so. I'm parched."

"What?"

"Your uncle. He's come back," Kat said with a wave at her husband, and Emma exhaled, grateful it wasn't Blackbourne she was waving at. Though why she should care, she did not know.

Mr. Carstead joined them and handed Kat a flute of champagne and Emma a glass of lemonade. "Thank you, Uncle."

"You're welcome." Thin, spare, and intimidating to most, Arthur Carstead spoke with a thick Welsh accent, which Emma sometimes found hard to understand and impossible when he was riled or angry.

"Now, I'll be off." He turned to Kat. "Unless you wish me to stay, my dear?"

"No, my dear," she said. "We're fine. Go play cards, enjoy yourself." Mr. Carstead bowed and disappeared, and Kat instantly grabbed Emma's arm. "Now we'll enjoy ourselves too by taking a turn around the room."

"How do you propose we do that?" Emma laughed. "We can barely move."

"Why do you think God gave us elbows?" She took a long drink of champagne. "Come now. We shan't see anyone standing against a wall. And no one will see us. We all can't tumble in front of an earl to get his attention."

"I did no such thing."

"I'm not saying you did so on purpose. I'm certain you were merely blinded by his brilliant neckcloth," Kat said and took another drink. "Speaking of infamous neckcloths. There he is."

"Lord Blackbourne? Where?"

"No, Lord Byron."

"You said neckcloth."

"I said infamous neckcloth. See how loosely he wears it?" She waved her flute at a tall dark-haired gentleman a few feet away. "I'm told some find it romantic." Her tone said she was not one of those barbaric individuals. Emma stared hard at the famous poet and wondered what made him so attractive to women.

"Stop staring, my dear. Or at least lift up your fan," she said, and Emma lifted the fan high so the tips of the feathers brushed her cheeks.

"Don't hold it like that."

"Why not?"

"Holding it thus makes a gentleman think he may approach you."

"You're joking."

"Not at all. It's called the art of the fan. One can carry on a whole conversation just by the way one holds it." Kat folded her fan shut and let it dangle from her wrist. "This position tells a gentleman he need not bother." She unfolded it halfway and raised it to her cheeks. "This tells one you're not interested."

"What position tells one they've had too much champagne?"

"There isn't one as one can never have too much of that." She took another sip. "Now you really mustn't hold it that way."

"Why?"

"Fully opened and covering everything but your eyes? That makes a gentleman think you're... interested."

"Interested in what?"

"Hold it thus in front of Lord Blackbourne and you'll find out." She took another sip and gasped. "There he is."

"Oh, no." Emma snapped her fan shut. "Do you think he saw me?"

"I hope so. He's the reason we're here."

"I'm not interested in Lord Blackbourne."

"Not him, but Lord Hefton. He's right over there."

Emma flicked a gaze heavenward and said, "From now on, Kat, I want you to say the gentleman's name. Aloud. His full name. No pronouns. Even their titles, if they have them, but don't you dare just say, 'there he is.'"

"Didn't I say so?" Kat tilted her head in a show of confusion. "But if you must know, he's James Edward Stanhope, the third Earl of Hefton and the—"

"Never mind. Where is he? Where is the gentleman you wish to buy a title from?"

"I'd scold you for your effrontery if it weren't true," Kat said and pointed at a tall amiable-appearing gentleman with wavy chestnut hair.

"He must enjoy his ale," Emma said.

"Why do you say that?"

"What else could explain his rather lumpy girth?" One at odds with his otherwise trim figure.

"That awful floral waistcoat, that's what." Kat sipped her champagne. "It gives him the appearance of a rhododendron bush in full flower."

"It's bright, I grant you, but I think it rather splendid."

"I'm not surprised."

As Kat eyed Emma's gown, Emma shrugged and said, "I like orange."

"Yes, well, we'll discuss your appalling inclination to wear colors at war with your complexion later. For now, we must not lose Lord Hefton."

Kat darted forward, and Emma dashed after her. Did she mean to tackle him? Heavens, but he's nimble. He must know he's being hunted. Finally, they stopped, and Emma almost barreled into Kat. "Good heavens," Emma said. "You nearly ran him to ground, Kat."

"If only I had run into him. He'd be forced into an introduction," she said and took a drink. "No matter. We're in luck." Her dark eyes twinkled behind her mask. "He's talking to a man who might be of help. Someone everyone knows. Someone who—"

"Name, Kat."

"Mr. George Brummell."

"The Beau?" Emma stared at Prince George's most famous ex-friend. "What gave him away? His understated dress? His perfect neckcloth?"

"Lord Hefton. I heard him say hello to him."

Emma laughed. She now knew from whom she inherited her keen ears. "What makes you think he can help you?"

"It's well-known Mr. Brummell is up the River Tick, far up the river, since getting the cut direct from Prince George. If I can persuade Mr. Carstead to help him, he might, in gratitude, arrange an introduction to Lord Hefton."

"My dear aunt, I'd no idea you had such a scheming mind."

"One develops such a weapon when one has three daughters to marry off. Oh, heavens. He's off again."

Kat charged forward, and Emma scrambled after her, grateful for Kat's height and the tall peacock feathers in her silver turban. Otherwise, she would've lost her in the crowd. A moment later, Kat skidded to a stop and Emma caught up to her and gasped out, "Who is he speaking to now?"

"I don't know, but he appears far less amenable than Mr. Brummell. In fact, he seems quite angry." A waiter passed, and Kat switched out her empty flute for another. "Perhaps if we get a little closer." She started forward but was knocked backwards by a large blousy woman, spilling the entire contents of her glass onto her bodice.

"I beg your pardon," Kat sputtered, but the lady ignored her and kept on her way, bumping all in her path. "What horrible manners. I've a good mind to go after her and demand she pay for my gown. Irish linen isn't cheap."

"You needn't bother. She's foxed."

"Obviously."

"One gets that way when one imbibes too much champagne," Emma said pointedly.

"That's it," Kat said. "More champagne."

"You don't need anymore."

"Not I, but you," she said excitedly. "You must get foxed and stumble into Lord Hefton."

"I'll do no such thing. Besides, you know champagne makes me giddy, and I must keep my wits about me just in case Prince George is here," Emma said. "I think you'd do better to find a towel, or you'll never be rid of the stain."

"Oh, dear, you're right." She swiped at her bodice with her fingers. "I must find a maid."

"Let's ask at the kitchen."

"No, I'll go alone. You must stay by Lord Hefton." Kat cast an eye on her prey. "Now that I've caught him, he must not escape."

She left, and Emma turned back to Hefton who dashed off. Blast. Emma rushed after him, and suddenly he stopped. In front of a boudoir. Emma's heart sank. Don't go in. Please don't—he went in.

Now what? She could not follow him into the tent, but what harm was there in standing next to it? In fact, she must do so or lose him. She moved closer and stood next to the opening flap. A trill of female laughter echoed behind the drapery, followed by the coarse laughter of a gentleman and the... tinkling keys of a pianoforte? Emma's ears perked up. Was someone playing "'Tis the Last Rose of Summer'?" Emma listened more closely. Not in the tent but... She elbowed her way to the other side and laughed in delight. There really was a pianoforte with a masked gentleman playing her favorite song. Unable to resist, Emma closed her eyes and sang along.

A few moments later the music stopped, and she opened her eyes. A crowd had gathered, and they burst into applause. Emma flushed with pleasure.

"Thank you, but the gentleman playing the pianoforte is just as deserving," she said and glanced at him. "Hold on. Where did he go?"

"Perhaps he disliked your singing," a female voice said, and Emma whirled around. Not like her singing. Impossible.

"I'm sorry?" Emma said, affronted.

"Not your voice, it's extraordinary," she said, staring at Emma through a silver and scarlet mask. "But the attention paid to you instead of him. You outshone him."

"Just like Lord Blackbourne..."

"You're acquainted with Lord Blackbourne?" she asked with a raised brow.

"A little. It's of no consequence," Emma said. "I am sorry about depriving the pianoforte player of his audience."

"Don't apologize. One should never apologize for one's talents. I never have."

"Do you sing?"

"I suppose I could if a role called for it."

Emma peered closer at the lady. "Are you an actress?"

"Tonight I am." She twirled around, her velvet dress swirling around her legs. "Can you guess who I am?"

Emma studied her. A tall, powdered pompadour wig, curled and decorated with a smattering of ribbons and tiny jewels, sat atop her head. She wore a low-cut silk gown twenty years out of fashion while a tiny silver watch hung by a silk ribbon from her waist. A beautiful lace brisé fan dangled from her wrist. "I'm sorry, but I'm afraid I don't know."

She lowered her mask revealing a white-powdered face, its paleness only relieved by a pair of startling jade eyes and a round beauty mark on one cheek. "The unhappy Marie Antoinette."

"Yes, now I see the resemblance." A tiny bouncer. Emma had never seen a likeness of the doomed French Queen. "I never thought to dress as someone else. Is that what one does at a masquerade?"

"What is a masquerade but acting? A place where one can reveal their desires—their true character—by hiding behind a mask," she said, and Emma detected a hint of cynicism in her words. "Take our pianoforte player, for instance. I'd say he's a gentleman who harbors a secret desire to play onstage but the ridicule he believes he'd receive from others won't allow him to do it. Instead, he comes here to play, hidden behind an extravagant volto mask. I expect he's another gentleman without the courage to do what he truly wants." She lifted her mask and surveyed the room as if looking for someone. "Yet, he holds actresses in such disdain."

What an odd thing to say. How could she know what he thought of actresses? "Perhaps he hasn't the confidence to play onstage."

"He plays well, does he not?"

"Not perfectly. I noticed a weakness in some of the notes. As if he wasn't sure he was pressing the right keys."

"You must have an ear for music."

"A family trait. One I share with my aunt." Oh, heavens. Her aunt. Lord Hefton. The boudoir. Had he come out? "Excuse me, I must go."

Emma whipped around the boudoir and slammed into a large gentleman. She reared backward and fell flat onto her bottom, her legs straight out in front of her.

How the devil had it happened again?

And not one single person offered her a hand up. She lifted her head. Even the cause of her current embarrassment had waltzed away without a backward glance. Say what one would about Lord Blackbourne, at least he had rushed to help her. A gallant gentleman in a snow-white neckcloth—much like the one worn by the man hurrying toward her now. Oh, heavens.

It couldn't be.

He moved closer, and Emma shook her head.

No, no, no. It can't be.

She laid her head back down and squeezed her eyes shut.

Oh, dear God, please don't let it be.

The gentleman settled next to her, and a familiar chuckle resounded from the depths of his chest. "Good evening, Miss Bryson."

A LAMENT—A CRI DE COEUR—REVERBERATED in Emma's soul. Surely a kind and loving God would not allow her humiliation two nights in a row. She lifted her head and saw Blackbourne settled on his haunches next to her, and she sighed. She was wrong. Again.

Still, she would not be intimidated. She would not allow the amusement lurking in his gray eyes to fluster her. Emma tilted her chin and stared right back. For a moment. Until she remembered Kat's admonition against staring—and the repercussions—and snapped her head down.

"Have you injured your neck again?" Blackbourne asked, his voice edged with concern.

"No, I'm fine. I'm just…" Emma searched for an excuse and his boots caught her eye. "I'm just admiring your boots. They're shiny. Exceptionally shiny. Almost like a mirror."

"I'm told one can see their reflection in them."

"Really?" Emma stared hard at one boot. A flustered and chagrined reflection stared back.

"Is something the matter?" he asked.

"Not at all." Emma straightened. She really must do better at not getting flustered by him. "Your valet did an excellent job."

"I'll tell him you said so," he said. "Now, let's get you up, shall we?" Emma nodded, and Blackbourne clasped her by the elbows and brought her to her feet. "Thank you," she said, shaking out the folds of her gown and pointedly ignoring his amused gaze.

"Do you find it as strange as I do, Miss Bryson," he said, "that we should meet again in such an extraordinary fashion?"

"I've no idea what you mean."

She knew exactly what he meant but thought it unmannerly of him to mention it.

"First, you fall."

Very unmannerly.

"Then a short discussion on my apparel ensues to be topped off by a compliment to my valet."

Emma sighed. It did appear that way.

"Do you suppose it has some sort of significance we're unaware of?"

"Hardly," she retorted. "Unless being knocked to the ground by a rude, unmannerly coxcomb is somehow significant." She glared at the coxcomb not five feet away.

"You think the Prince a coxcomb?"

"The Prince?"

"No. The Prince."

A sinking feeling enveloped Emma. "Are you saying the gentleman who bumped into me, who knocked me over, is—no, you're teasing me."

"You must've heard the creaking?"

Emma sucked in a breath. She had heard it. A low drawn-out creak, like a tree falling to the ground. She had been knocked over by Prince George. "I can't believe it."

"Trust me. It is him."

"No, I can't believe he knocked me over and ignored me." Ignored her voice.

"You must forgive him. I believe he'd just caught sight of Mr. Brummell." Emma followed Blackbourne's gaze to the well-dressed gentleman Kat had pointed out earlier. "No one enrages him more, except, perhaps, his wife." Emma laughed then sobered. This was no time for joking. Prince George was getting away. She must do something. She must get his attention. She must *sing*. She closed her eyes and belted out, "'Tis the Last Rose of Summer." Two full verses. There. That should have got his attention.

She opened her eyes to find Blackbourne staring at her, his mouth slightly ajar. "Are you certain you didn't injure your brain, Miss Bryson?"

"Where did he go?"

"The Prince? Into that boudoir."

Blast. "I should've sung a third verse."

"Ah, now I see," Blackbourne said. "You sang to get his attention."

"How else would he know who I am?" Emma shoved her mask atop her forehead. "How did you know it was me?"

His gaze trailed down her throat, swept over her bodice, and returned to her face. Her hot, flushed, face.

"You've other delightful attributes that distinguish you."

Good heavens. Marie Antionette was right. A masquerade did reveal a gentleman's true character. Emma covered her décolletage with her hand. "My lord, I don't think—"

"Your necklace."

"I'm sorry?"

"I couldn't help but notice it last night."

"Right. My necklace. That's what you were staring—"

"Now," he said. "Where is your company? I can't imagine you've come here alone."

"Assuredly not. I came with my Uncle and Aunt Carstead."

"Where are they now?"

"Mr. Carstead is playing cards, and my aunt spilled some champagne on her gown and went to find help in cleaning it."

"Why didn't you go with her?" The hint of suspicion in his voice surprised Emma, and she said, "She asked me to... I mean, she dashed off so quickly."

"I see." He studied her for a moment, and Emma didn't think he believed her. "Until she returns, I suggest you join Lady Heyer and I at our table."

"Lady Heyer is with you?"

"Not at the moment but she'll join us soon."

Emma bit her lip and debated whether to sit with him.

"You may safely join me, Miss Bryson. We are acquainted after all," he said, as if reading her mind. "Though you might wish to lower your mask."

Oh, heavens. How could she have forgotten? Emma yanked it down. Hopefully, no one recognized her.

"Miss Bryson?" A gentleman poked his head around Blackbourne, spikes of blond hair sticking up over his mask like dry grass. "Miss Emma Bryson?"

Blast. What should she do? Ignore him? Acknowledge him? Barrel out of the Saloon in a panic? Blackbourne decided for her. "Shall we find Lady Heyer?" he asked and extended an arm.

"Yes, thank you." Emma placed her hand on his sleeve. No reason to speak to a stranger. What could he have to say of interest anyway?

"The same Miss Bryson who sang so gloriously last evening?" he asked.

Emma stopped. On second thought, it'd be rude not to acknowledge him.

Blackbourne said, "I should warn you..."

Warn her against what? Praise? Admiration? A compliment about last night's performance? Frankly, her pride could use one about now. Mr. Claimore having been so meager with his own. She turned to the stranger. "Thank you, you're too kind. Mister...?"

"Mr. Vasec, at your service." He bowed and flashed Emma an obsequious smile. "I must tell you when I first heard your voice, I thought to myself, this is a voice worthy of the salons of Europe."

Emma preened. If only he had written her review. It would have been filled with compliments. No gratuitous comment about her fall, no comparison to a pigeon, no mention of a particular earl.

"And here you are with Lord Blackbourne again."

"Oh, right. Yes." Emma smoothed the folds of her gown.

"Just like last night. How... fortuitous."

"A coincidence," Emma said.

"A rather interesting coincidence," Mr. Vasec said. "At least many of my friends would find it so."

"I think you could find other, more interesting things to share with your friends," Blackbourne said, and Emma detected a hint of a warning in his voice.

"Such as, my lord?"

"My boots. I'm told they're exceptionally shiny."

Mr. Vasec glanced at the boots. "They are indeed."

"That is a charming detail you may share with your friends."

"Thank you, my lord. I'll be happy to do so."

"Now, Miss Bryson, I believe I see your aunt. It's so easy to get separated in this crowd." Blackbourne tucked Emma's hand into his arm. "Shall we?"

Mr. Vasec bowed his head goodbye, and Emma gave him a chilly nod in return. A moment later, Blackbourne steered her into a booth hidden under the staircase and sat opposite her. "I imagine you're a bit confused about Mr. Vasec."

"I dare say. What a silly man. Why must he regale his friends about a masquerade?"

"His so-called friends are gossipmongers. You must've read his article this morning." Blackbourne settled back against the booth. "A voice that travels higher and farther than a carrier pigeon?"

"No, you're wrong. Mr. Claimore wrote those odious words, not—"

"Nom de guerre."

"I'm sorry?"

"During wartime, some Frenchmen found it practical to take a 'nom de guerre' or war name to hide their true identity from the enemy."

"They fought under a false name?"

"For very practical reasons. It lessened their chance of getting shot if they were ever captured. It appears Mr. Vasec did the same for his writing endeavors." A slight smile curved his face. "He is Mr. Claimore."

"How despicable," Emma said. "Why didn't he just introduce himself as Mr. Claimore?"

"Perhaps he thought you'd shoot him," Blackbourne said.

"He thought correctly," Emma said forcefully, then flushed. "I mean..."

"One can forgive him that deception, but one finds it more difficult to forgive his other affectation." His eyes turned slate gray. "Really, Miss Bryson, have you ever met anyone who spells Claimore with an 'I'?"

Emma couldn't help it. She laughed. What an absurd thing to say.

"How pretentious!" he continued. "Why not spell it with a 'y' like the fearsome Scottish ax? One would be quite intimidated by a gentleman bearing that name."

"I can't see Mr. Vasec wielding such a heavy weapon." Emma grinned then a horrific thought struck. He had a more potent one. His pen. What would he write tomorrow? "Do you think he saw me fall?"

"I'm afraid many in the room did."

"Then he also saw you helping me up. It's last night all over again. I can't have another article about my falling, about *you*, and not my voice." Why had she even spoken to him? Why had she let her conceit, her pride in her voice, overcome her sensibility?

"I predict Claimore's article will be full of praise tomorrow."

"Do you think he heard me singing to Prince George?"

"I beg your pardon. I was talking about my boots." His eyes danced with amusement. "But why not your voice also? It's as brilliant as my boots."

"How kind of you to say so," Emma retorted, then a thought struck. "Is that why you mentioned your boots? To keep him from writing anything about us?"

"Us?"

"You know what I mean."

"I've learnt that, if one gives the press a morsel to chew on, it generally keeps them from the buffet."

"I can't eat just one piece of marzipan, my lord. I always want more," Emma said. Would Claimore be satisfied with a morsel, or would he want more? Or were there other journalistic appetites being whetted? Taking notes? Planning to reveal all in their article tomorrow? She would not share her marzipan with them.

"Thank you, my lord, but I can't take the risk of being seen sitting alone with you."

"Please stay, Miss Bryson," he flashed her a charming smile, which stopped Emma for a moment. "Allow me to order you some dinner."

"Thank you, my lord, but no. I must be going." Emma slid down the booth and was about to stand up when a shiny Hoby boot slammed right next to her thigh.

EMMA STARED AT THE shiny boot and her shocked face stared back. Did Blackbourne mean to keep her in the booth? Imprison her. To thwart her leaving again? The boot shifted closer to her thigh. Apparently, so.

How infuriating. How rude.

"How extraordinary." A male voice interrupted Emma's internal fulmination, and she whipped her head up to find Mr. Brummell by the table, a quizzing glass lifted to one eye. He stared at the boot and lowered his glass. "My dear Blackbourne," he said. "How does Simms do it?"

Blackbourne shrugged. "His secret I'm afraid, Brummell."

"Perhaps he'd be kind enough to share this little secret with Robinson?"

"You've my permission to ask him." Blackbourne brushed a nonexistent piece of lint from his coat. "And my apology now for his refusal." Brummell seemed surprised but then bowed stiffly and walked away.

"Now, Miss Bryson," Blackbourne slid his boot off the bench and straightened. "What do you think of the lobster?"

Emma blinked. He had just blocked her in the booth. Imprisoned her. Thwarted her just as surely as he had thwarted her the night before and his only thought was... dinner? She sputtered, "Lobster?"

"I beg your pardon. Have you eaten already?"

"No, I haven't but that's not—"

"Then you must try the lobster. The Saloon is famous for it. Just like their champagne. A perfect combination," he said. "A woman should never be seen eating unless it be lobster salad and champagne, the only true feminine and becoming viands." He sat back. "I'm quoting Byron, of course."

"Byron?"

"Lord Byron. He dabbles in poetry. Are you certain you didn't injure your—" He waved in the general direction of her head.

"I know who he is," she snapped. "I've seen his neckcloth."

"An abomination. Simms would never countenance it."

His lightheartedness caused Emma's anger to be replaced with perplexed exasperation. "My lord, do you not realize how unmannerly it is to block a lady—"

"Ah, Blackbourne, there you are." A gentleman's voice interrupted Emma, and a flash of brightly colored waistcoat caught her eye. Good heavens. Lord Hefton. How could she have forgotten? The evening was turning into a complete disaster.

"I'm returning Lady Heyer to you safe and sound," Hefton said. "As promised."

"Thank you, Hefty."

"Now, if you'll excuse me." Hefton backed away.

"No, Hefty." Lady Heyer held on to his arm. "Please stay with us."

"I'm afraid I can't, my dear. There's a gentleman I simply must speak with, but I promise to join you later." He gently disengaged her hand, bowed, and left.

"How vexing," she said. "I'd hoped to at least keep him from the card tables, having failed at keeping him out of the boudoirs."

"You mustn't hover over him so, Amelia," Blackbourne said. "He knows what he's about."

"I can't help it. I'm afraid he's following in Stephen's footsteps." Her gaze went to Hefton, who had joined a group of men. "Especially in the company he keeps."

"Speaking of company," Blackbourne said. "Miss Bryson has joined us."

"Miss Bryson?" Lady Heyer turned an extravagant yellow beaded mask—an exact match to her yellow gown and gloves—on Emma. "Is that you? How delightful."

She sounded more surprised than delighted. "Thank you, my lady. I'm sure you must wonder—"

"She's lost her aunt," Blackbourne said.

"Mrs. Carstead," Emma said. "You met her this morning."

"Yes, I had that... pleasure." She sat next to Blackbourne. "I apologize for my surprise, but I'd no idea you were coming out this evening."

"I'd no plans to do so, but Mrs. Carstead thought I could help... could use some amusement."

"I decided to attend at the last minute myself." Her gaze returned to Hefton. "I'm only glad Blackbourne agreed to escort me. I know he doesn't enjoy a masquerade."

"How could you know that?" Blackbourne stared at his sister.

She shrugged. "You aren't wearing a mask."

"He must not have anything to hide," Emma said and flushed. "I've been told that's why some wear masks."

"Yet, you're wearing one, Miss Bryson," Blackbourne said. "I wonder what that could mean?"

"It means Miss Bryson and I plan to enjoy the masquerade," Lady Heyer said, and Emma nodded her agreement.

"And I merely left mine at home," he said, and Emma wondered at the curtness in his voice. "Now," he said, "shall we order something to eat?"

The amiable manner in which he asked sparked a debate in Emma's mind.

She knew she should find her aunt. Or follow Lord Hefton. Or even stand by the boudoir and await Prince George. She especially knew being seen long in Blackbourne's company would add fuel to the gossipmonger's fire, yet she had a strange compulsion to stay. "I suppose I am a bit hungry."

"Champagne and lobster it is." Blackbourne waved down a waiter.

"Lemonade for me, please," Emma said. "I don't care for champagne."

"I've never heard of such a thing," he said. "It makes me think you've never tried it."

"I have once. French Champagne my uncle had gotten as a surprise for my aunt. It was supposedly quite special, but I can't remember why."

"Veuve Clicquot, 1811. The year of the comet," Blackbourne said. "Some think it caused an unusually fine vintage of grapes to be harvested that autumn."

"All I know is it made me giddy."

"Now that is the bubbles." Blackbourne said. "Now that is something special about French Champagne. I think the Portuguese wine served here might be more to your liking."

"You should listen to him, Miss Bryson. If anyone understands wine, it's Philip," Lady Heyer said. "Even our cousin, Lord Worthington, a connoisseur himself, bows to his superiority."

"Worthy would never admit to anyone being superior to him in anything."

"He might not but your parlor trick always proved it."

"Parlor trick?" Emma said, intrigued.

"More like a wine-tasting trick," Lady Heyer said. "When I was younger, Philip would entertain my friends and I by having our steward give him three different glasses of wine to taste. Not only could he tell us what sort of wine it was, but where it was made and its vintage. We even placed small wagers on the outcome."

Good heavens. Blackbourne's wager, Lady Heyer's gambling, and their cousin Hefty in deep with card players. Was it a family of gamesters?

"It was a delightful time. Blackbourne House was never as lively as those nights. Full of life and laughter and then..." Lady Heyer sighed. "The circumstances of our lives change whether we desire it or not."

Emma agreed. Her mother's death was one such circumstance. She had not wanted her life to change—and she was not ready to move on.

"Though I was happy to marry dear Heyer, I must admit I dreaded leaving Blackbourne House. It's mostly shuttered now. How many rooms have you kept open Philip?"

"Enough for a single gentleman to live quite comfortably. There's no reason for more."

"True, even our mother, Lady Blackbourne, doesn't live there now. She prefers her townhouse in Mayfair."

"She prefers being close to her friends," Blackbourne said and laughed. "It makes it much easier for them to get together and discuss the faults of their children. Is she come back from Italy yet?"

"Yes, I'd a note from her earlier. A mad unplanned trip, Miss Bryson. I don't know how she does it. There and back in five weeks. I'm sure such a trip would've exhausted me and I'm twenty-five years younger."

Blackbourne chuckled. "Lady Blackbourne would never let something as inconvenient as her age stop her from doing whatever she wanted."

The siblings laughed and a strange sense of envy spread through Emma. Their affection for their mother and each other was obvious and something she missed profoundly. If anything, her mother's death had thrown her own loneliness into relief. Aside from Malcolm, she had no one left from her childhood with whom to reminisce.

"Why shouldn't she do as she pleases?" Lady Heyer said. "Her children are grown. It's been an age since we all lived together at Blackbourne House. Perhaps someday it'll be filled with laughter again."

"When your children are old enough to come and stay with their uncle, I'll entertain them with the same games as I did with you."

Emma started. How odd. Her children? What of his own? Did Blackbourne expect no heir? Ever? Was it truly to be a marriage of convenience? A cold loveless marriage conceived to win a bet—but not children?

"Why not play one now? Shall you try your luck tonight, Amelia?"

"What do you say, Miss Bryson?" Lady Heyer perked up. "Shall we?"

"I would like to see if he really is the connoisseur he claims to be." He could not possibly excel at everything like Kat claimed.

"You've been challenged, Blackbourne."

"And I shall rise to it." Blackbourne waved a waiter over and quickly told him what he needed. The waiter left, and Lady Heyer turned to Emma and said, "We must attend closely, Miss Bryson. He mustn't be allowed to trick us."

"Don't worry, my lady." Emma grinned. "He shan't get anything past me."

"Won't I?" Blackbourne said.

"No, my lord. I shall watch you like a hawk."

"I can't imagine a lovelier set of eyes to have on me."

Emma's cheeks burned at his unexpected compliment, and she was grateful for the waiter's return, even with half the denizens of the Saloon in his wake.

"Word has got out about your wager Blackbourne," his sister laughed. "You'd better win, or they'll be very disappointed."

The waiter placed a tray with three goblets of wine on the table. He lifted the first glass, but Lady Heyer raised her hand. "Wait."

"Is there a problem, Amelia?" Blackbourne asked.

"I think we should be allowed to see the wine poured into the glasses." She grinned at Emma. "To be fair."

"The waiter seems trustworthy enough," Blackbourne said.

"Well, I think he should be blindfolded," Emma said.

"You wish to blindfold the waiter, Miss Bryson?"

"Not him. I meant you."

"Ah, it's me you don't trust." He leaned back. "Understandable, we hardly know each other."

"It's not that," she said, flustered. "Lady Heyer said you could do it by taste alone."

"She has you there." Lady Heyer grinned.

Blackbourne studied Emma for a moment, then whispered to the waiter who gathered up the tray and disappeared through the crowd. "Now, Miss Bryson. About your desire to see me blindfolded." He lifted a linen napkin from the table and extended it toward Emma.

"You can't possibly expect me to do it?"

"How can you be certain my eyes are covered unless you do?"

Those uncovered gray eyes held a challenge—and Emma determined to meet it. She grabbed the napkin and went and stood behind Blackbourne. She bit her lip. How did one tie a neckcloth around a gentleman's head? Emma wrapped it around his forehead and held it against his temples. Blackbourne's warm fingers covered hers.

"Shall I hold it for you?" he asked.

"Uh, thank you," she said and quickly knotted it and stepped back.

"Can you see anything, Blackbourne?" Lady Heyer waved a hand in front of his face.

"Nothing," he said. "Miss Bryson has completely blinded me."

"Has she?" Lady Heyer said enigmatically, and Emma's cheeks warmed.

"The waiter has come back," Emma said, then under her breath, "Just in time."

The waiter placed a tray laden with three empty goblets and three linen-wrapped bottles onto the table. "Will this do, my lady?" he asked Lady Heyer.

"Perfectly." She nodded. "Please proceed."

He removed the linen from one bottle and, at Lady Heyer's nod, poured a glass and placed it by Blackbourne's hand. "There you go, my lord."

"Thank you," Blackbourne said and picked up the glass, and the crowd hushed. He swirled the liquid around in the glass a few times, making more of a production of it than Emma thought necessary, and brought it to his lips. "Madeira... made on the island of the same name... 1803."

"Well done, my lord," the waiter said, and a roar of appreciation rippled through the Saloon. He took up the second bottle, poured it, and handed the goblet to Blackbourne.

Blackbourne sipped and set down the goblet. "I'm afraid I have the advantage of this one as I've a few bottles of it in my own cellar. Still, an excellent choice and one that would make one lady in particular quite giddy. A sight I would love to see."

He grinned directly at Emma, and she just stopped herself from kicking him. "We want to know the vintage, my lord, nothing else," she said.

"Champagne, French, Veuve Clicquot, 1814."

"Well done again," the waiter said as he lifted the third bottle and filled the remaining goblet. "Good luck, my lord."

Blackbourne sipped. "I see you've saved the best for last," he said. "Brandy, more specifically, Armagnac brandy, produced in France, 1810."

The waiter nodded, and the crowd applauded. Blackbourne held up a hand. "Shall I describe its color too?" The room quieted. He took up the goblet, sipped, tilted his head as if in thought. "Smooth, thick, rich. Yes, all these suggest it's the same lovely caramel color as the eyes of a lady sitting opposite me."

A knowing laughter rippled through the crowd, and Emma had a sudden desire to crawl under the table... and straight out of the Saloon. "Describing its color wasn't one of the requirements, my lord," she hissed.

"Perhaps not." He removed the blindfold and pierced Emma with a pair of amused slate-gray eyes. "But I am correct."

His gaze held her. She could not look away. Even as her cheeks burned, and her stomach tightened, and her breath fluttered, trembled, and stayed trapped in her chest.

"It seems you've won," Amelia's voice broke through, and Emma could finally breathe.

"What's my prize?" Blackbourne said while his gaze lingered on Emma, compelling her to turn away.

"Oh dear," Amelia said. "I fear trouble is brewing." She nodded her head at Hefton and slid out of the booth. Blackbourne caught her by the arm. "Be careful."

"I only wish to speak to him."

"I meant be careful of others."

"Don't worry." She jangled her bracelet. "Everything I'm wearing is paste."

"I'm glad you took my advice. Still, take care," Blackbourne said. "I wouldn't want you to have anything else stolen."

Lady Heyer's gaze fluttered over Emma and back to Blackbourne. "You're more in danger of having something stolen than I am." On that cryptic remark, she left and joined Lord Hefton.

Emma spoke without thinking, "Why would you advise Lady Heyer to wear fake jewelry?"

"A lesson from my past," he said tight-lipped. "I should say, a lesson from my aunt's past."

"Really?" Emma did not believe him. His reaction spoke of a more intimate lesson than one from an aunt. "What happened?"

"The poor lady had her jewels stolen by highwaymen and determined to never wear real ones when traveling again. She had pastes made of all of them, even those of little monetary value."

Emma could believe that and touched her pendant. It had only sentimental value, but she would be devastated if it were stolen. It meant more to her than singing—than even fulfilling her promise. Her father had given it to her mother upon their engagement, and it was the last thing her mother had given to her.

"Do you think thieves are here? Is that why you told Lady Heyer to be careful?"

"I wouldn't be surprised to find I'm sitting next to one right now."

Startled, Emma shot a look at the next booth. A pair of young men sat across from each other, one tugging at his neckcloth, the other pushing his food around his plate like a child. In the other booth, a gaggle of older ladies chattering their way through dinner. "They all appear harmless enough."

"They're usually the most dangerous. One doesn't suspect them."

"How would one know then? How does one avoid them?" She grabbed her pendant again as if to hide it.

"In such a crowded place? Try not to get bumped." He laughed.

"I'm sorry?"

"It's how a bulk and file works. Shall I explain?" he asked, and Emma nodded.

"It's quite simple. One thief, called a *bulk*, holds the mark—the person they're stealing from—whilst the other thief, the file, steals their jewelry."

"How despicable. To purposely bump into—wait, I was bumped earlier, remember? By Prince George," she said excitedly, then straightened. "Or was it him?"

"You heard the creaking."

"That means nothing. I've been told many gentlemen wear a cors—I mean masks and pretend to be someone else."

"A bulk disguising himself as Prince George to steal jewelry at a masquerade? How intriguing. How brazen. How... improbable."

"Why?"

"You still have your necklace." He pointed to her throat. "To go to all that trouble, to bump a lady, to knock her down even, and yet fail to steal it? How humiliating! No self-respecting bulk could ever face his fellow thieves after that."

Emma laughed. He did say the most outrageous things. "Except you forget, my lord. It isn't the bulk's job to steal the necklace but the file." She studied him. "Come to think of it, you did come upon me awfully fast. Almost as soon as I hit the floor."

"My dear Miss Bryson, are you suggesting I'm the file?"

She arched a brow. "You clearly know how it all works."

"Thus, I know the file would come from behind."

"You could approach me—or anyone—from the front. No one would suspect you of being a thief."

"That's the key, isn't it?" he said. "To be a creditable thief, one must appear unassuming, even innocent."

"Nothing you'd ever be accused of," Emma said without thought, relieved when Blackbourne laughed.

"I would hope not," he said. "No, if I'd wanted to steal your necklace, I could've done so last evening. When we were in much closer proximity."

Emma blushed.

"No, Miss Bryson, I'm afraid I acquire my jewelry in a rather boring manner, from a jeweler." He stared at her from under his eyelids. "I assume that's how you acquired your necklace?"

Emma lifted her pendant. "No, actually I—"

"Oh, my dear, there you are." Kat's anxious voice startled Emma, and she jerked her head up. Oh, heavens. Kat stood by the table. "I was certain something terrible had happened to you," she said. "That perhaps you'd been kidnapped, and I demanded Mr. Carstead leave his card game and help me find you."

Her uncle? Emma's heart raced, and she dared to take a peek behind Kat. Mr. Carstead stood there. Red splotches covered his cheeks, his eyes bulged, and his head swiveled back and forth between Emma and Blackbourne.

Oh, heavens. Here it comes.

A torrent of Welsh words shot from his mouth like a cannonball, colorful, loud, and completely incomprehensible to Emma. Except one.

Offer.

EMMA'S HEART POUNDED. Quite flew out of her chest. Had her uncle just demanded Blackbourne make her an offer? Marry her?

"Uncle," she said, grasping her pendant in agitation. "There's been a mistake..."

"Mrs. Carstead." Lady Heyer materialized out of nowhere, and Emma sighed in relief. "How delightful to see you again."

"Your ladyship, hello." Kat dropped a rather unsteady curtsy, and Emma wondered how many glasses of champagne she had drunk.

"Perhaps introductions are in order." Lady Heyer hinted, and Emma hurried to do it. "Of course, yes," she said. "Lady Heyer, Lord Blackbourne, might I introduce you to my uncle, Mr. Carstead?" Her uncle bowed stiffly at Blackbourne. "And this is my aunt, Mrs. Carstead."

Kat made another unsteady curtsy, and Blackbourne stood. "Miss Bryson said she lost you, Mrs. Carstead," he said amiably. "Understandable in such a crowd."

"Lord Blackbourne was kind enough to ask me to join him," Emma said.

"With Lady Heyer, of course," Blackbourne added, smoothly.

Mr. Carstead's eyes narrowed. Emma had no doubt he had seen Lady Heyer's arrival, but he said nothing. He had not become one of the wealthiest men in London by being foolish. And questioning the word of an earl would be foolish.

"Won't you join us, Mrs. Carstead?" Lady Heyer sat.

"Thank you, my lady," Kat said and slid into the booth next to Emma. "We'd be delighted."

Mr. Carstead did not appear delighted, and instead of joining his wife in the booth, he barked out something in Welsh. "He's returning to his card game," Kat translated, "and bids you all good night."

Mr. Carstead stomped his way through the crowd, and Emma turned to Kat. "I'm sorry if I caused you to worry," she said. "I know I was to wait by the staircase, but I was lured away."

"Lured away?" Kat asked, and Emma wished she would lower her voice and her champagne glass. "What—or should I say *who*—could possibly have lured you away?" She tittered and smirked and absolutely mortified Emma.

"Music," Emma hissed. "I heard a favorite song being played on a pianoforte."

"Was it his lordship playing? I'm not surprised," Kat gulped her champagne. "You're known to have very nimble fingers."

Emma died.

Expired.

Perished right there in the booth, but she still managed to say in a faint accent, "It wasn't his lordship playing."

"I'm afraid not," Blackbourne said. "When it comes to playing any musical instrument, I'm rather cow-handed. Not nimble, at all. I'm rather envious of those who are." He smiled at Emma.

"My dear niece is quite musical," Kat said. "But you know that already. You heard her sing at Lady Heyer's. I'm only sorry I couldn't hear her sing in such a beautiful salon."

"You've heard me sing plenty," Emma said with a grimace. "You attended that little musicale, remember?"

"I have but your voice is wasted in outdoor gardens and little salons. It's made for the salons of Europe."

Emma preened. No denying that.

"I can't imagine Miss Bryson sounding poorly anywhere," Blackbourne said. "I'd have to hear her sing in both places to make a proper judgment."

"Then you're in luck, my lord," Kat said. "She's to sing at Vauxhall next week."

"Aunt, please."

"Did I say something amiss? I clearly remember you telling me Mr. McBride had arranged another engagement for you."

"Yes, Malcolm did."

But that was before she had fallen and become the center of gossip concerning the Earl of Blackbourne. Hopefully, he had the good sense to ignore Kat.

"Must I wait so long?" he asked to Emma's chagrin. "How nimble are your fingers, Miss Bryson?"

"I'm sorry?"

"The pianoforte. Can you play it as well as you sing?"

Unlike her singing, no one had ever mistaken Emma's tinkling for virtuosity, but there was no reason for him to know it. She tilted her chin. "Yes. If not better."

"I thought as much. I've a shamefully neglected pianoforte at Blackbourne House. No one has played it for years. Perhaps you could come some evening and play it for me?"

Kat gasped and said, "I'm certain my niece would love to play for you, Lord Blackbourne."

Panic swelled in Emma, and she just kept herself from kicking her aunt.

"An excellent notion, Blackbourne," Lady Heyer said, then whispered to her brother who nodded. She turned to Emma. "Would tomorrow evening be amenable, Miss Bryson? I could easily serve as hostess."

Under no circumstances would she play for him. He'd know her bouncer in an instant. Oh, why must she speak so impulsively? So pridefully? "I thought you said only a few rooms were in use?"

"It'd be difficult, true, but if we kept it to a small party, just us, and perhaps Lord Hefton."

Kat gasped, and Emma did not restrain herself. She kicked Kat under the table garnering the attention of Lady Heyer. "You must come too, Mrs. Carstead."

"I'd be delighted, my lady." Kat's voice and body and peacock feathers all trembled in excitement.

"But you can't," Emma spluttered.

"Why not?"

"Because... Miss Carstead's engagement party." Emma snapped her fingers. "That's it. The party. Remember?"

"I'd quite forgot."

"Miss Carstead and my uncle surely haven't."

"I'm sure." Emma held her breath as a war of emotions battered Kat's features. Frustration, dismay, and rebellion made an appearance before she—and her peacock feathers—drooped in defeat.

"I'm afraid I must decline, Lady Heyer," Kat said, and her voice cracked. "Alas, I'm having an engagement party for my sister-in-law, Miss Carstead. An excellent match. One we're all quite excited about."

"Thank you for the invitation, Lord Blackbourne," Emma said, hoping to forestall her crying. "But as you can see, we've plans for the evening."

Kat rallied. "You needn't attend the party, my dear."

"It's the polite thing to do."

"Fustian. You've never even met her."

"Surely, I can be of some help?"

"Why would I need your help when I have servants? Mr. Carstead is hardly grudging when it comes to servants." Kat smirked at Blackbourne, and Emma flushed at her tactlessness.

"You'd do me a great favor, Miss Bryson, if you'd agree to come," Lady Heyer said. "My brother rarely entertains, and I'm certain such a momentous happening would even induce Lord Hefton to join us. And having him there and not... anywhere else would mean so much to me."

"My dear Lady Heyer," Kat said, "I'm certain my niece would *never* deny Lord Hefton the chance to hear her play."

A sinking feeling enveloped Emma. There was no getting out of it. Her aunt wanted her to go. Lady Heyer wanted her to go. Lord Blackbourne wanted her—what did he want from her? Why the invitation to Blackbourne House? Did it matter? She had been trapped, thwarted by him, again. If only metaphorically. She mumbled, "Thank you, my lord, I'd be happy to come."

"Excellent." He stood. "Now that Miss Bryson has been safely returned to her aunt, I think we'll be on our way."

"Yes, now that I've a party to plan." Lady Heyer stood. "I shall visit you tomorrow morning, Miss Bryson, with Doctor Hamilton."

"And I shall see you tomorrow evening," Blackbourne said. "I'm looking forward to hearing you play." Emma clasped her amber pendant, in irritation. He seemed to glory in making her uncomfortable. To fluster her. To intimidate her. Now, that would not do. She released the pendant, stared straight into Blackbourne's slate-gray eyes, and declared, "I'm looking forward to it too, my lord."

EMMA HELD HER TONGUE until Blackbourne and his sister had melted into the crowd before turning to her aunt. "How the devil could you betray me like that, Kat?"

"Betray you? I did no such thing."

"Surely you saw how desperate I was not to go to Blackbourne House?"

"Surely you saw how desperate he was for you to come?" She crowed.

"Fustian." Emma shifted in her seat, uncertain if it was fustian or not. "He was merely being kind to Lady Heyer. She'd said earlier how much she missed Blackbourne House and the parties that were once held there."

"Lady Heyer could roam the halls of Blackbourne House anytime she wishes." Kat shot down that ridiculous notion. "You, on the other hand, only have tomorrow night. So, you must make the most of it."

Emma blurted, "I can't go."

"Why in heaven's name not?"

"Lord Blackbourne is expecting me to play the pianoforte."

"He's expecting more from you than that." She grinned.

"It doesn't matter. I'm not going. It'd be humiliating. I haven't played the pianoforte for years. Since before Papa died."

"Are you saying you haven't played at all for almost six years?"

"I've had no reason to," Emma said defensively. "Mama preferred I sing and if I needed accompaniment, then Malcolm was always willing to play."

"There must be one song you're proficient at. One you could fudge your way through." Kat tapped her fingers on the table. "I remember my brother loved Robbie Burns. You always used to play his songs whenever I came for a visit. Surely, you remember one of them."

Emma bit her lip. "I suppose if I must play something..."

"Excellent! Pick one and we'll go home and practice." She jumped out of the booth. "Practice all night. Practice till the very tips of your fingers bleed."

"Are you mad? Your children are abed now."

"Who cares about that? It's more important you play one song, competently, for his lordship. If my children must endure a midnight concerto, then so be it. It's musical. It's good for their souls. It might very well be good for their futures. Especially Elizabeth's. Lord Hefton will be there." With one pull she succeeded in dragging Emma out of the booth and pushing her into the swirling throng. "Now go."

Emma stumbled forward and bit back a laugh. Kat would have Mr. Carstead and the carriage in front of the Saloon in minutes and would even drive it to Blackbourne House tonight if she could. Tomorrow would be too soon for Emma. Next year would be too soon. Which Robbie Burns song should she play? Which one had she played the most? Showed her to the best advantage? Which one—*bam*! Emma's chin smashed into a chest. She reared back and was suddenly grabbed by the elbows.

"Oh, thank you." Emma straightened. "Why, you're the pianoforte player. I recognize your mask."

His head dipped forward in a yes.

"Thank you for keeping me from falling. You can't know how grateful I am." Emma joked.

He tilted his head but said nothing.

"I enjoyed listening to you play. The song was a particular favorite."

Nothing. Completely mute. And Emma wondered if the elaborate masks covered his ears too.

"I really must be going." She stared hard at his hands, still gripping her elbows. A moment passed, and Emma said louder, "I must be going." when without warning he released her and disappeared into the throng. How strange and rude. Emma dropped her jaw a bit at his rudeness.

"Emma." Kat's voice cut into her irritation. "Come along my dear. Your uncle has already called for the carriage."

"Of course." Emma quickly forgot the pianoforte player's rudeness and followed her out of the Saloon.

Half an hour later, Emma flew up the stairs, her satin domino sailing behind her, and bustled into her bedchamber.

Jo sprang from a chair by the hearth. "Are you all right, Miss Bryson?"

"Yes, yes, fine." Emma dashed to her trunk and threw open the lid.

"Are you sure, lass?" Jo asked. "You seem flustered. Did something happen at the masquerade?"

"No, nothing. I'm perfectly fine." Emma tossed a pair of linen shifts over her shoulder.

"Och, now I'll have to iron those again." Jo grabbed the shifts and a set of unmentionables Emma threw over the side of the trunk.

"And those," she said. "Tell the truth, lass, you had a wee dram of champagne tonight, didn't you?"

"Oh, for heaven's sake Jo, I had some lemonade, that's all." Emma flung an Indian silk shawl into the air, and Jo grabbed it. "Then you've gone mad, lass. Stark raving mad."

"I'm not mad, either." Emma sat back on her heels. The music sheets must be in there. She had packed them herself.

"Then what are ye clawing through yer trunk for?" She squatted down by Emma.

"Robbie Burns." Emma dived back in.

"Och, no, nae mad at all." Jo patted Emma's shoulder. "Wee Robbie isn't in there, lass. He's been in the grave for years."

"Not really him, Jo, but his song sheets. Here they are." Emma sprang to her feet, the sheets clasped in her hands.

"What do you need those for?"

"To practice."

"Now?" Jo placed the discarded items back in the trunk. "Ye have gone daft."

"I must, Jo. I've been asked to dine at Blackbourne House on the condition I play the pianoforte for his lordship."

"Play for yer dinner?" Jo straightened. "What sort of gentleman demands a lady perform for him before she's allowed to eat?"

"It's nothing like that. It just happened to come up in conversation that I could play the pianoforte—"

"But ye can't."

"Thank you, Jo."

"Then why'd his lordship ask ye to?"

"Someone might've given him the impression that I could."

"Not anyone who's ever heard ye play."

"It doesn't matter how it came about," Emma snapped. "It only matters that I practice."

"It's nearly three in the morning."

Surprised, Emma went to the mantel and peered at the clock, its glass covering casting back her reflection. Gone was the annoyed countenance she had seen in Blackbourne's boot earlier; it was replaced by a rather harried and frantic reflection and... "Oh, my God, it's gone."

"What's the matter, lass?"

"It's gone, Jo." Emma whirled around. "My necklace. It's gone."

CHAPTER 3

E mma lay limp and exhausted on the bedchamber chair. Jo had opened the window, but no morning breeze came through, only a heat as heavy and oppressive as Emma's spirits. Her prized pendant, the symbol of her parents' marriage, their fidelity, their love, was gone.

And it was all her fault.

Hot tears scalded her eyes. Why was she always so reckless? So impulsive? Why hadn't she taken better care?

"I hope we aren't disturbing you, Miss Bryson," Lady Heyer said, and Emma turned to find her, Kat, and Dr. Hamilton by her chair. She hadn't even heard a knock.

Emma straightened and wiped her eyes. "No, of course not."

"As you can see, Dr. Hamilton has come to examine you."

"Would you like to move to the bed, my dear," Dr. Hamilton said in a kind voice. "You might be more comfortable."

"She's comfortable enough in that chair, I'm sure," Kat piped in. "It's an exact copy of one at Carlton House that I've heard Prince George sits in every night. If he's happy with—"

"I'm fine where I'm at, Doctor," Emma interrupted. "Please just... proceed." None of it mattered. Not her examination, nor where she or Prince George sat. She just wanted everyone to leave.

Dr. Hamilton peered into her eyes, checked each limb, and checked her heart with his stethoscope. "How does your neck feel now?"

"Fine."

"Might I look anyway?" He clasped the sides of her head and moved it up and down. "Does that hurt?"

"No."

"Or this." He tilted her head from side-to-side.

"No."

"Excellent. Well, now this is strange. There's a tiny scratch around your neck. I don't remember seeing it the other evening," he said.

The question in his voice compelled Emma to go to the mirror. There was a line around her neck. A thin almost imperceptible red line.

"I'd the same sort of scratch on my wrist," Lady Heyer said. "The morning after my bracelet was stolen."

"Stolen?" Emma's eyes caught Lady Heyer's in the mirror.

"Don't worry, Miss Bryson. It healed quickly. Mine is barely noticeable now," she said in a reassuring manner and said to Hamilton. "The poultice you recommended, Doctor. Perhaps a similar one would help Miss Bryson."

"An excellent suggestion, Lady Heyer," he said. "Might I give you the recipe, Mrs. Carstead?"

A discussion about ingredients commenced between the two, but Emma barely heard any of it. Other thoughts crashed through her brain. Stolen... Blackbourne... paste... bulk... file... bumped. Emma's knees buckled.

"Are you all right, my dear?" Hamilton grabbed her by one elbow and Lady Heyer the other, and they helped Emma stagger to a chair.

"Have a piece of marzipan, my dear," Kat said. "It always makes you feel better."

"I don't want any."

"Good heavens, check her for a fever, Doctor."

"No, please. There is nothing wrong with me."

Nothing except her gullibility and too trusting nature, just as Malcolm had said. It had never once occurred to her that her necklace had been stolen, even after Blackbourne's warning about not getting bumped.

Bumped. Emma sat forward. "I was bumped."

"You bumped your head?" Hamilton said.

"What? No, I mean I was bumped last night, first by Prince George..."

"The Prince Regent bumped into you?" Kat asked, astonished.

"Yes and knocked me to the floor."

"I don't believe it."

"Believe it, Kat. I heard the creaking."

"I mean I can't believe you met Prince George and said nothing to me." Kat staggered backward, a hand on her chest, and Hamilton helped her to a chair. "How could you not tell me?"

"It's of no importance. He wasn't the bulk."

"My dear," Hamilton said in a kind voice. "Are you certain you didn't hurt your head?"

"Trust me, Doctor. I'm in complete control of my senses." Except her sense of anger. An exceptional anger that brought heat to her ears and a vice-like grip to her chest. "I've been berating myself all morning for something that wasn't my fault. I wasn't negligent. I wasn't careless. I wasn't thoughtless."

"What are you rattling on about, Emma?" Kat asked.

"I'm saying I didn't lose my pendant." She stood. "It was stolen."

IT HAD TAKEN HALF AN hour for Emma to convince everyone to leave. Half an hour to retrace her steps through the Royal Saloon and determine who had bumped into her last. To know who stole her necklace.

At that moment of revelation, Kat entered the salon, a newspaper in her hand. "I've read the paper front to back and there's not one word about your encounter with Prince—my dear," she said. "What's the matter? You've gone quite pale."

"I know who stole my necklace."

"Well, go on. Tell me."

"The pianoforte player."

"The rogue who lured you away from Lord Hefton?"

"The very same. I bumped into him on the way out of the Saloon. I was distracted, thinking about which song to play, and didn't even notice him until he had me by the elbows. He held on to them just long enough for the file to steal my necklace."

"Blackguard."

"I must find him, Kat. It's the only way to get my pendant back." Emma stood and paced. "But how?"

"You must hire a thieftaker. A dear friend of mine hired one after her ring was stolen. A large, beautiful pearl set on a gold filigree band. I loved it so much that I begged Mr. Carstead for one exactly like it except with a bigger pearl—"

"Kat, please."

"She hired a thieftaker, and within a fortnight, she had the ring back and the rogue transported to Botany Bay."

"Transported?"

"He's lucky he wasn't hung. It was a very expensive ring though not as expensive as mine. Mr. Carstead had tiny diamonds added to—"

"Never mind that, Kat. How does one find a thieftaker?"

"Mr. Carstead."

"My uncle is a thieftaker?"

"How droll you are," she said. "No, but he'll know how to hire one. You're in luck too, as he's in the library today."

Emma and Kat rushed to the library and found Mr. Carstead ensconced behind his walnut desk, a pile of papers spread out before him, and a scowl on his lips. The scowl deepened at the interruption but did not deter Emma. She told him everything that had happened, then said breathlessly, "I've been told you know how to hire a thieftaker."

"Aye, if one is worth hiring." He studied Emma with a keen eye. "Do you know the pianoforte player's name?"

"How could I? We never spoke."

"What he looks like?"

"I don't know. He wore a mask."

Disbelief sped across her uncle's features, and he muttered something in Welsh. Emma turned to her aunt for translation. "Kat?"

"He said it'd be a waste of good blunt to hire a thieftaker if you can't even describe the thief."

He nodded at Emma and returned to his stack of papers by way of dismissal. Emma and Kat returned to the salon, and Emma sank onto the couch. "There must be some way to find him, Kat," she said. "Some way to identify him. If only he'd other distinguishable features like Lord Blackbourne's brilliant neckcloth."

"Or his silver at the temples," she sighed. "Or his long nimble fingers."

"Nimble fingers." Emma sat forward. "That's it."

"One wonders what his lordship does with them."

"Not him, Kat. The pianoforte player. He played in a distinctive manner. I can't describe it but if I heard him play..." Emma jumped up. "I must return to the Royal Saloon tonight. Do you think my uncle could arrange it?"

"No doubt, but you forget the engagement party. It's the reason I can't join you at Blackbourne House."

"Oh, heavens. I'd completely forgotten. Well, it doesn't matter. I can't go now."

"Not go? Are you mad? Lord Hefton will be there."

"I'm sorry, Kat, but I must find my pendant."

One small—very small—silver lining. She wouldn't have to play the pianoforte.

"Lord Blackbourne is expecting you. Surely, you wouldn't want to disappoint him?"

"He'd hardly be disappointed." Emma dismissed that ridiculous notion.

"You wouldn't say such a thing if you'd read Mr. Claimore's newest article." Kat held up the paper, and Emma snatched it from her hand. What had that coxcomb written? Emma found the article and read aloud, *"Miss B—n, dazed by her fall and the extraordinary gleam of Lord B—'s boots, the fallen songbird was again helped up by his lordship. A providential act reminiscent of the sort he once performed for his wife."*

"His wife?" She dropped the paper. "Why didn't you tell me he had a wife?"

"Why should I?" Kat said, then frowned. "She's dead."

"Dead?"

"Of course, she's dead. He could hardly marry again if she was living."

"Yes, no, of course," Emma said, rattled. "How did she die?"

"Her carriage overturned in a storm the night of their first anniversary. What a tragedy! By all accounts Lord Blackbourne was devastated."

"How long ago?"

"Must be going on eight years. He fled to his country estate and only returned for his sister's wedding two years ago. He's stayed at Blackbourne House ever since, but he's never entertained. That's why his invitation to you is so fascinating. He's never done so for any other lady, not even his mistress, Lady Wallingford."

"Mistress?" Emma sputtered. "I assume this mistress is still alive?"

"Don't be silly. Who'd want a dead mistress?"

"You should've at least told me about her."

"Why? It's obvious he isn't going to marry her. He's all but given her a carte blanche."

"A carte—what?"

"Blanche. It's French for blank card, or something like, or so Elizabeth told me. She speaks excellent French. Though I've never been able to work out why a gentleman gives his mistress a blank card. I'd rather be given jewels. Or a little house in Mayfair. Or even—"

"Kat."

"I only know a gentleman would never give one to a lady he means to make his wife."

"Fustian. I'm sure gentlemen have married their mistresses before."

"Then why make such a public wager?"

"That is a mystery."

"Hardly. It's to let eligible females know he's on the marriage mart, and it's worked, too. Brilliantly. If you thought the Saloon a crush last evening, you should attend a function he's known to be at. You couldn't push your way in. Though perhaps you could."

"What do you mean?"

"After witnessing his singular attention to you last evening, I'm starting to believe, nay, have a great hope, that he has chosen you as the means to win his wager."

"Don't be ridiculous, Kat," Emma said. "He isn't going to offer for me. It's all speculation. Brought on by a fevered imagination."

"I'd hardly call my imagination fevered," Kat said, affronted.

"Not you, but Mr. Stanley Claimore. Of all the foolish and, dare I say, libelous things to write." She picked up the paper. "I wonder what Blackbourne thinks of his late wife being mentioned?"

"I'm more interested in what he wrote about his future wife." She read aloud, "*A gallant, perhaps even providential, act—*" She looked at Emma. "I wonder, was his coming to your aid, again, a providential act or an act of Providence?"

"Oh, for heaven's sake, Kat."

"Exactly! Heavens!" she laughed. "I think it is in the stars for you to marry Lord Blackbourne."

"The stars have nothing to do with it. One must be free to make such a momentous decision as one's choice of spouse."

Besides, even if he was standing outside eager to propose, she would reject him. Admittedly, he was charming and handsome, and made her laugh, but what sort of marriage would it be based on a wager? A loveless one, that's what, and not one she aspired to. She wanted one like her parents had, the sort of love the amber pendant represented.

The pendant.

Finding it was her priority now. Not her promise and certainly not anything to do with the Earl of Blackbourne.

"I'm sorry to disappoint you, but I won't be going to Blackbourne House. I must return to the Royal Saloon, and yes, I know you can't take me, but I know someone who can. Malcolm."

"Mr. McBride? You place far too much trust in that gentleman."

"You do not know him as I do, aunt. He's never let me down. He knows what this pendant means to me."

She had no doubt he would help her again tonight.

A RUSTLING SOUND DRAGGED Blackbourne's attention from his baked eggs to the door. A maid trembled in its frame. A new girl, already? No surprise there. Mrs. Collins, his housekeeper, probably had the agency on retainer, ready to hire any number of servants the moment he gave the go ahead. Which he had done a few hours earlier.

Blackbourne laid down his fork. "Is something the matter, Miss...?"

"Betty, my lord," she curtsied. "Nothing's the matter, at least I don't think—it's just, there's a lady waiting in the—"

"The lady is waiting no longer." A tall, stylish woman swept past the frozen maid into the room.

"You may go, thank you, Betty." The maid curtsied and darted away. Blackbourne stood and raised a brow at the intruder. "It's difficult enough getting decent help without you frightening them off, Mother."

"If you had decent help, my dear," she said with the quirk of a well-formed brow. "A footman would've answered the door, and that little mouse of a housemaid would've taken my hat and gloves."

"She's still learning, and as you can see, it's all sixes and sevens here this morning."

"That's all well and good, but as you can see, I'm still holding my hat and gloves. Though come to think of it, I'd not trust a new maid with them. Yellow calfskin. Very desirable."

Blackbourne laughed. "Would you mind, Thomas?" The footman bowed, took Lady Blackbourne's hat and gloves, and disappeared through the door.

Blackbourne pulled out a chair for his mother. "Have you eaten?"

"I have, thank you." She sat and stared at the sideboard. "Though the ham does smell delicious. You did well to keep Pierre."

Thomas returned, and Blackbourne motioned to him to fill a plate for Lady Blackbourne and sat.

"One slice of ham only, Thomas, with a bit of baked eggs too, if you please," Lady Blackbourne said. "And perhaps a scone."

"What brings you here so early?" Blackbourne picked up his fork. "Not that you aren't welcome, it's just unusual."

"Can't a mother visit her only son?" She spread a napkin across her lap. "One she hasn't seen in a month's time?"

"It isn't your filial fondness I'm questioning but the timing." He chuckled. "I've never seen you anywhere before two in the afternoon."

"I've brought you a gift from Italy. A statuette of Venus. It'll fill the little alcove in the foyer perfectly."

"The one that's sat empty for years? One that could've remained so for a few more hours?"

"It'd make an excellent conversation piece if one were to have guests over."

Blackbourne chuckled. Not surprised she knew of the party. "You mean, like this evening?"

She swallowed a bite of baked egg. "I must say I'm a bit taken aback. For nearly a decade, Blackbourne House has been closed up, shuttered, has enjoyed fewer visitors than a mausoleum and now, suddenly, you're hiring servants and throwing parties. All for a common singer."

Singer, yes, but common? He was starting to think otherwise.

Lady Blackbourne stabbed her fork into a piece of ham. "I wonder what's brought all this about?"

He shrugged. "I'd a sudden desire to hear her play the pianoforte."

"She plays, does she? This person seems quite accomplished. Singing, playing, acting."

Blackbourne raised a brow. "She isn't an actress."

"Then why was she speaking to one last night?"

"How could you know that?" Blackbourne chuckled. "Everyone was wearing a mask."

"You weren't, my dear." She popped a bit of fruit into her mouth.

"You astound me. You're back one day, and you know more about events in London than Bow Street."

"What can I say? I'm blessed with curious servants."

"Spies you mean."

"It wasn't just any actress she spoke to either, but Miss Burkes. Surely you remember that scandal? Amelia's friend from school? Little Jayne Mayfield, as that is her real name, devastated her father by tramping off to Sheffield to become an actress."

That was a surprise. What was their connection? Had they met at Sir Thomas's birthday party? "Are you certain it was Jayne Mayfield she spoke to?"

"Quite," she said, spreading some jam on a scone. "Worthington is making a fool of himself over her."

Another surprise. "I didn't know my cousin was back in London."

"Followed her back. He's making a complete cake of himself. Showering her with all manner of expensive gifts. Flowers, jewelry, French Champagne."

"*French* Champagne? Oh dear, he must be serious."

"Ha! Bribery, nothing more."

Blackbourne chuckled. He had done the same, once, after a disagreement with Francesca. He had surprised her with an 1812 bottle of Veuve Clicquot. She had been placated and rather amorous. How would Miss Bryson react to such a gift? Giddy came to mind. It'd have to be a Veuve Clicquot 1811. The year of the comet.

"Why the smile, Blackbourne?"

"Nothing." He straightened. "It's not unusual for Worthy to be besotted by an actress. In a month's time, he'll be on to someone new."

"Your aunt thought as much three months ago. Yet Miss Burkes is still very much around. Mark my words. She's holding out for marriage." She nibbled on a scone. "I wonder if that's what she and Miss Bryson were discussing. Their mutual schemes to marry two of the most eligible bachelors in London."

"Trust me. If Miss Bryson had any designs of that nature, she didn't show it."

In fact, she appeared desperate to avoid Blackbourne House altogether. Which begged the question—why? Did she have other plans for this evening? One her aunt did not know about—but a band of thieves would?

"Ha! She's as good an actress as Miss Burkes. That outrageous bump into the Prince Regent? Tell me that bit of Shakespearean farce wasn't planned."

"Bow Street, Mother." Blackbourne laughed. "You should offer them your services."

"All for naught, I'm afraid. She's much too young and dark for Prinny."

"You know this, how?"

"He might've written a poem about me," she said with a coy laugh, then quoted,

On Richmond Hill there lives a lass,
More bright than May-day morn,
She paused and patted her still bright and sunny hair.
Whose charms all other maids surpass,
A rose without a thorn.
She sighed. "Awfully romantic of him to use my name, Rose too."

"Awfully clever of Leonard McNally to do so, as he is the person who wrote it."

"Did he?" she said in a tone that found it questionable. "Well, it wasn't him who whispered that poem into my ear to try to secure my affections. Naturally, having already married your father, I demurred." She chewed her scone in a reflective way. "I wouldn't be surprised if it wasn't what drove him into Mrs. Fitzherbert's arms."

"Are you saying it was the denial of your charms that impelled Prince George to enter a scandalous and illegal marriage to a Catholic?"

"I'm only saying I rebuffed him, and he wasn't happy." She emitted a coy laugh, then sobered. "That's why you must be careful on whom you bestow your attention, Blackbourne. Miss Bryson can't be unaware of the significance of your invitation to dine here, not if she's read Claimore's article, 'Reminiscent of the acts he performed for his wife.'"

Blackbourne bristled. Claimore should never have mentioned Clarissa. "I'm certain Miss Bryson won't read anything into it." Even if she did, *he* meant nothing romantic by it.

"I hope not." She put down her fork and stared at him. "I'd hate to see you fall for her tricks."

"I'm too old to fall for any tricks—"

"But still young enough to make a foolish match. Your wager?"

"A private bet between gentlemen."

"Private?" She snorted. "Hardly. The broadsheets have had a field day with it." She tilted her head. "Though I suspect you knew that would happen. What does Lady Wallingford think of it?"

"We've never discussed it. Why would we?"

"You've favored her company for months. She'd have expectations."

"Trust me, she's not about to give up her freedom as a widow to marry me."

"She would if she thought she'd have to give up being your mistress. She's like her mother in that way," she said bluntly. "Do you have plans to see her any time soon?"

"Tomorrow, I hope."

He had a few more questions about the Mayfield party that he hoped she could answer.

"Could you deliver a gift from her mother? Lady Tisdale couldn't pull herself away from Italy, or an Italian count, so she sent it with me. A delightful fan, as charming as any made in France."

The door swung open, and Simms stood at the entrance.

"Good morning, Simms," Lady Blackbourne said.

"Welcome home, your ladyship." Simms bowed.

"Hard to believe Hefty's atrocious waistcoat was mentioned in the *Morning Chronicle*," she said with a shake of her head. "Let alone praised."

"It does cause one to despair."

"At least his lordship's boots were praised too. That should give you some small comfort and keep you in the running."

Blackbourne chuckled. Naturally, she knew of his valet's wager too. "Is there something you needed, Simms?"

"Your newest coat has been delivered, my lord. The blue superfine. Shall I ready it for this evening?"

"An excellent choice as usual, Simms," Lady Blackbourne said. "You know what suits your master."

The door opened again, revealing Betty. She curtsied and held out a silver salver. "This was just delivered for you, sir."

Thomas took the card and gave it to Blackbourne, who read it. Then read it again. Then a third time.

"Is something the matter?" Lady Blackbourne said.

"It seems you brought the statue over for naught, Mother." He slipped the note into his pocket. "Miss Bryson is unable to attend this evening. It seems her necklace was stolen."

She put down her fork. "I don't believe it."

Neither did Blackbourne.

"Declining an engagement with you simply because a paltry amber stone was stolen?"

"Bow Street, Mother." Blackbourne laughed and turned to his valet. "There's your answer, Simms. I shan't be wearing the new coat."

"I expect your plans haven't changed at all, my lord," Simms said, "only the venue."

"Thing is, I'm not certain where the venue is now."

"That's the beauty of a well-cut coat, sir. It can be worn anywhere." Simms walked to the door. "Though if you could wear it somewhere public, hopefully to be raved about in the morning papers, I'd be most appreciative. We both have a wager to win."

THE HOUSEMAID HAD BARELY got out the words, "There's a visitor waiting in the salon," before Emma flew out of her bedchamber and down to the salon. "Malcolm," she said, rushing over to him. "I knew you'd come."

"I'll always come when you're upset," he said and enclosed her hands in his own. "I know how much the pendant meant to you."

"Now to have it stolen," Emma said. "I still can't believe it."

"Are you quite certain about that?" Malcolm asked. "Have you searched everywhere? Your bedchamber? Your clothes? Under your pillow?"

"No, I *know* it was stolen." She tilted her head and bared her throat. "See the scratch? It proves someone tore it off my neck."

He ran a finger over the scratch. "Does it hurt?"

"Hardly. I didn't even know it'd happened until Dr. Hamilton pointed it out." She paced. "If only it had hurt, I might've known then what happened and stopped the file from leaving with it."

"File?" He stopped. "Where did you learn such slang?"

"Lord Blackbourne. He explained how it all worked."

"He dared to use thieves' cant when speaking to you?"

"It wasn't like that. Lady Heyer mentioned she was wearing paste jewelry, and I asked why, and he told me she'd done so at his suggestion, as he knew there were thieves everywhere, even the Royal Saloon, which quite shocked me."

"Hold on. You were with him last night?"

"Yes, after I lost my aunt, he kindly asked me to join him and Lady Heyer."

"He just happened to find you in that mob? I wonder what he's about?" he mused, aloud.

"If you're thinking I'm the means to his winning his wager, you're daft," she said, exasperated by the turn of the conversation. "I'm certain Lord Blackbourne has no interest in marrying me."

"No, but his interest might lie elsewhere..."

Emma gasped. Did he think Blackbourne meant to seduce her? How ludicrous. "I'm certain he has no plans of that nature."

"You're too gullible and trusting to see it."

"I'm not as naïve as you think," she snapped. "I'm interested in only one gentleman, and it isn't Lord Blackbourne."

"Now, who would that be?" he asked.

His soft tone dismayed Emma. She had noticed the change in his attentions since coming to London. Less childhood friend and more... more what? More grown-up? More possessive? More romantic? Emma thrust that thought from her mind. It was nothing she desired. Too much of her life had changed already.

"The thief who stole my pendant," she said. "I'm determined to find him."

He stared as if she had sprouted two heads. "You can't possibly know who he is."

"But I do. He's the pianoforte player. I recognized his mask, and I'm certain if I returned to the Royal Saloon—"

"Return to the Saloon? Are you mad?"

"But I must. It's the only place he'll play according to Marie Antionette."

Now he stared as if she had three heads. "Who?"

"A lady there dressed as Marie Antoinette. She explained everything. Why he played there. Why he hid behind a mask."

"Even if all that were true, and I'm not saying it is. He won't be there tonight. There's no masquerade."

That stopped Emma, and she thought for a moment. "Perhaps I could speak to the lady again. Perhaps she noticed something about him, some other way to identify him."

"Will she be dressed as Marie Antionette again? I assume she wore a mask too."

"Oh, no, I saw her face, but..."

"But?"

"It was covered in white powder."

"Good heavens, lass, you spoke to a Cyprian."

"A what?"

"I'm afraid I must reveal my own knowledge of cant. A Cyprian, Emma, is a prostitute."

"Oh, dear. I thought she was only an actress."

Malcolm laughed. "Some find no difference between the two."

"If thieves and prostitutes can enter the Royal Saloon so easily, I wonder why my aunt thought it so difficult."

"It is difficult for the wife of a tradesman but not a Cyprian. They're always welcome. Their powdered faces and dampened gowns are akin to a voucher for Almack's." His lips curved into a smile, and Emma laughed.

"Now, I think I've relieved you of your innocence enough," he said. "I am sorry your pendant was stolen, Emma, and you know I'll do what I can to help, but don't waste your time pursuing the thief. You'll never find him."

"It's all I can think to do to find my pendant."

"There's another way. Pawnshops. The Adam Tiler will be certain to sell it."

"*Adam Tiler?*"

"He's the person to whom the file hands off the stolen item."

"Good heavens, there's a third thief?"

"His lordship didn't mention that?" Malcolm said in a mocking way. "Perhaps he isn't as knowledgeable about these things as he pretends."

Emma ignored his petty remark and remained focused on her necklace. "So, you're saying this *Adam Tiler* would've sold my pendant in a pawnshop?" she asked, and he nodded. "Then we must go now." She headed for the door, but Malcolm grabbed her arm.

"You must give him time to sell it," he said.

"How long?"

"Sometimes weeks."

Weeks? Then even more time scrounging through pawnshops—there must be hundreds in London—whilst hoping no one else buys it first? No, she could not wait. She must at least try to find the pianoforte player.

He walked to the door and turned back. "I'm sorry this happened, Emma, but try not to worry. We'll leave London soon enough and put it all behind us."

Leave London? What did he mean? He must know she would never leave without her pendant. Emma pushed aside his strange comment. She had more important things to consider—like how to return to the Royal Saloon. A hired coach could get her there but how could she get in? If only she had money or connections or... a powdered face...

Like a voucher for Almacks.

A scheme formed in her mind. First, she must get a tin of white powder without drawing suspicion. Send a maid? No. Too risky. Kat would hear of it and would demand to know who it was bought for—and why. No, Emma must go and buy it. She'd hire a hackney now and hire the same driver to take her to the Royal Saloon later. She would have him wait around the corner and once the party was in full swing, she would sneak out the servants' door.

Impulsive, risky, and even mad—and she would do it.

❦

BLACKBOURNE PACED THE Heyer salon and waited for Amelia. If anyone could help shed light on Miss Bryson's claim of a "stolen" necklace, it was her. Why had she claimed it? Why not make up an illness, or say she was sore from her fall? He chuckled. Pride. She'd never mention anything about her fall to him.

Had he raised her suspicions by his knowledge of thieves' cant or showing interest in her necklace? Another thought struck. Had she discovered the lady she stole the necklace from was his mistress?

No matter what reason had raised her suspicions, her canceling had solidified his belief that she was involved with the thieves. It only remained to be seen whether she was the bulk, the file, or the Adam Tiler.

For a moment, doubt niggled him. Could he be wrong? She seemed too artless, too gullible to be a thief. Of course, one could easily be deceived by a woman's guile. Clarissa had proven that.

The door opened, and Lady Heyer hurried into the room. "I'm sorry for making you wait, Blackbourne, but ever since this happened," she placed her hand on her belly, "I find I'm exceptionally tired."

"A welcome fatigue," he said. "I'm certain Heyer will find it so."

"I'm sure," she said and settled onto the couch. "But you've not come to speak of an event that's a good six months away but something more immediate. Tonight's party?"

"There won't be one." He joined her on the couch. "Miss Bryson sent a note, canceling."

"I'm disappointed but not surprised. I think realizing her necklace had been stolen quite shocked her."

"Are you certain she was shocked by it?"

"Quite obviously so. The blood drained from her face so quickly she barely made it to the chair. Hamilton practically had to carry her."

"Really?" Perhaps she was the actress his mother claimed. "Then what happened?"

"She rattled on about Prince George knocking her over and suddenly stood up and declared her necklace had been stolen."

"Did she elaborate on this dramatic pronouncement?"

"Not at all. In fact, she became quite adamant we all leave."

Why insist they leave? Was she afraid she could not keep up the act? Afraid they would question her more deeply?

"She's to sing at Vauxhall next week," Amelia pulled Blackbourne from his thoughts. "Perhaps I'll attend. If she still performs."

"Why wouldn't she?" He sat forward. "You don't think she's planning to leave London?"

"No, I just think her fall might have injured her confidence."

Blackbourne swallowed a laugh. Confidence in her voice was one thing Miss Bryson did not lack. No, if she left London, it had to do with the necklace and a fear of getting caught. Still, until she was caught out, he must ensure she stayed in Town. "Perhaps I can arrange something that'd help her regain her confidence."

Somewhere Bow Street could catch the thieves in the act. He snapped his fingers. "Worthy. His ball is next week. I'll have him invite her to sing."

"That's very kind of you."

"Merely helping Miss Bryson get back on her feet, as it were."

"Let's hope Worthy agrees to it. He's supposed to announce his engagement that evening."

"That's the first I've heard of it."

"That's because he isn't enthused about the bride."

"He is enthused with an actress," Blackbourne said with a laugh "One you might know. Miss Jayne Mayfield?"

"My old school friend? But how delightful."

"Our mother doesn't think so. She's certain Miss Mayfield has only returned to London to try to catch Worthy in a parson's trap."

"Or to mend fences with her father before it's too late," she said. "I've heard the baronet's health is failing."

"Francesca said nothing of it. She attended his birthday party recently with her uncle. By the way, have you heard if anyone had anything stolen at your party?"

"I would hope not," she said, appalled. "Why?"

"Just curious." Blackbourne stood. "Anyway, if you'll excuse me, Amelia, I must speak to Miss Bryson."

"You can't mean to visit her now?"

"Why not?"

"At least wait until the proper time. You mustn't be too enthusiastic," Amelia said with a smirk. "You might put ideas into someone's head."

"Trust me, Miss Bryson will think nothing of it."

"I was speaking of Mrs. Carstead," she said, and they both laughed.

"I suppose it wouldn't hurt to wait another hour or two. There are other things I could do." Like question Francesca, again. Perhaps she had seen something odd at the Mayfield party. Or seen someone acting suspicious. Someone acquainted with Miss Bryson... Blackbourne stood. "Good day, Amelia."

A short time later, Blackbourne pulled up a block from the Wallingford townhouse in surprise. A hackney coach sat in his usual spot. A short stout man stood next to it, glancing at his pocket watch. Blackbourne leaned forward. Surely, he could not be waiting on Francesca. She never took a hackney. A moment later, she came out of the townhouse and hurried into the coach, followed by the gentleman.

BLACKBOURNE STOOD BY the mantel in the Carstead salon, surprised Mrs. Carstead had not yet appeared. After all, he had been in the house a full minute. As if on cue, the door swung open, and she darted straight for him.

"My lord," she said, curtsying. "How delighted I am to see you."

"Thank you. I apologize for not sending a card first, but I was concerned about Miss Bryson."

"You needn't apologize. You're always welcome," she said. "Please have a seat."

Blackbourne sat on the sofa, the cushions stiff and uncompromising. He shifted his hips.

"It just arrived two days ago." Mrs. Carstead said by way of explanation. "Almost an exact reproduction to one in Lady Stanley's salon."

Blackbourne lifted his eyebrows in surprise. "You're acquainted with Lady Stanley?"

"Not precisely. A few months ago, my daughter, Elizabeth, and I were taking a ride when our carriage broke down in front of her townhouse."

"Oh, dear."

"She was kind enough to let us wait in her salon whilst my driver arranged for another carriage. Though I hated to impose as I knew her son, Viscount Tilbury, had come down from Eton."

"Had he?"

"Oh, yes. Just the day before. One would've thought he'd be eating breakfast at that time, but apparently, he was still abed."

"No doubt he'd spent the night out with friends."

"I hadn't thought of that." Kat nodded.

"Perhaps your next carriage accident will happen in the afternoon."

"Let's hope. Anyway, you've not come to speak of my trials, but of Emma." She sat in a chair opposite Blackbourne. "As I'm sure you're aware that she's had some rather shocking news."

"Her necklace..."

"Stolen! One can hardly countenance it," she said. "Poor Emma is quite up in the boughs about it. I've offered to replace it. A paltry amber stone would be nothing to Mr. Carstead, but it had some sentimental value I believe."

He doubted it was the pendant that had Miss Bryson upset but the stolen chain. He tightened his jaw.

"Is something the matter, my lord?"

"No, I was just sympathizing with Miss Bryson. Might I tell her so, myself?"

"Of course, you'd wish to see her. I'll send a maid. Might I offer you some tea whilst we wait?"

"Thank you, yes."

Mrs. Carstead pulled the bell cord, and a few moments later a maid arrived. "Please tell Miss Bryson she has a visitor. A very important visitor." She flashed Blackbourne a smile. "And have Mrs. Frank bring some tea and to use the Limoges set."

A few minutes later a maid returned pushing a cart laden with a teapot, cups, and plate of biscuits. "I'll pour." Mrs. Carstead shooed the maid away. "How do you like your tea, my lord?"

"Plain please."

"Exactly how Emma takes it." She arched a brow. "How interesting."

Blackbourne would rather hear it was interesting from Miss Bryson. What the devil was taking her so long? Was she avoiding him? He glanced at the doorway.

"I'm certain she will be along any moment," Mrs. Carstead said and then sat. "You must give a lady time to make herself presentable."

Blackbourne sipped his tea. Or time to disappear.

An awkward moment passed. "Would you like a macaroon?" asked Mrs. Carstead.

"Thank you, no." He would like to see Miss Bryson. How unpresentable could she possibly be?

A rustle came from the door, and Blackbourne glanced up. Blast. Just a maid.

"Excuse me." Mrs. Carstead went into the hallway but left the door open. "What do you mean she isn't in her bedchamber?" She hissed. "Find her maid. She'll know where she's got to." She returned to the salon, her hands clutched together.

"Is something the matter, Mrs. Carstead?"

"No, I don't think so, but I'm afraid Emma might've gone out," she said, agitated. "But I can't imagine where..."

Blackbourne could. "Perhaps she's gone to visit friends."

"She only knows one other person in London, Mr. McBride, and he came to visit earlier."

"Could she have left with him?"

"No, he left alone. I made certain he did not overstay his welcome."

"Does she have a carriage at her disposal?"

"Naturally, she can use our carriage whenever she likes, but she didn't ask for it. Perhaps she went out for a walk," she said with a pensive look at the window. "Emma is a great walker."

Where did she walk to? A nearby jeweler? A pawnshop? Perhaps a ride around the neighborhood was in order. Blackbourne placed his cup down and stood. "Thank you for the tea, Mrs. Carstead," he said. "I believe I've imposed on you long enough."

"I'm sure she'll be back by this evening, Lord Blackbourne," Mrs. Carstead said. She seemed about to panic. "I know it's a bit unorthodox, and even forward of me, but you're welcome to come back then."

Blackbourne raised a brow at her audacity. "Isn't there some sort of party this evening?"

"You'd be most welcome at any party, my lord."

"Thank you, I'll keep it in mind." He bowed and strode out the door.

An hour later, he entered his study and threw his hat and gloves onto his desk. Miss Bryson must be a bloody great walker. He had circled her neighborhood twice and had not seen her anywhere. Where the devil was she?

"Is something the matter, my lord?"

Blackbourne turned to find his valet by his desk. "Too many unanswered questions, Simms," he said. "And the two women who hold the answers are both inconveniently missing."

"Missing, my lord, or simply not where you wish them to be?"

"It amounts to the same thing."

Francesca did not concern him—though her riding in a hackney with a gentleman was odd—but Miss Bryson? She was avoiding him on purpose. And would continue to do so until she thought he had given up.

"If one truly wants to find someone, one must go where that person is."

"First, one must know where that person—hold on." He did know where she would be that evening. And it was the one place her conniving aunt would ensure she stayed. "You know I think I shall wear the new coat this evening after all."

"You've found the venue, sir."

Blackbourne smiled. "Indeed, I have."

CHAPTER 4

E mma turned her head in both directions and admired her white powdered face in the mirror. It hid her identity well but not her irritation. How could Kat have been so tactless as to invite Lord Blackbourne to the party? Of course, he would not come—why would he?—but the threat alone had forced her to alter her plans. She could not slip out the servants' entrance and risk being seen. Her aunt would be told immediately and would insist she rejoin the party. No, she must leave a different way. The window above the back garden caught her attention. Why not? If Malcolm could enter through it, then she could leave through it.

The mantel clock struck half past nine, and Emma jumped up. She must go. The jarvey would only wait so long. But first... Emma picked up her glass, poured the water down her bodice and let out a yelp. Good God. There must be other ways to capture a gentleman's attention besides this torture. She grimaced. She wasn't out to catch a gentleman; she was out to catch a thief.

Emma pushed up the window, and it creaked. She stopped, her heart pounding. Don't be such a ninnyhammer. It was far too noisy downstairs for anyone to hear anything, even Kat.

She pushed it all the way up and glanced out. In daylight, the garden was a beautiful canvas of purples and reds and yellows and greens, but dusk and a heavy fog had painted everything a gloomy gray. Emma squinted. She could hardly see the ground. How far down was it? How sturdy was the branch? Why did no one have a bedchamber on the ground floor?

She whirled away from the window. She couldn't do it. She took a deep breath. She could do it. She must do it.

Emma returned to the window and hiked up her gown. She put one leg through the window and then the other, and sat on the sill, both legs dangling against the house.

Steady. Take a breath. Don't look down.

She grabbed the branch and pushed off. The branch bent low, and Emma's stomach dropped. The branch swung up, and her stomach entered her throat. She waited until it stopped, then exhaled. Now. Just. Pull. Yourself. Into. The. Tree.

A moment later, Emma sat on the trunk, and giddiness swelled in her chest. She'd done it. She was in the tree. Now to get to the ground. Gathering her courage, Emma stepped down gingerly from one small branch to another and had put her foot on the last one when a loud crack reverberated through the garden.

Emma's stomach lurched into her throat, and she thumped onto the ground. Colored lights exploded behind her eyelids. Her pulse pounded in her brain.

Suddenly, a dark shadowy figure rushed through the bushes, and Emma swallowed a scream. It wasn't her pulse she had heard.

It was footsteps.

EMMA SQUEEZED HER EYES shut. Please go away. Please, please go away. The footsteps pounded closer, and a deep voice said, "Miss Bryson?"

"Lord Blackbourne?" Emma popped her eyes open. "What are you doing here?"

When did he get here? Had he seen her fall out of the tree?

"Checking to see if you're injured." He squatted down beside her.

"Why would you think such a thing?"

"You did just tumble out of that tree."

"I did no such..."

He pulled a leaf from her skirt.

"I'm not sure how that got there."

"Probably the same way your fan got caught on a tree branch."

"Don't be ridiculous. My fan is on my wrist where it—" Blast. She scanned the ground. Blast. Blast. She peered into the branches and sighed. There it hung, illuminated by a large shaft of moonlight.

"Do you see it?"

"One can hardly miss it. Wide open as it is." Emma struggled to keep the bitterness from her voice.

"Is that significant?"

"According to my aunt, it means I'm interested in... in a hand up." Emma stuck out her hand, but to her surprise, Blackbourne ignored it. "My lord?" she said, growing more annoyed by the second.

"Oh, dear," he chided her. "I see you've forgotten last evening's conversation."

"I'm sorry?"

"First, you fall, then I find you, then a discussion on my apparel ensues, followed by a compliment to my valet. Then I help you up."

"You're joking?" His demeanor spoke of one who was not joking, but who was enjoying himself.

"Fine," Emma said. "I don't need your help." She placed her hands against the ground and pushed. "I can get up... ouch."

"Is something amiss?"

She tugged on her pelisse. "It seems I've snagged my coat on something when I, uh..."

"Fell out of the tree?" He grinned at her, and Emma responded with a glare. How infuriating. No matter. She would wait him out. She could be just as stubborn as he. A minute passed. No, she couldn't. She needed to get to the Royal Saloon. Fast. "Fine. You win," she said, annoyed. "Your coat is lovely and well cut."

"And?"

"And you may tell Simms I said so."

"He'll be delighted." He loosened her pelisse from a tree root and pulled her to her feet then grimaced. "Though I'm not nearly as delighted. The coat is so well cut that I can barely move my arms."

He feigned straining his arms, and Emma laughed against her will. He was so ridiculous. "It does look constraining," she said.

"More like imprisoning."

"Then why do you wear it?" Emma shook the wrinkles out of her gown.

"You think I'm allowed a choice in the matter?"

"I'd think a grown man could make his own decisions when it comes to his dress. I don't ask anyone's opinion on what I wear."

"If only I had your freedom Miss Bryson, but I'm afraid I'm constrained by more than a well-cut coat," Blackbourne said. "Society, expectations, my valet's wager."

"My heavens," she said without thought. "Even your servants wager?"

"What can I say?" He shrugged then peered closely at her. Emma's cheeks grew warm under his perplexed gaze. "My dear Miss Bryson," he said. "Have you powdered—"

"Hush," Emma said.

"I'm sorry?"

"Be quiet," she hissed and pointed to the patio.

"Oh, I see," he whispered. "The doors have opened." Suddenly, two ladies walked out, and Emma dove behind the bushes. Blackbourne scrunched down beside her. "I take it you don't wish to be seen."

"We are in the garden, alone, my lord," she hissed and peeked through the shrubbery. How long would they stay out? Would others follow suit? Would she be stuck, scrunched beneath the shrubbery like a frightened rabbit, till the blasted party was over?

"They're discussing something," Blackbourne said in a low voice. "Do you think they heard us?"

"No. They're discussing the flaws of the bridegroom."

"You can hear their conversation?"

"I've very keen ears," she said. "Unfortunately, so does my aunt. Let's hope she doesn't come outside."

"I think she'd be quite happy to find us out here... together."

"My uncle would not. And you'd not like it if he did."

"Do you think so?" His enigmatic tone confused Emma.

"Let's stop talking so neither of us finds out."

"Perhaps we should move our conversation to my curricle. It's just there, outside the garden gate."

"What luck."

"Luck or providence?"

"A happy circumstance, my lord, and nothing more," she said firmly. They stole their way forward using various trees and shrubs as cover and slipped out the gate. He went to the curricle, pulled up the hood, and motioned her over. He helped her onto the seat and joined her. The hood did not stop a stout breeze from whipping through Emma's dampened gown, and she shivered.

"Are you cold?"

"No, I'm fine." Emma clamped her chattering teeth together.

"I don't think you are." He shrugged off his coat.

"My lord, what are you doing?"

"We'll just cover you up in this."

"Absolutely not." Emma backed away. "Please put your coat back on."

"I was recently told that a grown man should make his own decisions on what he wore and when. What better time to declare my independence from the tyranny of my valet than in aid of a shivering lady?"

A breeze cut through her again. "I suppose that's true," she said and allowed him to wrap his coat around her. The soft warm wool settled onto her bare shoulders and Emma found she could not shrug it off. Nor did she want to. She tugged it closer. "Thank you."

"You're welcome. I must say, Miss Bryson, as partial as I am to a grand entrance, and a lady climbing out a window and down a tree is even better than a lady falling on a ballroom floor, I must ask..." He stared hard at her. "What possessed you to do such a dangerous and foolhardy thing?"

A brief debate warred in Emma's mind. Should she tell him of her plan? Could she trust him? Did she have a choice? Time was running out. She squared her shoulders and said, "I'm returning to the Royal Saloon to find the thief who stole my necklace."

Nothing. No response. She waved a hand in front of his face. "Are you all right, my lord?"

"No, I'm well, I'm just a bit taken aback."

"You can't be that surprised. I sent you a note."

"It said nothing of you returning to the Royal Saloon to find a thief."

"No one was supposed to know." She scowled.

He laughed but said nothing. He merely studied her, and Emma's heart pounded. Now what? Would he force her to return home? Would her plans be thwarted by him for the third time? He surprised her by asking a question. "What makes you think your necklace was stolen?"

"I was bumped."

He stared blankly at her, and Emma shook her head. First, his dazed reaction to her plan and now this. She had no idea he could be so thick. "Last evening you told me to keep my jewelry from being stolen I must avoid getting bumped."

"Oh, right."

"Unfortunately, I couldn't do so. I was in a hurry, you see, to return home to prac—to choose a song to play this evening."

"You did mean to come to Blackbourne House? I wasn't slighted?"

"No. I'm sorry if you thought so." Emma peeped at him, uncertain if he was serious or not.

"Then I still have hope of hearing you play the pianoforte?"

"Uh, yes, of course." She cleared her throat. "Anyway, in my rush out of the Royal Saloon I was bumped, my lord. Bumped and held fast by a bulk."

"Now things are beginning to make sense. You think you've been the victim of a bulk and file."

"I don't think. I know."

"You must have other reasons than being bumped to think this?"

Emma shifted his coat away and exposed her neck. "This."

"Did you injure your neck again?"

"I never injured—no, it's not injured, but there's a scratch. Hamilton noticed it this morning. A thin red line where my necklace should've been." She tilted her head. "Can you see it?"

Blackbourne swept a tendril of hair away and leaned in closer, his breath warm against her throat. A shiver—not caused by a breeze—coursed through Emma. "I'm afraid it's too dark," he said. "I can't see any scratch."

Desperate, Emma grabbed his hand, removed the glove, and guided his finger to the scratch. "Then you must feel it."

Feel it, he did. Twice. The second time he ran his warm and nimble finger over the scratch slowly and Emma's cheeks warmed. Her whole body warmed. Surely, steam would rise from her gown any second.

Finally, he leaned back, and Emma exhaled.

"Is something the matter?" he asked.

"No. What? I'm sorry," she said, still overheated. "Did you feel it, or must you try again?"

"No, there is a scratch." He sounded surprised. "Just as you said."

"I'd not lie about such a thing," she said, affronted.

"Then why all the subterfuge tonight?"

"My uncle couldn't take me back, and when Malcolm refused—"

"Malcolm?"

"My cousin, Malcolm McBride."

"The fellow who arranged your singing at Vauxhall?"

"You remember? Yes. He manages the New Castle Theater and so couldn't take me." A small plumper. But that must be the real reason he refused to take her.

"So, you decided to go on your own by climbing out your window and shimmying down a tree."

"I meant to go out the servants' entrance, but when Kat told me she had invited you, I thought it best not to tempt fate by going downstairs."

"Fate?"

"A turn of phrase," she said, exasperated. Really, the constant allusion to fate and the stars was getting ridiculous. "I merely wished to avoid anyone who might stop me from returning to the Royal Saloon."

"Say you do get there. How, exactly, will you recognize him? You said he was masked."

"His pianoforte playing. I'm confident I shall recognize it. There was a weakness in certain notes."

"Your keen ears." He nodded. "Well, you certainly have thought it out. I assume you had a way to get back to the Saloon?"

"I made arrangements with the jarvey who drove me to the linen drapers earlier," Emma said. "He should be waiting a wee bit up the lane. At least if he hasn't left. I didn't expect to be delayed." She scowled at him again. "Though you could make it up to me."

"Yes?"

"By taking me to him."

"My dear Miss Bryson," he said. "I can't possibly allow you to take a hackney to the Royal Saloon."

Anger shot through Emma. Thwarted by him. Again. "Of course, you wouldn't," she snapped. "Why would you? It isn't your pendant that's—"

"I'll take you there, myself."

"I'm sorry?"

"I'll take you to the Royal Saloon."

"But... you can't take me."

"Why not?" He raised a brow. "We're already in my curricle."

"Yes, I know you could, but..."

But why would he? Curiosity? Boredom? Or a less altruistic reason? She didn't believe he meant to win his wager by offering her marriage, but was Malcolm right? Did Blackbourne mean to seduce her? Would he use her current desperation to do it? She needed to know what price—if any—she would have to pay. "I'm exceedingly grateful, my lord, but why would you help me?"

He turned toward her, his eyes half closed and bearing a small smile. Emma's stomach dropped. Malcolm was right.

"What can I say?"

"Just say it, my lord," Emma blurted and turned away, unable to face him. "Just say what you expect. Just say what you desire."

"I'm bored."

She whipped around. "I'm sorry?"

"I said I'm bored."

"I heard what you said," she snapped. Malcolm was only half right. He was bored, just not bored enough to seduce her.

"Is something the matter?"

"Nothing." Nothing, except that she, apparently, was not attractive enough to be seduced by the great Earl of Blackbourne. "Is that the only reason?"

"Do I need another?"

"Of course, not."

Not that she wanted to be seduced by him but why wouldn't he want to?

"You seem disappointed."

"Not at all."

Was it her looks? Her dress? She'd removed the prim lace that had edged the bodice—no Cyprian worthy of the name would cover her décolletage—but even without it, the dress was still boring.

"Though I do need something in return."

She blinked. He did mean to seduce her.

"A small favor, trivial even. It won't take but a moment."

Was a lady's virtue nothing but a triviality to him? A moment's diversion?

He tugged a white square from his pocket, and Emma sucked in a breath. There it was. The blank card. The carte blanche. Her heart raced. "I'm sorry my lord, but I can't do it," Emma said. "I refuse to take the card."

"What card?"

"The blank card you're holding that signifies... hold on." She peered closer. "Is that a... handkerchief?"

"Yes."

"A white, perfectly square handkerchief?"

"Simms. He insists they be starched and properly folded."

Kat and Malcolm had done it. They had driven her insane. "What do you want me to do with it?"

"Wipe the powder off," he said and handed Emma the cloth. "Might I ask why you covered your lovely face in such an outlandish manner?"

"I was told it'd help me get into the Royal Saloon," she said, wiping her cheeks. "Like a voucher to Almack's."

He stared in amazement, his mouth slightly opened. "My dear Miss Bryson, it is nothing at all like that."

"I suppose it might have been said in jest." Emma folded the handkerchief and gave it to Blackbourne. "Thank you."

He slipped it into his pocket. "Do you truly not know the risk you took to your reputation, to your very person, by going to the Royal Saloon alone with nothing but a powdered face to hide behind?"

"I'd no choice, besides, I thought it hid my identity quite well."

"It didn't," he said bluntly. "I recognized you immediately."

His remark stung. "Perhaps I didn't apply it very well. I've never painted my face before."

"Obviously." He picked up the reins. "To excel at any art, even the art of painting one's face, it must be practiced, like singing or playing the pianoforte."

Ha! Little did he know her powdering skill far exceeded her skill at the pianoforte. Hopefully, he would never know.

He set the carriage in motion. "Speaking of which, now that we are returning to the Royal Saloon, perhaps I might still hear you play."

Emma squelched a sudden desire to jump off.

A QUARTER OF AN HOUR later, Blackbourne eased the curricle into a side street and pulled up.

"This isn't the Royal Saloon, my lord," Emma said with a worried glance around.

"It's around the corner."

"What are we doing here?"

"My coat," he said. "I don't think you'd wish to be seen wearing it."

It had been so warm and comfortable she had forgotten she had it on. She slipped it off. "Thank you for letting me borrow it."

"You're welcome." Blackbourne struggled into it, turned, and inspected her.

"Am I presentable?"

"Perfectly," he said. "But you still must have something to cover your face since you, ah, misplaced your fan..." He laughed and took out a box from under the seat. "Perhaps this will do."

He handed her the box, and Emma opened the lid. A delicate bone and lace fan trimmed with dyed blue ostrich feathers lay in the box. "It's beautiful."

Beautiful and exotic and expensive. Who did it belong to? Who had he bought it for?

"Italian craftsmen. They're as talented as the French. Or so I'm told." He put the curricle in motion. "Keep the fan up at all times, at least until I've arranged a private boudoir for us."

"I can't—I won't—go into a boudoir with you, my lord."

"Yet you were willing to risk worse by coming here alone?" He raised an eyebrow. "What if we arrange for a maid to join us? Will that satisfy you?"

"I suppose, but how will I find the pianoforte player?"

"The same as if we weren't in one. Your keen ears." He pulled the curricle to a stop and jumped down. They had arrived at the Royal Saloon, and the enormity of her situation struck Emma. So much could go wrong. She could be recognized. Lose her reputation. Ruin any chance she had of fulfilling her promise. All on the off chance she would find the thief. For a split second she froze.

"Miss Bryson?" Emma glanced down. Blackbourne had his arms lifted to her. "We should probably hurry."

"Of course." She bit her lip.

"Don't worry. I won't let you fall," he said. "Trust me."

She must trust him. If she were to get her pendant back. She must trust the Earl of Blackbourne. She moved into his arms, and he swung her down to the ground.

"Shall we?" he said and cocked his arm.

"Yes." Emma slipped her hand through his arm and walked into the Royal Saloon.

EMMA SIGHED. BLAST it all. It appeared the Royal Saloon was as popular as the night before. Would he come to play, maskless, in such a crowd? There was only one way to find out. She started forward, but Blackbourne grabbed her arm. "Let me speak to the proprietor about getting a boudoir first," he said. "And open your fan all the way."

"You obviously don't know what you're asking," Emma muttered but followed his direction.

True to his word, Blackbourne arranged everything, and a moment later, he held open a tent flap, and Emma, Blackbourne, and a maid entered the boudoir.

"Now, I shall get us some refreshments." He left and Emma sat at the table. The maid plopped down on a stool in the corner. If he wanted to seduce Emma, that tiny, freckled girl would not be a hindrance. Not that it mattered. He obviously had no plan to do so.

Blackbourne returned and handed Emma a glass. "Lemonade."

"You remembered," she said, surprised. "And you're having an Armagnac brandy."

He took a sip. "As did you."

Emma's cheeks warmed. His very public compliment and the magnetic pull of his gaze were difficult to forget. "It was only a day ago."

"Strange. It seems like I've known you much longer," he said. "Perhaps it's the rather extraordinary manner of our meetings."

"There's nothing significant about any of them," she said, but then, "I'm grateful for our meeting tonight. I'm not sure I could've got into the Royal Saloon without you. So, thank you."

"Thank me after we've found the thief."

Did he really mean to help her? "I hope we do find him tonight." Emma said. "I only wish I'd more than a few weak notes on a pianoforte to identify him, like a distinctive coat or your brilliant white neckcloth."

"Do I stand out that much?"

"Yes," Emma said without thought, and he grinned. "Well, no more than Mr. Brummell, or Prince George with his creaking corset, or even Lord Hefton with his loud garish waistcoats." She stopped. That was his cousin. "I mean, it's my aunt who thinks they're garish."

He laughed. "As do a few others."

"In truth, I rather like them."

"As do I, but please, don't tell Simms. He'd never allow me to wear anything quite so loud."

Emma laughed. "Come now, my lord. Show some mettle. You liberated yourself from your coat earlier. Why not do the same with your dull, boring waistcoat?"

"Are you suggesting I remove it, Miss Bryson?" His hand went to the vest's buttons.

"What—no." She shot a glance at the maid. "Absolutely not."

"This evening alone, you've divested me of my coat, personally removed my glove, and now you're suggesting I take off my waistcoat." He leaned back. "I've no idea what to think of you."

"You mustn't think of me at all," she said. "I've a horrible habit of saying whatever comes to mind. Some think me impulsive."

"One must be to climb out a window and shimmy down a tree." He sipped his brandy. "I'm not sure I know any other lady who'd go to such lengths to find a necklace."

Emma knew his statement was more of a question, and she answered simply, "It was a gift from my mother."

He straightened. "Your mother?"

"You're surprised my mother would give me a gift?"

"Not at all. My own mother gave me one just today. A rather deplorable statue of Venus. Please don't tell her I said so." They laughed, and he sobered and said, "It must hold great meaning for you. To do all this."

"It was an engagement present from my father, and I promised..." She hesitated. Could she trust him with that too? "I promised to wear it when I sang for the Queen."

"Queen Charlotte?"

She nodded. "My mother always claimed my voice was beautiful enough to sing for her."

"It is," he said, and Emma was touched by his sincerity. "It also explains your bump into the Prince last evening."

"I did no such—" His eyes turned slate gray, and Emma realized he was teasing her. "Well, obviously my ruse didn't work as some other gentleman insisted upon coming to my rescue." She rolled her eyes, and Blackbourne laughed.

"Is that why you were upset about Claimore's review?" he asked.

"Yes. Not that it matters now. Finding the pendant is more important. Though I'm not sure what else to do. This was my only scheme so far."

"I could put an advert in the *Hue and Cry* describing your missing necklace if you wish."

"Thank you."

"We could visit a few pawnshops."

We? A strange excitement filled Emma. Did he mean to keep helping her? "We must wait a few days," she said. "Give the Adam Tiler time to pawn it."

"*Adam Tiler?*"

"He's the third thief charged with selling the stolen items."

"I'm impressed."

"Don't be," she said. "Malcolm told me."

"He must know how the mind of a thief works."

"He knows how my mind works," she said and laughed. "He saw how hysterical I got at Sir Mayfield's party. The chain had broken, and my pendant had fallen to the ground. I thought I'd lost it forever, but he found it. He got another chain too, so I could wear it whilst I sang."

"Mr. McBride gave you a new chain that night?" Blackbourne asked abruptly.

"Within the very hour," she said. "I don't know how he managed it."

"I wonder too," he said. "Mayfield Manor is rather rural."

"He's always been resourceful."

"That must be it. If only we had his resourcefulness now," he said and consulted his fob watch. "I wonder now if the thief is even coming."

He stood as if to leave, and Emma panicked. She could not leave yet. She might not get another chance. "I know someone else we could speak to," she said. "A Cyprian."

"My dear Miss Bryson," Blackbourne said with a raised brow. "I'd never imagined you to be friends with a prostitute."

EMMA SQUIRMED UNDER Blackbourne's amused look. "I don't know if she was a prostitute or a Cyprian, or an actress—"

"An actress?"

"Yes. As she was dressed as Marie Antoinette," she said. "Anyway, I spoke to her after the thief played the pianoforte."

"Was she near the instrument the whole evening, do you think?"

"Possibly. And that's why we should speak to her. She might've noticed something about him. Some other way to find him."

"Why not?" he asked. "They might even be partners."

Emma gasped. "You think she's the file?"

"Why not? Ladies can be as duplicitous as men."

"You think ladies are deceitful?"

"Actresses, I mean."

Emma didn't think he meant that at all. "I doubt she'd be dressed as Marie Antionette tonight."

Blackbourne surprised Emma by going to the tent opening and pushing open the flap. After glancing around, he motioned for her to join him. He pointed to a lady across the room. "Is that her?"

Emma studied her. Same build and height, and the unpowdered face seemed familiar. "It might be... I'd need to see her eyes to be certain." Emma started forward, but Blackbourne stopped her. "You mustn't go out," he said.

"She can't come in here. Even with the maid, I'd rather not be found in a boudoir with you."

"True." He thought for a moment and apparently decided Emma could risk it. "Keep the fan up and don't mention your necklace."

"Why not?"

"If she's the file, we mustn't give it away that we know," he said, and Emma nodded at his good sense.

"We'll restrict our conversation to questions about the pianoforte player."

Emma placed her hand on Blackbourne's arm, they exited the boudoir, and within seconds they were in front of the lady. Emma admired her jonquil gown with its periwinkle ribbon circling the bodice but was less enthused about the matching yellow gloves. It seemed every lady in Town had them. The lady glanced over at Blackbourne, and her large jade eyes widened. Emma's heart pounded. It was her.

Blackbourne bowed. "Good evening, Miss Mayfield."

Emma started. He knew her? How did he know her? How well did he know her?

"Lord Blackbourne." She curtsied. "Though I believe you were still Viscount Linley when last we met. How is dear Amelia? It's been so long since our schooldays."

Emma's shoulders eased. Of course! A school friend of Lady Heyer's.

"Lady Heyer is in excellent health."

"Ah! I heard she'd been caught in a parson's trap."

"I take it you've not?"

She shrugged. "I find the chase more amusing."

"I expect there are many gentlemen who'd enjoy chasing you." Blackbourne flashed a devastating smile.

"The more carriages, the more exciting the race." Miss Mayfield glanced at a blond gentleman across the room, then turned back to Blackbourne. She touched his sleeve. "I understand you're an excellent whip, my lord."

"I've been told I have very nimble fingers," he said, feigning modesty as he looked at Emma. Embarrassment shot through her but quickly turned to irritation. She hadn't climbed out a window, tumbled out of a tree, and hid in a boudoir with Blackbourne to stand by while he flirted with another woman. She crossed her arms and said boldly, "My necklace was stolen."

"Oh, dear," Miss Mayfield said. "I'm sorry to hear it, Miss...?"

"Miss, uh, Cameron." Emma avoided Blackbourne's gaze. "Anyway, I'm hoping you could help me."

"I'd love to but how could I?"

"Because you know who stole it."

Miss Mayfield bristled. "I may be many things, but a confidant of thieves isn't one of them."

"Oh, no, I certainly didn't mean to imply anything of the sort," Emma said. "I meant the gentleman playing the pianoforte last night. He stole my necklace."

Miss Mayfield thought for a moment, and then her head jerked back. "Why, you're the lady with the lovely voice."

"Yes, thank you."

"I knew I recognized you." Miss Mayfield cut her eyes at Blackbourne then back at Emma. "But I thought your name... never mind. How can I help?"

Emma said. "I'm hoping you remembered something about him or even that you spoke with him."

"I'm afraid I must disappoint you. He totally ignored me." She waved her fan in an indifferent manner. "I couldn't get his attention at all."

"I don't believe you, Miss Mayfield," Blackbourne said, and Emma started. Surely, he wasn't calling her a liar. "No gentleman in his right mind could ever ignore you," he said, and Emma groaned.

"Well, if I might be allowed a little vanity." Miss Mayfield tilted her head coyly. "He might've paid me some attention."

"I knew your particular charms would never go unnoticed," Blackbourne said, and Emma swallowed a snort. Not in a dress that tight. Her charms were practically spilling out of it.

"Anything you remember about him would be appreciated," Blackbourne said. "No matter how inconsequential."

"I'd be happy to oblige you, my lord," she said, toying with her necklace. "I'm not sure where to start. He was wearing a mask."

"Let us start with that," he said. "Can you describe it?"

"A volto mask. Large and extravagant and colorful."

"What of his hair then? Do you recall the color?"

"Dark, like yours, but not as wavy and no hint of silver at the temples."

"A Blackbourne peculiarity."

"A most delightful one."

"Thank you."

Oh, for heaven's sake. Emma interrupted, "The color of his eyes?"

"I'm afraid I couldn't see them. The slits in his mask were so thin, it's a wonder he could see out of them."

"About his neckcloth," he said. "Anything memorable about it?"

"No, just an ordinary neckcloth, though quite dull in comparison to yours. I expect many are." She shaded her eyes. "How do you keep it so bright?"

"The fields of Islington." Emma said. "Simms insists on hanging the linen there, away from the London soot."

"Simms?"

"My valet," Blackbourne said. "Do you recall anything particular about his coat, Miss Mayfield?"

"Rather ill-fitting if I remember. Not nearly as well cut as yours, my lord."

"Less imprisoning, would you say?" Emma asked.

"I suppose one could say that." Miss Mayfield said in a confused manner.

Emma grinned. "Simms insists on a well-cut coat."

Blackbourne said, "How tall would you say he was?"

"Almost as tall as you." Miss Mayfield moved close to Blackbourne and tilted her head upward, and Emma fumed. She needn't be that close to judge his height.

"On closer inspection," she said. "Perhaps not." She didn't move backward, only cast another glance at the blond gentleman who now stood and appeared to be glaring their way. "You're a good inch taller."

"My boots, I'm certain," he said. "Perhaps he was wearing shoes and not boots."

"No, he wore a lovely pair of Hoby's too. Though not nearly as shiny. My goodness, one can almost see their reflection in them."

"Simms again," Emma said. "He's a magician with boot blacking."

"You seem to have a rather intimate knowledge of his lordship's apparel."

"Oh, no." Emma removed her hand from Blackbourne's arm. "Not at all. It's just…"

"It's just we've fallen into a discussion about my valet a few times," Blackbourne chuckled.

"How odd. I'm sorry to have disappointed you both, but except for his mask, I'm afraid there isn't enough to distinguish him from any other gentleman."

"There is one way," Emma said. "His pianoforte playing."

"Miss Bryson has the ability to distinguish subtle differences in which notes are played," Blackbourne explained. "She has lovely keen ears."

"Thank you." Emma feigned modesty but tucked a stray tendril of hair behind one keen ear in case he wanted a better view of it.

"How extraordinary," Miss Mayfield said.

"I wouldn't say extraordinary." Emma preened.

"I certainly couldn't do it," Miss Mayfield said.

"Nor I," Blackbourne said.

"Well," Emma said. "I suppose one *does* have to be born with it."

"Perhaps you could show us lesser beings how it's done?" Blackbourne pointed to the pianoforte.

"It's of no consequence." Emma flushed. "Thank you for your help, Miss Mayfield. We needn't bother you any further."

Miss Mayfield glanced at the blond gentleman again and placed a hand on Blackbourne's sleeve. "What should I do if I think of anything else?"

"If we need your help again, I'm sure we can find you." Emma tugged on Blackbourne's free arm.

"Miss... Cameron has decided, and I must defer to her wisdom." Blackbourne and Emma returned to the boudoir.

They sat, and Blackbourne said, "I think that went quite well."

Emma swallowed a snort. Perhaps his flirtation with Miss Mayfield had gone well but not—hold on. Emma sat upright. "It just occurred to me," Emma said. "I sang for a Sir Mayfield, recently."

"His daughter."

"His daughter is a Cyprian?" Emma asked, astonished.

"Worse," he laughed. "An actress." He finished what was left of his brandy. "Was she at Sir Mayfield's party?"

"I didn't meet any of the guests," Emma said. "Though I think I'd remember her. Such large jade eyes and everything..."

"Jade, yes," he said but appeared caught up in his own thoughts. He strummed his fingers on the table. "But if she were..."

"If she were what—?" Emma's question was interrupted by the sound of the tent flap opening. She swiveled around. The angry blond-haired gentleman stood at the entrance. His flashing gray eyes—so much like Blackbourne's—directed on his lordship.

"Blackbourne," he growled.

"Worthington." Blackbourne said, and Emma slammed her fan against her cheeks. Lord Worthington?

"Let us speak outside." Blackbourne stood and the gentlemen left the boudoir, and Emma lowered the fan. How could she hear their conversation now? Keen ears or not, she still needed to open the flap. A risk she could not take. But the maid could. Emma called her over. "I need you to poke your head out and listen to those two gentlemen. I want to know every word they say."

The girl shrank back in horror. "I can't do that, miss."

Emma dug a coin out of her reticule and pushed it into the girl's hand.

"I'll do what I can." She poked her head out.

"Well?" Emma whispered. "What are they saying?"

"I can't hear much. They're too far away, but the tall blond one's waving his arms around like one out of Bedlam. The handsome dark one is talking now. Calmer, like. Now the mad one is pointing at some lady in a tight gown. A very tight gown. Good lord, miss, do ye think she can breathe?"

"Oh, she can. It's the gentlemen that's been made breathless."

"Now the mad one is yelling... you blackguard, you... I've a good... call you out."

Emma gasped. Is he challenging Blackbourne to a duel? "What did the handsome gentle—I mean, what did Lord Blackbourne say?"

"I can't hear your handsome lord. He's talking too low."

"He isn't my lord." But he was handsome, and Emma wanted to know what he was saying. Needed to know. She stuck her head out of the tent, tilted her head to the pair and heard... the pianoforte?

Now? Right now? Of all the ill-luck. No, it's good luck. It's the reason she was here. Emma shut her eyes and concentrated. All she needed was a few notes.

"Miss Bryson?"

Emma opened her eyes. Blackbourne stood next to her.

"What are you doing?" he asked.

"Someone was playing the pianoforte—why are you pushing me?"

"I'm not pushing you," he said, though one of his hands was firmly in the small of Emma's back. "I'm merely moving your lovely but thoroughly uncovered face back into the boudoir."

How stupid could she be? "Do you think anyone recognized me?"

"Only Miss Mayfield." He closed the tent flap. "Your attempt at a nom de guerre, notwithstanding. Miss... Cameron."

"Do you think she'll say anything?" Emma sat on the bench.

"No." He joined her at the table. "She's far too occupied with her own affairs to concern herself with yours."

"Lord Worthington?" Emma leaned forward in eager anticipation of a good coze.

"Yes," Blackbourne said, disappointing Emma by not saying anything more. He, instead, took a drink of brandy, then asked, "The person playing the pianoforte just now. I assume it wasn't our thief as you didn't rush out and confront him."

"No, unfortunately."

"A shame."

Even more a shame because it had caused Emma to miss the rest of the conversation between him and Lord Worthington. Would he really duel over Miss Mayfield? When he already had a mistress? No wonder he hadn't tried to seduce Emma. Even he would find it difficult to juggle three mistresses.

"Even so, I think we did rather well tonight, don't you think?"

"Yes, I suppose we did."

He finished his brandy, set down the glass, and stood.

"Are you leaving?"

"We both are," he said. "I brought you, remember?"

"Right, yes, but shouldn't we discuss what we learned and not risk forgetting something?"

"There's more risk of someone discovering your empty bedchamber." Blackbourne pulled out his fob watch and showed it to her. "It's nearly dawn, Miss Bryson."

Good heavens. The night had flown.

CHAPTER 5

The next morning, Emma sat in bed, sipping her cup of chocolate, the ruins of her breakfast on a tray next to her. She had pleaded a headache to avoid going downstairs—to avoid pesky questions from Kat. Questions that had kept her from sleeping.

Would Lord Blackbourne really duel over an actress? What would his mistress think about it? Or was Lady Wallingford as cynical as he? Where had his cynical and depressing view of women—of love—come from? His cynicism helped explain his wager. If he believed ladies were duplicitous and only marrying him for his title, then why shouldn't he think it reasonable to marry to win a bet?

She nibbled a bit of scone. Why help her? Was it truly just boredom? To take her to the Royal Saloon, rent a boudoir, and even question Miss Mayfield. No, there was more to Lord Blackbourne's actions than boredom, but... what?

"Did ye join the party last night after all, Miss Bryson?" Jo interrupted Emma's thoughts.

"No. I had a megrim, remember."

"Aye, but how'd this stain get on the front of yer dress?"

"I must've spilled a glass of water."

"It's missing a wee bit of lace too." She clucked. "The only gown that did ye any favors, ruined."

"It hadn't done me any favors last night," Emma muttered into the scone.

The door opened, and Kat stood in the aperture. "Thank heaven, you're awake." She darted over to the bed. "A letter has been delivered for you, from Lord Worthington."

123

Emma almost dropped her cup. Good heavens. Had he recognized her in the boudoir? "Are you certain it's from him?"

"Quite. I recognized the footman's livery. Maroon and gold." Kat handed the letter to Emma. She stared at it for a moment.

"Go on," Kat said in an excited voice. "Open it."

Emma broke the wax seal and read it. "He's asked me to sing at his ball."

"How exciting."

"Thank God," Emma laughed with relief. "I thought it had something to do with last night."

"Last night?" Kat raised a brow.

Oh, dear.

"Out with it, Emma."

Emma toyed with the fringe of her blanket. "I might've snuck out and returned to the Royal Saloon."

"How could you do such a thing? Didn't you realize the danger? Did anyone see you? Recognize you?" Kat paced. "This could be worse than your jilt."

"You needn't look so worried. I promise you we were very discreet."

"We?"

Blast.

"I meant I," she said. "I was very discreet."

"You said we, Emma. Quite clearly." She crossed her arms. "Did Mr. McBride take you? I knew he couldn't be trusted. I'm afraid he'll no longer be welcomed at this house, Emma."

"It wasn't Malcolm, but Lord Blackbourne."

"His lordship took you to the Royal Saloon?"

Kat's demeanor transformed from irritation to joy so quickly that Emma laughed. "I suppose he's still welcome?"

"One can hardly banish an earl, my dear." Kat sat on the side of the bed. "How did you meet him without anyone knowing?"

"I climbed through the window—"

"You climbed through the window?"

"How else was I to leave without being seen? I started down the tree and must've slipped on a branch and fell. The next thing I knew, he was beside me."

"Lord Blackbourne was in my very own back garden, and I never even knew it." She shook her head then gasped. "That explains the fan. The gardener said there was one hanging in the tree. I accused him of drinking." She opened the curtain. "I can see it and look! It's wide open, signaling interest. How clever you were to arrange a rendezvous by hanging one from a tree."

Emma burst out laughing. "Are you mad? I did no such thing."

"Whatever you say my dear." She dragged Emma to the settee. "Tell me everything. Leave nothing out."

Emma found she wanted to talk about it. To clarify her own feelings. To banish some of her confusion. Within a moment, she had recounted everything from Blackbourne's appearance in the garden to his bringing her home. She left out his flirtation with—and possible duel over—Miss Mayfield. Why should Kat care about that? Why should Emma care?

"Go on," Kat said eagerly. "Then what happened?"

"Luckily, the garden patio doors weren't locked, and Blackbourne waited until I was safely inside."

"I mean did anything of significance happen?"

"I'm not sure what you mean."

She knew exactly what Kat meant.

"Did his lordship ask you any pertinent questions, say, about your plans for the future?"

"Not that I recall." Emma pretended to think. "Though he did make me an offer—"

"I knew it," Kat crowed. "I knew he'd offer for you."

"Ye didn't say yes, did ye?" Jo wailed.

"Of course, I said yes!" Emma said slyly. "I'd be foolish to refuse his offer to... put an advert in the *Hue and Cry.*"

"Joke all you want, young lady," Kat said. "But mark my words, he'll be putting a different sort of notice in the papers soon enough. Banns."

"I think you're reading too much into everything," Emma said. "He's simply bored."

"Ha! A bored gentleman doesn't arrange for one to sing at the Worthington ball."

"You think Lord Blackbourne asked him?"

"Who else?"

A strange warmth filled Emma, and it was not caused by her chocolate. Is that what they were discussing so calmly and not Miss Mayfield? No. She shook her head. He was helping her out of boredom and nothing more. He had said it himself.

"You must make the most of this opportunity. You must be agreeable."

Emma put down her cup. "Aunt, if Lord Blackbourne wishes to say something to me, I'll certainly listen, but I'll make no move—"

"Exactly. Don't move. Stay perfectly still. Trust me, Emma, a gentleman wants a wife not an acrobat from Astley's circus."

"Don't worry. I'm determined never to fall for him."

"Fall for him?"

"I meant in front of him. Or anyone. Nor will I hold my fan a certain way."

"How will he know you're interested?"

"I'm not and I'd refuse his offer, anyway."

"Are you mad?"

"Perfectly sane. I refuse to wed a gentleman simply so he may win a bet."

"Or demands ye sing for yer dinner," Jo said. "Ye cannae trust such a man, lass."

It struck Emma that she had trusted him. Trusted him to take her to the Royal Saloon. Trusted him with her reputation. Trusted him with her promise. None of which meant she could trust him with her future happiness. "My thoughts, exactly, Jo."

"Please, Emma," Kat said. "I'm desperate. Elizabeth received a letter from that soldier yesterday. I'm certain it speaks of his return now that Napoleon has ruined everything by quitting the field."

"Kat!" Emma said in a shocked voice. "We should all be happy the war has ended."

"Yes, yes, naturally, but if it had only lasted a few more weeks, I could've arranged something with Lord Hefton. Especially now that you're such a close friend of Lord Blackbourne."

"We are hardly bosom bows," Emma snapped. This was becoming too ridiculous. Too complicated. She threw the covers off and stepped out of bed. "And I don't wish to discuss it anymore. I must get dressed. I have somewhere to go."

"With Lord Blackbourne?" She pulled the window curtain aside as if to show the fan.

"No. I'm going to search pawnshops. Alone."

"Alone? In broad daylight? What if you are recognized? People might think you poor or, worse, they'll think your uncle is mean in his care of you."

"I'll be very discreet," Emma said with a laugh. "But if it makes you feel better, I'll take Jo with me."

Their lack of enthusiasm did not deter Emma. She needed to search for her pendant and keep her mind off a particular earl.

BLACKBOURNE WALKED across the Wallingford salon, the clip of his boots making a slight echoing sound. What had happened to the carpet? He settled on the couch, placed the box with the fan next to him, and smiled. The fan he had lent Miss Bryson. A lady unlike any he had ever known. To dress as a Cyprian, climb out a window, and risk heaven knew what to return to the Royal Saloon alone. All on the slight chance of finding a thief? Amazing. It'd only taken a few hours in her presence to know she was not a thief—but she was unwittingly helping one.

Malcolm McBride.

If McBride had given her the gold necklace the night of the Mayfield party, then he must've stolen it from Francesca. But why steal it back at the masquerade? And what of Amelia's bracelet? He knew Miss Bryson had not sung at that soiree. Yet, his instincts told him all three thefts were connected. And he knew the connection. Miss Jayne Mayfield. An actress without a stage, disowned by her family, and with no obvious means of income. Yet, she refused a carte blanche from Worthy.

Her attempt to make Worthy jealous by flirting with him had worked. Worthy was furious. But to threaten to duel? Good God, the man was besotted.

Miss Bryson hadn't threatened a duel, but she had been annoyed by the flirtation. Jealousy had burnished those caramel eyes to a deep luminous brown.

"Dear Philip, it is you," Francesca said.

"Hello, Francesca," he said and stood. "I'm sorry to have come unannounced, but I've been tasked with a delivery." He pointed to the box.

Francesca grinned and hurried over. She opened the box and lifted out the fan. "How beautiful." She opened it wide and turned to Blackbourne, her eyes peeping coyly over the blue-dyed ostrich feathers. "Thank you, darling."

"I'd love to take credit, but it isn't from me. Lady Tisdale sent it back from Italy with Lady Blackbourne."

"Ah." She folded the fan and set it aside. "As usual, my mother could not bring the gift herself."

"I understand she's finding the Italian air quite invigorating."

"I doubt it's the air that has her 'invigorated.'"

"At least your gift is useful. My own mother brought back a statue of Venus for me."

"The goddess of love? How interesting."

"To some, I suppose," he said. "Anyway, I tried to deliver it yesterday afternoon..."

"Why didn't you come in? I'm always waiting for you."

"I saw you leave in a hackney coach."

"Oh, yesterday *afternoon*. I'd a few errands to run, and I was meant to use my uncle's carriage, but he'd already made other plans, so I ordered a hackney."

"The gentleman?"

"I'm sorry?"

"The gentleman who followed you into the coach."

"Ah, right, that. There was a misunderstanding on whose hackney it was." She turned away. "In the end, we decided to share it."

Her quick entry into the carriage did not speak of a last-minute accommodation to Blackbourne. "Lucky for you, you were going in the same direction."

"I'm not certain where he was going, but I knew where I was," she said. "To find my stolen necklace."

"Does the thief know this?"

"No, but my jewelers do," she said with a laugh. "I believe the thief will recognize its worth and realize he'd get much more from a jeweler than from pawning it. So yesterday, I went to every jeweler in London and told them of my troubles. Mr. Rundell was so kind. He promised to personally keep an eye out for it."

"May the thief be as sensible and cunning as you, Francesca." She preened as if he had complimented her gown, and Blackbourne laughed. "Speaking of your necklace, I've a few questions about the night you lost it."

"Do you remember who else attended the Mayfield birthday party?"

"I didn't know most of them. They were older friends of Sir Mayfield."

"Do you remember if Miss Bryson came with anyone?"

"The singer? Why would I? I barely remember she was there."

Blackbourne bristled, annoyed by her easy dismissal of Emma. "As it turns out, she's had a necklace stolen too."

"Really?" She straightened. "When? Where?"

"At the Royal Saloon two nights ago."

"The poor thing. I hope it wasn't something she set store by."

It dawned on Blackbourne that Francesca would recognize the notice he'd told Emma he would place, and it had never occurred to him to do it for her. "By the by, I put a notice in the *Hue and Cry* today, describing your necklace. It should run tomorrow."

"You are serious about finding it." She turned back to him in surprise. "Thank you Blackbourne, I'm... grateful."

"It isn't completely altruistic. I do have that wager with Hefty, remember."

"I do. I remember all your wagers..." she said, her features soft and vulnerable.

Blackbourne winced. It was obvious which wager she meant. Had his mother been right? Did Francesca expect an offer? Should he be honest now and tell her he had no plans to marry? Or ignore her comment and let things go on as they are? He compromised. "If I ever do decide to marry again, Francesca, you'll be the first to know."

EMMA DESCENDED THE stairs to the foyer where her maid stood sullenly by the door. "Are you ready, Jo?"

The maid turned around, her mouth dropped, and her eyes bore holes into Emma's gown.

"Is something the matter?" Emma glanced down at her outfit. "Marzipan crumbs?" She brushed a hand across her chest. She knew she should not have eaten that last piece.

"Nae, I just cannae believe ye've broken yer promise to Mrs. Carstead."

"I'm sorry?"

"About being discreet," she said. "Ye could see that bright-green spencer all the way from Scotland."

"Never mind my outfit." Emma laughed and tugged on her pair of blue gloves, ignored Jo's heavy sigh, and said, "Have you got the list of addresses?"

"Aye." She handed the paper to Emma. "But we'll never 'ave time to visit them all."

"It's why we should've left an hour ago." Emma motioned for the footman to open the door and stepped out.

"What if we get lost?" Jo stopped at the door.

"We won't, but if we do, someone will help us." An image of a gentleman in a brilliant neckcloth flashed through her mind. She shook her head. *Stop being so fanciful.* "Come along, Jo," Emma said. "Or must I ask the footman to carry you outside?"

The footman balked and Emma laughed, but Jo remained unmoved—and in the house. The maid peered at the sky. "A storm's brewing."

Emma looked up. She was right. The London sun, never one to give off much heat, was even less generous today, hidden as it was behind a bank of dark clouds. She pulled her spencer tighter and had a sudden desire for Blackbourne's warm topcoat.

"This is nothing, Jo," she said. "How many times have we walked along the moors and got caught in a storm?"

"This feels different. Not at all like at home."

"Don't be silly, storms are the same every—" A peal of thunder stopped Emma. Or was it thunder? She tilted an ear. No. Horses hooves. Suddenly, a curricle swerved around the corner, pulled up in front of the townhouse, and stopped.

"Lord Blackbourne?" Emma said. "What are you doing here?" Kat would never believe it wasn't planned.

Blackbourne jumped down from his curricle and handed his reins to his tiger. "Good afternoon to you too, Miss Bryson." He laughed.

"Yes, good afternoon." She bowed her head. "Forgive my manners, I'm just surprised to see you."

"Is that why your mouth is hanging open?"

Oh, God. Emma clamped it shut.

He glanced around her. "As is the front door."

"I've just come out."

"Out a door? How extraordinary," he said. "Have all the windows been nailed shut?"

"Hush." She laughed and nodded at Jo who stared suspiciously at Blackbourne.

"Really, my lord," Emma said. "What are you doing here?"

"To make good on my offer—"

Jo gasped and came full into the doorframe. "I thought ye said he'd nae offered for ye, Miss Bryson—"

"He didn't, Jo," Emma said, mortified by her maid. "And I certainly never said he did."

"I'm shocked, Miss Bryson, and even a little hurt," Blackbourne said, "as I clearly remember making you an offer."

"What?" Emma turned to him to find Blackbourne's slate-gray eyes upon her and a smile playing on his lips. "Oh, that's right you did," she said. "I found it so inconsequential I'd quite forgotten about it."

"I suppose an offer to escort you to pawnshops would be considered of no significance."

"Oh, that offer."

"Did I make another?"

"No, I—never mind." She must not let him fluster her. "We were just on our way to visit some now. We have a list."

"So, you did reject my offer."

"Aye, so you see there's no need for your services, my lord." Jo stepped outside, her cheeks bright red. "I'm happy to accompany my mistress."

"Now you are?" Emma asked, amazed at the audacity. "What of the storm, Jo?"

"It's cleared a wee bit," she said with a leery eye on Blackbourne and not the sky.

"Hardly. I expect to be pelted with rain any second."

"What's a wee bit of rain?" Jo shrugged. "It's nae that far to the hackney."

"Why walk at all when there's a perfectly serviceable curricle just a few feet away?" Blackbourne flashed a charming smile at Jo. "We could even all squish up together."

Emma rebelled at that thought. She knew she would be squished up against the cold hard railing of the carriage seat and not Blackbourne. Jo would insist on sitting between them. Yet, how could she demand Jo stay behind? She muttered, "I suppose that'd work."

"Excellent. Now, to save time, I suggest we first visit a pawnshop managed by Mother Cummings."

Emma hunted down the list. "I don't see her name."

"Your aunt's servants wouldn't have heard of her, but Bow Street has, as she's a fence."

"A fence?"

"A dealer in stolen goods."

"As in my stolen necklace?" Emma got excited. "Are you saying this fence might have my pendant?"

"You catch on quickly, Miss Bryson."

"Where is this pawnshop? How long will it take us to get there?"

"Not far. It's in St. Giles."

"Oh, nae, lass, we cannae go there." Jo pulled Emma back. "It's too dangerous."

"Your mistress will be perfectly safe. My tiger knows how to defend himself and us if it comes to it." He pointed to the boy struggling to keep Blackbourne's huge bay under control.

"That scrawny boy couldn't defend us against anyone," Emma said with a scoff. "But you could."

Blackbourne raised a brow. "Do you think so?"

Emma coughed. "So I've heard."

"James might help in another way," Blackbourne said. "As a chaperone."

"Then Jo needn't come at all," Emma said excitedly and turned to her maid. "I mean, thank you anyway, Jo, but as you can see, I no longer need you to accompany me."

"Shall we, my lord?" Emma headed toward the curricle.

"First, I need you to do something for me."

"There's always a catch with this one," Jo whispered to Emma. "First ye must sing for yer dinner..."

"Hush, Jo." Emma turned to Blackbourne. "Yes?"

"I think you should change out of that spencer before we go."

"I told ye, lass," Jo muttered, and Emma bristled. "I think it suits me just fine."

"It's perfectly lovely," he said, and Emma glowed with pleasure at the compliment. "It's the length I have issue with. Far too short. You need a pelisse that covers your gown. One you won't mind getting a bit dirty."

It struck Emma that he had planned to come here. The pelisse, James. Everything. Why did this make her happy? "Give me a moment to change."

Moments later found Emma sitting by Blackbourne in the carriage, the tiger perched behind them, and Jo glaring from the sidewalk.

"I plan to take less populated roads as there is less risk of us being seen. So, it might take longer to get to St. Giles." Blackbourne picked up the reins and set the carriage in motion. "I hope you don't mind."

Emma eyed his profile. The strong jawline. The well-shaped nose. The delightful dash of silver at the temples, and she nodded.

"You're nodding. I take it you don't mind?"

She laughed to herself. No, she didn't mind. She didn't mind at all.

A SHORT TIME LATER, Blackbourne pulled the curricle to a stop, and Emma glanced around, eagerly. "I've never been to a pawnshop, my lord, which building is it?"

"Philip," he said, confusing her.

"I'm sorry?"

"I think we've earned the right to use our Christian names, don't you?"

"Oh, I suppose so... Philip," she said, unsure of the new intimacy. "Which building is it?"

"We aren't quite there yet, Emma." He smiled. "We must walk the rest." He jumped down and grasped Emma by the waist. His fingers burned through her pelisse and thin muslin gown and a thrill shuddered through her. Less unsure about that intimacy. Nimble fingers, indeed.

He set Emma on the ground and disappeared behind the carriage. "What are you doing back there?" Emma asked with a wary glance around the alley.

"I'll be just a moment." He returned dressed in a shabby, albeit well-cut, topcoat. His linen shirt partially untucked, his beaver cockeyed, and his neckcloth askew.

"Are you following Byron's lead now?"

"Do you find it romantic?"

Yes. But she would never tell him so. She shrugged. "If I were you, I'd worry more about what Simms thinks."

"It'd send him to his sickbed." He grabbed a fistful of dirt from the road and rubbed it into his fawn pantaloons.

"And that would kill him."

"We'd do well to blend in."

"I see." She grabbed a fistful of dirt and decided to kill her own maid by rubbing it into her pelisse.

A moment later, Blackbourne crooked his arm, and Emma slipped her hand through it as they headed deeper into St. Giles. The walk revealed a world Emma had never seen. Run-down shanties and lean-tos all built on top of each other, a man asleep on the ground, and a woman with an empty bottle next to her. Ragged pinch-faced children huddled together, and rodents scurried through the fog around them. It unnerved her and filled her with compassion. Her country childhood had been so different. "It isn't anything at all like my wee village."

"Poor St. Giles, such a discredit to his blessed name. A hospital named for him has been on the site since the Middle Ages. Patron of lepers and cripples. The lepers were cured—only to be replaced by all manner of brigands and thieves."

"A shame such a place bears the name of a holy saint—but handy that so many thieves are confined to one area."

Blackbourne's laugh was interrupted by a shrill female scream and the sound of smashed crockery. A man stumbled out of a nearby shanty, blood streaming from his nose. He swore and swayed and stumbled about and came within inches of Emma. Blackbourne deftly pulled her back, and the man shuffled away.

"Foxed," Emma said.

"No doubt." Blackbourne nodded. "Speaking of which, I wonder if you could feign being drunk?"

"Why?"

"To fool Mother Cummings."

"A ruse?"

"Yes," he said. "Do you think you could do it?"

She could. She loved Kat dearly, but she had seen her tipsy often enough. Emma swayed back and forth and stumbled into Blackbourne.

"Oh dear."

"What?"

"I didn't expect Mrs. Siddons, but I was hoping for more than an impersonation of a sick cat."

Emma bristled. "I'm sorry you found my performance wanting. Not all of us can be actresses," she huffed. "Perhaps Jayne Mayfield would be more to your liking."

He grinned, annoying Emma.

"I suppose we must improvise," he said and suddenly pulled her against his side, tight against his side, and Emma gasped. What sort of gentleman did that?

"Now," he said, "cling to me as if you'd fall. Without my support."

She threw him a glare for his poor joke but did as bid and allowed him to half walk, half carry her in an awkward, embarrassing and utterly delicious manner.

"Ah, here we are," he said.

"Already?" she asked. "Have you been here before?"

"Yes."

His voice sounded flat and tense, and Emma wondered what had brought him here. She placed her hand on his arm. "I'm grateful you have."

He stared in surprise—and something else. Wonder? Confusion? Emma quickly removed her hand and turned her attention to the building.

"What a depressing place to live," she said. She eyed the long ramshackle building, windows embedded haphazardly into its façade, and a pair of dilapidated wooden steps leading up to its doorway.

"It's a boardinghouse too, remember."

"What a depressing place to live," she said.

He stared in surprise—and something else. Wonder? Confusion? Emma quickly removed her hand. "Shall we?"

"Let's." Blackbourne knocked on the door, and a moment later, it opened. A thin plain woman stared out through the crack. "Aye?" she growled.

"Good afternoon, my... my..." He stumbled forward, pulled back, stumbled forward again, put his hand on the door frame, straightened and said, "My dear lady, I wish to procure a necklace for my... for my..." Blackbourne dragged Emma forward. "For her."

Emma held her breath as Mother Cummings—if it was her—raked her over with one gimlet eye. Would she have her pendant? Would she sell it to them?

"Ye be wanting a sparkler for yer rum mort?" she said, and Emma grimaced. It was like speaking with her uncle.

"In truth I... in truth, I..." He hiccupped. "Yes."

Mother Cummings opened the door wider and stared at Emma with crossed arms.

"He's a love, ain't he?" Emma poked Blackbourne in the arm and cackled hard. Mother Cummings retreated a foot. "Ye ain't about to get sick, is ye, gel?" she said. "I'd a sick cat 'at looked like ye just afore she cast up her accounts all over me good tog."

"Oh, for the love of... I do not look at all like—"

"Like she's ill." Blackbourne intervened. "She's just enjoyed a bit too much..." He made a drinking motion with his hand.

"As have ye." She eyed Blackbourne's neckcloth. "Steenkirk."

What the deuce did that mean? Exasperated, Emma turned to Blackbourne for translation. "Is only Byron allowed to wear his neckcloth askew?" he asked and placed a hand on his chest in feigned indignation.

"Don't you mind her, my lord," Emma said. "I think it quite romantic. In fact, I ken it could be a bit looser." She laughed and shocked herself by tugging at his neckcloth.

Blackbourne grabbed her hand. "You've nearly taken it off, my love."

"I couldn't help myself," Emma flirted.

"I'm not complaining. It just isn't the best time."

Emma wondered what would happen if it were the right time. Mother Cummings interrupted, "Ye be wanting a sparkler, or no?"

"I beg your pardon. You can comprehend my sudden distraction," he said with a leer at Emma. "Yes. I'd like a sparkler. One with a stone that matches my lady's lovely eyes."

Emma held her breath. What if she had more than one amber pendant? What if she produced a different one? He must describe it in enough detail. Did he remember its size, its coloring? She elbowed Blackbourne. "Be sure and get one I fancy."

"One that is oval."

Excellent start.

"Full of depth."

Good.

"With a deep shade of... emerald."

"Emerald?" Emma yelped.

"Oh, I beg your pardon, love." He looked apologetic. "More of a jade, then?"

"Neither my lord." She gave him a playful but hard slap on the arm. "You know my eyes aren't green."

"I must've been thinking of another ladybird." He made a broad wink at Mother Cummings, and they both cackled, and Emma fumed. He had two seconds—*two seconds*—to compare her eyes to an amber stone or else... Suddenly, he tilted Emma's chin up and gazed deeply into her eyes. Deep into her eyes. And like the night at the Royal Saloon, Emma could not turn away.

"A deep rich caramel color." A slow smile spread across his countenance. "Like Armagnac brandy." His arm still around her, he turned to Mother Cummings. "I'm in need of a sparkler with an amber stone."

"An' she's in need of a good smack," Mother Cummings said with a smirk.

"I agree, Mrs. Cummings," Blackbourne said. "A good smack is exactly what she needs."

He gave Emma a wicked grin, and she pushed him away, appalled. Would he hit her to keep up the act? Would he take the role of a drunk lover too far?

"Mayhap you'll also be needin' a keep for you and your canary bird?" Mother Cummings said, again outdoing Mr. Carstead in incomprehensibility.

"A room for the evening?" Blackbourne said, and Emma emitted an outraged yelp. "I don't think the lady appreciates your kind offer."

Did he appreciate it? Really, how far would Blackbourne take this charade? First a smack and then letting a room? Would she be forced to keep up the sham by entering the room with him? With Mother Cummings leering after them? Outrage and a bit of panic set in, and she disentangled herself from his arms and crossed her own.

"I'll not enter any keep with anyone," she said emphatically. "I'm here to find my necklace and nothing else."

Mother Cummings squinted hard. "What do ye mean, find?"

Emma threw a frantic glance at Blackbourne.

"She meant buy," he said smoothly. "Or should I say, she wants me to buy it for her." He grimaced, but Mother Cummings was having none of it.

"Ye ain't a prig napper, are ye?" she said.

"I've no idea what a prig napper is."

"I don't believe ye," she said. "Scat noo', else I'll call me cuffin to rub ye both down with an oaken towel." She whipped around and slammed the door.

Emma stared hard at the door, willing Mother Cummings to come back out. To no avail. Her impulsive tongue had again caused her trouble. Had it ruined her chance to find her pendant? Why must she always speak without thinking? "What the blazes do we do now?"

He descended the steps. "I expect we should leave."

"Leave?" Emma rounded on him. "Why?"

"Simple. I don't wish to get rubbed down by an oaken towel by her cuffin."

"I'm sorry?"

"She's threatened to set her husband on us."

"I'm appalled."

"As am I," he said. "I find it shocking she has a husband."

"I meant I'm appalled you think we should just leave."

"There isn't much else we can do." He started down the alleyway, and Emma scrambled after him. "We can't leave," she said. "We won't get another chance."

"No, we won't. But someone else will."

"Who else knows what my pendant looks like? Even you only had a glimpse of it."

"The pendant, yes, but the chain is unique, distinctive. It'll make it easy to identify."

"I suppose." Emma dragged her feet. They reached the end of the building and Emma suddenly stopped. "Hold on." She grabbed Blackbourne's arm. "Do you hear that?"

He listened. "Is someone playing a pianoforte?"

"A spinet, actually. It isn't the instrument, but how it sounds." Emma rushed down the side of the boardinghouse, stopped, and listened again. She crept forward and crouched under a dirt-covered window. Blackbourne joined her, and she could barely keep her excitement contained. "Our thief is in there."

"Are you certain?"

"Yes." She moved her fingers as if playing along. "It's the same weakness in certain notes."

"Is he playing 'Tis the Last Rose of Summer'?" he asked, surprising Emma with his memory again.

"No, but I'm certain it's him." She returned to the window. "If only I could see him." Emma ran a finger across the pane, the grime thick and hard and stuck like plaster. "May I borrow your handkerchief, my lord?"

"I'm afraid I've left it in my other coat," he said.

Blast. Emma balled her fist and attacked the grime.

"Now, that won't do at all," he said.

"What won't do—what are you doing?"

"I'm removing my neckcloth."

"I can see that, but why are you?"

"Simple, you need a cloth," he said, the neckcloth now completely off. "Why so priggish now? You nearly tore it off yourself just a moment ago."

"I know but that was…" She stopped. The collars had fallen back onto his shoulders, revealing his throat. A strong muscular throat.

"Miss Bryson?"

She jerked her head up. "Yes?"

He extended the neckcloth. "The window."

"Right." Good heavens. Get composed. Do not let a bit of flesh, no matter how virile, how masculine, how delightful, distract her. She balled up the linen and within a minute, had managed a peephole. She put her eye to it. "There's someone sitting at the bench, but his back is turned, and... oh, no!" She ducked and whispered, "He's stopped playing... he's walking around the room." She listened. "He's moving something across the floor and now... how strange." She peeked through the hole and gasped.

"What do you see?"

"Nothing." She turned to Blackbourne. "He's gone."

Blackbourne put his eye to the hole. "You're right. The room is empty."

"Why didn't I hear the door open?"

"I'm not sure..."

"Still, he must come out the front door." Emma dashed down to the end of the building and poked her head around the corner. Blackbourne caught up with her.

She stared hard at the entrance. "Where is he?"

"Give him time."

Minutes passed and Emma's frustration mounted. "Do you think there's another way out?"

"I wouldn't be surprised if there were many hidden doors and escape routes," Blackbourne said. "He must've left another way."

"What do we do now?"

"No reason for despair, Miss Bryson. Thanks to your lovely keen ears, we know the masked gentleman does indeed live here. We shall simply return tomorrow."

Wait until tomorrow? When her pendant was here and just waiting to be found? "No, we won't."

"We won't?"

"No. I came to find my pendant, my lord, and find it I will."

"I admire your determination, Miss Bryson, but I'm not sure there's anything else we can do."

"There is something." Emma took a deep breath. "We can search his room."

CHAPTER 6

Emma's heart pounded. Search his room? What the devil was she thinking? Why had she blurted out something so outlandish? So outré? So utterly outrageous? She eyed Blackbourne. Surely, he'd never agree to breaking into a boardinghouse room.

"I think it sounds like a capital idea."

"You do?"

"Why not?" he said. "We know which room it is, and as you're an expert at climbing out of windows, I expect you'd be an expert at climbing in one too."

"Climb through the window?" she said stupidly.

"How else are we to get in?"

"I hadn't thought about it." She hadn't thought he'd agree, either. It had been an irrational impulsive even emotional thought, not a sane one. She bit her lip. "I suppose it is the only way."

He sighed. "If only you'd taken Mother Cummings up on her suggestion."

"Yes." Emma perked up. "Perhaps you could ask her again?"

"You wish me to let us a room?"

"It must be you. She'd never rent it to me."

"She might not even do it for me now."

"I'm certain you can charm her still," she said. "She did say you were handsome."

"Caught that did you?" He grinned.

"It's the only word I understood," she said. "Never mind. We'll try it your way."

They returned to the window, and Emma peeked through the peephole. "It's empty," she said and turned to find Blackbourne's coat folded and laying on the ground.

Good heavens. No cravat, no coat. What's to come off next—his waistcoat? "What are you doing?"

"I'm rolling up my shirt sleeves."

"Obviously, but why?"

"I believe we've already had a conversation about a tight-fitting coat," he said. "If I'm to crawl through a window of that size, I must be able to move my arms."

Emma stared at his bare arms. His bare, muscular, sinewy arms.

"Emma?"

"What? Yes. I'm sorry."

"We haven't much time." He pointed to the window.

A moment later, Emma was in the boardinghouse room. Strips of faded and torn wallpaper covered the walls. A small bed with a checkered blanket sat in one corner and a wardrobe opposite it. "I knew it," she announced with glee and dashed across the room to a far wall. "That, Philip, is a spinet not a pianoforte."

"I'm impressed." He sounded sincere and not the least cynical or even amused.

"Oh, thank you," she said, and heat mounted her cheeks. "But you needn't be. I played on a similar one quite often when I was younger. It belonged to a relative of mine, Mrs. McBride."

"Any relation to Malcolm McBride?"

"His mother," Emma said, surprised at his memory. "She often asked me to play."

"So, you're an expert on both instruments?"

"I suppose one could say I play both equally well," Emma said and pulled on the cuffs of her pelisse.

"Go on then, give it a go."

Oh, God. Would she ever learn? "We haven't time."

"Right. No *time*." He smirked. "Then we better hurry. Luckily, there isn't much to search through," he said. "I'll take the wardrobe."

"I'll check the bed." Emma dashed to it and lifted the pillow.

"You think the thief would hide stolen jewelry under a pillow?" Blackbourne pulled open the wardrobe doors.

"It's where I hide my jewels."

"I hope no one else knows it."

"Only Malcolm." She ran her hands across the worn blanket.

"You must trust him very much."

"Naturally, I do," she said and bent down to scan underneath the bed. "We've known each other since we were children." She stood and put her hands on her hips. "Nothing," she said, frustrated.

"We still have the trunk." Blackbourne shut the wardrobe door.

"Right." She went to it and lifted the lid. A quick survey of the top tray revealed nothing but two pairs of gloves, a silk fob, and a folded neckcloth. She removed the tray. Two stacks of neatly folded shirts and waistcoats sat in the bottom compartment. She ran a hand underneath the shirts, and her fingers grazed a wooden box. Her heart pounded. Could it hold jewelry? She lifted it out, opened it, and gasped.

"What is it?" Blackbourne joined her. "Did you find the necklace?"

"No, these." She held up the box.

"Dueling pistols. Wogdon and Barton to be exact." He studied one of the pistols. "And stolen from Sir Mayfield."

"How do you know?" She sucked in a breath. "Have you dueled with him?"

"No," he said, bemused. "His name is engraved on the silver plate."

"Right, that makes more sense..."

"I wonder how long they have been missing?" Blackbourne mused.

"Does it matter?"

"It could," he said slowly. "It's been a theory of mine that these thieves target mainly private homes. Amelia's bracelet was stolen at a soiree."

"But mine was stolen at the Royal Saloon."

"I did say mainly."

"Should we return the pistols to him?"

"Steal them back?" He cocked a brow. "Absolutely not. The thief must remain ignorant of our presence here, or we'll never get your necklace back."

"Right." And that was the most important thing. She replaced the box beneath the shirts and returned the top tray to its place. About to stand, her eye caught the folded neckcloth. Could it hide a necklace within its folds? Emma lifted the cloth, then suddenly straightened, and cocked an ear.

"What's the matter?"

"Footsteps." Emma shut the trunk lid and jumped up.

Blackbourne moved behind the door, and Emma quickly joined him.

The footsteps pounded closer. Suddenly Blackbourne pulled Emma against his chest. *Tight* against his chest. What sort of gent—it didn't matter. Emma prayed. A moment later, the footsteps echoed down the hallway, and she slumped against Blackbourne. "That was close," she whispered.

"Yes," he said, and his arms encircled her. Emma reveled in the aroma of sandalwood for a moment before she stiffened.

And so was he. Too close.

She pushed away. "We should go."

"Now? Shouldn't we—"

"No, we should not. We absolutely should not." Emma did not elaborate on what they should not do but rushed to the window and clambered through. Without waiting for Blackbourne, she hurried to the alley.

"You seem in a hurry, Emma," he said from behind her.

"We can't get caught together."

"The person had already walked by."

Emma stopped. He was right. Why was she running? What was she running from? She regained her composure and waited. He had managed to get his coat back on and was buttoning it up.

"The neckcloth is still a mess." She pointed out. A delightful Byronesque mess.

"Which one? Mine or the one you're holding?"

"Oh, no," Emma said. "I took it from the trunk. I thought my pendant might've been hidden in it. Do you think the thief will notice it's missing? Should we take it back?"

"And risk getting caught? How would we explain that?"

"I can't keep it. I don't want to be transported."

"Transported?"

"Malcolm said one could be transported for stealing a piece of cloth."

"First, Bow Street must know you took it," he said. "And I've no plans of turning you in."

"What should I do with it?"

"Give it to me. I'll show it to Simms. He's quite knowledgeable about fabric. Perhaps he could tell us something about its owner." He took the cloth and slipped it into his pocket. "As fun as it is playing at thieftaker, it's much better to leave it to the experts."

His tone was jocular, but his words struck Emma's heart. Playing at thieftaker. To Blackbourne it was a game. A sport. A way to lessen his boredom. Malcolm had warned her—so why did she suddenly feel so deflated?

"Don't worry," he said. "We can trust Simms with our secret."

"I'm sure but that wasn't what I was thinking."

"What were you thinking?"

She was thinking how the last two nights had been exciting and terrifying and exhilarating, and it had nothing to do with her pendant but everything to do with him. Would she even see him once she found her pendant? Or would he move on, find something—or someone—else to relieve his boredom?

"Emma?"

"I'm thinking, if I'd understood you and Mother Cummings, I wouldn't have blurted out what I did, and she would've sold you my pendant instead of our breaking into a stranger's room and my taking this cloth."

"That's what you were thinking?" He sounded skeptical.

She turned away. "Something of that nature, yes."

"Pedlar's French."

"I'm sorry?"

"An idiom used in St. Giles," he said. "Steenkirk, cuffin, prig napper, smack, all pedlar's French."

"I see. Sometimes when my uncle gets riled, he speaks in Welsh, and my aunt must translate," Emma said. "I doubt she knows pedlar's French."

"It'd be odd if she did." He took her arm.

"If only one had a dictionary," she said, and they started to walk. "I don't suppose Mr. Johnson has written one?"

"Not that I'm aware." He laughed. A moment later, they reached the carriage.

"Any trouble?" Blackbourne asked his tiger.

"No, milord," the boy said and climbed onto the back of the carriage.

Blackbourne helped Emma into the carriage, climbed up, took the reins, and made their way out of St. Giles.

A short time later the carriage stopped and jolted Emma. "Home already?" she asked. "That was fast."

"You did seem preoccupied."

Yes. With thoughts of him.

He jumped down, and a second later, he took her by the waist and helped her down. Did Emma imagine his hands lingered longer than needed? He escorted her up the sidewalk and halfway to the front door before he pulled her toward the back garden. "My lord, where are you going?"

"I assumed you'd enter through your window."

"Thank you, no." She laughed, and his joking manner revived her spirits a bit. "I came out the front door and shall return the same way."

"I'm never certain with you, Emma," he said. "You baffle me."

She just smiled and entered the townhouse, closed the door, and leaned against it. He equally baffled her, and she wished she had a dictionary or an aunt to explain him.

Polite and well-mannered but audacious.

Generous and kind yet cynical.

Open and friendly, but inscrutable.

An enigma.

Emma sighed and headed up the steps. One thing was certain—she must tread carefully around him. She must not let her impulsive heart fall for him. If only he weren't so much more interesting than any gentleman of her acquaintance.

BLACKBOURNE SAT AT his desk in the library and swirled the brandy in the tumbler, the lead glass darkening the liquid to a deep caramel brown. The color of Emma's eyes.

"The Ravenscroft, my lord?" Simms interrupted. "Forgive my surprise but I've not seen it out of the cabinet since the late earl was alive."

"It reminds me of someone." His mind wandered back to that someone.

Innocent and impulsive yet daring.

Humorous and honest yet determined.

Original and unorthodox yet conventional.

An enigma.

Simms made a polite cough. "You sent for me."

"Yes, I'm sorry." Blackbourne placed the glass on the table and pulled himself together. He mustn't let his attraction to Emma steer him from his purpose. To capture the thief. To capture McBride. A sudden thought struck. How would Emma react to McBride's capture—and his part in it? He pushed the thought aside and turned to Simms. "I'd like you to look at something." He pointed to the stolen cloth lying on the table next to his chair.

Simms lifted the cloth up, revealing a book underneath. "*The 1811 Dictionary of the Vulgar Tongue*," he said. "An odd choice for reading, my lord."

"I got it from the booksellers. A gift for Miss Bryson."

"I'd keep that fascinating bit of information from Lady Blackbourne," Simms said.

Blackbourne chuckled. "The cloth?"

Simms lifted it high and examined it from all angles like an exotic bug—one he wasn't convinced had died. "Where did you get this?"

"Miss Bryson acquired it, quite by accident, from a boardinghouse room."

"Were you in this room with Miss Bryson?"

"Yes."

"Another fascinating bit of information I'd keep from her ladyship."

"Nothing untoward happened, I assure you."

"Except Miss Bryson stole this."

"She was holding it when we were forced to make a quick escape." They needn't have made that quick of an escape. No, she had run from something else.

"She was quite upset about it. She thought she'd be transported for stealing," Blackbourne said. "She wanted to return it, but I thought we might learn something of its owner from the only expert on gentlemen's attire I know."

"You flatter me."

"You thought I meant you? I beg your pardon. I meant Robinson. I was hoping you could show it to him at your weekly luncheon. It's tomorrow, isn't it?"

"His lordship appears to be in a rather joking mood today. I wonder what—or who—has put him in such a good mood?"

Blackbourne chuckled. He was in a great mood. One he hadn't been in for years. He pointed to the cloth. "Well?"

"It's lawn. At one point a very fine lawn but too much laundering has taken its toll. Notice the thinness of the thread."

The command wasn't rhetorical—Blackbourne knew he was expected to look. He dutifully did as bid. "Why would someone keep such a ragged neckcloth?"

"Two possibilities. It belongs to an older gentleman who's worn it many times. Or a younger gentleman who only owns the one and thus launders it quite often."

"A gentleman?"

"One would almost have to be to afford it. Miss Bryson is correct. One could be transported for stealing it."

"That's rather harsh."

"The alternative is worse." Simms feigned wrapping a noose around neck. "Hanging."

"I shall keep that interesting bit of information from Miss Bryson," Blackbourne said, compelling a smile from Simms.

McBride was not a gentleman—so how did he get the neckcloth? Had he stolen Mayfield's cravat the same night he stole the pistols and Francesca's necklace?

"If there's nothing else, my lord...?" Simms headed for the door.

"There is, actually," he said, and the valet turned back. "Do I, perchance, own any floral waistcoats?"

"His lordship really is in a jokey mood today." Simms laughed, then sobered. "Dear heaven, you're serious."

He shrugged. "Someone suggested I might try something new."

"Did she, indeed?"

"Fashions do change, Simms. Take Lord Byron for example. I understand he's taken to wearing his neckcloth quite loosely."

"As loosely as his morals?"

Blackbourne chuckled. It amused him how servants took morality more seriously than the upper classes. "My wearing a floral waistcoat won't alter my principles."

"Your principles, no, but possibly your plans for the future," he said in an enigmatic tone. "I'll see what I can do, sir."

"Next week? In time for Worthy's ball?"

The valet sighed. "Must you?"

"Take heart, Simms. The morning after the ball my waistcoat will be as lauded in the broadsheets as Lord Hefton's. You do want to win your bet, don't you?"

"Strange we both might win our bets due to Lord Hefton's unique style."

Blackbourne's objection was stopped by a voice from the hallway.

"Are you there, Philip?" Lady Blackbourne asked.

"Mother," he said. "Do come in. I wasn't expecting you."

"I thought I'd stop by and see if you'd placed the statue of Venus in the alcove."

"Not yet."

"I hope the goddess of love hasn't found a home in some other alcove." She tilted her head. "Perhaps in a boardinghouse room."

"Your spies have been busy." Blackbourne laughed. "We were searching for Miss Bryson's necklace."

"Is that all you were looking for?" She sat and pointed to the book. "What's that?"

"A gift," Blackbourne said. "For Miss Bryson."

"Hmmm." She read the title and arched a brow. "I'm shocked you bought it for her."

"You find it objectionable?"

"Hardly. I merely meant you could've borrowed mine."

Blackbourne shook his head. "No doubt you bought it the moment it hit the bookseller's shelves."

"Oh, I didn't buy it," she said. "It was given to me by a dear friend. An officer in the army. Wellie had just returned from camp..."

"Wellie?" Blackbourne interrupted. "Please don't tell me you're referring to Arthur Wellesley, the Duke of Wellington."

"Fine, I won't tell you." She laughed, coyly. "Wellie—I mean, my friend—had returned to London for a few days of much-needed leisure and, of course, couldn't wait to see me. While stopping at a wine merchant's he saw this book at a bookseller's stall nearby. He thought it'd be great fun to read together. If I remember correctly, and I always do, it was great fun." She twirled a lock of fair hair around a finger. "You know, we must've spent that whole night together, reading and laughing, and... well, you get the idea."

"Yes—and the idea I'm getting is of a mother I never knew existed. First Prince George and now Lord Wellington. Heavens, madam, I'd no idea you were quite so admired."

"Such fustian. So a few gentlemen enjoyed my company, nothing remarkable in that." She laughed merrily, then sobered. "I understand more than you think my dear."

"Do you?"

"I would hate for you to be forced into marriage."

"I shan't be forced into anything." But what if it wasn't forced? What if he chose to marry Emma? "But might I ask, strictly out of curiosity, what do you find objectionable about her? Is it her person? Her common background?"

"Her fashion," she countered. "Heavens knows what she'd wear to her wedding. Probably something in yellow. Or that ghastly orange she wore to the Royal Saloon." She shuddered. "I'd be embarrassed to attend."

He laughed. "I'd take the pressure off you by going to Gretna Green."

"Eloping, are you mad?"

"Who said anything about eloping? Miss Bryson is Scottish. She might prefer to marry in her own country."

"My dear boy, you'll be married at St. Georges, or you shan't get married at all."

"Finally, we agree." Blackbourne took the book from his mother and walked to the door. "I shan't get married at all."

CHAPTER 7

E mma threw the covers off and climbed out of bed. Enough thoughts about muscular arms and bare throats and silvery temples. Especially of a gentleman interested in only one thing—solving a crime. Well, she wanted to solve it too, and she knew someone who could help. Blackbourne wasn't the only person with a servant. Emma had befriended a Scottish maid the night she had sung at Mayfield Manor. Molly had kept Emma's voice supple with copious cups of lemon tea and her nerves in check with entertaining stories about home. Emma would ask her about the pistols. She rang the bell for Jo.

An hour later, the hackney pulled to a stop in front of Mayfield Manor, and Emma stepped out. "Wait in the carriage, Jo," she said. "I won't be long."

Emma hurried to the servants' door and had just raised her hand to knock when a voice called from behind, "Miss Bryson?" Emma whirled around. Molly stood next to her, holding a basket.

"Molly! Hello," she said. "You're just the person I wanted to see."

"Me, miss?"

"Aye. Do you have a moment to talk?"

"I don't know. The missus keeps a sharpish eye on us." She glanced around as if expecting Lady Sarah to pop out of the bushes. "But she's got a visitor in the parlor now, so if ye make it quick..."

"I will." Emma spoke fast. "I can't tell you how I know this, and I might even sound mad, but I've reason to believe Sir Mayfield's dueling pistols were stolen."

"Stolen?" she gasped.

"Yes. Perhaps even the night I sang here. Have you heard anything?"

"Nae, not a word."

Blast. Emma had hoped for a simple yes. "Did anything strange happen the night of the party? Was there anyone there you didn't recognize?"

"Almost everyone," she said with a grin. "I've nae worked here long." She shifted the basket in her arms. "But come to think of it..."

"Yes?"

"I did see a lady hovering outside the library that night," she said. "A bonnie lass. Pretty reddish hair, all pinned up and smooth. Not at all like this frizzy mop of mine."

Emma started. Jayne Mayfield had auburn hair. "Was it Sir Mayfield's daughter, do you think?"

"I cannae say. I've never set eyes on her." She leaned in close. "I understand she was told never to return."

Emma balked. "Sir Mayfield banished his own daughter?"

"Oh, nae! 'Twas the missus. She claimed her running off to the stage upset the master, but Mrs. Coats, the housekeeper, thinks the missus was just jealous of her."

"Why?"

"I was told Miss Mayfield reminds him too much of his late wife."

"I see." Emma paced and scratched her chin. "Is it possible Miss Mayfield came back to the house to get her jewelry?"

"She had nae reason! Mrs. Coats had already snuck it all back to her. She was close to the lass, ye see." A panicked look crossed her face. "But that's a secret. If the missus was to find out..."

"Don't worry, Molly. I'll not say a word."

If Mrs. Coats was willing to risk her position to do such a thing, perhaps other Mayfield servants were just as bold. Perhaps one of them was even a thief. "Do any of the footmen play the pianoforte?"

Molly laughed. "Now that's a mad question, miss."

"I know, but trust me, I've good reason—"

"Och, noo, he's come out." Molly stared wide-eyed over Emma's shoulder. "An' he's coming this way. I've got to go."

"No, no, wait." But the maid dashed through the door.

Blast. Why the devil must he come out right then? Emma whirled around and gasped. "What are you doing here?"

"I imagine the same reason as you," Blackbourne said. "To ask about the pistols."

His answer dismayed Emma, and her spirits sank a bit. Why hadn't he asked her to come with him? It really was just a sport to him. A game. An elixir for his boredom. Still, finding her pendant was the important thing, and he was helping with that. She swallowed her hurt and said, "Well, did you find out anything?"

"Only that the party had been deemed a great success," he said. "At least according to Lady Sarah."

"She said nothing about the pistols?"

"Nor of anything else being stolen."

Emma paced. "It amazes me that no one has noticed they're missing."

"I'm not surprised. Sir Thomas has been ill lately. He probably hasn't touched them for months. Which means the pistols could've been stolen anytime, even weeks ago." Blackbourne eyed Emma. "You look skeptical."

"Would his pistols have been kept in his library?"

"It's not unheard of," he said. "Why?"

"The maid I was just talking to told me she saw a lady hovering outside the library the night I sang."

"Interesting," he said. "Did she know the lady?"

"No. Only that she was beautiful with reddish hair."

"Marie Antoinette," Blackbourne said. "Again, you appear to disagree."

Emma repeated what Molly had told her about Mrs. Coats.

"She might still need money," he pointed out.

"Do you truly think she'd steal from her own father?"

"One never knows whom to trust." His face hardened like ice and made Emma wonder just how deep his cynicism went. Was it embedded so far into his soul as to never be free of it?

"Well," he said. "It seems we've come to another impasse." And like a chameleon, he had returned to his usual cheerful manner.

"Yes," Emma said and sighed. "And it's quite frustrating."

"But we are making progress," he said. "Shall I return you to your aunt's?"

"Thank you, but I've a hackney waiting."

"The one with your maid glaring at us from the window?"

"The very one." Emma grinned and suddenly wished the carriage and her maid to perdition. She would much rather ride with him. "Well, I suppose I should be going."

"Yes, but... would you wait a moment?" He disappeared around the corner, leaving Emma in a state of confusion. He soon returned carrying a small package wrapped in brown paper and tied with a beautiful orange ribbon.

"A gift," he said and handed it to her. "A small remembrance of our boardinghouse visit."

Emma flushed with delight. "Thank you," she said and tugged on the ribbon, but he stopped her. "Perhaps you should wait to open until you're alone," he said.

"Why?"

"Let us just say some might find the gift objectionable."

"Oh, I see." She nodded. "Like an insane maid?"

He chuckled. "Or an equally insane mother."

They walked to the hackney, and Blackbourne helped Emma in and closed the door. To her surprise, he leaned in through the window. "Miss Bryson," he said, "might I call on you this afternoon?"

"Why, yes, if you wish." Her heart pounded, and Jo stiffened next to her.

"I do wish it as I've something of importance to discuss with you," he said, his low grave tone mitigated by his dancing slate-gray eyes.

Emma bit back a laugh and said, "I can't imagine what it could be."

"Can you not?" He gave her a lover-like look. "Let me offer"—Jo sucked in a breath—"a hint," he said. "It's something I believe will secure our future happiness."

"You've quite intrigued me, sir," Emma said, and Jo huffed and crossed her arms.

"Have I?" he said. "Until this afternoon." He gave Emma a wink and departed.

Emma watched him walk away with a lightness in her heart she hadn't felt a few minutes before. He truly was an enigma. A warm and funny but cynical enigma.

Blackbourne rounded the corner, and Emma signaled the jarvey to go and leaned back against the seat, holding his gift in her lap. Emma pressed her fingers into it. Obviously, it was a book. But what sort of one? She gazed out the window, her mind a whir. A book of verse? Poems? Letters—what the devil? She sat forward, her gaze directed at a shop.

"What's the matter, lass?" Jo peered out the window.

"Nothing. I just thought I saw someone I knew." What was Malcolm doing on this side of town? Why had he gone into that shop? Who was the lady with him?

"Do ye want the driver to go back?"

"No, I'm sure I was mistaken." Emma sat back. As much as she wanted her curiosity satisfied—she did not want Malcolm's roused. He'd be equally curious to know why she was on this side of town—and with whom. No, she did not want to argue with him right now. She wanted to get home. To open a gift. To dwell on the mystery that was the Earl of Blackbourne.

THAT AFTERNOON, EMMA sat in the salon, *The Dictionary of the Vulgar Tongue* in her hands. She did not know what made her happier—the gift itself or Blackbourne's remembering her dismay and small joke. Would any other gentleman have done so?

He had even written a list of the pedlar's French words that had vexed her and their meaning and had marked other words in the book he thought would interest her. They had not. In fact, she hadn't even bothered to look them up as her mind had become absorbed with one word. Smack.

Emma's heart fluttered. It meant kiss and explained Mother Cummings knowing look. She leaned back against the sofa, the book clasped against her chest. What if he had smacked her? Would she have smacked him back?

"Why the smile?" Kat asked, and Emma jerked up. "I didn't hear you come in." She tucked the book behind her.

"Don't think to hide anything from me, my dear." Kat joined her on the couch. "What is it?"

"It's a book," Emma said and retrieved it. "A gift from Lord Blackbourne."

"Why in heaven's name would you hide that?"

"He thought some might find it objectionable."

Kat skimmed the title, and her brows lifted. "He's right. I do find it objectionable."

"You do?" Emma laughed. "*You?*"

"Naturally! Granted you're not engaged—yet." Emma rolled her eyes. "But I don't think a gift of a diamond or even a small ruby would've been amiss."

"Oh, Kat." Emma shook her head and laughed. "In truth, I much prefer this gift as it will help me find the only jewel I do want."

"A dictionary?"

"It will help me learn pedlar's French."

"French? Who needs to learn that now? Haven't you heard? Napoleon has lost. Surrendered. Left the field." She jumped up and paced.

"You can't possibly be upset that the war is finally over," Emma said, stunned.

"No, no, don't be silly. Of course, I'm happy about that," she said but did not convince Emma. "I'm merely upset that its end will have Lieutenant Gibson darkening my door again very soon." She sat and exhaled a frustrated sigh. "Oh, if only Elizabeth had met Lord Hefton."

"As to that," Emma said. "Do you really wish her to marry a gamester?"

"I wish her to have a title, and he has one now."

"Now? What do you mean?"

"Of course, you don't know, but he only came into the title about seven months ago after his elder brother died. He's barely out of mourning. I wish he'd stayed in it a bit longer as he'd never have dared wear that garish waistcoat during—"

"Aunt, enough about the waistcoat," Emma said. "How did his brother die?"

"I'm not certain. I only know it was in France."

"How awful. Was he fighting with Wellington?"

"Oh, no, Stephan wasn't the soldier, but James. Though naturally, he's had to give it up."

"Hold on. Lord Hefton was an officer?" Emma asked. "Does Elizabeth know it?"

"What does that matter?"

"Why, it might make her more amenable to meeting him."

"Or let her think we've no objections to her marrying one," Kat said. "No, she can find out all about his past after they're married. But first they must meet."

"I agree, but I'm not sure how it could be arranged."

"Quite easily," she said with a shrewd look at Emma. "They could be introduced at an engagement party or a wedding..."

"They have no common acquaint—oh good God. You can't possibly mean Lord Blackbourne and me. I hardly know him." She clasped the book. But what she did know she liked—she liked very much.

"How well did you know Mr. MacIntosh before you so foolishly agreed to marry him?"

"Exactly. Foolishly. Look how that turned out. I'll not be so impulsive again." She would make certain she was truly in love and that the sentiment was returned.

"Nor will I be the means of someone winning a wager."

"Don't you think his choice of a gift might speak of a certain attachment for you?"

Emma almost trembled at the thought. What if he had? It would certainly change things. She dampened her enthusiasm a bit. She wanted more proof than a book—delightful as it was. "I've other reasons to decline at least for now. My pendant. My promise."

Malcolm.

Had she misunderstood his affection all these years? A friend would be happy for her to marry well, but his recent actions made it obvious he would not be. If she married Blackbourne—or any gentleman—she would lose his friendship and her last link to her childhood.

A tap sounded and a maid entered. "There's a gentleman waiting to see Miss Bryson."

Blackbourne? Emma's heart raced. Was it visiting time already? She looked eagerly to the door.

Malcolm entered and bowed.

"Oh, hello," Emma said and tried to hide her disappointment.

"Mr. McBride?" Kat said. "I didn't know we were to have the pleasure of your company today." Her tone said very well that she did not consider it a pleasure.

"Impulsive, I know," he said. "But I found I'd a spare hour before I must attend to some business at the theater."

"The theater's a bit of a walk from here, isn't it?" Kat said. "Are you certain you've time for a visit?"

Emma knew her comment to be a barb aimed at his lack of a carriage and knew it hit its mark.

"Don't worry about me, Mrs. Carstead," he said in a tight voice. "I've hired a hackney to come here at a quarter of one."

"Well, then, please, have a seat."

Malcolm joined Emma on the couch. "I hope this was a pleasant surprise for you anyway."

"You know I'm always happy to see you," Emma said. "In fact, I thought I saw you yesterday. Entering a shop on Essex Street. You held the door for a lady?"

"You've caught me out," he said. "It was a small jewelry shop. I was looking for your pendant."

Emma's heart warmed. She knew he could not be indifferent. "I wish you'd told me. I would've come with you."

"As it turns out, it wasn't there." He glanced at her lap and raised a brow.

"Getting in a bit of reading today?"

Blast. Why hadn't she tucked the book away? "Yes, I, uh, got it from the lending—"

"From Lord Blackbourne," Kat said. "A gift."

Malcolm read the title, and his face flamed. "A gift or an insult?"

"A gift," Emma said, exasperated at them both. "I'd made a wee joke about Mr. Johnson and a dictionary. I'm surprised he even remembered it."

She was not. He remembered everything.

"He answered your little joke with a vulgar one of his own," Malcolm said in a heated voice. "But why not? He'd no trouble speaking cant in front of a lady, so why not give you a book of this nature?"

"Oh, Malcolm, really."

"I've half a mind to call him out for it."

"Oh, for heaven's sake," Emma snapped. This was getting ridiculous. "Don't be such a goosecap."

"He'll get bored with this game, Emma," he said suddenly. "With you. Trust me."

A small catch in his voice brought forth Emma's compassion. "You're worrying for nothing." She patted his arm. "Let's have a nice visit. Will you play for me? I really should practice." She stood.

"Is that all it'll take to regain your affection?"

"You've never lost it." She went and stood by the pianoforte. Malcolm appeared hesitant but finally stood and joined her.

"It's been a while," he said and rubbed his gnarled hand. "I've not even played for my mother, though she's asked."

"How is Mrs. McBride, Malcolm?" Emma asked, happy to have a distraction. "Have you heard from her?"

"I received a letter from her yesterday. She's doing better than she has for many years." He smiled. "She's even planning a visit to my aunt in Brighton."

"How wonderful," Emma said, happy for him. She knew he worried about his mother since his father had disappeared years before. "Do you think she'll come to London? I'd love to see her."

"Perhaps I could persuade her."

"If you'll both excuse me, I've other things I must attend to," Kat stood. "I'll send a maid in."

Just then the door swung open, and a footman stood in its frame. "Lord Blackbourne to see Miss Bryson."

"On the other hand." Kat grinned. "I haven't finished my tea."

EMMA'S MIND WHIRLED in confusion. Blackbourne had promised to visit so why the surprise? Why the sudden tightness in her chest? The rapidness of her pulse? The inability to breathe?

Kat hurried to greet him. "My lord, what an unexpected pleasure."

"Thank you," Blackbourne said. "I hope I haven't interrupted anything." His glance settled on Emma.

"No, no, not at all." Emma clasped the music sheet tighter. "I mean, yes, we were about to practice for the ball."

"We?" Blackbourne turned a pleasant gaze to Malcolm.

"Yes. I don't believe you've met my cousin," Emma said. "Mr. McBride."

Malcolm bowed. "My lord."

"Ah, Mr. McBride, of course," Blackbourne said. "I believe I owe you, my thanks."

Malcolm's brows furrowed. "I can't imagine why, my lord."

"For the pleasure of hearing Miss Bryson's magnificent voice. I understand it was you who arranged it all."

"Oh, that," he said. "With some help, yes. My role in it all was quite small."

"Like Friar Francis in *Much Ado about Nothing*, the smaller roles are usually more pivotal. Anyway, please don't let my presence stop you from practicing," Blackbourne said. "I've long desired to hear Miss Bryson play."

"No, no. We can certainly do so later." Emma tossed the sheets onto the holder and hurried away from the pianoforte. "Perhaps we should ring for tea, Kat."

"Of course." Kat rang the bell. "Please, my lord, have a seat."

Blackbourne sat on the couch and appeared as comfortable and unperturbed as if he was in his own salon. Emma sat beside him, and Malcolm sat beside her. He looked as uncomfortable and perturbed as if in a lion's den. An awkward silence ensued. Emma could think of nothing to say and was irritated at her aunt's silence for once. Finally, a maid entered with the tea cart, and Emma jumped up.

"I'll pour," she said and grabbed a cup. "How do you take your tea, my lord?"

"The same as you, Emma, plain." Kat answered for him. "It's nice to have something in common."

"I couldn't agree more, Mrs. Carstead," Blackbourne said, and Emma wanted to throttle them both. She filled the cup and handed it to him. His warm hand brushed against hers, and she sucked in a breath.

"Is something the matter?"

"No, nothing."

Only her hand trembling even more than when she had tied the napkin around his head. Only thoughts of bare forearms and exposed necks invading her brain. Only the word *smack* crushing every other thought. Emma served the others and sat, a piece of marzipan in her fingers.

Blackbourne sipped his tea and set down the cup. "I understand you manage a theater, Mr. McBride."

"Yes, the New Castle. I'm surprised you know it. I must be spoken of in some circles." He cast a significant look at Emma.

"Is it possible to rent a box, say, tomorrow evening?"

Malcolm's eyebrows lifted. "It could be arranged."

"Excellent. I'll send my man around later." Blackbourne turned to Kat. "It wouldn't be any fun to attend alone. Perhaps you could join me, Mrs. Carstead, if you haven't another engagement."

"I'd cancel it if I did."

"I'm flattered you think so highly of my company."

"I do my lord. I most certainly do. I assume you'll be inviting others—"

"We'd love to join you, my lord," Emma interrupted, mortified. "I've been dying to attend the theater since I came to London."

"You haven't been? Not even to the New Castle?" He looked blandly at Malcolm, who turned to Emma and said, "I'm sorry. I've been neglectful."

"Don't apologize, Malcolm. Neither of us has had the time."

"Still, I promise to take you before we leave London."

"You mean to leave London?" Blackbourne asked.

"Yes, at some point."

"And you, Miss Bryson." Blackbourne turned to Emma. "Are you leaving?"

"Not any time soon," she said with a glare at Malcolm. What the deuce was he about? Did he think to warn Blackbourne off by insinuating she meant to leave London with him? "And not before I find my pendant."

"Don't worry, Emma, I'm certain I'll find it." Malcolm gave Blackbourne a baleful look.

"How do you plan to do so, Mr. McBride?" Blackbourne sipped his tea. "Do you know the thief personally?"

"One only needs to know where he sells his bounty."

"Like pawnshops?"

"Or jewelry shops."

"I can't imagine Mr. Rundell would buy anything from a thief."

"It isn't the thief who would try to sell it."

"You do know a bit about how it all works."

The tension thickened, and Emma whispered to Kat, "This is awful. We must do something."

"Why?" she asked, grabbing a biscuit. "This is far more entertaining than Drury Lane."

Not to Emma. It was downright nerve-racking. "It's twenty of one, Malcolm," Emma said. "Don't you need to get to the theater?"

"You did say it was important." Kat finally said something useful.

"You're right Mrs. Carstead, it is. Quite important." Still, he hesitated. He remained sitting.

"Your coach is probably here," Emma prodded.

He sighed and stood. "I shall arrange your box, my lord."

"Thank you."

"I'll walk you out," Emma said and tried not to push Malcolm out of the salon. Once in the foyer, he stopped. "I should've taken you to the theater, Emma," he said. "I didn't know you desired it."

"Don't worry. We'll go another time." She opened the door. "Oh, good. Your carriage is here."

"So, it is." He hesitated.

"You mustn't make him wait."

"No." He stood another moment. "I'll see you tomorrow night."

He stepped out the door, and Emma quickly shut it, somewhat ashamed she had rushed him. Only a wee bit as she wanted to talk to Blackbourne about the book... about the note...

Emma hurried to the salon and sat back on the couch.

"I've never been to the New Castle Theater," Kat said. "Mr. Carstead has a box at Drury Lane, but we rarely attend as he is so busy. Though I'm sure he'll be delighted to join you, my lord." She glanced back and forth between Emma and Blackbourne. "In fact, I think I'll write him a note to ensure he makes no other plans." She put down her cup and stood.

"I'll find Jo and send her in." Before Emma could say a word, she flew out of the room.

APPALLED, EMMA TURNED sheepishly to Blackbourne. "I'd apologize about my aunt's behavior but by now you know her character."

"Mrs. Carstead is rather trusting," he said.

"No, she's rather scheming," Emma laughed. "She has no intention of sending Jo to us." He raised a brow, and Emma's cheeks warmed before she stood. "Perhaps I'll open the door a wee bit."

He raised the brow higher, and Emma sat back down. They had been alone together in places far more conducive to seduction. If he were so inclined. Which he was not. "It's just I don't want you to think..."

"Think what, Emma?"

"Our meetings have been rather..."

"Extraordinary? Unorthodox?" he said. "Providential?"

"Perhaps." She acknowledged the possibility that fate might be at play. "At least I haven't fallen in front of you in a while."

"You haven't, have you? I wonder if your newfound poise signifies anything?"

"Hardly new, I've never fallen in front of anyone but you," she said. "And I intend to keep it that way."

He laughed. "To disprove any significance to our meetings or to exercise your free will in defiance of it?"

"My motives are not so philosophical. I've merely grown tired of embarrassing myself."

"You've left no room for the feelings of others on the matter."

"Surely your own feelings aren't affected by something so arbitrary."

"Mine? No. I meant Simms," he said. "Since you refused to fall, I'll not hear one word about my sartorial splendor this afternoon." He waved a hand down his body. "His effort has been all for naught."

She laughed and returned to sit by him. "No matter the reason for our meetings, my lord, I'm grateful for your help," she said. "With no expectations for anything in return."

"You don't think I have expectations?"

Her heart stopped. "Do you?"

He smiled. "I expect to find your necklace."

"Oh, yes. Of course." Why had she thought something else?

"If Mr. McBride doesn't do so first. He might have more of an idea where to look in London than I."

"I can't imagine why. He only came last year from Sheffield."

"Sheffield?" he said rather sharply.

"Yes, he managed a theater there."

"How interesting."

He lifted the book off the couch. "Does he know about this?"

"I was holding it when he arrived," she said. "He thought it an insult."

"Do you think it?"

"Not at all. I loved it," she said. "But I understood the joke."

"I thought you might." His whole countenance seemed to lift. "Have you learned any interesting words?"

"Some, yes," she said. "I read your list."

"I thought one word in particular might excite you," he said, and his eyes lingered on her lips, making Emma's pulse race. *Smack*. He must mean *smack*.

Emma moistened her lips. "What word would that be?"

He lowered his head toward her, and Emma closed her eyes. His breath warmed her cheek, and he whispered, "Plant."

"Plant?" she snapped open her eyes.

He leaned back. "Do you have something against plants?"

"What—no, of course not, I love roses or daisies or..."

"Oh, you thought I meant plant as in actual plants," he chuckled.

"What other kinds of plants are there?" Her voice came out sharper than she intended but really...

"I'm surprised you don't know," he said. "I marked it in the book."

"I must've missed it."

"Shall we look it up now?" He flipped through the book. "Ah, here it is. *Plant. The place in the house of the fence where stolen goods are secreted. Any place where stolen goods are concealed.*"

It took a minute for his words to sink in. For the word's definition to dawn on Emma. "A place a thief could hide a stolen necklace," she said slowly. "As in a boardinghouse room?"

"Exactly." He closed the book. "Now, doesn't that excite you?"

Yes, it excited her. It excited her very much. She was so close to recovering her pendant that she could almost feel it hanging from her throat. She jumped up. "If we go now, I could even wear my pendant to the Worthington ball."

"How does tomorrow evening suit you?"

"Today would suit me better," she said. "But tomorrow is—hold on. Haven't we just promised to go to the theater?" His eyes turned slate, and suddenly his scheme dawned on Emma. She nodded in appreciation. "A ruse."

"Precisely." He laughed. "The first part was easy. The second part is a bit trickier. We must get up a large party."

"Is there enough time?"

"Between the two of us, I think we could manage it."

Us. We. Emma's heart soared straight up into the boughs.

"I'm certain Amelia will come as well as my cousins, Hefty and Worthy, and a few friends. Now what of you? Mrs. Carstead won't change her mind, will she?" he asked, and Emma grinned. "And Mr. McBride will stop to check on us."

"No doubt," Emma muttered.

"Is there anyone else you could invite?"

"My cousin, Elizabeth. If she hasn't any plans," she said, knowing full well Kat would make certain she did not.

"Now, if everyone attends, we'll be able to make our escape quite easily."

"Our" escape. He had annoyed Emma by thwarting her escape twice before but now she could not wait to escape with him.

"Now that all is understood, I think I'll be going." He stood and walked to the door. He turned back to Emma and said, "I'm looking forward to tomorrow."

So was Emma.

CHAPTER 8

The next evening found Emma relaxed back against the carriage seat, listening to Kat and her uncle talking across from her. Elizabeth sat next to her, quiet as usual. Emma had tried to talk to her about her soldier earlier, tried to discover her true feelings, but she had only spoken in general terms. Emma had no idea if her cousin felt the same strange excitement around him as she did around Blackbourne.

Was it him—or was it their unorthodox and even dangerous meetings that caused her heart to flutter erratically? She gazed out the window. What would it be like to spend time with him under ordinary circumstances?

A drive in Hyde Park... an ice at Gunter's... a waltz at Almack's...

Emma straightened. Good heavens, no. Not a waltz. Not any dance. Imagine the disaster! Poised and handsome, Blackbourne walks across the ballroom to her, his neckcloth dazzling and brilliant and bright. She shades her eyes. He asks her to dance. The musicians play a waltz, he takes her in his arms, swings her around and...

She falls.

Tumbles head over slippers to the floor.

And drags Blackbourne down with her.

Emma shuddered. Oh, no.

No, no, no. Absolutely not.

She would never dance with Lord Blackbourne.

"Stop woolgathering, Emma," Kat's voice interrupted Emma's developing nightmare. "We're almost there."

"Do you think Lord Blackbourne and his company have arrived yet?" She tried to contain her excitement.

"I hope not," Kat said. "I want to be settled in our box long before Lord Hefton arrives."

Elizabeth jerked forward, her gloves slipping off her lap to the carriage floor, and Emma grinned. Kat had given the game away.

"That's why you must keep your gloves on, Elizabeth. They're so easy to drop." Kat berated her daughter. "A new pair too. Yellow calfskin. Everyone is wearing them. Quite exotic."

"Hardly exotic if everyone has a pair," Emma said and garnered a smirk from Elizabeth, who had picked up the exotic gloves and tugged them on. "I've never understood why one would wish to dress like every other lady out there."

"That's quite apparent, Emma. I swear you just reach willy-nilly into your trunk and grab whatever article of clothing is closest."

"Don't be ridiculous."

"What else could explain you bringing that fan with that gown?"

"It's new."

"It's ghastly."

"It's Italian."

"Your other fan would've suited much—oh, never mind. I forgot." Kat tittered. "You misplaced that one."

Emma ignored Kat's knowing grin. Blackbourne would appreciate this fan. Should she make a joke about not leaving it in a tree? Hold a "conversation" with it? What would she say? Would she be discreet? Coy? Flirtatious? Or would she open it wide on purpose and let him know she's interested? Her pulse raced. Admit it. Emma was interested. Very interested, indeed.

BLACKBOURNE SETTLED against the seat of his barouche landau and idly listened to his sister and Miss Mayfield chattering opposite him. He had been relieved when Amelia had agreed to invite her. It fulfilled his end of the bargain he had made with

Worthy to arrange a meeting with Miss Mayfield, in return for Worthy asking Emma to sing.

Worthy would be happy—but what of Emma? Would she be surprised? Would she wonder why he had invited her? Would her eyes darken with jealousy again?

"I see by your smile that you were amused by Miss Mayfield's story from our schooldays, Philip," Amelia said.

"I—yes, of course, very amusing." He sat forward.

"Jayne mimicked our schoolmistress's expression perfectly," Amelia said. "She always had a talent for pantomime."

"Thank you, Amelia, but please stop, I beg you," Miss Mayfield said. "You're quite putting me to the blush."

Blackbourne doubted it. Her countenance spoke of pride not embarrassment. "Have you been to the New Castle, Miss Mayfield?" he asked politely.

"No. In fact, it's been a few weeks since I've attended any theater."

Since she'd been on stage, she meant.

"I've only been there once, myself," Amelia said. "With Lady Blackbourne, before she went to Italy. Is she to join us this evening, Philip?"

"No, thank heaven. Lady Stanley has proved herself our friend by inviting her to Drury Lane."

"And Hefty?" Amelia looked anxious. "Have you heard from him?"

"He's promised to come, as have a few others."

"With Miss Bryson and her party, our box should be quite lively."

"Quite," Blackbourne said. "I even expect her cousin, Mr. McBride will stop by." He watched Miss Mayfield for a reaction, but she made none. Hardly surprising, she was an actress. Still, they must know each other. The Sheffield Acting Company could not be that large.

Discovering McBride had worked in Sheffield had added to Blackbourne's belief that Jayne Mayfield was McBride's "Adam Tiler."

Blackbourne grimaced. The situation was becoming complicated. If Miss Mayfield and McBride were the thieves, how would this revelation affect Worthy and Emma? Especially Emma. Just how close was she to McBride? He pushed the bothersome thought aside. He need not worry about it yet. He still needed proof. Proof he hoped to find tonight. In a boardinghouse room. A frisson of excitement coursed through him. Alone—with Emma.

CHAPTER 9

A quarter of an hour later, Blackbourne descended from his carriage and turned to help out Miss Mayfield and his sister. "I'd no idea this theater was so popular," he said to Amelia.

"I'd some little notion of it." She straightened her jonquil silk wrap on her shoulders. "Lady Wallingford mentioned it. She attends quite often, you know, with her uncle."

Blackbourne raised his brows in surprise. "I did not know it."

"Don't worry, she won't be coming tonight," Amelia said. "I chanced upon her today at Rundell's. Her uncle is ill again, and she means to stay with him."

"Thank God," he said, relieved. He had neither the time nor the inclination to deal with Francesca tonight.

"So, you are free to pursue Miss Bryson's necklace... or even her," she said with a gurgle of laughter. Blackbourne ignored her insinuating comment but declined to deny its possibility.

"Come along, ladies." He took each by the arm. "I believe our box is this way."

They made their way through the crowd and had just found their box when a female voice called out, "There you are Blackbourne." He let out an exasperated sigh.

"Hello, Mother," he said. "I thought you were to attend Drury Lane with Lady Stanley."

"I said she'd taken a box at a theater, not which theater." She gazed curiously at Miss Mayfield and then pointedly at her hand still nestled in Blackbourne's arm. "Care to introduce me to your... friend?"

"You remember Miss Mayfield, Mama," Amelia said. "She and I were school fellows."

"I remember her quite well. How do you do, Miss Mayfield, or should I say Miss Burkes?"

"Miss Mayfield will do, thank you, your ladyship." She curtsied but kept her hand firmly attached to Blackbourne's arm. He chuckled. She had spunk, he had to give her that.

"Come along, Jayne." Amelia tugged Miss Mayfield away from Blackbourne. "I think I see another acquaintance of ours. I'll talk to you later, Mama."

"You can be certain of that, my dear," Lady Blackbourne said and turned to her son. "What were you thinking, Blackbourne, bringing that actress here?"

"It's a theater, madam," he said and laughed. "One could find many actresses here."

"On stage, my dear, not clinging proudly to my son's arm," she said. "And not one who's causing my dear sister so much grief. Is Worthy coming?"

"I hope so."

"And Lady Wallingford?"

"I'm told her uncle is ill again."

"Lord Cheatem? Fit as a fiddle. I saw him at Gunter's earlier, eating an ice. He wasn't alone. Miss Portnoy was thoroughly enjoying an ice too. A lemon, I believe."

"Perhaps the ice made him ill."

"More likely it's an ice that has made Lady Wallingford ill," she said. "The lemon one enjoyed by his companion."

"Why should that bother her?"

"Miss Portnoy has been on the shelf for ages, but she's still young enough to produce an heir. If that were to happen, then Lady Wallingford would lose those funds her uncle has all but promised her."

"I'm sure she wishes her uncle happy."

"Happy, yes, and unmarried. When do you expect Miss Bryson?" She raised her silver quizzing glass to her eye and glanced around. "Frankly, I'm surprised she isn't here yet."

"Shouldn't you return to your friends, Mother?" Blackbourne laughed. "Your glass will be put to much better use when the play starts."

"Afraid I'll see something you don't wish me to, Blackbourne?"

"My dear Mother, you only see what you want," he said with a chuckle. He bowed her away and entered his box. His mother's appearance had reminded Blackbourne to claim the chairs in the darkest back corner to keep prying eyes—with quizzing glasses or not—from seeing when he and Emma snuck away.

EMMA TWIRLED AROUND in excitement, captivated by every colorful nook and cranny of the theater. Dozens of elegant people streamed by, bedecked in satins and silks and jewels, and a potpourri of floral perfumes wafted in their wake. Emma longed for only one scent, sandalwood. Was Blackbourne here yet?

"Come along, Emma," Kat said, and Emma fell into step behind her and Mr. Carstead. Kat's turban, adorned with tall peacock feathers, turned this way and that, and Emma almost laughed. Searching for Lord Hefton, no doubt. Emma stole a glance at Elizabeth, whose grim appearance said she knew it too.

"There you are." Malcolm appeared at Emma's side.

"My aren't you dashing," Emma said and admired his buff pantaloons and bottle green topcoat.

"Are you surprised?" he asked with a grin.

"Not at all, except perhaps your neckcloth," she said cheekily. "I've never seen it tied so elegantly." Or so bright. Was it new?

"The Oriental, or so I'm told," he said and grinned. "Now, what do you think of the theater?"

"It's fantastic."

"I'm glad," he said. "Shall we find your box?" He crooked his elbow, and Emma slipped her hand through it. A short walk and a flight of stairs later, he stopped in front of a box door. Without even entering, Emma knew it was situated directly in the center of the theater and easily visible from the stage. She pursed her lips. Had Malcolm done it purposely to keep an eye on Blackbourne and her? As if Blackbourne would seduce her in public. Or anywhere. Emma tapped her fan against her hand. Perhaps he needed some encouragement. Perhaps a "conversation" about the matter was in order.

Malcolm knocked on the door, opened it, and everybody crowded in. Emma immediately found Blackbourne, handsome in a navy topcoat and fawn pantaloons.

Malcolm whispered, "It's impolite to stare, lass."

"I'm not."

She was. Blackbourne's brilliant white neckcloth—and the muscular neck beneath—had drawn her eyes like a beacon. Her presence must have attracted his attention, as Blackbourne left his group and approached Emma. "Good evening," he said.

"My lord." Malcolm made a slight bow. "I hope everything is to your liking."

"Oh, it is." Blackbourne's gaze centered on Emma, and a strange giddiness enveloped her. "Very much so."

Suddenly dizzy and rather hot, Emma gripped Malcolm's arm. She had no intention of falling but why take the risk.

"It seems most everyone is here," Blackbourne said, and for the first time, Emma noticed Lady Heyer nearby in conversation with two gentlemen and—Miss Mayfield? Emma shot him a questioning look, but he merely shrugged and said, "Shall I make the introductions?" A tiny knot formed in Emma's stomach, and she reluctantly followed him. Would Miss Mayfield recognize her from the Royal Saloon?

Blackbourne introduced Lady Heyer and his friends from Eton, Mr. Wesley Gates and Sir Edward Tilney, to Malcolm and Emma. He turned to Miss Mayfield and said, "Miss Mayfield, might I introduce you to Mr. McBride."

Malcolm arched a brow. "Miss Mayfield, is it?"

"It is." She tilted her chin as if daring him to claim otherwise.

He only smirked in reply and said, "A pleasure," and stepped away.

"And this, Miss Mayfield," Blackbourne said, amusement tinging his voice, "is Miss... Bryson."

"Miss Bryson, is it?" Miss Mayfield mimicked Malcolm.

Blast. She did recognize her.

"Yes, right." Emma coughed. "Nice to meet you." She made a quick retreat and joined Malcolm, whose annoyance was palpable.

"He would be so unmannerly as to invite an actress to sit in his box with you," he said in a heated voice.

"He must have his reasons."

"No doubt," he said musingly. "But what could they possibly be?"

Emma could think of two. Blackbourne meant to interrogate her about the pistols—or to make her his mistress. Neither idea sat well with her.

"Shall we sit?" Blackbourne asked. "We wouldn't want to miss the start of the play."

"I believe that's my signal to depart," Malcolm said. "I hope everyone enjoys the play." He bowed and departed.

"What do you think of these chairs, Emma?" Blackbourne pointed at a pair of velvet-covered chairs in the dark back corner. "I find they are perfectly situated." He grinned, and Emma comprehended his meaning and grinned back.

"Oh, I quite agree, my lord," she said and quickly sat.

Lady Heyer, Miss Mayfield, and the gentlemen settled into the seats in front of Emma. The Carsteads sat *en famille* in the front of the box. Kat threw her reticule on the seat next to her, and Emma laughed. Blackbourne wasn't the only one thinking of advantageous seating. If Lord Hefton did come, she knew where he'd be forced to sit.

Just as all were seated to their satisfaction, a knock sounded. "Another guest?" Kat asked. "How delightful." She grinned and turned toward the door as two footmen entered. They set up a small table, removed a cold collation of ham and various delicacies from the baskets, and then stood at attention by the table.

"Please, everyone, help yourselves," Blackbourne said. "Shall I get you a plate, Emma?"

"No, I'm too nervous and excited to eat."

"Perhaps I've something to help settle those nerves." He stood and retrieved a small box. "Marzipan?"

"Oh, thank you." She grinned and took a piece and marveled at his memory.

Emma sat back and nibbled on her candy. The low hum of voices reverberated through the box. Only she and Blackbourne remained silent. She glanced at him. Perhaps it was time she started a "conversation" with him. Would he "converse" back? What would he say? Would he compliment her gown? Her eyes? Only one way to find out. She fortified herself with one last bite of marzipan and snapped open her fan, wide. She shifted in her chair toward him and lifted the fan to her nose. Employing a seductive voice, she said, "My lord—"

"You're close with Mr. McBride?" Blackbourne suddenly asked.

"What?" She stopped midwave. "I'm sorry?"

"Mr. McBride. You seem close."

"I suppose we are," she said. "We grew up together. Our mothers are—were cousins."

"Ah," he said. "That explains the grip you had on his arm."

He noticed that too? Did it bother him? Was he jealous? She lifted the fan. "Oh, that," she said, peeping over the feathers and batting her lashes. "I'd become a bit overheated."

"Do you find the box stuffy? Should I open the door?" He stood.

"No, please sit." Had she held the fan wrong? She adjusted its position. "It isn't the box that's caused the heat, my lord." She batted her eyelashes.

"Is something in your eye?"

Good heavens—could he be that obtuse? "I don't have anything in my eye," she said, exasperated. "I was just trying to start a conversation."

"Excellent," he said and crossed his legs. "What do you wish to talk about?"

She stared, dumbfounded. He was that obtuse.

"Emma?"

"Right, yes." She thought quickly. "The... neckcloth." She put down the useless fan. "Was Simms able to tell you anything about it?"

"Only that its worn and faded condition could mean two things. Its owner is elderly, and the neckcloth is as old as he, or he is young but poor and wears the neckcloth daily and thus launders it often."

"I suppose that might be helpful," she said. "What did you do with it?"

"I had Briggs return it to the boardinghouse room," he said. "Speaking of which..." He stood. "I need to take care of something."

"Right now?"

"Oh, absolutely I must." He leaned in close and whispered, "If we're to make our escape."

He flashed a brilliant smile and departed, and Emma quite floated to the ceiling. *Our escape.*

"Since my brother has abandoned you, Miss Bryson, why don't you join us," Lady Heyer's voice brought Emma back down to her chair.

Emma could think of no reason to decline, so she joined them but did not join the conversation. She sat and munched her marzipan until her eye caught sight of Miss Mayfield's bow pin watch. She furrowed her brow. Was it the same one she had worn at the Royal Saloon? Had the housekeeper returned it to her?

"Do you like it?" Miss Mayfield asked.

"I beg your pardon." Emma straightened. "I didn't mean to stare. I've never seen one like it before."

"Made in New York. My mother was an American, you see."

"I didn't know that."

She tilted her head. "Why should you?"

"No reason." Time to change the subject. Emma thrust out the box of candy. "Would anyone care for a piece of marzipan?"

Lady Heyer and the gentlemen declined, but Miss Mayfield said, "I'd love some, but I'm afraid it doesn't agree with my constitution. In truth, one bite nearly killed me."

"How awful."

"It was," she said. "The doctor thought it the almonds and forbade me to ever..." To Emma's surprise, Miss Mayfield paled, then reddened, then paled again. She began to blink rapidly. Emma twisted around to see what caused such an odd reaction. Lord Worthington stood in the doorway, his broad shoulders blocking much of the light from the hallway and his gaze on Miss Mayfield. In an instant, Emma knew why Blackbourne had invited Miss Mayfield, and happiness flooded her.

Worthington stepped aside, and Blackbourne entered. "Miss Bryson," he said and approached her. "Might I introduce you to my cousin, Lord Worthington."

Emma jumped up and curtsied. "I'm so pleased to finally meet you, my lord," she said. "And to thank you for inviting me to sing at your ball."

"I'm delighted to have done so, Miss Bryson," he said. "I've heard nothing but acclaim for your voice."

"I've heard nothing but acclaim for your music room, sir. I understand it rivals that of Carlton House."

"Like His Royal Highness, I consider myself a great lover of the arts." His gray eyes, so much like Blackbourne's, traveled over to Miss Mayfield who appeared to be blinking herself to death. "I hope to prove worthy of your patronage, my lord."

"Shall we sit?" Blackbourne asked, and Kat threw her gloves atop her reticule on the seat next to her. Emma stifled a laugh. Lord Worthington had no intention of sitting with the Carsteads. He proved her correct by sitting next to Miss Mayfield. That lady turned away from him, her cheeks again pale, and her blinking under control.

Blackbourne and Emma settled back onto their seats, and Blackbourne picked up the playbill. "We're to be entertained with a tragedy first."

"It appears so," Emma said. Now what the devil had Lord Worthington said to upset Miss Mayfield?

"My cousin is not a small man," Blackbourne said with a chuckle. "Would you like to change seats to see the stage better?"

And miss the drama unfolding right in front of her? "No, no, I'm fine." She grabbed a piece of marzipan and tilted an ear toward the couple.

"Just say the word and I'll speak to the manager at Drury Lane," Lord Worthington said.

"You don't think I'm capable of getting hired on my own?" She snapped back. "I played every starring role in Sheffield. Every single one."

Emma gasped. Sheffield? Did she know Malcolm?

"I remember," he said. "And if *you* remember, I never missed a showing."

"Then you must know I'd not settle for anything less," she retorted. "Even on Drury Lane."

"You wouldn't be a bit player for long."

Emma nibbled. He sounded besotted.

"Thank you for the confidence, my lord."

"I'm merely surprised you haven't even tried for a part."

Now he sounded exasperated and even petulant.

"It's not why I've come to London," Miss Mayfield said.

"Why have you come to London then?"

Emma leaned closer. Yes, why?

Miss Mayfield glanced back, and Emma looked at the ceiling. "I don't wish to discuss it any longer, my lord," she hissed.

"Miss Bryson?" Blackbourne said, and she jerked her head around.

"What?" She straightened. "Oh, hello." A tall imposing lady elegant in a silver and white evening gown and sporting an icy-white silk turban stood next to Blackbourne.

"Might I introduce you to my mother, Lady Blackbourne?"

"Of course." Emma stood and curtsied. "Your ladyship."

"Miss Bryson." She tilted her head, and Emma expected the chunk of ice on her head to slide off, but it stayed frozen in place. "That's a... lovely fan. Orange and brown feathers. One doesn't see that too often."

"It's Italian," was all Emma could think to say.

"How like them to pair it with a blue satin gown and marzipan?"

"I'm sorry?"

"I believe you've a few specks there, on the bodice," she said. "Hardly noticeable."

Mortified, Emma swiped at the crumbs.

"I see Worthy is here, Blackbourne." She dismissed Emma and her gown with ease. "Your aunt would not be pleased."

"Yes, but Worthy is," he said, then under his breath, "For now anyway."

Emma started. What did Blackbourne mean by that?

"I expect your friends are missing you, Mother," Blackbourne said cheerfully.

"My friends have intrigues of their own to occupy them, but I take your meaning," Lady Blackbourne said, and with one final imperious look at Emma, she swept out of the box.

Blackbourne motioned to Lady Heyer, who surprised Emma—and even more so her aunt—by engaging Kat in conversation. "My dear Mrs. Carstead..."

"That should keep everyone distracted, at least for a while," Blackbourne whispered to Emma and pointed to the door. "Shall we?"

It struck Emma that Blackbourne must have told Lady Heyer of their plans, and this stayed her departure for a moment. What would she think of Emma's being with Blackbourne in a boardinghouse room? Alone. Then it struck her even more forcefully that she did not care. She didn't even care if this confusing, yet exhilarating relationship came to nothing; she would enjoy every moment she spent with Blackbourne.

"Yes, let's," she said and followed him out the door.

A QUARTER OF AN HOUR later, Emma stood on the street in St. Giles and waited impatiently as Blackbourne gave his tiger instructions and walked to the carriage boot.

"My lord," she said. "We haven't much time."

He returned and handed Emma a folded garment. "Wear this over your gown. I wouldn't want it to get ruined."

"Don't worry, it's already covered in marzipan," she said with aspersion, and he laughed.

She unfolded a finely tailored and obviously expensive rose satin pelisse. "It's beautiful. I can only imagine the sensation the lady caused when she wore it."

"I suppose," he said and shrugged. "But unlike Brummell, I find it's the person who makes the clothes and not the other way around," he said, and Emma took it as a compliment to herself, not her dress, and warmed. "Still, won't she who—"

"Its owner has no need of it anymore," he said. "Trust me."

His brusque tone told Emma it had belonged to his wife. Which made no sense. Why would he give Emma his late wife's gown to possibly ruin—if he had loved her as much as rumored?

"We should hurry."

"Of course." She slipped on the pelisse and placed her arm through Blackbourne's. They hurried through the streets, the noise and bustle and the bursts of drunken laughter, the same as before. "You haven't said how you plan to get us by Mother Cummings," Emma said.

He laughed. "I plan on avoiding her altogether."

"You don't mean we are to climb through the window again?" Emma tried to contain her excitement. He would have to remove his coat.

"You might prefer to do so, but I wish to be a bit more dignified," he said, "by entering through the door."

"Oh."

"You sound disappointed."

"You must admit it's a bit boring."

"But much less conspicuous," he said. "Here we are."

The boardinghouse loomed before them, and Emma headed for the door, but Blackbourne stopped her. "My lord?" she asked, but he ignored her and pulled a cheroot from his pocket and lit it.

"Must you smoke now?" she hissed.

He ignored her and puffed on the cheroot until its lit end flashed bright in the darkness. He took one last puff, threw it to the ground, and glanced around.

Within seconds, a tall gangly man appeared out of the shadows, and Emma grabbed Blackbourne's arm. "My lord?"

"Don't worry. It's the runner, Briggs. He's been watching the boardinghouse for us." He loosened Emma's hand with a pat and said, "Wait here a moment."

Blackbourne joined Briggs, and the two men conversed in low tones, but Emma still caught a few words. Safe... cuffin... Jenkins... Blackbourne repeated that name twice, and Briggs nodded. A moment later, the runner disappeared and Blackbourne returned to Emma.

"Is everything all right?" she asked.

"Perfectly," he said. "We're safe to go in. Mother Cummings has gone for a pint at the Stout Pig with her cuffin."

Emma grinned. "Her husband."

"You've been reading your dictionary."

She preened. "I might've learned a word or two." Smack being the other.

"Dazzle me with your knowledge," he said. "What others?"

"Never mind," she said. "What of the thief?"

"He's gone too."

"To the Stout Pig?" Emma joked, but Blackbourne did not return her smile.

"I only know he isn't here." The pair entered the boardinghouse and crept through a dark narrow hallway until Blackbourne stopped. "This is it."

"Are you certain he isn't home?"

"Yes, but just in case, put one of your keen ears against the door."

Emma complied, then nodded. "It's empty."

They slipped in, and Emma dashed to the trunk and lifted the lid, but a tapping sound stilled her hand. Blast. Was someone at the door? She twisted around and found Blackbourne tapping on the wall. "What are you doing?" she said in a loud whisper. "You'll get us caught."

"It's the only way I know of to find a plant." He tapped. "The echo."

"Should I do it too?"

"No, you continue there. It'd be difficult to hear with two of us doing it."

He tapped again, and Emma turned her attention to the trunk. Everything appeared the same except for one thing. "My lord," she said. "Are you certain Briggs returned the neckcloth?"

"Yes." He tapped. "Why?"

"It isn't here."

"The thief must be wearing it. You shan't be able to steal it again," he joked, and Emma grinned, shut the lid, and joined Blackbourne at the far wall. "Any luck?"

"Not so far." He tapped.

She wandered over to the spinet and was surprised to find on its top a pair of yellow gloves, two half-empty crystal flutes, and a box with naught but crumbs in it. "I think our thief has been entertaining a lady," she said. "A very stylish lady."

"Why?"

She held up the gloves. "She left these."

"Or the thief stole them."

"Ladies' gloves?"

"If he can break into a house and steal a gentleman's dueling pistols, he can steal gloves from a lady's bedchamber," he said. "Or from under her pillow."

He gave her a pointed look, and Emma laughed. "My jewels are quite safe as only you and Malcolm know where I keep them," she said, and embarrassment heated her ears. It now seemed such an intimate thing to have shared with him. To hide her discomfort, she picked up a half-empty flute and joined him. "Parlor trick."

"I'm sorry?"

"If Simms's expertise on cloth could tell us something, then yours on wine should be able to do the same," she said. "If you're the expert you claim to be."

"Are you questioning me? If that's a challenge, Emma, then I accept." Blackbourne removed a handkerchief from his pocket, wiped off the edge of the glass and sipped. "It's lucky you didn't taste it—it would've made you giddy."

"Champagne?" Emma said, no longer amazed—but strangely excited—that he remembered things about her.

"Yes. A rather expensive bottle too. Not many people can claim to have it."

"He clearly wanted to impress her. I mean he's impressed me." She pointed to the box. "If those aren't the remains of marzipan, then I'm Marie Antoinette."

"Marie Antoinette, how... apt." He seemed lost in thought for a moment. "Perhaps it isn't the thief who brought the champagne but the lady."

"Why? As a gift? A bribe? To get him foxed?" Emma's inhaled, and she asked in a breathless tone, "To get him to do her bidding?"

"Her bidding? Why Emma, it almost sounds as if you have some experience with an affair of this nature." He sounded flirtatious and, dare she think it, even interested, and instantly, Emma snapped open her fan. "I might have some experience, my lord," she said.

"I'm sorry but I don't believe you."

Emma snapped the fan closed. That's it. She was done with it—unless to smack him on the head with it.

"Perhaps I've not had an affair," she said. "But I have had a romantic entanglement of sorts. I was engaged once."

"Were you?" He tapped.

"Yes. And I jilted him." There. She'd said it. It was all out in the open. She held her breath and waited for his reaction.

None came. One would think such a dramatic confession would cause one to stop tapping. "I jilted him," she repeated louder. "At the altar."

"You must've had a good reason," he said in a mild tone. "One doesn't do such a thing on the spur of the moment."

"You know me well enough by now to know I do," she joked and was rewarded with a smile.

"Was the engagement itself just as impetuous?" He tapped.

"Yes, I mean, I knew it was coming, but it still caught me by surprise."

"Why did you agree to it?"

The question surprised Emma. No one had ever asked her. "I'm not sure," she said slowly. "I suppose I didn't want to be alone."

"Understandable." He tapped. "Your mother had just died."

"Yes, she had, but that's still no reason to have—hold on," she said and pulled him around. "How did you know that?"

"I've a confession of my own," he said. "I had you investigated the moment I learnt Amelia had hired you."

"Oh."

"She was no longer under the protection of my roof, and as Lord Heyer was away, it fell to me to find out who she was allowing under her own." He dropped his hands to his sides. "I hope you understand."

"Of course."

"Good." His shoulders sloped minutely as if relieved by his confession, and he turned back to the wall. "Do you miss her?" He tapped.

"My mother? Terribly."

"It's difficult to lose a parent. Everything seems to change, afterward."

"I didn't want anything to change. I was perfectly happy."

"Is her death, and your promise, the reason you sing under her name and not your own?"

"Oh, no. That was Malcolm's idea. He thought my jilt would be troublesome if it became known," she said. "Though why anybody in London would care about the romantic life of a doctor's daughter from a wee village in Scotland, I couldn't say."

He tapped. "It's a shame our past mistakes should have such an influence on our present."

Did he mean Emma's past—or his own? "I don't know about you, my lord," she said, "but I've learned from mine."

"How so?"

"I shan't be as impetuous from now on," she said forcefully. "I'll not agree to an engagement for any reason except love."

He did not look at her but nodded slowly, and Emma knew he understood she referred to his wager.

"I suppose there's a time and place for impulsive decisions," he said. "Deciding whom to marry isn't one of them."

"You were married once." It was out before she could stop it. What would he think?

The tapping slowed. "I see I'm not the only one who's been investigating."

"Oh, no, I haven't... I didn't... It's just people—"

"People talk," he said. "Yes, I was married. Once." He tapped the wall, and it sounded harder to Emma, louder, and the echo more distant, like he was pulling away. He must've loved her very much.

"I'm sorry, I shouldn't—"

"Hush."

Emma raised her brows. "I just wanted to apolo—"

"No, listen." He tapped the wall. "Surely, with your keen ears you heard that?"

"An echo?" she said. "Have you found the plant?"

"We'll know in a moment." He tapped a little farther down the wall and stopped at the wardrobe. He stared at it for a moment and pushed it away. The wall came with it.

"That's the sound of moving furniture I heard." Emma said excitedly. "But how clever."

"It's even better than that. He's bolted the door to the wardrobe, so it opens with it. Once inside, he uses this handle." He pointed to an iron handle attached to the inside of the door. "To pull it shut."

"Well." Blackbourne's eyes danced. "Shall we?"

Emma nodded.

Blackbourne bent low to enter the room, and Emma slipped in after him. He pulled the door closed, plunging them into semidarkness. Only a shaft of moonlight filtered through the dirt of a small window kept it from total darkness. Blackbourne pointed to it. "That's how our thief disappeared."

Emma could see how even a man could slip through it if he removed his coat and his neckcloth and his...

"Emma?"

"Yes."

"No time for woolgathering. We need to search the shelves. I'll take the top shelves."

"Right." Emma kneeled by the lower shelves and pulled each object out, one by one, and held it up to the light. "There must be a dozen necklaces here with a dozen different jewels but not one amber pendant," she said in frustration. "Any luck, up there?"

"Not so far. The top shelf seems to be the place for rings and bracelets and stolen watches. Hold on." He pulled out a silk handkerchief, unfolded it, and lifted out a chain. He held it to the shaft of moonlight. Flecks of gold glinted off a unique gold-braided chain. He grinned. "I think we've found it."

"Thank you!" She took it and quickly checked it. "Oh, no."

"What's the matter?"

"There's no pendant. Perhaps it's lying on the shelf. Can you check?"

He swept the shelf with his hand. "I'm sorry."

"But it doesn't make any sense. Why would the thief sell the pendant and not the chain?" She handed it back to Blackbourne.

"You don't wish to keep it? It looks to be quite valuable."

"I wouldn't know."

"Wasn't it a gift from Mr. McBride?"

She shrugged. "It means nothing to me."

"I'm happy to hear it."

"Why?"

He seemed caught off guard by her question. "I... because we mustn't take it," he said. "Else the thief will know someone had found his plant."

"We might've been found out anyway," Emma whispered. "I hear footsteps."

In a blink, Blackbourne slipped off his coat, climbed the ladder, pushed his coat out the window, and squeezed through. He helped Emma out, shut the window, and they ran down the crowded alley.

Emma glanced back. "Someone's poked their head out the window. What if he follows us?"

"Then we must hide."

"Where?" she said, panicked.

Blackbourne stopped, pushed her against a wall, and muttered, "In plain sight," and crushed Emma's lips with his own.

Crushed. Plundered. Ignited.

And all thoughts of her pendant, of the thief, of life itself fled.

An eternity passed and he lifted his head but kept her against his chest, tight against his chest. What sort of gentleman—just the sort Emma liked. She pressed in closer and slid her arms around his neck. "Do you think he's gone by?"

"I'm not certain," he said, and his eyes swept Emma's face. "But just in case..."

His lips found hers again. Soft and warm, hard and hungry, probing and inviting, Emma moaned softly. Her fingers went to the silver at the temples, and suddenly, he released her. "We should return to the theater," he said in a ragged voice.

"We should," Emma said, but neither moved. A surreal moment passed before Blackbourne stepped away and slipped.

"Careful." Emma grabbed his arm. "You might fall."

"Too late, I think," he muttered and took Emma by the arm and led her down the alley.

THE CARRIAGE DRIVE back to the theater was quiet and dreamlike, as if the whole earth held its breath, and Emma wished it would last forever. She wanted to hold on to this extraordinary feeling and feared it would disappear with their return to the box. Her fear proved true. Kat's high shrill voice met her the moment she entered.

"Thank God you've returned, Emma," she said. "Elizabeth is missing."

"What do you mean?"

"Exactly what I said. Missing. Gone. Disappeared," she said, and her voice and the peacock feathers rose higher with each syllable. "The foolish girl has vanished into thin air."

Emma looked to her uncle for an explanation, but he merely let out an exasperated sigh.

"Kat, please, sit down." Emma sat and tugged her aunt down next to her. "Now tell me exactly what happened."

"There we were in the middle of what I thought a quite pleasant conversation with Lady Heyer, when Elizabeth jumped up and darted out of the box. I hadn't a second to wonder what had come over the child when who do you think appeared?"

Emma didn't need to think—she knew. "Lord Hefton."

"Yes." Kat's agitation increased. "Of all the ill luck."

Ill luck or planned escape? "Perhaps Elizabeth saw some friends and ran out to greet them."

"My imperturbable daughter doesn't drop everything and dash out of a theater box to see a few friends. She even dropped her gloves. Again. Miss Mayfield picked them up and said she was certain Elizabeth would not want to lose them. She knew how dear they were, as she had recently lost a similar pair. I retorted that Mr. Carstead could well afford to buy as many gloves for his own daughter as needed."

"Oh, Kat—"

"Then Lord Worthington said he'd happily replace a lost pair of gloves for any lady he cared for too, but I knew he wasn't speaking of Elizabeth. Why would he? He barely knew the gel, and besides, he was staring right at Miss Mayfield when he said it. And she retorted he was free to buy gloves for any lady he wished. And I interrupted them both to remind them there were far worse things than losing a pair of gloves, like having one's daughter kidnapped."

"Kidnapped? Don't be absurd, Kat," Emma said. "I'm certain she is safe."

"She isn't safe at all. Not from the smooth words and charming manner of Lieutenant Gibson. Oh, if only Lord Hefton hadn't gone away with Miss Mayfield—"

"With Miss Mayfield? Why?"

"After the ridiculous rattling on about gloves, Lord Worthington stormed out. Miss Mayfield seemed agitated and out of sorts, so Lord Hefton offered to take her home."

"How kind of him."

"Kind?" Kat squawked. "It should've been Elizabeth he was taking home."

"Kat, lower your voice." Emma glanced at Blackbourne and Lady Heyer.

"I'm sorry, I'm just so upset. I'd a hard enough time convincing Mr. Carstead to come, and I'm now certain he'll insist we leave once Lizzie returns," she said. "Though why I should care now, I don't know. I'm certain Lord Hefton won't return now that Miss Mayfield has got her claws into him."

"Trust me, Miss Mayfield has no interest in Lord Hefton," Emma said.

"How could you know that?"

"Did she flirt with him? Did she open her fan at him?"

"This is hardly a time for joking, Emma."

"You're right. I'm sorry." It's not as if the fan really worked.

A noise came from the doorway, and Kat and Emma turned. Kat sighed. "It's only Lady Blackbourne," she said in a bitter tone while Emma wiped her mouth. Her ladyship joined her children, and a moment later, they all joined Emma and Kat.

"I hadn't noticed your pelisse, earlier Miss Bryson." Lady Blackbourne said, and Emma panicked. Was it wrinkled? Covered in marzipan? Covered in dust from the plant? "Yes, I felt a bit of a draft."

"It's not a color I'd expect you to wear."

"Mother—" Blackbourne said.

"I merely wished to say I quite like it."

"Thank you, Lady Blackbourne, but in truth, it isn't mine. A friend lent it to me."

"Your friend has excellent taste."

"Yes, he does," Emma said without thinking.

"He?"

Blast. "I meant *she*."

"She meant me, Mama," Lady Heyer said. "You may keep it if you wish, Miss Bryson. Mama is right. It does become you."

"I'm no longer cold. In fact, I'm rather overheated." Emma stood, slipped it off, and placed it on the chair. "Thank you for the use of it, Lady Heyer."

"I saw Hefty leaving with Miss Burkes," Lady Blackbourne said. "Does Worthy have competition?"

Kat wailed and Emma pinched her arm.

"Not at all," Lady Heyer said. "Miss *Mayfield* merely became indisposed, and Hefty offered to take her home."

"I'm surprised you didn't offer to do so, Philip. You're usually so attentive. I wonder what you were about?" She targeted Emma with a stare.

"Have you come to join us, Mr. McBride?" Blackbourne asked.

Now Malcolm too? Emma sighed and turned around to find him in the doorway, red-faced, flustered, and staring hard at Emma. Thank heaven she had taken off the pelisse. His observational skills were on par with Lady Blackbourne.

"Malcolm, hello," she said. "Is everything all right?"

"Yes, everything is fine now, I believe," he said, and his features relaxed, returning to their usual pallor. "I just wanted to see how everyone is enjoying the play."

"Everyone is enjoying themselves immensely," Emma lied. "Would you like a glass of wine?"

"No, thank you," he said. "I can only stay a moment. I must return backstage."

"Surely, Mr. Jenkins can handle things for now."

"Mr. Jenkins?" Blackbourne said.

"He's Malcolm's partner."

"That explains it."

"Explains what, my lord?" Malcolm lifted an eyebrow.

"The name of the theater company. I read it on the playbill, and I've wondered about it all evening."

"I'm happy to have satisfied your curiosity, my lord."

"You have," Blackbourne said and brushed a piece of lint from his sleeve. "Tonight, anyway."

A tic formed on the side of Malcolm's jaw for a second before he said, "Enjoy the rest of the play." He bowed and turned to leave, nearly knocking over Elizabeth as she stepped into the box.

"There you are." Kat turned her wrath on her daughter. "Do you have an explanation for your atrocious manners?"

"Leave her be, Katherine," Mr. Carstead said in a sharp, unusually clear manner. Elizabeth went and stood by her father, a sly smile on her face. "We can speak about it at home." He tilted his head toward the door and fulfilled Kat's prognostication that he'd insist they leave.

With half the party leaving or having already left, the remaining group decided to end the night too. Amid the general melee of finding reticules and gloves, Emma found herself alone with Blackbourne.

"Quite an adventuresome evening, Emma," he said.

"Yes." She kept her eyes forward. "One I won't soon forget."

He leaned in close and whispered, "Neither will I."

Emma's heart quite flipped over her chest.

CHAPTER 10

The next afternoon, Emma sat on the couch, her music sheets in her hands. She knew she should be practicing, needed to practice, but thoughts of Blackbourne and the surreal escape from the plant kept intruding. Were all kisses so warm? Penetrating? Delicious?

"What's delicious, lass?"

Emma shot up, and the music sheets scattered across the floor. "I didn't hear you come in, Jo."

"I brought yer tea." She put a tray down. "Ye didn't come down for luncheon."

"Yes, well," Emma said, flustered. "I've been practicing my singing."

"I must've lost my hearing as I didn't hear a sound."

"I was just going over the music." She gathered the sheets from the floor.

"I expect his lordship would rather hear yer voice."

"Thank you, Jo. I'll keep that in mind."

The maid poured tea into a cup and handed it to Emma. "Have ye decided which gown you'll be wearing to sing at the ball?"

"The green satin," she said and took a sip of tea. "And my new Indian shawl."

"The one with every color of the rainbow except green?"

"That's the one."

Jo groaned. "I'll take it down and iron it."

The maid left, and Emma set down her cup. Jo was right. She must practice. Her vocals must be in top form. Prince George might be there and—why had Blackbourne kissed her a second time? She relaxed back against the couch. Had he done it just to hide her? It had not felt like a-hiding-her-from-a-thief kiss. Oh, no. Not at all. It had been searing. Torrid. Hot.

"What's hot, my dear?" Kat asked from the doorway, and Emma sat up. Did no one ever knock?

"My, uh, tea," she said.

"Let it cool down for a minute." Kat sighed and sank down onto a chair.

"Is something the matter?" Emma asked, though she knew the answer. Lord Hefton and his effrontery in taking Miss Mayfield home last evening and not Elizabeth. "You seem out of sorts."

"Perhaps I am suffering a bit of the blue devils today, though I can't imagine why." She drooped her arms over the chair like wet feathers. "I'm usually in such high spirits."

"Fustian. You know exactly why." Emma set the music sheets aside. "It's Lord Hefton, isn't it?"

"If only they had met. Things would be so different this morning."

"Please don't take what I'm about to say amiss." Emma took a breath. "I think, Aunt, you must let Elizabeth decide for herself."

"Decide for herself?" Kat darted up. "Have you gone mad?"

"If she truly loves this soldier..."

"Bah! Even if she does love him," she said. "She'd get over it once she's Lady Stanhope."

Had Blackbourne ever gotten over his wife? Emma had tried not to think how he had turned away from her when she blurted out that he was a widower.

"Besides, how can she decide anything if she's never even met Lord Hefton?" Kat interrupted Emma's thoughts. "I'm certain they'd suit if only I could get them in the same room together."

On this point, Emma agreed. She had been in the same room with Blackbourne, and she thought they suited very well. Very well, indeed.

"Why the smile, Emma?" Kat stopped in front of her. "Do you think Lord Hefton will be at the ball?"

Emma did not like the sudden gleam in Kat's eyes. The hard calculating gleam of someone who'd fake a broken carriage axle in front of the Worthington mansion the night of the ball. She could not let that happen. "Perhaps I can invite Lord Hefton to come to Vauxhall," she said quickly. "I'm to sing there next week, remember."

"Oh, my dear Emma." She fluttered down next to her on the couch. "Would you?"

"Of course! You and uncle have been so kind... it's the least I could do."

The least she could do to keep her from humiliating Emma by invading the Worthington ball.

"And another few days would give me time to ensure Elizabeth comes too." She nodded in thought. "We needn't mention our plans to anyone."

"It'll be our secret." Emma laughed. Kat had finally realized which parent Elizabeth resembled the most.

"Thank you, my dear." Kat went to the door, paused, and turned back to Emma. "I only wish for Elizabeth to have the opportunity to fall in love with an earl," she said. "Just like you."

She strode out the door and left Emma gaping after her. What she said was true. She had fallen for the Earl of Blackbourne. Quite literally. Emma was head over slippers in love.

BLACKBOURNE SWIRLED the brandy in the Ravenscroft tumbler, its caramel color again reminding him of Emma's eyes, its smooth warm taste of her kiss. He wasn't fooled. He had enough experience to know she had no experience—despite her claims of being a jilt. Her reaction to his first kiss showed her innocence, but the second showed her aptitude. Indeed, she learned quickly. Heat had shot through her lips and seared his own like fire. He recalled the soft moan, the shocked and even disappointed look when he pulled away.

"My lord?"

"I'm sorry, Simms." Blackbourne straightened. "I didn't hear you come in."

"You did appear preoccupied."

"And you seem a bit perturbed." He set down the glass. "What disaster has befallen you?"

"Your waistcoat has been delivered." The disdain in Simms's voice caused Blackbourne to laugh. "Is something the matter with it?" he asked. "Won't it fit?"

"Oh, no, it's cut perfectly. I understand Weston himself oversaw its construction..."

"But?"

"But really, my lord, must you wear it to the Worthington ball?" he asked in a pained, agitated voice. "It's so very public and this waistcoat is so very... loud."

"But that should please you. It's bound to be commented upon in all the morning broadsheets." He unfolded himself from his chair and stood. "I wouldn't be surprised to find you two points ahead tomorrow."

"Or three down. You do realize the comments must be complimentary?" he said. "Comparing your waistcoat to a set of floral draperies hanging in a library would not be so."

"Would floral draperies really do in a library?" Blackbourne joked. "I must ask Lady Blackbourne."

Simms arched a brow. "Whom do you speak of my lord? Her ladyship your mother or the future Lady Blackbourne?" He walked to the door. "I understand they have different styles."

The valet departed, and it surprised Blackbourne that he did not feel the need to chase after him, to protest the possibility of there being another Lady Blackbourne—and who that lady would be. Had he fallen in love with Emma Bryson? He'd not go that far, but he did know this: Thoughts of his wife no longer tormented him, nor did his chest tighten at her name. It had been remarkably easy to loan Emma the pelisse. Why had he even kept it or any of Clarissa's things? He'd have his housekeeper remove all reminders of her tomorrow. He pulled aside the curtain to see the sky clear and bright except a single dark cloud hovering over the horizon. But he must remove something else—or someone else—himself. Francesca.

CHAPTER 11

Blackbourne walked across the Wallingford salon, his shoes making a clipping sound on the floor, and he idly wondered what had happened to the carpet. He reached the fireplace, rested a hand on the mantel, and stared into the empty grate, his thoughts about the carpet overtaken by more immediate concerns. How to tell Francesca their affair was over and just how honest he should be about it.

"Hello, Philip."

Startled, Blackbourne turned. Francesca stood next to him, stunning in a green and gold satin gown. Stunning and striking and completely artificial. Had she always been so calculating in her dress? In her manner?

"You're staring, darling," she said with bemusement. "Were you not expecting me?"

Blackbourne pulled himself together. "That's the thing, isn't it," he said. "Admit it, you've always made me wait at least ten minutes before coming down."

"Why should you always wait on me?"

"It's never bothered me, Francesca."

"That's kind of you to say, darling, but it's begun to bother me," she said. "And I think it's time for a change."

It was, and he must tell her so tonight after the ball.

She slipped her arm through his and led him to the couch. "You can't imagine how much I'm looking forward to this evening," she said and sat. "I plan to do nothing but eat, drink, and dance."

"Naturally, I must claim the first one." Blackbourne joined her.

"You may claim as many as you wish as I plan to dance every set," she said. "I swear I've done naught but play cards with elderly roues for weeks now."

"I'm sure your uncle appreciates your company."

"True, but now I realize in my desire to be a useful niece, I may have neglected others." She glanced at him from under her lids. "I shan't allow that to happen anymore." She gave him a beguiling smile and placed a gloved hand on his knee. A yellow glove like every other lady in London wore—except Emma.

"Shall we go?" he asked abruptly and stood.

"Right now?"

"Yes, I don't wish to be late."

"I see." She pursed her lips briefly, then she shrugged, and held out her hand. Blackbourne clasped it and for the first time noticed the gold-braided bracelet clasped around the glove. He raised his eyebrows in question.

"I would've preferred to wear both, but since I can't yet, I mean to have everyone admire my bracelet at least."

Everyone—or one person in particular? Had she noticed the shift in his affections and to whom? Would she make their relationship known to Emma? A queasiness formed in Blackbourne's stomach, and a sliver of apprehension niggled at him. He should have broken off their affair sooner.

EMMA TWISTED HER BODY back and forth in front of the mirror. Perfection. Sheer perfection. Contrary to Jo's predictions, the dark rose gown and brightly colored wrap suited her magnificently. Her skin glowed and her eyes sparkled more than usual. But was it her clothes that caused it—or something else? What had Blackbourne said? *The person made the clothes...*" and Emma agreed.

Especially a person in love. She would glow and sparkle just as much robed in sackcloth and ashes.

"Emma, you've a visitor," Kat said from the hallway, in an irritated tone, and Emma knew the visitor was Malcolm.

"I can insist he leave if you do not wish for company," Kat continued.

"No, I'll see him." Emma sighed, and a moment later, she entered the salon.

"Malcolm," she said. "I wasn't expecting you. The Worthington ball is tonight, remember?"

"It's why I've come. I've brought you something." He held up a small velvet sack, and Emma gasped. Had he found her amber pendant?

"I know it isn't your pendant." He dashed that thought quickly. "But I think you'll still be pleased." He pulled out a thin gold chain strung with three pearls from the bag and let it dangle from his hand. "I thought of you the moment I saw it."

"You needn't have got me anything." She turned away abruptly, loath to take such a gift from him.

"Don't you like it?"

"Yes, of course I do, it's beautiful."

"Here then, let me put it on you."

There really was no reason to refuse that she could tell him.

Malcolm clasped the necklace around her throat, his fingers warm and lingering. Emma shifted away uncomfortably before turning around. "How does it look?"

"Perfect against your skin."

Emma clasped the pearls, cold and hard beneath her fingers, and thought her skin had lost a little of its glow.

"Prince George shall be so overcome by your beauty he shall immediately invite you to sing for Queen Charlotte."

"If only," she said, releasing the pearls and relieved to speak of something else. "Tonight might be my last chance."

"Not necessarily, love," he said.

"Of course you're right. I could always try again next Season."

"I meant Queen Charlotte isn't the only queen in Europe." Malcolm smiled. "You could always sing on the Continent."

"Don't be ridiculous, Malcolm..." Emma laughed and then sobered. "Oh, dear, you're serious."

"Why not?" he said. "You'd dazzle in the salons of Europe."

"I shan't deny that, but... Come now, don't be silly. How would I even get there? Where would I live?"

"I'd arrange everything," he said. "As before."

Annoyance erupted in her breast at his presumption that she would drop everything and go, and she rebelled. "I'd never ask it of you."

"You didn't ask before."

"True but that was before."

Before Blackbourne.

"Before you lost your pendant?" he asked quietly.

"Exactly," she said. "You know I won't leave until I've found it."

"You needn't worry about that, lass," he said. "I'm certain I will find it."

As opposed to Blackbourne. He knew their rivalry was no longer over that, but he would never acknowledge it—and still she could not tell him. Not yet. What did another day or two matter?

A footman appeared. "Miss Bryson, the carriage is waiting," he said, and Emma sighed in relief at the interruption.

"Thank you," she said and turned to Malcolm. "I must go now." She strode to the door.

And he must let her go

CHAPTER 12

The Worthington ball was a crush. Stylish ladies and elegant gentlemen filled every chair and every space against the walls and every eye seemed turned on Emma. A flame of panic lit inside her. Would she fall again? Would these stares turn to gawks? Was Claimore here? Emma took a deep breath and snuffed out the flame. It did not matter. Nothing could ruin this night—not even Prince George's apparent absence—as Blackbourne was here.

She had found him easily enough, and it wasn't the brilliant neckcloth, or silver at the temples, or even the delightful new floral waistcoat—that she just knew he wore for her—that caught her attention. It was just him. Sitting between his mother and sister in the front row and smiling directly at her.

Emma signaled to the pianoforte player, and the music started. She took a deep breath and sang. Her voice came out strong and clear and bright, and she did not miss one beat through five songs. On the final note of her final song, her voice soared heavenward, and the crowd came to their feet, and she did not fall off hers.

The applause reverberated through Emma's body, and she basked in the adulation until a hand on her elbow brought her out of her reverie.

"We'll have no untoward movements," Blackbourne said. "Not after that superb singing."

Emma giggled. "I might fall from the reaction alone."

Or his nearness.

"Absolutely beautiful, Miss Bryson," Lady Heyer came into view, her blue-green gown swirling around her legs like a wave. "But I did not expect any less."

"Yes, well done, Miss Bryson," Lady Blackbourne joined them. "Everything I heard was true. Your voice is magnificent."

"Thank you, your ladyship."

"I particularly enjoyed the last song. I've never heard it before."

"It's called Ae Fond Kiss. It was a favorite of my father's and written by a fellow Scotsman. Mr. Robert Burns. Have you heard of him?"

"I can't say I have, but I do know an excellent modiste by that name," she said. "Miss Cecilia Burns has a delightful little shop on the Pall Mall and an exceptional eye for color."

"Mother—" Blackbourne said with a warning shake of his head.

"What, my dear? I thought Miss Bryson might be interested in finding a new modiste."

"You're very kind," Emma said with a laugh. "But I'm quite satisfied with my own."

"Miss Bryson needn't worry about her dress when her voice speaks for her," said a female voice she did not recognize, and Emma turned around to find a stunning creature sheathed in green smiling at her.

"Miss Bryson," Blackbourne said, and Emma wondered at his sudden tension. "Might I introduce you to Lady Wallingford?"

Emma stifled a gasp. This exotic long-limbed lady with the ream of reddish-gold hair was Blackbourne's mistress?

"How delighted I am to finally meet you, Miss Bryson," she said. "I've heard nothing but praise about your voice."

"Thank you." Emma curtsied and marveled that Blackbourne had spoken to the woman about her.

"Lady Wallingford," Lady Blackbourne said. "You'll be glad to hear your own mother is still enjoying the fine Italian weather."

"Is that what she's enjoying?" She arched a well-formed brow. "I've always found her to be more of an indoor sort of person."

"Just so," Lady Blackbourne laughed. "Did you receive the fan she sent back from Italy? I asked Blackbourne to give it to you."

"Thank you, yes," she said, and Emma could not restrain a grin. The borrowed fan had been a gift for her—but *not* from Blackbourne.

"I'm rather surprised to see you aren't carrying it, this evening," Lady Blackbourne said, her brows knitted together. "I dare say it would've gone perfectly with that gown."

"Yes, well," she said and sounded annoyed. "We aren't here to admire my dress but Miss Bryson's voice."

"And what a voice it is." Lord Worthington joined the group. "One worthy of the London stage. Would you ever consider it, Miss Bryson?"

"Or even the Continent. You'd dazzle in the salons of Europe." Lady Wallingford joined in the conversation, and Emma blinked in astonishment. It was as if she and Malcolm were of one mind.

"What do you say, Miss Bryson?" Lord Worthington asked.

"Thank you both," she said. "But I sing for my own pleasure."

"Speaking of pleasure," Lady Blackbourne said, "I thought there was to be an announcement tonight, Worthy."

A flush covered his cheeks. "You were... misinformed, Aunt," he said in a tight voice. "Now, if you'll excuse me. I must see to my other guests."

"Oh, dear," Lady Blackbourne said. "I certainly didn't mean to upset him. You never know what he'll do when he gets in a pet. Go and speak to him, Blackbourne."

"Perhaps it's time we did have a word," he said, and Emma started. Surely, he would not tell Worthy he thought Miss Mayfield was a thief. He still had no real proof.

She grabbed him by the arm and hissed, "You aren't going to speak to him about Miss Mayfield?"

"No." He grimaced. "Not yet anyway." He left to join his cousin, and now Emma grimaced. They were too far away for even her keen ears.

"Is that Lady Stanford I see over there?" Lady Blackbourne said.

"The lady standing conveniently close to Blackbourne?" Lady Heyer asked.

"That's the one. You know, I haven't spoken to her in a dog's age."

"You had tea with her last week."

"Tea dear, not conversation." Lady Blackbourne grinned and went and joined her friend, and Emma pursed her lips. If only she had a friend conveniently close to Blackbourne.

"Ah, Hefty. I'm delighted to see you," Lady Heyer said, and Emma whirled around. Lord Hefton stood next to his cousin. Tall and handsome and—sporting a new waistcoat? Emma wrinkled her nose. A rather boring and conventional waistcoat. At least there weren't any alarming bulges protruding from this one. It trimmed him down and even enhanced his handsome features.

"Is this the famous singer I've heard so much about?" he said.

Emma whipped her head up and found his gray eyes—so much like Blackbourne's—on her and lit with amusement. Oh, heavens. Had he caught her staring at his waistcoat?

"Yes, I'm not sure if you've been introduced," Lady Heyer said. "Miss Bryson, this is my cousin, Lord Hefton."

"My lord." Emma curtsied.

He flashed an amiable smile. "Your voice is as magnificent as Blackbourne claimed."

"Thank you," Emma said and caught the quick scowl that marred Lady Wallingford's features.

"Is this the infamous bracelet, Lady Wallingford?" Hefton turned to her, and her countenance brightened. "It is, my lord," she said. "And I am quite delighted with it." She held out her arm, and sparks of gold glinted off a beautiful, braided chain. "I told

Blackbourne I simply must show it off tonight even without the necklace."

"Yes, why aren't you wearing it?"

"You've not heard, sir?" she said in a tragic whisper. "It was stolen."

Emma gasped, and they both looked at her. "I beg your pardon," she said. "But my necklace was stolen too, recently."

"I'm sorry to hear it, Miss Bryson," Hefton said.

"That's kind of you, sir, but don't worry, I'm determined to find it," she said with a tilt of her chin. "I must. Though it is only a small oval amber pendant, my mother gave it to me."

"You needn't apologize for wanting to get back what is yours," Lady Wallingford said. "I plan to get mine back too, though my reason isn't so sentimental. There's a wager on it."

"You wagered on your necklace?" Emma asked, shocked. She would never have risked her pendant on a bet.

"Oh, heavens no, not I, but Blackbourne," she said with a gurgle of laughter. "It's why I must get it back. He's never lost a bet."

"So, I've heard."

"I'll do anything to ensure he never does," she said in a defiant tone, and Emma knew she did not mean the bet about the necklace.

"He'd lose one if he thought it'd win him a better prize," Lady Heyer said in a pointed manner.

Lady Wallingford's eyes flashed briefly before she turned to Hefton. "I understand this wager wasn't his idea, but yours, Hefty," she said with a smile. "What were you doing in Rundell and Bridge that day? Buying something pretty for a conquest?"

"That'd suggest an interest in one particular lady." He laughed. "No, as it happens, I was looking for a ring," he said. "A jewel I want back as much as you ladies want yours."

A shadow crossed his face, and Emma wondered if he lost it at the gaming tables and now regretted it.

Lady Wallingford only smirked. "Is there a wager on finding it too?" she asked.

"No. A promise." He clamped his jaw shut, indicating he would speak no more about it.

"Well then," Lady Wallingford said. "I suppose we must content ourselves with a different wager this evening."

"I find I'm rather bored with this subject," Lady Heyer said, casually waving her fan around. "Can't we speak of something more interesting?"

"But this is interesting as it's about Miss Bryson."

"Me?" Emma said. "Why?"

"I understand the book at White's is full of bets on whether you'll fall again tonight," she said. "I hope you aren't shocked."

"Not at all." A whisker. It did shock her a little, but she feigned indifference with a shrug. "I've already sung, so I'm quite safe."

"We do still have hours of dancing before us," she said with a glitter in her narrowed eyes that Emma immediately mistrusted. "Speaking of which, it appears the music is about to start, and I must remind someone who promised me the first dance."

She glided away as if he had promised her something more, but Emma knew better. It was only the first dance and nothing else.

"I'm certain Blackbourne wishes to dance with you, Miss Bryson," Lady Heyer said.

"Do you think he wagered on me falling?" she joked.

"I'd not be surprised. Though I doubt he'd go so far as to trip you."

"I'd bet a monkey Lady Wallingford would," Emma said. "She did say she'd do anything to ensure he wins."

"That'd have the opposite effect of what she wants, as that would assuredly land you right in Blackbourne's arms," she said. "Physically and metaphorically."

"If it does happen, I'll be sure to pull him to the floor with me," Emma said cheekily. "Just for making a bet about me."

"Oh, please do, Miss Bryson." Lord Hefton grinned. "I would love to read of his embarrassment in the morning broadsheets. I'm taking a mail coach to Brighton, and I shall need to be entertained."

"You're not leaving again Hefty?" Lady Heyer said.

"Only for a few days. I shall be back Wednesday afternoon. Come along, Cousin," he said and took Lady Heyer by the arm. "You also promised to dance with me."

EMMA WATCHED THE DANCERS, nibbling on a piece of marzipan, and tried to ignore the battle between pride and desire that raged in her mind. Pride—why should she dance and risk a fall, just to satisfy a roomful of gamesters? And desire. Oh, how she wanted to dance with Blackbourne.

And do so as well as Lady Wallingford. She stuffed the last piece of marzipan in her mouth to quell her jealousy. That lady floated across the floor. No tripping over inanimate objects, no sudden missteps, no flailing backward onto her backside. She danced with self-assurance and poise. Great poise. A gift recently denied Emma by a capricious Deity.

Emma glanced around. Others seemed just as captivated by the couple. Would they gawk just as much at her? She grimaced. No doubt they would, but for a very different reason. Suddenly, neither pride nor desire raged through her but cowardice. She did not want to be gawked at again. In a fit of impulsiveness, she whirled round and dashed from the ballroom.

"Where were you off to, Emma?" Blackbourne's voice came from behind.

Blast. She turned around. "I... wanted to see the music room again."

"It's in the other wing." He caught up to her. "Shall I take you there?"

She raised her brows in surprise. Perhaps he did not wish to dance after all. "Yes, please."

"Excellent," he said and took her arm. "I've been hoping to hear you play the pianoforte."

Blast again. "On second thought," she said and stopped. "Perhaps we ought to—"

"Return to the ballroom?" he finished her thought. "I was hoping you'd say so. The next set is forming." He leaned closer and said, "It's the waltz."

Emma groaned.

"Don't you know it?"

"Of course I do," she snapped. She also knew it was scandalous, indecent, and quite... intimate. "I'm just surprised your aunt Worthington would allow it. It's considered objectionable by some."

"The Patronesses of Almack's approved it, so I think we are quite safe as long as two feet are kept between the partners." He winked and leaned in close. "Though the temptation to dance even closer would be quite... overwhelming."

This time desire overtook pride and trounced cowardice. Blast everyone. Emma would dance with him.

A FEW MOMENTS LATER, Emma wondered what had worried her so. Blackbourne was an excellent dancer. He swung her around with the ease of a bird in flight. Slid across the floor with the smoothness of an ice skater. Performed the intricate steps with the proficiency of a—suddenly Blackbourne stumbled backwards, and Emma grabbed him by the waistcoat and pulled him upright.

"What happened?" she asked.

"I must've tripped," he said in such a confused manner that Emma worried he might do so again and quickly wrapped her free arm around his back.

"Luckily you caught me."

"I had to." Just as she had to pull him a little closer. "I wasn't about to let you pull me to the floor so you could win a bet."

"Oh, dear. You've caught me there too," he said, and their eyes met and held and lingered.

"We really should sit down," he broke into their trance, but Emma remained unmoved. "Let's give it at least a minute," she said. "Just in case."

She splayed her fingers across his warm firm chest too. Just in case.

"As delightful as this is," he said, "we're attracting quite a bit of attention."

Emma dragged her gaze from him and glanced around. Why must people gawk at them? Had they nothing better to stare at? She muttered, "I suppose we should sit."

Blackbourne led her off the dance floor and to a chair. "Don't let their rudeness upset you," he said.

"You should be more upset than I," she said smugly. "I didn't fall, which means you lost a bet."

"I expect to lose another one soon." He turned to her and bent a smile on her. "At least, I hope..."

His stare intensified and Emma's pulse galloped. She did not miss the significance of his remark. Emma gave her pulse a moment to slow to a canter and said, "Lord Hefton will be disappointed I didn't fall."

"He made a wager at White's? How unlike him."

"I don't know about that, but he hoped I'd pull you to the floor with me." She grinned. "He wanted to read of your embarrassment in the papers tomorrow."

"Now that is more like him." He laughed. "I daresay this evening has gone quite well, Emma, except for the absence of Prince George, of course."

"I must admit to being a wee disappointed."

"He's quite fond of Vauxhall," he said. "Perhaps you'll bump into him there."

"I'll do what I must," she said and grinned. "Will you be there?"

"I wouldn't miss it," he said, and an enticing picture of her future emerged in Emma's mind. Blackbourne and she in a dark hidden corner of Vauxhall Garden alone... when another thought invaded.

"Do you think we could sneak away and search the plant again?" she asked. "I just know my pendant is in there."

The question seemed to catch him off guard. "I don't think so," he said slowly. "It'd be difficult to sneak away."

"We do have experience sneaking through a darkened garden," she joked.

"Vauxhall will not be as dark as your uncle's garden. Lanterns will be set ablaze on nearly every bush, and it'll be much more crowded," he pointed out. "No. Far too risky."

"What's a bit of danger?" she asked in a persuasive tone. "It hasn't stopped us before."

He turned and looked directly at her. "That was before the thief caught a glimpse of my face in the alley."

"What?" Emma gasped out. "Do you think he recognized you? Recognized us?"

"I'm certain *your* face was covered."

"Thank heaven, you thought to kiss me," she blurted. "I mean..."

"Yes. Thank heaven," he said. "In truth, it's a shame the thief isn't here now." His voice came out low and intimate and inviting, and a shiver cascaded through Emma. Thank heaven, she was not standing, else Blackbourne would have won his bet.

CHAPTER 13

Emma pushed aside the curtains and the rays of morning sunlight touched her cheeks. Warm and pleasant, and nothing like the heat that had burned through her body when she had danced with Blackbourne. Its memory compelled Emma to turn from the window, and she put her arms out and turned... turned... turned... right smack into a body. She stumbled backwards. "Kat," she yelped, embarrassed. "Why didn't you knock?"

"I did," she said. "You must not have heard it over the imaginary music you were dancing to." She smirked.

Emma pulled at the fringe of her nightgown. "I was not dancing."

"Fustian. You were reliving your waltz with his lordship." She sat on the settee. "Well, go on. Show me how you kept him from falling."

"How the deuce do you know that?"

She held up a newspaper. "Mr. Claimore."

"What did that coxcomb write?" Emma snatched the paper and read aloud, *"The always entertaining Worthington ball was made more so by an extraordinary voice—"* Emma eyed Kat over the paper. "Well, that part is true," she said smugly and continued, *"And the even more extraordinary sight of a disheveled and flat-footed Lord B—e nearly tumbling to the floor, with only the quick actions of a songbird saving him from embarrassment."*

Kat stomped her feet in glee. "You saved him."

"Perhaps," Emma said with a laugh and continued, *"If only she had saved him from his atrocious waistcoat."* She folded the paper and joined Kat on the settee. "Why would I save him from it?" She grinned. "He wore it for me."

"I shan't hold it against him," Kat said. "He can even wear it when he comes to make you an offer."

"I believe he will make me an offer," Emma said, and Kat inhaled a breath. "But not until after the Season ends."

"And lose his bet? Why would he do that?"

"He knows it'll prove he has real affection for me."

"Wearing that ridiculous waistcoat wasn't enough?"

Emma giggled. "I suppose that does say something."

"Then why should he wait?" Kat asked. "I mean, really, Emma, why be so selfish."

Emma bit her lip. She had not thought about it that way. "I suppose it is a bit selfish of me to insist he lose his—"

"I'm not speaking of him," Kat interrupted, "but me. The sooner you accept his offer, the sooner I can throw an engagement party and invite Lord Hefton."

"I should've known." Emma burst out laughing. "I'm sorry, Aunt, but I shan't be the means of you entrapping Lord Hefton. I'm afraid you must devise another scheme."

Emma wished the words back in her mouth as Kat seemed to take it for permission. She stood and paced, her hands clasped behind her back. "You are already acquainted with him," she pointed out.

"I am."

"I'm certain he'd be happy to meet whenever you wished."

"I suppose, but..."

"You could even send him a card to meet somewhere today."

"Not today, I couldn't," Emma broke in, relieved to stop the nonsense from going any further "He's in Brighton until Wednesday."

"What? Why?"

"I hardly know him well enough to ask," she said pointedly, but Kat was no longer attending and had resumed her pacing. "To leave now," she muttered. "Of all the ill luck."

Emma did not consider it ill luck, but a reprieve for Elizabeth. Though Emma did agree she should meet him. He was kind and amiable and even a bit mysterious with his lumpy waistcoat and missing ring. Her cousin could do far worse than to marry such an intriguing gentleman. But it must be her choice. Just like it was Emma's choice. There should be no manipulation where love and marriage were concerned, either by a calculated wager or an interfering mother.

WITH A NEW SENSE OF optimism about his future putting a spring in his step, Blackbourne strode into his library and straight into the muzzle of a gun. He stepped back. "My dear, Simms," he said. "Have I upset you in some way?"

"Not at all. I'm merely cleaning your pistols. Every third Thursday, remember, whether they've been used or not."

"Is it that time already?" He made his way to his desk. "I suppose I've been distracted."

"Distracted. Disheveled." He tightened his lips.

"Oh, dear. You've read the article." Blackbourne sat. "Now I really insist you put the pistol down."

"I've no intention of shooting you, my lord. No matter how deserving."

"I, for one, am surprised you weren't shot last evening, Blackbourne." Lady Blackbourne appeared in the doorway.

"Mother, how delightful. Do come in and tell me whom you think should've shot your only son."

"Why, Lady Wallingford, of course." She sat on the settee and removed her gloves.

He did not even feign surprise at his mother's knowing what had transpired after he had returned Francesca to her townhouse. "She was quite civil about it if you must know."

"For now, my dear," his mother said and sat on the settee. "Hell hath no fury like a woman scorned... or a valet." She smiled at Simms.

"I was not scorned so much as ignored, my lady. I warned him the waistcoat would garner more opprobrium than compliments." Simms placed the gun in its case. "And I had nothing to do with the disheveled neckcloth. It was a perfectly tied Oriental when he left the manor."

"No doubt," she said soothingly. "One can hardly blame you that a lady decided to paw your master on a ballroom floor."

Blackbourne leaned back in his chair and laughed. "No one pawed at me. In fact, she was helping me to stay upright."

"By holding on to you for over a minute?"

"She was ensuring I didn't fall."

"She was ensuring her capture of London's most eligible bachelor."

"You can hardly know her motives."

"Of course I can," she said. "It's how I captured your father."

"My father stumbled about on a dance floor?"

"Oh, no, not him, he was far too steady a man to do that. It was Conte Volta."

"Conte Alessandro Volta? The inventor of the voltaic pile? The battery?"

She made a coy shrug. "Who do you think inspired him to invent it?"

"According to my professor at Oxford, it was his experiments with frog's legs, but I expect you're about to disabuse me of that notion."

"I was fifteen and had been waiting all evening to dance the minuet with Allie," she said, and a far-off look came into her eyes.

"The music started, and he was instantly at my side and pulling me to my feet. The second he clasped my hands a jolt of electricity shot through us, stunning us both. Dazed, Allie stumbled. To keep him from tumbling over, I held on to him. Perhaps a bit longer than necessary." She tittered. "I quite enjoyed it, but it infuriated your grandfather. He had poor Allie thrown out of the salon. As he was dragged out, Allie yelled to me that one day he'd discover the reason that jolt burned through us."

"I wonder now that I'm not the son of an Italian conte," Blackbourne said. "But what does it all have to do with my real father?"

"To keep Allie and I apart until he left the country, your grandfather forced me to stay in my bedchamber. A whole month, Blackbourne. He even set a guard outside the door. Not that it deterred me. I climbed out the window."

Just like Emma.

"Why the smile, Philip?"

"It's just you and... never mind," he said. "Go on. What happened next?"

"Much to my surprise, your grandfather had placed a servant in the garden. Such little trust he had in me." She shook her head in feigned despair. "Anyway, I was returned to my bedchamber. Your father, hearing of my distress, sent me a lovely posy of flowers every day of my captivity. Every day, Philip, without fail. The rest is history."

"What a history you've had, madam," he said and chuckled.

"One that led to an excellent match." She grinned. "Something I dearly wish for you." Blackbourne quirked a brow and laughed. "I know which way the wind is blowing, my dear, even if you don't," she said. "And I've long thought what you needed was a lady who kept you a little off-balance..."

"But?"

"Be careful my dear." She put a hand on his arm and squeezed it. "You've known her for such a short time."

Yet it seemed as if he had known her forever.

He patted her hand in return and gave her a warm smile. "I shall keep that in mind."

The short time of their friendship did not worry Blackbourne. Malcolm McBride did. He lived in the boardinghouse room and had climbed out of the plant after them. He had given Emma the pearl necklace Blackbourne had seen in the plant. He was the thief Blackbourne had chased all Season—and now had no idea what to do about him.

CHAPTER 14

The applause from the audience echoed up into the gazebo, and though she reveled in it, Emma did not need their praise to know she had sung better tonight than she ever had—and only one thing explained. Sheer happiness.

Emma stared out into the darkness. A soft wind blew through the trees, setting hundreds of lanterns dancing like fireflies. Had it only been a few weeks since she had first sung in Vauxhall Garden? Since this whole exhilarating life-changing adventure had begun?

She stepped off the gazebo and found Blackbourne, dapper in a dark green coat and brilliant neckcloth, standing with Lady Blackbourne and Lady Heyer. She joined them, and the usual accolades about Emma's voice were dispensed with and accepted with equal graciousness.

"We are a small party this evening," Lady Heyer said. "With Hefty still in Brighton and Worthy heaven knows where."

"Off chasing your school friend, I'm sure." Lady Blackbourne appeared displeased.

"No Mrs. Carstead tonight, Emma?" Blackbourne asked.

"She had hoped to come, but they had another engagement." Emma glanced around, more interested in who was here than who was not.

"Are you looking for someone?" Blackbourne asked.

"Prince George." His presence the only thing that could improve upon this already perfect night.

"I see." He thought for a moment. "You know, I believe I saw him walk down that way earlier. Shall we try to find him?"

"Oh, yes." Emma tucked her hand into his arm.

"Where are you going?" Lady Blackbourne asked.

"To find Prince George."

"Prinny? I would love—"

"You know, I saw the most beautiful flowering bush earlier," Lady Heyer quickly interrupted her mother. "Down this pathway, I believe."

"A flowering bush in Vauxhall Garden?" Lady Blackbourne rolled her eyes. "A rare treat indeed."

"Then I insist you see it." Lady Heyer dragged her the other way.

Blackbourne and Emma walked a short distance. "Are you certain Prince George went this way?" Emma said.

"Oh, I've quite forgotten about him."

She stopped. "Then what are we looking for?"

"Oh, a little peace, a little solitude," he said. "Or a little dark hidden alcove where we could talk or do whatever else comes to mind."

His gray eyes held an invitation, and Emma's pulse quickened. What she would do in a dark hidden alcove immediately sprung to her mind. She'd tear his brilliant neckcloth from his throat and place her lips... Ooohh, there was a perfect alcove.

She eyed Blackbourne, but he kept walking. Perhaps it wasn't dark or hidden enough. He did seem to have a care for her reputation, and it would be compromised if anyone caught her ripping his brilliant neckcloth off and pressing her... Another excellent spot.

Again, he kept walking, and Emma's frustration mounted. Just how dark and hidden did this blasted alcove need to be?

They trod farther up the path, past other promising spots, and it hit Emma. She would have to take matters into her own hands—by falling into his. At the ball, Lady Heyer had assured her that Blackbourne would catch her—it was time to put that theory to the test. A moment later, Emma found the perfect spot. She threw herself backwards, flapping her arms dramatically, and fell straight into a bush.

"Emma, are you all right?" Blackbourne rushed to her.

"I'm fine." Just irritated that her body was entangled in some branches instead of his arms.

"Lucky for you, you fell against the bush," he said, and she glared at him as he raised a brow. "Would you rather have fallen to the ground?"

"I'd rather not be stuck in a bush."

"Allow me." He gently untangled her hair, then suddenly stopped, and stared down at her. Emma stared back. His gray eyes smoky, his lips slightly parted, his neckcloth inches from her. Oh, blast it all. Just do it. She reached up and...

"My Lord Blackbourne, is that you?" A gentleman asked, and Blackbourne snapped up. "Unbelievable," he muttered, and Emma agreed. It was unbelievable that someone interrupted her just when his neckcloth was this close to being torn off and... She glared her frustration at the gentleman.

"I thought it was you," he said in a jolly laughing tone.

"Indeed, it is, sir." Blackbourne turned around. "You caught me."

"I'm more interested in whom you've caught."

"Yes, of course." Blackbourne pulled Emma forward. "Allow me to introduce Miss Emma Bryson," he said. "Miss Bryson, His Royal Highness, Prince George."

Emma gasped. Prince George had caught them, had seen... How humiliating! She stared hard at his waistcoat. Why the devil hadn't the whalebone corset creaked?

"Do you like my waistcoat?"

"I'm sorry?"

"You seemed captivated by it."

"It's lovely and quite fitting," she said without thought, and heat mounted her cheeks. Would he take her comment amiss?

"Never underestimate the importance of a good tailor," he said with a good-humored laugh. "Wouldn't you say, Blackbourne?"

"Certainly, my valet would agree."

"Bah! Your valet." He emitted a very unroyal-like snort. "Tried me damndest to win Simms away from Blackbourne, Miss Bryson. No amount of money moved him."

"What can I say? I've very loyal servants."

"Perhaps I'll exact my revenge another way." He clasped Emma's hand and brought it to his lips. "By winning a more delectable prize."

Blackbourne reached for her hand and brought Emma to his side. "Not everything is a prize to be won, Your Highness."

"This coming from you?" He leaned back on his heels for a moment as if in thought. "I'll wager I can get her attention. I heard you sing tonight, Miss Bryson. Your voice is divine."

A thrill went through her. "Thank you."

"I've rarely heard anything quite as beautiful. I would very much like you to come to Brighton next week and sing for me."

"Brighton?" Emma repeated stupidly.

"Yes. I'm removing there in a few days. The heat! It's far too hot in London."

"I'd be honored to sing there, Your Highness," she said, her mind whirring. It was happening.

"I hope you don't mind, but my lady mother, the Queen, is there now, enjoying the seaside. I think your voice would please her even more," he said, and Emma just kept her knees from buckling. It truly was happening. All of it.

"I shall do my best." Emma could barely get the words out.

"One should always strive to please one's mother," Blackbourne smiled at Emma.

"Ah, yes, your charming mother, Blackbourne." Prince George gazed off into the distance. "A rose without a thorn." He returned to the present and said, "You must tell Lady Blackbourne I expect her to come too."

"I'm sure the... sweet lass of Richmond Hill would be delighted."

"Excellent." Prince and his coterie moved on down the path and out of sight.

Emma turned to Blackbourne. "Am I dreaming?" she asked. "Did everything I've wanted just come true?"

"You may expect an official invitation tomorrow."

Oh heavens! A letter from the Prince of Wales. Kat will be in transport. It was almost all too much, and only one thing marred her excitement. Her missing pendant.

"Is something the matter, Emma?" Blackbourne said. "I'd ask if you were worried about singing but—"

"No, not that," she said with a laugh. "I was just thinking I wish I had my mother's pendant. She would've been in raptures about all this. My singing for Lady Heyer, at Vauxhall, meeting Prince George. Meeting you..."

They stared at each other. "You do know what it means when the Prince removes to Brighton?" he asked, and she shook her head. "It signals the end of the Season."

He said nothing else. In truth, nothing else needed to be said. He had made his intentions clear in so many other ways. Emma simply placed her hand through his arm, and they headed down the path, together.

THE COUPLE TOOK A LONG circuitous route back to the gazebo, and while it may have passed some time, it did nothing to bring Emma down from the clouds. She barely even noticed when Lady Blackbourne and Lady Heyer had rejoined them.

"My daughter promised me a flowering bush," Lady Blackbourne said. "But I see it's you who found one, Miss Bryson."

"I'm sorry?" Emma tried to focus.

"You've a few leaves in your hair."

That brought Emma down to earth. "Oh, right, thank you," she mumbled. "I must've—I mean..."

"I've just spoken to Prinny." Lady Blackbourne interrupted Emma's babbling. "He's told us a bit of news."

"Yes, congratulations Miss Bryson," Lady Heyer said. "I'm so happy for you."

"Thank you," Emma said. "I can hardly believe it, myself. I'm to sing for the Queen."

"You must be careful of what you sing for Her Majesty. She's quite prudish," Lady Blackbourne said. "Might I suggest 'The Lass of Richmond Hill'?"

"I know that song," Emma said. "Leonard McNally wrote it."

"Did he?" she asked archly. "No matter who penned it, I expect your voice will do it justice."

Her compliment astounded and touched Emma. "Then I shall be happy to sing it."

"Do you plan to join us... Rose?" Blackbourne asked.

"Why not? I haven't been to Brighton Pavilion in years. I understand Prinny's taken my advice and hired that Nash fellow to fix it up a bit."

A rustle came from the pathway, and everyone turned. Emma half expected to see Prince George again, but a woman emerged instead.

"Lady Wallingford?" Lady Blackbourne said in a rather sharp tone. "I didn't know you'd be here tonight."

"Why would you, Lady Blackbourne? I'm hardly a member of your family," she said, a hint of snideness in her tone. "I knew Miss Bryson was singing tonight, and I wanted to tell her something."

Blackbourne tensed beside Emma, and she almost giggled. Did he think she would shock Emma by speaking of their affair? "Yes, Lady Wallingford?"

"I thought you might like to know that I've found my necklace." She lifted a diamond pendant that hung from a gold-plaited chain around her throat and showed it to Emma.

"I'm delighted for you," Emma said and meant it.

"And you, my lord?" She tilted her head at Blackbourne. "Are you delighted?"

"Naturally." He stared hard at her. "Also a bit surprised."

"I don't see why. I told you I had friends looking for it. One such friend said he thought he saw it at a jeweler, and I was thrilled to find he was right."

"If only I had such a friend," Emma said.

"I'm sure you do," Lady Wallingford said. "Well, my lord, when shall we meet at the jewelers?"

"I'm sorry?"

She held out her wrist, and the gold bracelet she had worn to the ball glistened against her skin. "They do match, don't they?"

"I've quite forgotten about that wager."

"Does that mean you'll lose another one? Gracious, how many does that make now?" She laughed. "The Blackbourne I knew would never countenance losing. I thought we had that in common. I still hate to lose... anything."

"One must first be in possession of something to truly lose it," Blackbourne said.

"I thought I had it."

"One shouldn't wish to lose their dignity, either," Lady Blackbourne intervened. "And one can never make a scene without doing so." She took Lady Wallingford by the arm. "Come along, my dear. I understand there's a delightful flowering bush somewhere down this path."

The two departed, and Emma stared after Lady Wallingford with understanding. Blackbourne had obviously given her up as a mistress, and it had devastated her. Emma knew her own reaction would be the same.

CHAPTER 15

Emma had just raised her morning cup of chocolate to her mouth when a scream echoed up from the foyer. She placed the cup on its saucer, leaned back against her seat, and counted backwards, "Five, four, three, two—" the door swung open, and Kat rushed in.

"Good morning," Emma said pleasantly.

"Don't you good morning me, miss. What is this?" She waved a letter about her head.

"How should I know? Do you think it important?"

"Of course! I'm certain it's from the Prince of Wales." She sounded almost triumphant as if she had won the letter in a duel.

"Is it?" Emma suppressed her excitement, barely. "I suppose I'll get to it sooner or later."

"You'll open it this very second."

"Kat, really, I've barely woken up... my chocolate is getting cold..."

"Right this instant."

"If you insist." Emma rolled her eyes but in truth could contain her excitement no longer. Here it was, in her hand. The invitation she had hoped and prayed for since leaving Scotland. She tore it open and read through it.

"Well, what does it say?" Kat hovered over Emma's shoulder.

"It says I've been invited to sing for His Royal Highness the Prince of Wales, at Brighton Pavilion next Wednesday."

The women screamed in unison. Kat recovered first. "How did this all come about?"

Emma shrugged. "I met Prince George at Vauxhall last evening."

Kat gasped. "You did not bump him again?"

"No. In fact, it was he who bumped into Lord Blackbourne and myself just as we were about to... Anyway, he asked for an introduction, told me he had enjoyed my singing, and now this." She waved the invitation.

"I can't believe it. My niece singing for Prince George at Brighton Pavilion."

"It's even better than that. The Queen will be there."

The women screamed again, and Kat even cried a bit. "I'm truly happy for you, my dear," she said and squeezed Emma's hand. "I only wish the same happiness for Elizabeth."

"She will be happy, Kat. If she's allowed to choose her own partner."

"She must first know she has other choices." Exasperated, she took a deep breath and continued, "And then, if she still refused Lord Hefton, I'd reconcile myself to it."

Emma squeezed her hand. She knew how difficult that would be for Kat and Malcolm. She could put it off no longer. She must tell him. She loved Blackbourne.

A FEW HOURS LATER, Emma had her chance. Malcolm sat across from her in the salon, holding the note she had sent him. "Well, go on, lass," he said. "What's the important news you have?"

He appeared leery, even suspicious, but Emma did not allow that to dampen her excitement. She told him everything about meeting Prince George—except precisely when—and said, "I'm to sing for the Queen," and thrust out the invitation.

He read it aloud, and his smile got bigger with each word. "Congratulations, lass," he said. "I'm happy for you."

"It's all thanks to you, Malcolm," she said and meant it.

"I ken your voice had more to do with it," he said, then stood and tapped the invitation against his palm as if in thought. "But next Wednesday?"

"Is there a problem?"

"No, everything is happening a bit sooner than expected... or hoped."

"I feel like it's taken forever." Emma laughed. "I thought it should've happened much sooner."

"I meant I hoped to find your pendant before then," he said. "You'll sing without it?"

"If I must." She shrugged. "I doubt Prince George will ask again, and later, after I'm married, I won't—" She stopped and wished the words back in her mouth.

"You expect to be married soon?" Malcolm asked quietly.

She tilted her chin. "Yes."

"I see." He turned and walked to the mantel. "I take it the Earl of Blackbourne has made you an offer."

"Not yet, no, but he will once the Season is over, and I'll accept him."

"You've declared your feelings?"

"Not directly."

"I'm amazed." He turned and glared at her. "I'd thought your impulsive tongue would've spewed those words out the minute they entered your head."

"Malcolm!" She knew he'd be upset, but he had no right to speak to her so derisively.

He did not apologize, only continued in the same manner. "Does he know you're a jilt?"

"Yes, he does," she shot back and took a deep breath to suppress her rising temper. "He also knows I'm no longer that lonely impulsive girl, that I've... moved on."

"Have you?"

"Yes," she said, exasperated and growing tired of the conversation. "We all must move on from our past. Whether it be good or ill."

"In a few days, we'll all be moving on," he said enigmatically.

"I hope you move on to happiness too, Malcolm." She squeezed his hand, but he did not return the gesture. "If you'll excuse me," he said and pulled his hand from Emma's. "I must return to the theater." He walked to the door and stopped. "I still think his lordship is using you, Emma. If not to win a bet, then for some other reason. And I'll prove it."

His snide comment did not bother Emma—she trusted her own feelings—but one thing he had said did. Her pendant. She did want it around her throat when she sang for Queen Charlotte, and she knew it was in the boardinghouse room. They must've just missed it. If only they hadn't been interrupted the last time. But if they hadn't been interrupted, they might not have escaped through the window and down the alley. And kissed. She did not regret that.

She would go to the plant and search for it one more time. Why not? It would be easy. She knew how to get into it from the outside window. Her decision made, Emma wrote a quick note for Jo, and grabbed her gloves. If she hurried, she could be there and back before tea.

HALF AN HOUR LATER, Emma stepped out of a hackney coach, pressed an extra coin into the jarvey's hand, and started down the alleyway. "I'll be back soon," she said over her shoulder. "A quarter an hour at most."

"Mind ye are, miss," he yelled back. "I'm not one to dawdle in St. Giles."

Emma hurried to the boardinghouse and stopped outside the plant window. She quickly built a make-shift staircase with a few crates, climbed up the steps, pushed open the window, and slipped into the plant.

She pressed an ear against the little door. Empty. Relieved, she turned her attention to the bottom shelves. A moment later, she stood and bit her lip. How strange. They were both as empty as the room.

Had everything been moved to the top shelves? Adjusting the ladder, she climbed up and swept her hand across them. Nothing. No silk handkerchiefs. No snuff boxes. No jewelry of any kind.

What the devil had happened to it all?

Dismayed, Emma clambered down the ladder, set it against the window, and climbed back out onto the crates. Placing her foot on the bottom step she twisted an ankle and fell to the ground. Blast. She pushed herself up onto her hands and knees, turned halfway, and rammed her head against a pair of shiny boots.

Exceptionally shiny boots. She could see her reflection.

Emma followed the boots up past the fawn breeches, past the blue superfine coat, past a brilliant neckcloth, and looked straight into the glowering face of Lord Blackbourne. Shock pushed her back on her haunches, and she spluttered, "What the deuce are you doing here, my lord?"

"I might ask you the same thing." He grabbed her by the elbows and pulled her to her feet.

"Searching for my pendant, obviously."

"So, you took it upon yourself to traipse through St. Giles alone?"

"I had no choice." She met his heated gaze with one of her own. "You said you couldn't risk it—"

"You thought you could?" he thundered.

"Yes, I did, actually," she thundered back.

"Whilst attracting attention from God knows who." He waved his arm around the alley. "Did anyone see you?"

"No."

"Did *you* see anyone?"

"What? No."

"Good." A weight seemed to come off his shoulders, and he even smiled at Emma. "Very good."

"Hardly, my lord. My pendant wasn't in the plant. In fact, nothing was there."

"What do you mean?"

"Everything is gone. The jewelry. The candlesticks, the watches. There's nothing left." She tried to stifle the panic in her voice.

"Are you certain?" he asked sharply. "Did you check every shelf?"

She shot him a withering look that told him the stupidity of that question.

"How strange. Why sell everything now?" He stared at the plant window as if the answer would climb out of it.

"Does it matter?" Emma said. "I'll never find my pendant. It's gone forever." The catch in her voice appeared to snap him out of his thoughts, and he turned to her. "Don't despair, Emma," he said. "I'm certain you'll still find it."

"Do you think the thief will just hand it to me?"

"Something of that nature," he said in an odd tone and added, "Lady Wallingford got her necklace back, remember."

"That is true," Emma said slowly, and her spirits revived a bit. "And I do have a few days to check jewelry shops."

The walk to the carriage helped restore Emma's equilibrium if not her sense of humor, and she managed to joke, "I see my jarvey has disappeared just like my pendant."

Blackbourne laughed. "Happily, my tiger is a bit more stout-hearted." James, standing by the horse, puffed up at his remark.

"You do have very loyal servants." Emma climbed into the carriage.

"As do you." He joined her on the seat. "It was your maid who braved the manor to tell me where you'd gone."

"I must confess I'm grateful."

"You should be. It's an awful long walk back to your aunt's." He smiled and set the carriage in motion. "Speaking of long distances, how do you plan to get to Brighton?"

"I hadn't thought about it, though I'm sure my aunt would be happy to take me." But did she want Kat in Brighton? Emma panicked. "Perhaps it'd be better if I took the Mail Coach."

"Or I could take you."

"Oh, would you?" Emma asked, relieved.

"Naturally you must put up with my poor company," he said.

Emma laughed and then said, "On second thought..."

A short time later they arrived at the Carstead mansion. Blackbourne helped Emma down, and they walked toward the door. Suddenly, it swung open, and Kat poked her head out. "Emma is that you?" she said. "I've been worried all—oh, hello my lord. How delightful to see you."

"Mrs. Carstead." He nodded.

"I'm sorry for my surprise, but Emma never said anything about—"

"About our ride in Hyde Park?" Blackbourne shook his head at Emma. "Why didn't you tell her?"

"It slipped my mind, Kat. I'm sorry."

"No reason to apologize, my dear, none at all." She smiled at Blackbourne. "I know my niece was quite safe in your capable hands. You're known to be an excellent whip. Very nimble fing—"

"Thank you for the ride, my lord." Mortified, Emma shoved her aunt into the house.

CHAPTER 16

The next morning, Blackbourne paced the library, still seeking the answer to the question that had caused him to toss and turn all night. Why had McBride sold everything in the plant? Blackbourne could see no reason to sell everything now. The door swung open, and a footman entered. "I was told to bring this box to you, sir." He placed a large velvet box on the desk.

"Thank you, Thomas." Blackbourne said and opened the lid. Dozens of bright jewels sparkled up at him from their silk bedding. Emeralds. Rubies. Diamonds. Almost the entirety of the Blackbourne jewels.

A moment later, Amelia glided into the room. "I came as requested, Philip..." She stopped and eyed the velvet box. "Oh, I see." She sat on the settee and folded her hands in her lap. "Will Miss Bryson choose her own wedding set, or will you give her the Blackbourne sapphires?"

He laughed. "That's a question that won't be answered until after the Season ends."

"You'll lose your wager?"

"It's a matter of trust."

"It's also a matter of a thousand pounds." She laughed. "If you weren't deciding on an engagement present, then why have that box brought from the bank?"

"I wanted to give Emma something to wear in Brighton since she has not found her pendant."

Yet. He knew McBride still had it.

"It's why I asked you over. I can't decide. What do you think?"

"Aunt Mary's ruby pendant," Amelia said instantly. "I know it's been in the family for generations, but you can trust Miss Bryson with it. She won't pawn your jewelry... unlike Clarissa."

Blackbourne stilled. "How did you know?"

"I remember the night she left. I was still living here, you remember."

"You were in your bedchamber in the other wing."

"I came down to the landing when I heard the carriage return. I wanted to see Clarissa in her gown again. I heard everything. Why she left. What she'd done."

Clarissa had sold all her jewelry. Every piece he'd given her. To flee with her lover. She would've got away, too, if he hadn't caught them whispering together at the masquerade, finalizing their escape. Upon return to the manor, they had argued, and she had fled in his carriage during a storm. A mile down the road, it had overturned and killed her.

He had managed to get most of the gems back. He'd found many at Mother Cummings's boardinghouse where he learned Clarissa had sold them for a mere pittance to flee London.

He straightened. Is that what McBride was doing? Did he plan on leaving London soon?

"Newer and better things are happening now," his sister startled him.

"Yes," Blackbourne said and pushed aside his problem with McBride. "For both of us." He smiled. "Have you told her yet?"

"That she's to become a grandmama?" Amelia smiled and put a protective hand over her belly. "Heavens no. I'm waiting for my husband."

"For the official announcement?"

"For protection. I don't anticipate her taking it well."

"As well as she'll take my engagement to Miss Bryson. Perhaps I should wait for Heyer's return too."

Amelia laughed and said, "When should I have Emma for tea?"

"After I talk to Rundell, I'll let you know. I'm going to have an engraving made on the pendant."

A word. *Impulsive.*

"Be certain to take the original and not the paste." Lady Heyer stood and walked to the door. "One can hardly tell the difference."

AN HOUR LATER, BLACKBOURNE entered Rundell and Bridge jewelry shop and wandered over to the counter. A whiff of Night Jasmine drifted across the room and reminded Blackbourne of Francesca. Even after their last meeting, he was happy she had got her necklace back, as it gave him hope that he'd find Amelia's bracelet. As far as Emma's pendant, he must rely on McBride's character, unfortunately.

A clerk approached, and Blackbourne waved him off with a request to speak to Rundell, personally. A moment later, the jeweler stepped out from behind a curtain and rushed over to Blackbourne. "I'm sorry my lord," he said. "I was helping another customer in back."

"Afternoon, Rundell," Blackbourne said. "I'd like a word engraved on this." He took the ruby necklace from his pocket. "How long will it take?"

He studied the jewel. "I'll have it ready by tomorrow morning," he said. "Shall I have it delivered?"

"Thank you, yes." Blackbourne turned to leave but was stopped by the sight of a familiar profile across the room. Miss Mayfield stood at the counter. "Surely, these are worth more," she said to the clerk and pointed to a set of sparkling jewels laying out on a handkerchief before her.

Blackbourne straightened. Were those jewels her own—or ones stolen by McBride? Could Amelia's bracelet be amongst them? He turned to Rundell and whispered in his ear. The jeweler's call for the clerk caught Miss Mayfield's attention too, and she turned around. Her large jade eyes flashed at Blackbourne, and he bowed.

Soon, the sale was made to everyone's satisfaction. Miss Mayfield took possession of the cash, and Blackbourne took possession of her jewels. He quickly searched through the handkerchief. Damn. No ruby and sapphire bracelet nor amber pendant. Had she sold it to another jeweler? Did she have more jewelry to sell? Was she going to another shop now?

Blackbourne shoved the jewels into his pocket. "Tomorrow, Rundell," he said and dashed out the door. He just caught sight of Miss Mayfield entering a hackney coach before jumping into his own. He followed close behind and was disappointed when her cab pulled to a stop in front of the Cork Street Hotel instead of another jewelry shop. Blackbourne stopped half a block away and turned around in time to see Miss Mayfield ascend the hotel steps. A man came out of the hotel and started to talk to her, and Blackbourne shot forward.

What the devil was McBride doing here?

McBride and Miss Mayfield exchanged a few words, and Blackbourne had a sudden desire for a pair of keen ears. It did not matter. He did not need to hear their conversation to prove what he had suspected all along. Miss Mayfield was the Adam Tiler.

Blackbourne sat back against his leather seat, his heart heavy. How the deuce was he to tell Worthy, and worse, how could he avoid telling Emma?

"COME ALONG, EMMA." Kat stood in the salon doorway. "The carriage is waiting."

What? Emma jumped off the settee. It couldn't be time. Lady Heyer's invitation had said two o'clock. She glanced at the ormolu clock. "It's only eleven!" she said. "A full three hours before her ladyship's carriage is to be here."

"Not her carriage, but ours. I thought it such a beautiful day that we should go for a ride."

"You're roasting." Emma laughed. "I'm not going anywhere."

"Don't worry, we'll be back in plenty of time for you to change for tea."

"I'm already dressed." In one of her favorites. A bright pink muslin with green cupped sleeves and a wide yellow sash.

"Are you?" She raised a brow. "Well, no matter. The ride will take your mind off the wait," she said. "And mine off your deplorable sense of color."

Her aunt's insult aside, a ride might do her good. Emma had done nothing but fidget since receiving the invitation that morning. "Fine, I'll go," she said. "But I'll never forgive you if I miss Lady Heyer's carriage."

The pair walked outside, and Emma found Elizabeth seated in the carriage. Warning bells shot off in her head. "What is going on, Kat?" Emma hissed. "Where are we going?"

"I told you, my dear." Kat settled into the carriage. "For a ride."

Emma sat back against the seat, certain there was more to it. Her suspicions were proven true when a short time later the carriage pulled into the cobbled courtyard of Blossoms Inn.

"Why have we stopped?" Emma shouted over the sound of carriages pulling into the courtyard, disembarking passengers, and vendors hawking their wares.

"I thought you might like some marzipan." Kat stepped from the carriage.

"We've come to an inn, Aunt." Emma followed Elizabeth out. "Not a sweet shop."

"It's upstairs," she said. "In the room I've rented."

"Why have you—never mind." Emma started to cough. "This dust is horrible. I hope it doesn't ruin my dress."

"A little gray dusting would be an improvement," Kat said. "Come along."

The group made their way upstairs to a warmly appointed room and found a table already spread out with ham and scones, tiny pies, jars of fruit, and a box of marzipan.

"Enjoy a scone, Elizabeth," Kat said, then dragged Emma to the window, and whispered, "The coach from Brighton should be here any minute."

A sinking feeling settled in Emma's stomach. "And?" she asked warily.

"I think Lord Hefton might enjoy a little refreshment."

She knew it. Why the deuce had she ever told Kat about his trip? "You cannot mean to accost the poor man in public."

"Oh, not I, but you."

"Are you mad?" Emma yelped and garnered a curious look from Elizabeth. "I'll do no such thing."

"You must, Emma. I'm desperate. That horrid soldier has been granted a furlough and, even now, is on his way to London."

"I don't give a fig if he's standing at your doorstep this very minute."

"Perish the thought, but if he is, then you really must invite his lordship," she said. "It might be my last chance."

Why even continue the conversation. Kat would not take her home, and it was too far to walk. "I daresay I don't have a choice," Emma spat out, "since you've good as kidnapped us."

"Kidnapped? Now you're the one funning," she said.

"You better hope he approaches us, Kat, because I won't embarrass him or myself by waving him down like someone out of Bedlam. And if I miss Lady Heyer's carriage no amount of marzipan will make up for it." She returned to the table, picked up a piece, and nibbled it as she paced.

Four pieces later, a shout came from the yard, followed by the *clop-clop-clop* of horses' hooves pounding the cobblestones. Kat pushed Emma to the door. "Enjoy your meal Elizabeth," she said. "We won't be but a moment."

They rushed outside only to wait impatiently amid a flurry of stable boys, barking dogs, and passengers retrieving their luggage. The last passenger, a small, faded woman, climbed down from the top of the coach. Emma squinted. Could it be? "I don't believe it, Kat," she said. "But I think—"

"Oh, my goodness, there he is," Kat interrupted in a breathless tone, and Emma whirled around. Lord Hefton emerged out of the dust, and Emma smiled, then frowned. Why must he have worn that unflattering waistcoat today?

He stopped in apparent surprise. "Miss Bryson," he said. "How delightful to see you."

"Thank you, my lord," she said. "I'm relieved you think so."

"Why wouldn't I be?" he laughed.

"No reason." She turned to Kat. "You remember my aunt, Mrs. Carstead?"

"I do." He bowed. "Mrs. Carstead."

"My lord." She bowed her head at him and elbowed Emma.

"Oww," Emma said. "I mean, you look tired, my lord," she said. "Would you like to join us for some refreshments upstairs?" She pointed to the window and noticed Elizabeth peeking through the curtain.

"That's very kind of you, but I..." He glanced at the window, and his lips spread into a smile. "You know, I believe I could use a little refreshment."

A moment later, Kat rushed first through the door, "Elizabeth, my dear," she said. "You must meet..." She stopped and glanced around the room. "Elizabeth?"

"Is something the matter, Mrs. Carstead?" Hefton asked.

"She's gone."

"Who's gone?"

"My daughter." She twirled around. "I can't imagine what's happened to her."

"Perhaps she's been kidnapped again," Emma said in a joking fashion.

Her aunt said, "Do you think so?"

"No! I was merely attempting a joke."

"One should never joke about an heiress worth 30,000 pounds," she snapped but immediately realized her tactlessness. "I beg your pardon, my lord. But it does make her the target of unscrupulous characters."

"And unscrupulous suitors, I'd imagine," he said with a slight smile.

"Exactly right, my lord," she said. "Thank you."

Emma rolled her eyes, "She's been kidnapped by neither. She probably caught sight of a friend and went to speak with them."

"She must be rather spirited," Hefton said. "I imagine whoever she's with would have their hands full."

"He would, my lord," Emma said.

"Are we speaking of Miss Carstead's future husband or the kidnapper, Miss Bryson?" he joked.

Emma laughed and said, "Elizabeth would consider them one and the same."

"He'd get a pretty penny in return for his trouble," Kat retorted.

"Now, are you speaking of the kidnapper or the husband, madam?" Hefton smiled.

"Either, though naturally I'd prefer a husband."

A moment of awkward silence passed until Emma broke it by saying, "Please do sit, Lord Hefton, and have something to eat."

"In truth, I do have business I must attend to," he said, telling Emma he had come up just to meet Elizabeth, and his next remark proved it. "Perhaps I could meet the elusive Miss Carstead another time."

Kat perked up. "Oh, you may, my lord, at any time. Night or day."

"I shall try to make it a time convenient for all of us," he said with a smile and bowed his way out the door. Kat immediately began to wail.

"Calm down, Kat," Emma said. "Did he not just say he wants to meet her?"

"He should've met her today." She strode around the room, clenching her fists. "When I get my hands on that girl…"

"You can hardly punish her for not falling for your schemes." Emma picked up a piece of marzipan. "She'll be back soon."

"Oh, no, she'll make us wait for hours."

"Why?" Emma choked on the marzipan.

"It'll be her little way of punishing me."

Emma went to the window. "She'd better turn back around this instant."

If she didn't—and caused Emma to miss her tea with Lady Heyer—she'd punish Elizabeth herself.

AN HOUR LATER, EMMA entered the Heyer townhouse. She divested herself of her pelisse and gloves and hurried to the salon door. She stopped on the threshold and ran her hands down her second favorite day dress—a yellow muslin with ruche sleeves that Jo claimed washed Emma out—and composed herself.

Satisfied she got her heart rate down to a gallop, Emma entered the salon.

"Miss Bryson, please sit down," Lady Heyer said, and her smile turned to a small frown. "I do hope the trip wasn't too uncomfortable." She waved a hand at her own cheek, and Emma wondered just how red hers still were.

"Not at all," she said. "It's just that I had luncheon with my aunt and was a bit more rushed than I would've preferred."

Though that wasn't the only reason for her flushed appearance. She smiled at Blackbourne standing by the couch, his hands behind his back.

Lady Heyer poured a cup of tea. "Where did you go for luncheon?"

"Blossoms Inn." Emma took her cup.

"A rather busy place from what I understand," Blackbourne said and joined her on the couch.

"And quite dusty," she said, still annoyed she had to change her dress. "The strangest thing happened whilst I was there. I'm certain I saw a lady from my village arriving on the mail coach. Mrs. McBride."

"Mr. McBride's mother?" Blackbourne spoke sharply, and Emma nodded. "Did he mention his mother was coming to London?"

"Not a word," she said, surprised by his interest. "He did say she meant to visit a sister in Brighton, and the coach did come from there."

"Brighton?" Lady Heyer said. "I wonder you didn't see my cousin, Lord Hefton. He was supposed to come back today."

Blast. She had hoped to avoid sharing that information. She cleared her throat. "As a matter of fact, Lady Heyer, I did see him."

"How did he look?" She leaned forward eagerly. "Did you speak to him?"

"Yes, for a few moments. He seemed in excellent spirits."

"I'm glad he's come back," she said. "Miss Mayfield asked me to thank him for his kindness in taking her home the other night. She's leaving London soon—"

"Why?" Emma interrupted. "Is she not happy?"

"She's returning to the stage," Lady Heyer said. "If you'll excuse me. I need to check on something."

"I'm sorry for Lord Worthington," Emma said. "I think he was quite taken with Miss Mayfield."

"It was a bad match."

"Surely not because she's an actress?"

"No," he said. "Because she's a thief."

"I know you think so, my lord, but do you have any proof?"

"I have enough." He sipped his tea.

"It'd take *more* than enough for me to believe someone I loved and trusted was one."

"Would it?" He put down his cup.

"Yes, of course," Emma said, surprised by the question. "What proof do you have?"

"Their proximity at the Royal Saloon the night your necklace was stolen, for one. It tells me they were working together."

"Many people were by the pianoforte."

"The yellow gloves in the boardinghouse room, then."

"Every lady in London has a pair of those. My aunt has two," Emma said. "And even you said they might've been stolen."

"They were stolen. By her," he said bluntly. "But the most damning proof of her guilt, in my estimation was the Champagne, a Veuve Clicquot, 1812."

Emma recalled his doing the "parlor trick" at her request. "Is that vintage so unique?"

"Acquiring it certainly is. I know only one other person besides myself who has a bottle. Worthy," he said. "I'm certain he gave it to her."

This was more difficult to dismiss, but Emma's instincts still told her Miss Mayfield was innocent. She drummed her fingers on the arm rest. "Hold on." She sat forward. "The marzipan. I offered her a piece at the theater, but she refused. She said she'd almost died the one time she had eaten it. The almonds, you see. Her doctor warned her never to eat them again."

"She needn't have eaten any."

"Then why were there two plates with crumbs?"

That seemed to give him pause, and Emma waited for his counterargument, but Lady Heyer's entrance postponed it. She handed Blackbourne a velvet box and sat, a small grin betraying her excitement to Emma.

Blackbourne opened the box and withdrew a long, gold chain with a ruby dangling from it. "I've something for you, Emma," he said and handed it to her.

Emma held the necklace up, entranced by the deep red glow of the ruby. "It's beautiful," she said.

"There's an inscription."

She turned the jewel over. "*Impulsive*," she read, and a glow as deep as the ruby spread through her.

"I hope you'll wear it when you sing for Queen Charlotte," Blackbourne said, and they stared at each other briefly. "I will, my lord, thank you." Emma pulled her gaze from his and turned to Lady Heyer. "I must thank you too, my lady," she said. "None of this would've happened if you hadn't first hired me."

"As to that, you must thank Lady Wallingford."

Blackbourne's brows shot up. "What do you mean?"

"She recommended Miss Bryson to me after hearing her sing at Vauxhall," she said. "She even arranged everything with your manager."

"With Malcolm?" Emma said. "But... they aren't even acquainted."

"They must've met somehow. Perhaps at the New Castle Theater. She takes her uncle there quite often."

"Or at the Mayfield birthday party," Blackbourne said slowly.

Where or how Malcolm met her did not concern Emma—only his silence on the subject. Why had he not told her? But even that could not suppress her joy. "I suppose it doesn't matter where they met," Emma said. "I'm only grateful they did."

CHAPTER 17

Blackbourne pulled to a stop in front of the Wallingford townhouse, jumped from the carriage, and strode to the door. He could not get across Town soon enough. He had questions and only Francesca had the answers.

Did she know McBride?

Was she the Adam Tiler?

Had he been betrayed, again?

He banged on the door and waited. He banged again. A moment later, a young maid opened the door. "Yes, sir?" she said in a timid voice, and it struck Blackbourne he'd not seen an actual footman in weeks.

"Tell Lady Wallingford Lord Blackbourne wishes to see her."

The maid curtsied and scurried away, and Blackbourne entered the salon. He glanced around, and a sudden realization dawned. He knew the answers to his questions and even the *why*.

A noise came from the doorway, and Blackbourne turned. Francesca stood in the frame. "I never expected to see you here again, my lord. At least not this soon." Francesca sauntered to him. "Have you changed your mind about the jewelers? Or perhaps something else?" She brushed a hand down his arm.

"No," he said bluntly, and her eyes sparked in anger, and her hand dropped.

"I see." She turned away and walked to the couch. "Then why the surprise visit?"

"Because of a surprise visit I made somewhere else recently," he said. "A boardinghouse."

"You in a boardinghouse?" she laughed. "I'm sorry but that strikes me as quite funny."

"Not as funny as the items I found in it. Yellow calfskin gloves. Plates of marzipan. Glasses half filled with champagne. A rather expensive champagne. Veuve Clicquot 1812."

"You sound as if you've had a bit too much champagne, my love."

"I've found I prefer brandy," he said. "Coming into the salon, it suddenly struck me. The missing Waterford vase. The carpet out being 'cleaned.' A different servant every month." He looked at her. "You're in trouble, Francesca. Please tell me if I'm right. There can be no other explanation for you stealing from your friends."

Her silence told Blackbourne everything he needed to know, and he swore under his breath. To think he had accused Miss Mayfield and nearly lost his cousin's friendship. "Why?"

"For the money of course."

"What happened to Lord Wallingford's money? To your dowry?"

"The dowry my husband lost at the gaming tables?" she said in a bitter tone. "I suppose I must give him some credit. He went through his own money before losing mine."

"Why not tell me of your misfortune? I would've helped."

"I fully expected you to—before the end of the Season."

Blackbourne winced. The wager. His mother had been right. "What of Lady Tisdale? Could she not have helped?"

"Oh, I asked, and she responded by sending a fan. A beautiful Italian fan she thought would help me capture a gentleman. I didn't use it as she intended. I sold it. I thought I had already captured one."

Blackbourne ran his hand through hair and sat. He needed a minute to absorb everything. To try to understand how she—a lady of her stature—had become a thief.

"How did it happen, Francesca?" he finally said. "How did you become involved with McBride?"

"It's rather boring really," she said. "I was at the jeweler's, trying to sell a few jewels I'd managed to hide from my husband. I'd just come to the most agreeable terms with Mr. Rundell when Mr. McBride came in. He placed a beautiful diamond and sapphire bracelet on the counter. I recognized its value and its owner."

"Amelia's bracelet."

She nodded. "He thought he could get more from a jeweler than pawning it, except Rundell refused to buy it. I don't think he trusted him, and that's when it occurred to me that Mr. McBride and I could be of service to each other."

"He steals the jewelry, and you sell it," he said. "You're the Adam Tiler."

"You do love your cant."

Blackbourne ignored her derisive remark, walked to the hearth, and drummed his fingers on the mantel. McBride did not just hide jewelry in the plant. There were other stolen items too. Candlesticks. Silk neckcloths. Pistols. She was the red-haired lady outside the Mayfield library. He turned to her. "You helped McBride break into houses."

She shrugged. "Until then, he'd been charming maids to let him in. Or climbing through windows. It seemed much easier for me to let him in through a back garden door or the servants' entrance. Sometimes even the front door. He could dress like a gentleman when he chose to. No one ever questioned us."

"And then you invited your friends to his theater," he said, and she nodded. "In effect, you brought the ladies of the *ton*—and their jewels—to him."

"Except the nights they followed the Earl of Blackbourne somewhere else."

Blackbourne almost snorted at the irony. She lured them to parties to steal their jewels while he lured them to keep them from getting stolen. He shook his head in wonder at her audacity. "Taking your uncle was simply a ruse. You never were at his sickbed."

"Oh, he was abed often enough. Just not enough to keep him from Miss Portnoy's clutches," she snarled in response. "Methinks my time would've been better spent with you."

Time spent keeping him from Emma, she meant.

"McBride didn't steal your necklace," he said. "You gave it to him at the Mayfield party."

"He begged me for it. Miss Bryson's chain had broken, and she was in hysterics. She threatened not to sing and to return to Scotland. He was desperate, and I didn't think you'd notice it missing. Or care."

Blackbourne winced. A deserved barb.

"Why steal it back?"

"After your notice in the *Hue and Cry*, we realized you were looking for it. It was only a matter of time before you recognized it. You were in Miss Bryson's company so often."

He did not allow her snarky remark to nettle him but continued the interrogation. "Did you help McBride sell everything recently?"

She nodded.

"Why?"

"To buy passage to Australia."

"What the devil for?"

"It's all quite sweet. He made a promise to his mother too," she said. "To reunite her with her husband. He was transported years ago for stealing."

"McBride kept the family trade alive, I see," Blackbourne snorted. And it explained McBride's being at the Cork Street Hotel and Emma's seeing Mrs. McBride at Blossom's Inn. "When does he plan to leave?"

"He only needs enough money for one more ticket," she said, and an icy panic tightened around Blackbourne's chest. "For Miss Bryson?"

"You think he convinced her to come to London because of a silly deathbed promise?" She smirked. "One can't get on a ship to Botany Bay in Edinburgh."

"What makes him think she'd even go with him?"

"He hoped to convince her to sing elsewhere. He'd then pretend to make all the arrangements, and she'd believe him. She trusts him. The ship would be halfway to Botany Bay before she suspected a thing."

"Why now? Why not wait until the Season is over?" He paced in agitation. "Surely, there's more jewelry to be stolen? More people to swindle?"

"Maybe he thinks his love plans to marry someone else," she said. "Someone who recently had a large ruby engraved."

Blackbourne stopped. "Night Jasmine," he said. "You were in Rundell and Bridge."

"Selling another piece of jewelry to keep the creditors at bay." She picked at the fringe of a pillow. "So, it is an engagement present."

"No, but..."

"But it might as well be." She threw the pillow aside and stood. "Well, what now, my lord?" she said. "We know Miss Bryson's future but what of mine? Am I to be arrested? Led straight to the gallows?"

Her question stayed him. If he had Francesca arrested, McBride's involvement would become known, and Emma would be devastated. If he didn't do something soon, McBride might trick Emma onto the boat, devastating *him*.

"I must think a bit," he said. "I'll return tomorrow and tell you what I plan to do." He strode to the door and stopped. After all this—could he trust her to keep quiet? "Don't speak to McBride," he said. "I'd hate for things to go worse for you." He heard her swear softly, and he walked out.

BLACKBOURNE TURNED from the window, and the heat of the morning sun coming through the windowpane and joined his valet by the wardrobe. "Tell me, Simms," he said. "What has upset you more, my request to wear the floral waistcoat on the drive to Brighton or my plan to capture McBride?"

"If I must choose, I'd say the latter." Simms handed Blackbourne a linen shirt. "Dare I remind you of the last time you implemented a scheme concerning Miss Bryson? I suggested you shoot yourself in the foot. This one is even riskier."

"Au contraire. It's the perfect plan." He donned the shirt and tucked it into his buckskins. "I need only write Claimore a note later, telling him I gave Miss Bryson the ruby and hinting the Blackbourne sapphires were soon to follow."

"Thus, letting everyone in London know of the ruby in his article."

"More specifically, McBride."

"That Mr. Claimore will do exactly as you say, I've no doubt." Simms tugged a gray- and green-striped waistcoat over Blackbourne's shoulders. "It's the others involved in your ruse I don't trust."

"Lady Wallingford will do her part too. She does not want others to know of her treachery." It was galling enough he knew. "No, she'll use the paste ruby I'll give her today to convince McBride to switch it out for the real one."

"To steal from Miss Bryson." He handed Blackbourne his neckcloth.

"It's not like he hasn't done so before," he said cynically and knotted the cloth around his throat. "Afterwards, they'll meet at Rundell and Bridge, where I'll be waiting to confront McBride."

"And all of this is to what end, my lord?"

"To give McBride an option. Leave on the Mary Ann, without Emma, or hang."

"Have you taken into consideration Miss Bryson's reaction to finding out her cousin is a thief?"

"I hope she doesn't ever find out."

"Wouldn't it be easier to simply offer for her before you leave for Brighton?" Simms held open a topcoat and helped Blackbourne shrug into it. "That will ensure she won't get on the boat."

"She'd always wonder if I married her to win a wager."

"It's not like you to be so rash, my lord," Simms said with a shake of his head. "Don't you trust Miss Bryson?"

"Of course, I do. It's McBride I don't," he said. "Besides, an engagement wouldn't stop him. If he's determined to take her to Australia, he'd do so even if we were married."

"The Season is almost over."

"But the Mary Ann leaves in a few days."

"Too many things can go amiss, my lord."

"I appreciate your concern, Simms." Blackbourne smiled at the valet. "And if I had any doubts, I'd be asking you for my pistols now instead of my hat."

Simms sighed and handed him the beaver. "If you've truly decided to lose your wager instead of marrying Miss Bryson now, then I suppose I could lose mine too."

"How so?"

"By acceding to your wish to wear that abominable floral waistcoat to impress Miss Bryson. It all but ensures I shan't get any more points."

"You're a romantic, Simms."

"Hardly, sir." He held open the door. "I fully expect you to pay my debt."

AN HOUR LATER, BLACKBOURNE parked in front of the Wallingford townhouse. His anger at Francesca's betrayal had abated and might even disappear fully *if* she agreed to his plan. He did not have to wait for her entrance. He found her sitting on the settee in her salon.

"What is it to be, my lord?" she asked. "Banishment? Shunning? The Tower?"

"A bargain," Blackbourne said, and her eyebrows shot up in surprise.

"I'm listening," she said in a wary tone, and he laid out the scheme.

"You'll give him the paste ruby and tell him it's an exact match to the one I gave Emma. Emphasize its worth. That it's more than enough to start over in Australia."

"He'll wonder how I got it."

"Tell him the truth. From me."

"Ah, I'm to tell him you gave it to me as a gift. A paste ruby. I suppose it's true. Your love has been false."

"I never claimed otherwise," he said bluntly.

"True." Defeat marred her features briefly, then she rallied, and stood. "It appears you've thought it all through except McBride's reaction. Are you certain he will steal it?"

"He stole her prized pendant."

"That bloody pendant. It's what caused all this fuss in the first place." She walked around. "I suppose it could work. Malcolm does still trust me. He knows I want—wanted—nothing more than to see Miss Bryson gone. I might be able to convince him this would get us both what we want."

"Will you do it?"

"Do I have a choice?" she said with a short cynical laugh. "You've the power to ruin me. I wouldn't even have to be arrested. All it would take is one cutting word from the Earl of Blackbourne and I'd be shunned forever."

"You'll be well compensated," he said. "With a generous note from my bank."

She lifted a brow. "A limited carte blanche?"

"You'll be more than comfortable," he said. "I suggest you take a trip somewhere till things settle down."

"Trying to get rid of me, darling?"

"I'm merely suggesting a visit with your mother might be in order."

"Oh, no. I shan't go to Italy," she said. "Do you know how tiresome it is to live in the shade of a renowned beauty?"

"Another's shadow can only cover you as much as you let it, Francesca. You can step out from under it whenever you choose."

He'd come out from Clarissa's shadow.

"I suppose I've no right to ask, but is there a chance of getting the note soon?" she said. "Moneylenders can be so tiresome."

"You'll have it this afternoon."

Blackbourne pulled the paste ruby from his pocket, handed it to her, bowed, and left the townhouse, his anger now fully diminished. Part one was settled, now on to part two. He expected this to go even smoother. He mounted his horse and set it in motion toward Fleet Street and Mr. Stanley Claimore.

CHAPTER 18

E mma needed little prodding to do as Kat requested. She happily picked up the paper and read Claimore's article aloud for the third time, "*A large ruby recently bestowed on a Scottish nightingale makes one wonder if a set of matrimonial jewels won't be next. The only mystery being when. Before or after the end of the Season?*"

"Matrimonial jewels," she said and let out a girlish giggle that Kat joined her in. "As if that beautiful ruby wasn't proof enough of Blackbourne's intentions," she said. "Mr. Claimore must mention those too."

Emma knew they would be given after the Season, so why had Blackbourne told Claimore it was a mystery?

"I'm sure *I* don't need more proof," Emma said in a leading way, hoping Kat might know the answer.

"Yes, but others do need it," she said with a delighted laugh. "No doubt his lordship is tired of all those mamas throwing their daughters at his head."

"Of course!" Emma almost laughed in relief. She had forgotten why he made the wager in the first place. "He's sending them a message."

"You both have the most extraordinary ways of communicating." Kat opened the window. "I can't believe your fan is still there, dangling from my tree. Methinks you may safely remove it."

"No, I shan't remove it quite yet. Not until I remove to Blackbourne Manor." She giggled again.

"Then I shall keep my message from him, too, for a while." Kat pulled a card from her gown pocket and waved it. "Such a conventional way to invite one to Vauxhall Garden."

"Quite dull," Emma agreed, with a laugh.

"Do you think Lord Hefton will be there?"

"If he thinks Elizabeth will be there, I'm certain he'll be there too. He made it quite obvious he wished to make her acquaintance."

"She won't be there though. She has plans to visit a friend this evening."

"I thought she wasn't allowed to go anywhere after her disappearance."

"What can I say? Her father dotes on her, and he gave his permission."

"You don't seem upset."

"Why should I be?" She leaned forward and whispered, "My daughter thinks she's got away again, but I plan to invite Lord Hefton to visit us, here, tomorrow."

"Why are you whispering, Kat?" Emma whispered back.

"She hasn't left for her friend's house, yet." She tilted her head at the closed door. "And the child does get her keen ears from me."

"And her scheming ways." Emma smirked. "Still, I'm rather surprised you're risking it. I thought her officer was on his way to London."

"There is a God. I've been granted a reprieve. He's been delayed. A sick relative. He won't be coming to London as soon as I feared." She straightened. "No, no, my dear Emma," she now shouted at the door. "We shall miss Elizabeth, but I'm certain we will still have a most pleasant time at Vauxhall tonight."

EMMA HAD NOT EVEN WAITED for the applause to die down before she bowed to the crowd and rushed out of the gazebo. Blackbourne waited for her at the bottom of the steps, and he crooked his arm and led her to where her aunt and uncle and Lady Heyer waited.

Kat quickly pulled her aside. "I've yet to see Lord Hefton," she said under her breath. "Do you think he's had an accident?"

Emma laughed. "He probably had other plans."

"You were certain he'd come if he thought Elizabeth was here." She gave Emma an accusing look.

"He might not know."

"I knew I should've sent him a note somehow. How can I invite him to luncheon if he isn't here?"

"Where is Worthy, Blackbourne?" Lady Heyer said. "I thought he was to join us?"

"I'm afraid he's left Town."

"Oh, dear. Has Jayne's leaving upset him that much?"

"Yes, and that is why he's gone after her," he said. "At my suggestion."

Emma grinned at him, thrilled he had changed his mind, and wondered if she had played a small role in it. "That should make Miss Mayfield happy," she said. "She did say she found the chase more amusing."

"Which do you prefer, Emma?" he asked. "The chase or the capture?"

"Getting caught, my lord. Getting caught," she said, and Blackbourne smiled.

"And what of your friend, Mr. McBride?" Lady Heyer asked. "I thought he'd come, too, this being your last night at Vauxhall."

"He's busy. The theater..." Emma said, but in truth, they had not spoken since she told him she would marry Blackbourne. This hurt and bewildered her but did not stop her defense of him. "It's not like he hasn't heard me sing many times."

"Naturally, he has," Blackbourne said, his words replete with understanding, and Emma was grateful. He knew her affection for Malcolm.

"And in a few days, you are to sing for Queen Charlotte," Lady Heyer said. "What shall you wear?"

"Something without marzipan bits on it, I hope." Lady Blackbourne appeared out of the darkness. "Though that white muslin you wore to the theater would work splendidly if you replaced those ghastly yellow and pink ribbons with ones more suitable to your complexion." She studied Emma critically. "With a purple ribbon or even a dark rose."

"I quite agree, your ladyship," Kat said boldly, and Emma suppressed a gasp. The two had not been formally introduced. Lady Blackbourne let Kat know her displeasure by giving her a slow, measured stare, as if she were inspecting a mushroom—an encroaching mushroom.

Emma said quickly, "Might I introduce you to my Aunt Carstead, Lady Blackbourne?"

"Your ladyship." Kat gave Lady Blackbourne a deeper curtsy than required to make up for her faux pas.

"I'm happy to see you've agreed on what dress I should wear, but I'm afraid you'll be disappointed," Emma said. "I've a liking for the orange satin."

The appalled faces Kat and Lady Blackbourne turned on Emma were so alike it made her think they had been carried in the womb together.

"The gorgeous one you wore to the masquerade?" Blackbourne asked, and the twins now showed signs of apoplexy.

"The very one." Emma smiled.

"I'm afraid I must agree with my mother," Lady Heyer said. "You must wear the white muslin."

"Thank you, Amelia," Lady Blackbourne said. "Finally, someone with a bit of taste."

"Oh, don't misunderstand me, I love the orange gown, but I think it might outshine her ruby."

"You mean clash with the ruby, my dear," Lady Blackbourne said. "Though, I must admit Aunt Mary's ruby would look lovely against your complexion, Miss Bryson. Do you mean to wear the paste one?"

Paste? Emma recalled the conversation from the Royal Saloon, and she turned to Blackbourne. "The ruby you gave me belonged to your favorite aunt?" Emma asked, touched.

He smiled and simply said, "Yes." Then he turned to his mother. "And no, she isn't wearing it. It doesn't have the engraving."

"What's this about an engraving?" Lord Hefton appeared out of nowhere and smiled at the company. The particulars of the conversation were supplied, and Hefton turned to Emma. "You simply must wear the orange dress," he said.

Kat shocked everyone by saying, "Have you gone mad?"

"Not at all, Mrs. Carstead," he said with a laugh. "And I'm delighted to see you too."

"I beg your pardon, of course. Thank you."

"Are you here with your family?" He swept a glance behind her.

"Just Mr. Carstead and myself, I'm afraid."

His happy demeanor dissipated a bit. "I see."

"My daughter, Elizabeth, is visiting a school friend, though she should be back home tomorrow. Perhaps you could join us for luncheon?"

"I'd be delighted," he said, and Emma could not be any more delighted on how the evening had ended.

CHAPTER 19

E mma only just perceived the hand shaking her shoulder and her aunt saying, "Emma, Emma, wake up."

Emma rolled over. "What time is it?"

"Nearly eleven."

She sat up and rubbed her eyes. She had stayed out so late. It had been almost dawn when she had returned home and had barely made it into her bed before falling asleep. She hadn't even looked at her ruby.

"A letter has just been delivered for you." Kat sat on the side of the bed, and Emma pushed herself up. "Who is it from?"

"I don't recognize the wax stamp."

"Must not be from anyone of importance, then," Emma said with a laugh and turned the letter over in her hand. Had Malcolm arranged another place for her to sing before everything else had happened? Emma broke the seal, read the letter, and stared in astonishment at her aunt. "I must still be asleep as I'm dreaming. Lady Wallingford wants to meet—"

"Lady Wallingford?" Kat interrupted. "You mustn't go."

"You don't even know why she wants to meet..."

"It doesn't matter. She's read the article. She knows Blackbourne is lost forever," she said. "I don't trust her. She might turn violent."

Emma giggled. "I doubt she'll try to plant a facer on me at Rundell and Bridge."

"What do you mean?"

"She wrote to say there's a stone there that she knows I'd be happy to see returned." Emma put the letter down. "Don't you see? It must be my amber pendant."

"Neither Mr. Rundell nor Mr. Bridge would give your tiny amber stone a second glance," Kat said with a scoff. "How does she even know about it?"

"I told her at the ball, though I am surprised she remembered. I'm also grateful." Emma jumped from the bed. "I must hurry. Might I borrow the carriage?"

"I'm sorry, Emma, but Mr. Carstead has taken it to Middleton today. He won't be back for hours."

"Oh, well, could you send a footman for a hackney then?" She pulled a day dress from the wardrobe.

"I will, but I must tell you Emma that I don't have a good feeling about this at all."

Emma laughed her aunt's concern off. What was there to fear? Everything was going so well. The invitation from Prince George. The ruby from Blackbourne. Lady Wallingford finding her pendant. Emma's heart overflowed with happiness.

It was all too good to be true.

BLACKBOURNE PARKED his curricle a block from Rundell and Bridge, jumped down, and proceeded to the shop, a happy jaunt in his step. Really, Simms worried far too much. Everything was going exactly as planned. And so much sooner than he'd hoped! He pushed open the door, and the bell above it clanged out his entrance.

Francesca and Rundell stood by the middle counter, and Blackbourne joined them. "You arranged everything quickly," he said to her.

"Things do seem to fall into place for you, don't they?" Francesca said with a cold stare.

Blackbourne ignored her. He was minutes from having McBride in his grasp, and that was what mattered. He turned to Rundell. "Is everything ready?"

"It is my lord," the jeweler said and led Blackbourne to the backroom, closing the curtain behind them.

A few moments later, the bell clanged, and footsteps patted across the floor. Blackbourne tensed. Was it McBride?

"Finally, you've come," Francesca said, and Blackbourne relaxed. "Were you able to switch it?"

"With ease," McBride said. "Conveniently, almost the whole family was at Vauxhall last night. Not that they needed to be. Even if Emma had been in the room, I still could have got it," he said, and Blackbourne bristled at his arrogant tone.

"Are you certain? Mr. Rundell would know immediately if it's a paste."

"Let us test his skill, then, shall we?"

The counter bell rang, and Rundell looked at Blackbourne, who nodded. The jeweler pushed aside the curtain and stepped into the shop. "Might I help you?"

"I'm afraid I'm forced to sell another one of my jewels, Mr. Rundell," she said and managed to inject such sadness, regret, and even embarrassment into her tone that Blackbourne wondered she had never thought to join Miss Mayfield on the stage.

"How unfortunate, my lady," Rundell said. "Might I have a look at it?"

"This is an exquisite ruby. What's this? An engraving?"

Blackbourne sucked in a breath.

"A silly little word. I was almost embarrassed to even show it to you," she said, and McBride snorted.

"The engraving itself is excellent," Rundell said with a hint of pride, and Blackbourne swallowed a chuckle. "One can easily read the word. *Impulsive.*"

A second later, Blackbourne pulled aside the curtain and stepped into the shop. "Good morning, McBride."

Blank astonishment covered McBride's features before fear took over, and he glanced at the door. A clerk moved in front of it.

"Do you have somewhere to be?" Blackbourne moved from behind the counter.

"Not at all," McBride said coolly. "I'm merely surprised to see you here, and hiding in the back room, no less. Have you gone into the gem trade?"

"I'm in a trade of sorts." He smiled. "The business of catching thieves."

"A thieftaker?" He laughed. "Not quite as lucrative, I don't believe."

"But much more satisfying. Especially when one catches the thief in the very act."

McBride put a hand to his chest in feigned disbelief. "Dear me, you think I'm a thief—"

"Don't bother with the pretense, McBride." Blackbourne held up a hand. "Unlike Lady Wallingford, you'd never make it on the stage. No, you're the thief in question. You stole my sister's bracelet and Miss Bryson's pendant." He pointed to the jewel on the counter. "And last night you stole her ruby."

To Blackbourne's surprise he did not try to deny it. "You've no proof."

"Don't I?" Blackbourne picked up the ruby. "An engraving was made on the original, but not its paste. The same paste I gave to Lady Wallingford. To give to you."

McBride paled, and he flashed Francesca a look of hatred before he turned back to Blackbourne. "Emma will never believe you."

"I don't wish for her to find out," Blackbourne said. "I merely wish you to leave. I understand you've planned a trip to Australia..."

A string of oaths accompanied McBride's second look of hatred at Francesca.

"Leave on that ship," Blackbourne interrupted him, "without Miss Bryson, and nothing will happen to you."

McBride clenched his fists, and a tic appeared on his jaw. "If I refuse?"

"You'll hang."

The word hung in the air between them—as if to emphasize the severity of the situation—before McBride bowed and walked to the door.

"One more thing, McBride."

He stopped.

"I expect to see Miss Bryson's amber pendant around her throat soon," he said. "Very soon."

McBride left, and Blackbourne exhaled. He hadn't even known he had been holding his breath. "Now, Francesca, let us finish our business."

"We shall my lord," she said, her gaze not on Blackbourne but on the street. "But you've other business to attend to, first, I'm afraid."

"I can't imagine what," he said.

The door swung open, and Emma entered. Blackbourne's heart stopped. Francesca turned a sly vindictive smile toward him. "I imagine you do now," she said.

With great bitterness, he remembered his distrust of women.

EMMA NEARLY DROPPED her reticule in surprise. A pleasant surprise but still a surprise. "What are you doing here, my lord?"

"I could ask the same of you."

"I'm here to sell my jewelry, naturally," she joked, surprised he didn't smile in return. Confused, she continued, "I received a note this morning from Lady Wallingford saying she'd found my amber pendant." Emma smiled at her. "I'd no idea you even remembered my description of it, my lady."

"I'm sorry, Miss Bryson, I should've been a bit clearer in my writing," Lady Wallingford said. "It isn't your pendant I discovered here, but the lovely ruby Blackbourne gave you."

"I'm sorry?"

She pointed to the gem lying on the counter. "Is that not it?"

"It might be..." Emma peered closer at the ruby but did not pick it up. "But I'm certain my ruby is safe under my... in my uncle's lockbox."

"Your ruby or its paste?"

"You know about the paste?"

"Of course, I do," she said, as if everyone knew about it. "Dear Blackbourne gave it to me, and except for a rather endearing engraving, I'd wager our rubies look exactly alike."

Wrath turned Blackbourne's face dark. "Francesca—"

"What darling? I thought you liked wagers. Especially ones involving jewelry. Remember the one you made about my necklace and bracelet when this whole farce began?" She sighed and shook her head. "One should never trust a man, Miss Bryson."

"You'll regret this," Blackbourne ground out.

"Perhaps." She shrugged. "But if I do, it shall be in a nice little house in Calais." With one last cold stare at Blackbourne, she walked out.

Bewildered, Emma turned to him. "Is what she said true?"

"About Calais? Yes."

"Philip?"

"Yes, all of it, but you must allow me to explain."

Emma's chest tightened. She wanted an explanation but was suddenly afraid of what it'd be.

"This is your ruby, Emma." Blackbourne held it out to her, but she refused to take it. "McBride stole it last night and put the paste one in its place."

"Impossible. Malcolm is no thief."

"It's true. He also stole your pendant."

"*My* pendant?" she said and laughed—it was what that ridiculous claim deserved.

"He was the pianoforte player. It was his gnarled fingers that caused the weak notes. He played your favorite song to lure you to him. It was crowded, remember, and he could only steal it from you if he could find you."

This was getting even more ridiculous. "Now you've gone mad," she said. "Why would he steal a necklace he gave me?"

"It belonged to Lady Wallingford. One I'd given her. She gave it to him at the Mayfield party to help calm you down," he said. "He stole it back because they both feared I'd recognize it. They didn't know I already had."

"Why in heaven's name should that bother them?"

"Because they knew I'd discover they were the thieves I'd been chasing all Season."

A horrible thought struck. "Is that why you've been helping me find my necklace? To entrap Malcolm?"

"No. I didn't even know he was the thief when I met you."

"But you realized it later and never said a word to me?" Her words seemed to rile him, as he shot back, "Would you have believed me?"

"You never gave me the chance." She glared. "You didn't trust me."

Blackbourne's cheeks darkened at the sudden accusation. "You made it clear enough of your affection for McBride. I was trying to spare you pain."

"You could've found a way to tell me. If any of it was even true."

"I wanted to, but after he sold everything in the plant, I knew I was running out of time. He planned to go live with his father in Australia."

"You're mad. He disappeared years ago."

"He didn't disappear. He was transported for stealing," he said. "McBride planned to join him there with his mother—and you."

"Me?"

"It's the reason he convinced you to come to London. He means to take you with him."

"How, pray tell, would he do that?"

"Cajole, sweet-talk you, trick you, if need be."

"He'd never..."

"He could, and would, quite easily," Blackbourne said harshly. "He has your trust."

Emma's mind whirled, and her breath started coming in gasps. She placed her hands on the counter to steady herself.

"Some water, please, Mr. Rundell," Blackbourne said in a panic, and the jeweler hurried away.

He returned with the glass and pressed it upon Emma. She drank, slowly, refusing to look at Blackbourne. She needed to think. It was all too much to take in let alone believe.

"I wouldn't believe it either," he said simply. "I never thought anyone I loved would betray me, but I learned differently."

"No one's betrayed me except you," she said and put the glass down and stumbled to the door.

"Emma, please, listen to me," Blackbourne said, and she stopped. "Open your ears—your very keen ears—and listen to what I'm saying. You must believe me." His hands fell to his side. "You've closed them."

She had closed them—to his explanations. To his excuses. To him.

She ran out the door.

Half an hour later, she dashed up to her bedchamber. Her mind fixated on one thing. Her ruby. It would be exactly where she put it. She headed straight to her bed and stopped. What if it was the paste ruby?

What if Blackbourne had told the truth?

A knock sounded. "My dear, is something the matter?" Kat's worried voice came from the hallway.

"Not now, Kat."

"Was it not your pendant after all?"

"No. It was not the pendant."

"I'm sorry. Might I come in?"

"No. Not now," she snapped out. "I'm sorry, Kat, but I need to be alone."

Alone to check under her pillow.

Alone to find an engraved ruby.

Alone to weep if she did not.

BLACKBOURNE STUMBLED out of his carriage, headed straight to his study, and grabbed his bottle of brandy. He poured an inch into the Ravenscroft tumbler, tossed it down, and refilled it. He sank into his leather chair and stared blankly ahead. Emma had rejected him. Had ignored his explanations, his pleading. She left. Fled. Refused to hear him out. Just ran after McBride. The man she really loved. He finished the brandy in one gulp.

He'd always suspected it and now he knew it. She was no different from any other woman. No different from Clarissa. Was history repeating itself? Had Emma pretended to love him to get money to run off with McBride?

Bitterness and despair ate through his stomach like acid, and he had a sudden urge to throw the tumbler against the wall. He cocked back his arm, and the glass was suddenly taken from his hand.

"What the devil?" He whipped his head around. "What the blazes are you doing in here, Simms?"

"Stopping you from doing something you might regret."

"I won't regret it," he said with a snort. "Hell, it might even make me feel better."

"For the moment, yes. But come tomorrow you'll feel differently."

"I highly doubt it." Blackbourne covered his eyes with one hand and waved Simms away with the other. "Fine. Take it out of my sight then. I should never have taken it out of its cabinet. Have a maid put it back."

"I don't think we need to lock it away quite yet, my lord," he said. "But I will bring you another glass."

Simms disappeared for a moment, returned, and poured some brandy into the glass. "Here you are, sir." He slid it across the desk.

"Thank you."

"Might I get you anything else?"

"Yes," he said. "Solitude, Simms. I wish to be alone."

Alone with his thoughts.

Alone with his misery.

Alone to get blazing drunk.

"Very good, sir." The valet quietly pulled the door closed.

CHAPTER 20

C lothed in depression—and yesterday's clothes—Emma walked to the bedchamber window and pushed aside the curtain. The sun had come up, after all. She leaned her forehead against the pane and stared down into the back garden. A sliver of yellow caught her eye. Her lovely Italian fan. It no longer hung on the branch but lay muddied on the garden floor. She hadn't removed it. Malcolm had when he had climbed the tree, snuck into her bedchamber, and stole her ruby.

She dropped the curtain and turned from the window, searching for the paste. It still lay in the corner where she had thrown it. A dull ache filled the space in her chest where her heart should be. Blackbourne had told the truth, but she still needed to hear it from Malcolm.

Emma straightened her wrinkled clothes and smoothed her hair. She left no note, not even for Jo. As if Blackbourne would chase after her now.

Half an hour later, she stepped from the hackney, paid the jarvey, and told him not to wait. She had no idea how long she would be.

Emma walked through the narrow streets, and almost every step evoked a memory. The ragged children. The vermin. The drunk man bloodied by crockery. She approached the boardinghouse and other, more intimate memories surfaced. Blackbourne removing his neckcloth to clean a window—and then his coat because he trusted her enough to break into a room. The wild dash down the alley when they thought they had been caught.

Their kiss.

Why had she been so stupid? No matter that deep down she knew her decision to ignore Blackbourne's explanations had been impulsive and emotional—like dashing from the altar—it was still the wrong one. And there was no fixing it. She gathered herself together and entered the building.

She heard the spinet before she made it to the door. Heard "'Tis the Last Rose of Summer" playing. Heard the weakness in some notes.

She knocked. It opened, and Malcolm stood before her.

"Blackbourne was right, but I didn't believe him." Emma gasped. "You're the pianoforte player."

Malcolm leaned nonchalantly against the door frame. "Your keen ears."

No denial. Not even any anger. He seemed almost proud. "How could you, Malcolm? How could you steal my pendant?"

"You already know how," he said. "Or have forgotten the cant his lordship taught you?"

Emma blinked, amazed at his flippancy and the casual nature of his confession. "Then everything he told me is true."

"Is this your mother's spinet? Did I see her get off the coach at Blossoms Inn? Did you promise to take her to Australia?" Emma rattled off the questions and wondered if Malcolm could understand them—she was speaking so fast—but he nodded.

"Then your father is alive," she said. "But you led everyone to believe—"

"I led no one," he retorted. "I merely refused to refute the rumors that others spread. That he was dead. That he abandoned his family for another woman." He turned away. "It was easier than telling people the truth."

The catch in his voice caused Emma to respond with less rancor. "That he had been transported for stealing."

"His business was failing, you see, and he got a bit... desperate. An Englishman had swindled him and in retaliation he took a bolt of expensive lawn cloth—"

"You mean stole."

"I mean took. He owed my father money, so he took the cloth as payment, intending to use it to make neckcloths and sell them."

That's why he always wore that faded neckcloth. His father made it.

"Instead, he was arrested and banished to Botany Bay."

"I'm sorry for your father, but there was no reason for you to follow him into a life of crime. You had a respectable job."

"One that paid a pittance, and I needed more than that to keep my promise," he said. "And to pay for three tickets."

Emma stared in amazement. "Oh, my God. Blackbourne was right about that too. That is why you convinced me to come to London. Why you arranged everything."

"You'd never have done it, otherwise. Even with your deathbed promise."

Emma colored. "You're right Malcolm, but I was still in mourning, in shock. Given time, I would've done something."

"Like marry the first man who asked? You almost did, didn't you? And then you jilted him."

"You did something much worse," she retorted. "You broke into my bedchamber and stole my ruby."

"You broke into my bedchamber with Blackbourne."

Emma froze.

Malcolm nodded, slowly. "You just confirmed it. I wasn't certain. I didn't recognize the pelisse on the woman running down the alley." He shook his head. "Miss Emma Cameron alone in a boardinghouse room with a gentleman. What would your good father think?"

"He'd understand my reasons." She regained her composure. "I only came here to find my pendant. You lived here, Malcolm, on purpose, to sell stolen jewelry."

"I didn't sell everything." He reached into his pocket, pulled out her amber pendant, and handed it to her. "I was always going to give it back to you."

Emma turned the deep dark gold gem over in her hand. It represented more than just her parents' love now. She put it into her reticule and cinched the bag tight. She would not lose it again. "Goodbye Malcolm."

"You're leaving?" he asked, bewildered. "Just like that?"

"What can I say? I have a lot to do. Gowns to have ironed... a trunk to pack..." she said. "A promise to fulfill." She walked to the door.

"You'll regret your rejection of me," he said behind her.

"I'll regret a few things from the farce," she said. "But that won't be one of them." She walked out.

BLEARY-EYED, AND REEKING of yesterday's sweat, Blackbourne grabbed the bottle of brandy from the desk. and refilled his glass for what—the fifth time that morning? It did not seem to matter. No amount of brandy could fill the dull empty hollowness in his stomach.

"Lady Blackbourne to see you, my lord."

"Thank you, Dobbs."

The footman stepped aside, and Lady Blackbourne swept into the library. "I see you've finally hired another footman to help Thomas. Now I shan't be charging into your home unannounced."

"It doesn't bother me, Mother."

"It might bother the future Lady Blackbourne." She removed her gloves. "I am, of course, speaking of Miss Bryson."

"You know there'll be no marriage between us," Blackbourne growled out. "And I'm certain you know why."

"All I know is there's been a misunderstanding." She sat on the settee.

"Trust me," Blackbourne said with a snort. "I didn't misunderstand *her* at all."

"What would you call it?"

"Betrayal."

"Rather melodramatic," she said. "Have you spoken to her today?"

"Why? She wouldn't listen to my explanations yesterday. Why would she do so now?" he said. "She thought McBride the victim. She believed him over me."

She chose McBride over him. The dull ache grabbed at his guts, and he took another swallow.

"Dear me. I see Clarissa has damaged you far more than I had thought."

"She had nothing to do with it."

"She has everything to do with it. Her betrayal has wounded you. It's made you cynical."

"This isn't the same situation unless you're telling me Emma loves McBride."

"Naturally she loves him," she said, plunging a knife into Blackbourne's heart. "He's been a part of her life forever, but she isn't in love with him."

The knife retracted, a little.

"Certainly not enough to ever marry the creature."

The knife slipped out, completely.

"Miss Bryson reacted so impulsively because she thought you betrayed her, and you reacted to her reaction because of what Clarissa did to you." She gave her son a stern look. "You both could've behaved differently."

"Does it matter? It's too late. The damage is already done."

"Oh, dear, surrender then! Take off your neckcloth and wave it over your head like a white flag. Heaven knows it's bright enough." His mother pulled a face and pretended to shade her eyes, compelling Blackbourne to laugh.

"You can repair the damage, my dear," she said. "I'm certain Miss Bryson wants it fixed as much as you."

Still not convinced but willing to be, he put down his glass and said, "Do you think so?"

"Trust me. In matters of love, I've never been wrong," she said. "I married your father, didn't I? No woman was ever happier."

He raised a brow. "Did he know he was marrying an inveterate flirt?"

"Of course, he did. I could flirt with impunity because he trusted me. I never gave him any reason not to. Admit it. Deep down, you trust in Miss Bryson's affection for you. You know she's nothing at all like your wife."

In truth, he did. He also knew, deep down, that what his mother said was true. Emma had reacted impulsively to what she considered an unsubstantiated attack on a friend—and he had reacted defensively because of Clarissa. He regretted his reaction immensely. Perhaps Emma did too.

"You can speak to Miss Bryson tomorrow night and sort this whole mess out," she said. "I'm speaking of Brighton, of course."

"Do you think it wise we still go?" he said. "Perhaps I should give Emma more time."

"Time for what? To wallow in her own regret? No. Besides, Prinny has invited us, so we can't refuse." She stood and tugged on her gloves. "I, for one, plan to be as flirtatious as possible. Quite shameless. One will never know I'm about to become a grandmama."

Blackbourne laughed. "Amelia's told you?"

"Hardly. She's waiting for Heyer's return. For some odd reason she thinks I won't handle the news well."

"A more fashionable grandmama has never been known."

"Certainly, more fashionable than the future Lady Blackbourne," she said with a smile, and Blackbourne didn't take the stab amiss.

The future Lady Blackbourne.

His wife.

Perhaps it wasn't too late.

"As to that, I shan't have you advising her in any way," he said. "She'll wear what she pleases."

"And dress you as she pleases, I suppose?" Lady Blackbourne said. "Did you hear that, Simms?" She yelled out the door. "I fear we're stuck with floral waistcoats."

"I doubt we'll have to bear it long, my lady." Simms entered the library. "Someone I know once said that styles change. What is fashionable one Season might not be in the next. One could say the same for one's season in life. If they change together, then all shall be well."

"Very insightful, Simms," Blackbourne teased his valet in a gracious tone.

"Thank you but I've not come to share my wisdom but to deliver a note." Simms held out a card, and Blackbourne took it and read through it.

"What's the matter, Philip?" his mother asked. "You've turned positively crimson."

"It seems I've been challenged to a duel," he said. "By McBride."

"He has the gall to challenge you? Is he mad?" she asked. "You may safely ignore him. He isn't even a gentleman. No one would find it amiss."

"It's not that easy I'm afraid." He paced. "He's threatened to expose an incident from Emma's past."

"Which one? Her jilt or her clandestine visits to the boardinghouse with you?"

"I'm not surprised you know," he said. "But I would like to keep it from others."

"Even if the whole world knew, it'd not matter. Once she's Lady Blackbourne." She sorted that distasteful matter with a wave. "Take her to the country for a few months after the wedding, and all will be forgotten."

"I doubt she'd agree to it. She won't marry me just to save her reputation."

"You have no choice, then," she said. "When has this scoundrel demanded your presence?"

"Tomorrow morning."

"A full day's notice. How kind of him."

"It isn't kindness. The Mary Ann is leaving tomorrow evening."

He would ruin Emma and flee. The coward.

"Where is this debacle to be held?"

"Islington Field."

"Your pair of Mantons will be primed and ready, sir," Simms said. "I'll bring them to the field myself."

"That's very kind of you, Simms."

"It isn't kindness, my lord." The valet straightened. "I have laundry to hang."

CHAPTER 21

Emma waited patiently as the footman loaded her trunk onto the back of the Carstead carriage. After her return from the boardinghouse—and a small argument—her aunt had agreed to take Emma to Blossoms Inn to catch the mail coach the next morning.

"I'm sorry Mr. Carstead could not spare the carriage to take you," Kat said.

Emma smiled. Kat was sorry she could not go and take Elizabeth with her. "I'm just happy you and Elizabeth are awake to see me off."

"To think if you'd taken my advice and written Lord Blackbourne a note, explaining things," Kat said, "he might be taking you instead."

"We've discussed this, Kat."

As much as she would love for him to take her, Emma was not as confident he'd react well to a note. What if he didn't? What if he rejected her explanation? Her apology? Her pride could not take it.

"At least let me have the gardener hang your fan back up," she joked, and Emma smiled at the effort. Suddenly, the sound of horses' hooves captured Emma's attention, and she turned her gaze to the street.

"What's the matter?"

"I think a carriage is coming and quickly."

A moment later, a barouche turned the corner and pulled to a stop in front of the townhouse.

"Lady Heyer, what are you doing here at this hour?" Emma asked, and a glimmer of hope lit in her breast. Had Blackbourne decided to send her a message in a more conventional way, through his sister?

"I have news," Lady Heyer said, leaning out of her carriage.

"Yes," Emma said eagerly.

"I'm afraid it's not good."

"I only wish I'd seen the note from my mother sooner, but my indisposition had made me tired, so..."

"I beg your pardon, Lady Heyer," Emma interrupted. "But I must hear the news."

"Mr. McBride has challenged Blackbourne to a duel, and he's accepted."

"What?" Emma's heart dropped.

"It's true. He's threatened to reveal your jilt and your visits to the boardinghouse with Blackbourne."

"Visits to a boardinghouse?" Kat gave Elizabeth a sideways glance then and said in a low voice to Emma, "What on earth does she mean?"

"It means Malcolm has decided to ruin me," Emma said grimly. He had said she would regret her rejection of him. "He can threaten all he wants. It doesn't matter. I'll be back in Scotland soon enough and all this will be a bad memory. There's no reason for Blackbourne to duel him."

"I'm afraid my brother isn't as cavalier about your reputation as you are."

Emma recalled all the times he kept her reputation intact—when he could have easily let her go to ruin. But to duel over it? After she had rejected him? Insanity. "He's mad. I must put a stop to it. I'll write him a note, telling him it doesn't matter."

"I knew you should've written him earlier." Kat said in a sing-song voice.

"I'm afraid there isn't time," Lady Heyer said. "The duel is this morning. Almost this very minute."

"Now?" Emma said. "Where?"

"Islington Field."

"Where laundry is hung?"

"Yes." Kat's voice trembled. "And duels to the death."

Duels to the death. Emma's mind could not fathom it. "Hold on," she said. "Malcolm doesn't even own any dueling pis—" Oh, heavens. He did own a pair. A stolen pair. "We must go there now."

"You'll miss your coach to Brighton."

Miss her chance to sing for the Queen. Would it matter if Blackbourne was shot? If he was dead? Everything went still inside. "It's not the least important."

"We'll take my coach," Lady Heyer said.

"No, no, we must take mine," Kat said. "It's a beautiful barouche that seats four quite comfortably with a matched set of grays—"

"There's no time, Kat, let's just get in the blasted thing," Emma said, and a moment of pandemonium ensued until all ladies were settled in the carriage.

"Please hurry, Thomas," Emma said to the driver.

"You needn't worry, Miss Bryson," Lady Heyer said. "My brother is an excellent shot. He's never lost a duel."

"Yes, very nimble fingers," Kat said.

"It isn't his lordship's skill I doubt," Emma said. "It's Malcolm. He'll do anything to beat Blackbourne. Even cheat."

BLACKBOURNE SQUINTED through the slight hazy mist covering most of Islington Field. A hackney stopped on the far edge, and his stomach tightened. Was McBride finally here?

"It's Hamilton," Lord Hefton said, and Blackbourne relaxed. "Hopefully, he won't be needed."

He would not. Blackbourne had no intention of killing McBride, or even wounding him. Emma would never forgive him.

"You've still time to back out," Hefton said. "He isn't a gentleman."

"That's precisely why I must do it. A gentleman would never threaten to ruin a lady's life."

"It seems you shall get your wish," Hefton said.

Another hackney stopped beside Hamilton, and Blackbourne grimaced. He had nourished a tiny hope McBride would come to his senses, but that was not to be. The coxcomb was crossing the field with another man, presumably his second.

"Mr. Jenkins, I presume?" Blackbourne said, and that man nodded curtly. It all made sense. McBride's "partner" was the same man who'd shared the carriage with Francesca. "I suppose it's only fitting he's your second."

"Is Lord Hefton to be your second or your valet?" McBride turned to Simms and said in a derisive tone, "Had you nothing better to do than accompany your master to a duel?"

"It was no bother." Simms glared. "I had laundry to hang." He pointed across the field to where a maid was hanging linen, and McBride snorted. "The infamous snow-white neckcloths," he said and scrutinized Blackbourne. "Though I see you're wearing a darker one today."

"Obviously, you've no familiarity with the Code of Honor," Blackbourne said. "A bright neckcloth may cause distraction to the opponent."

"It certainly could blind a lady to a gentleman's faults."

"For my part, I've found ladies are more influenced by a neckcloth's knot," Blackbourne said lazily, and Simms nodded. "Steenkirk, my lord," he said. "Abominable."

"Just so, Simms." Blackbourne stared at McBride through half-closed lids. "When one ties one's knot so loosely, one shouldn't be surprised when a lady slips through it."

"Are we finished?" McBride snarled.

"We certainly are," Hefton intervened amiably. "We've set the marks at fourteen paces. I hope that's amenable, Mr. McBride?"

He nodded. "Let's get this over with, shall we?"

"Why, you sound as if you have someplace to be, McBride," Blackbourne said, garnering a sneer for his trouble.

Hefton and Jenkins checked the guns, handed them to the duelers, and joined Hamilton at the edge of the field.

Blackbourne saluted McBride and strode to his mark. Turning sideways, he waited for his opponent to get in position. Simms stood between them and lifted a handkerchief. Without pulling back the hammer, Blackbourne lifted his pistol and waited.

A split second later, a familiar piercing voice shattered the dawn, and Blackbourne's heart lurched. Emma. He whirled toward the voice, and suddenly a searing hot poker jabbed into his shoulder. He dropped his gun and fell to the ground.

EMMA TORE ACROSS THE field, her heart in her throat. Was Blackbourne dead? Had Malcolm killed him? She fell to her knees beside him. Blood seeped through his shirt near his shoulder, and without hesitation, Emma tore his neckcloth from his throat and pressed it against the wound.

"Simms will not be happy, you know," Blackbourne joked.

"He'll be less happy if you bleed to death."

"There's no chance of that." He squeezed her hand. "Thanks to you."

"Me?"

"Your voice distracted McBride," he said, and a smile crept across his face. "Higher and farther than a carrier pigeon."

To her surprise, Emma laughed. "Not a word about it to Claimore."

"I doubt he's here," Blackbourne said. "But I'm happy you are."

Emma avoided looking at him by lifting the neckcloth. The blood flow had stopped as had the wild beating of her heart. It had slowed to a manageable roar.

"He's the thief, Emma."

"I know," she said quietly. "I went to the boardinghouse."

"Alone, I suppose."

"I wanted him to tell me he wasn't... to explain... but... He was playing the spinet when I got there. I listened outside the door for a moment, and I knew..."

"Your keen ears."

"Yes. I might hear exceptionally well, but I don't always listen."

"No one wants to hear bad things about people they love. I should've told you of my suspicions," he said plainly. "I should've trusted you."

"I would never have believed you. Obviously." Their eyes locked, hers pleading and his full of love and understanding. Emma exhaled. For the first time in days, she could breathe.

A moment later, they were interrupted by an older bull-like gentleman dragging Malcolm forward, and Emma averted her gaze. No matter what, she did not want to witness his humiliation and pain.

"This scoundrel," the stranger said, shaking Malcolm. "Threatening to use a lady's past against her. Dishonorable. Very dishonorable."

"And you are, sir?" Blackbourne asked.

"John Townsend, my lord." He made a quick nod. "At your service."

"The King's former bodyguard?"

"Yes, and a dear friend of mine," Lady Blackbourne appeared from behind him. "Oh, don't give me that look, Blackbourne. It's completely innocent. At least on my part. I sent a note to him this morning saying there might be some trouble, and he was kind enough to come."

"Anything for you, my lady," he said in a brusque tone. "Well, my lord, what should I do with him?"

"Let him go." Blackbourne's tone was firm.

Townsend's dark brows came together. "I'd not recommend it, my lord."

"He'll leave England on the Mary Ann this evening, or he'll hang. It's his choice." Blackbourne turned to Emma. "It's your choice whether he leaves alone."

"Alone." The word came out quiet but firm, and Malcolm swore behind her.

"I'll see he's aboard that ship," Townsend said. "And that he doesn't get off it."

"Thank you, John," Lady Blackbourne said, and the man blushed profusely before he collected himself and dragged Malcolm away.

Once that drama had passed, the others who had been huddled together in different groups rushed over. Their sudden encroachment did not bother Emma. Unlike the mob that had gawked at her after her fall at Lady Heyer's soiree, this was a crowd of friends, and the obvious concern they had for her and Blackbourne showed in their demeanor.

Hamilton and Simms approached and helped Blackbourne to sit up against a tree. The doctor quickly checked the wound and declared it "a mere scratch" and "easily repairable."

"Unlike the neckcloth," Simms said repressively. "It's ruined."

"No worse than Emma's carriage dress," Kat declared. "It'll be difficult to get the grass stains out of it."

"No matter." Emma shrugged. "I shan't be traveling to Brighton today."

Blackbourne sat forward. "You missed your chance to sing for the Queen."

Emma experienced a moment of disappointment but shook it off. She might have missed her chance, but Malcolm had missed his shot, and that was infinitely more important.

"Fustian," Lady Blackbourne said, joining the group. "I'll speak to Prinny about your singing and to my laundress about those stains. Or you could have the dress remade into a curtain."

"That color would fare better against a window than her complexion." Kat joined the disparagement of Emma's gown, and both ladies nodded in agreement.

"You do have the damnedest luck, Blackbourne," Lord Hefton said. "Even when you lose a duel, you win."

"I can't argue with you there," Blackbourne grinned.

Hefton turned to Kat and Elizabeth.

"Mrs. Carstead, always a pleasure," he said, his gaze on Elizabeth.

"Thank you, your lordship. Might I introduce you to my daughter." Kat gave Elizabeth a little push forward. "Miss Elizabeth Carstead."

Lord Hefton bowed. "A pleasure."

"Sacre bleu!" Elizabeth dropped her gloves.

"That's some sort of greeting, anyway," he said. "At last." He smiled at Elizabeth, her face white, and her mouth open. She turned on her heel and fled.

"Elizabeth Mary Carstead," Kat yelled at her fleeing daughter. "You come back here, right this minute." She turned to Lord Hefton, her cheeks as red as wine. "I apologize for my daughter's appalling manners, my lord."

Hefton gazed after Elizabeth for a moment. "About luncheon, Mrs. Carstead," he said. "Would sometime this week be convenient?"

"Any day, my lord, any day," Kat said, and Emma hoped he did so soon, as she knew Kat would hold Elizabeth prisoner until he did.

"Well, Blackbourne," Lady Blackbourne said. "You've lost a duel, and with Prinny in Brighton, you've lost your bet. Perhaps, you and

Miss Bryson should discuss the ramifications of such a disaster," she said. "Come along, Amelia, Hefty."

Emma kept her eyes on the group as they walked away, suddenly too nervous to look at Blackbourne.

"It seems we've traded places, Emma," he said, and his quiet tone compelled her to look at him. "When we first met, it was you lying on the floor, clothing askew, surrounded by a crowd."

"You've an excellent memory, my lord. Too excellent," she said with an exaggerated grimace, and he laughed.

"It's easy to remember such an extraordinary encounter. Do you think there was any significance to it?"

"Heaven only knows," she said, acquiescing to his obsession about fate a little. "I certainly had no intention of falling at your feet that night."

"You might've fallen first," he said. "But I believe I fell the hardest."

"You could never have fallen harder in love than I," Emma declared impulsively.

For a moment, Blackbourne's eyes reflected her sentiment before he said, "I beg your pardon, but I meant the ground." He patted it. "It's quite hard."

"Would you like me to help you up?"

"Yes." He stuck out his good hand, but Emma folded her arms and grinned. "I'm waiting."

"Is that how it is?" he laughed and leaned back against the tree. His gaze rove over her.

"I've always found your choice in clothing quite charming and insist you send my compliments to your maid."

"Jo will quite hate that, you know."

"I expect she'll hate what I do next, even more." Blackbourne clasped Emma's hand and pulled her down to him. "My dear Emma," he said, "I would like very much to make you an offer..."

CHAPTER 22
Epilogue

E mma slipped into the music room at Brighton Pavilion, closed the door, and slumped against it. Lady Blackbourne had kept her promise to speak to Prince George, and now it was time for Emma to keep hers.

In less than half an hour, she would sing for the Queen.

Butterflies rampaged her stomach, and she took in a deep breath. Why the sudden nerves? The agitation? It was too ridiculous! Her voice was as pristine as ever, and it would sound even better in this room, with its domed ceiling and convex cones and plush carpet.

Emma walked to the pianoforte. A dozen music sheets lay scattered on its polished cypress top. She picked through them. The Prince certainly had an eclectic taste in songs—everything from the religious to the ribald. One song caught her eye, "'Tis the Last Rose of Summer," and a river of images flooded her mind. Stolen amber pendants and ruby necklaces, rickety boardinghouses and hidden plants, childhood playmates and betrayal.

Emma shook her head and straightened. That was all in her past, and she would not allow it to ruin her future. The door opened, and she turned around. Her future stood on the threshold.

"Good evening, my lord," she said and grinned.

"I thought you'd disappeared in here." Blackbourne strode across the carpet, a pair of wine glasses in one hand and a bottle in the other. "Preparing?"

"Perhaps."

297

"I can't imagine why," he said. "I'm certain your voice will be as magnificent as ever."

She preened but admitted, "I'm a wee bit afraid my nerves will get the better of me."

"Don't worry. I've brought just the thing to help." He placed the glasses on the pianoforte and held up the bottle. "Though it might make you a bit... giddy."

"Champagne?"

"Not just any Champagne, my sweet, but *Veuve Clicquot—*"

"I'm sorry?" she blurted. Surprised and even a bit hurt he would bring that particular vintage. "I mean really, my lord, of all the wines you could've brought," she chided him.

"Trust me, I brought the right one. This is Veuve Clicquot 1811, not 1812," he said with emphasis, and Emma relaxed. "And it's claimed this wine is the best that's ever been produced."

"What's so unique about it?"

"That year a comet was seen flying over the grape fields of France."

"Surely, you don't believe the mere sighting of a comet had some magical effect on the grapes?" she asked with a scoff.

"Or it had some physical effect on the soil as yet undiscovered by scientists," he said with a laugh. "Let us not get bogged down by the details but merely see if the claims are true."

"You've not tasted it?" she said. "You, a connoisseur?"

"I've been saving it for something special." He smiled and filled the glasses.

"Our wedding isn't for a few weeks," she said.

"I expect fulfilling a deathbed promise is just as singular." He handed Emma a glass and held up his own. "Shall we?"

"I really should wait until after I've sung," she said but took a sip anyway, and another, and another. Within a moment, her bones had warmed, and her joints loosened, and she grinned dizzily at Blackbourne.

"I believe you're now experiencing the effects of the, uh, comet."

Emma giggled, wanting to argue it was not the bubbly liquid that caused her giddiness, but him. The delightful silver at his temples... his perpetually amused eyes... his nearness...

"How are your nerves?"

"Quite settled, thanks to you," she murmured. "If only there was something I could do in return..." She peeped at him coyly over her wine glass.

"In truth, there is something I want..." He took Emma's glass and placed it next to his on the pianoforte. "Something I've desired for quite a while now..."

His eyes lingered on her mouth, and Emma's pulse raced. It had been too long since their lips had met. Still, she demurred, "What if someone comes in?"

"Then I expect they'll enjoy a good show."

"I beg your pardon?" Emma squawked. "I'd never allow anyone to view our lovemaking."

"Heavens, no! I meant your pianoforte performance," he said in a teasing manner. "You must admit I've waited a long time to hear it."

"You'll be waiting even longer," Emma said with feigned indifference. "I've a concert to perform." She started to stomp away, but Blackbourne caught her and pulled her against his chest. Tight against his chest, and Emma gasped.

"Tell me," he said. "What must one do to enjoy a... private recital?"

Pull one tighter against a chest, but Emma would not quibble. She threw her arms around his neck, lifted her face to his, and to her delight, he took it from there.

Blackbourne ravaged her lips, her throat, her face. Bone-melting heat surged through Emma like lava, and she worried her orange satin gown would burst into flame.

Too soon, Blackbourne pulled away, his eyes smoky and half shut, and his brilliant neckcloth crushed.

"Well, my lord," she said breathlessly. "I hope you enjoyed your little concerto." She brushed a tendril of hair from her cheek. She certainly had.

"I don't believe I've ever enjoyed one more."

"No?" She ran a finger down his topcoat. "Perhaps an encore is in order."

"If only," he said, then sighed. "Unfortunately, we must return to the salon. The Queen should arrive any moment."

"Perhaps she'll be late," Emma said. "A wheel might fall off her carriage, or a horse throw a shoe..." He laughed and propelled her out the door. A moment later, the pair entered the salon and joined Lady Blackbourne and Lady Heyer.

"I told you I'd find her," Blackbourne said.

"Where?" Lady Blackbourne eyed Emma's gown. "Tumbling about on some floor?"

"I've not fallen for weeks," Emma said, indignant.

"Your gown says differently, my dear. It's all askew."

Emma glanced down. It was askew. Delightfully so. She straightened it.

"You obviously joined in the acrobatics, Blackbourne," his mother said and pointed at his neckcloth. "Simms would be appalled."

A commotion at the door stopped Blackbourne's response, and the group turned. A footman announced the arrival of Prince George and his mother, the Queen. They entered, and after the usual salutations accorded Their Majesties were dispensed with, Prince George said, "Shall we remove to the music room? Her Majesty is quite eager to hear Miss Bryson." He smiled at Emma, and her heart pounded. It was happening.

The guests all made their way to the music room. Prince George escorted his mother to the front row, and after she had sat, he turned to his guests. "Please, everyone, be seated," he said and smiled at Blackbourne's mother. "My dear Lady Blackbourne," he said. "Might you join me?"

"One can hardly disobey a prince," she said coyly, and Blackbourne shook his head in laughter.

"Good luck, Miss Bryson," Lady Heyer whispered, and Emma inhaled. She did not need luck. She strode to the front of the room and turned to face the crowd and... froze.

The gapes and stares of the crowd rattled Emma, and for a split second, she thought she would fall. She gripped her amber pendant and sought out Blackbourne. He smiled and nodded in encouragement, and her composure returned. Emma Bryson released her pendant, smiled at the shrunken but dignified Queen, and sang.

Brilliantly.

Miss Carstead Drops Her Guard

MONEY IS THE ROOT OF all evil. Or was it the love of money? Did it even matter? Elizabeth Anne Carstead only knew it was the love of her money—her dowry of 30,000 pounds—that was the root of all evil in her life. She settled onto the carriage bench and enjoyed a smug smile.

Not for long.

She had done it. Snuck out of her London townhouse and caught the mail coach to Brighton. She had even convinced her old nursemaid to flee with her. The plump loyal servant joined Elizabeth on the bench and patted her hand. "Ye did it, pet."

"Almost, Higgins, almost. All that remains is the trip itself." Elizabeth took off her gloves and held them tight in her lap. "If the mail coach is as punctual as claimed, we shall be at the seaside before the sun rises..."

And a few short hours after that, she would see the person who impelled her desperate flight. Lieutenant Henry Gibson. Her soldier. The man she loved. The man she would marry, and not the so-called gentleman her mother had tried to force upon her all Season.

A gentleman more interested in a good game of cards than a good wife.

A gentleman in love with only one thing—her inheritance.

The gentleman stepping into the carriage right now.

Elizabeth shot forward. Was it him? He sat on the opposite bench, and a shaft of moonlight flashed on his waistcoat. A loud garish floral waistcoat.

"*Sacre bleu*," she blurted. It was him. James Edward Stanhope, the third Earl of Hefton.

"Is something the matter, Miss Cars—"

"Hush," Elizabeth hissed. Had he heard Higgins? She held her breath, but he made no reaction. She exhaled, leaned back, and tried to relax. Her pulse may have slowed, but her mind still raced with one question.

Why the devil was he riding in a mail coach?

She snorted. She knew why. His love of gambling—and lack of skill—had compelled him to give up his carriage. She squinted at him in the semidarkness. But why this particular coach? She snorted again. There could only be one reason.

Her mother. Katherine Cameron Carstead.

Elizabeth pursed her lips. She must've discovered Elizabeth's plans and contrived to get him on the coach too. Too mad? Too far-fetched? Too preposterous an idea? Not for the likes of her scheming and ruthless parent.

Well, Elizabeth had outwitted her many times before, and she would do so again. She need only keep her face hidden and her mouth closed. *Tres facile*. It was dark, and they had no reason to speak at all.

"I beg your pardon, Miss..." he said.

Elizabeth froze.

"I hate to bother you." He spoke a little louder. "But I believe these are yours." He held up a pair of yellow kid gloves in the moonlight. "You must've dropped them."

Elizabeth glanced at her hands. She had dropped them—just as she had when they met on the dueling field the week before. Would that spark his memory? How many ladies dropped their gloves in front of him each time they had met?

"Would you like them back?"

"Yes, thank you." Careful to keep her face hidden, Elizabeth took the gloves and pulled them on. She would *not* drop them again.

Another passenger entered. Hefton slid over, and the moonlight shifted to his long buckskin-covered legs. Legs now shockingly close to Elizabeth. She moved her own away.

"Forgive me, but I'm afraid I've nowhere else to put them," he said, and his voice held a hint of amusement. "I hope they don't bother you."

They did bother her. They bothered her very much. No gentleman had ever dared put his legs—his fine, shapely legs—this near her person. Not even Gibson.

"No, it's fine. They're fine. Your legs are fine. I mean your legs are fine where they are not that you have fine legs. Not that you don't have fine legs but..."

Good heavens—stop babbling. He'll think her an idiot. Worse, spew enough words at him, and he might recognize her voice. Though they had only spoken briefly, she had often been complimented on her melodious and distinctive voice. Why take the chance? "No." She altered her tone. "They don't bother me."

"Good," he said, and Elizabeth just discerned a furrowed brow. Excellent. Her ruse appeared to work.

"Since we've already met..."

"Have we?" she asked, panicked, and forgot to change her voice.

"Yes, well, our legs, anyway." He laughed.

"Oh, of course." She lowered her voice again, and his brow furrowed again.

"That being said, allow me to introduce the rest of me." He bowed his head. "Lord Hefton. At your service."

His introduction took Elizabeth aback. One would think the dropped gloves, her distinctive voice, her name would impel some recollection on his part.

"And you are?"

"I beg your pardon, I'm Miss... Miss Higgins." Her nursemaid gasped, and Elizabeth elbowed her in the ribs.

"Miss Higgins, did you say?" He sounded skeptical.

"Yes."

"A lovely name."

"Oh." He really did not remember her. "Thank you."

The coach lurched forward. "Off we go." He leaned back against the seat. "One boon of riding at night is the possibility of getting some sleep." He settled back against his seat and appeared to shut his eyes.

Elizabeth stared in amazement. Sleep? Here? Now? She bit her lip. It would make the trip go faster and had the added benefit of forestalling any more conversation. She might as well do the same. She lay back against the cool leather seat and shut her eyes—and popped them back open. Really, how could one sleep with the gentleman her mother would force her to marry, snoring just two feet away?

Don't miss out!

Visit the website below and you can sign up to receive emails whenever celeste de sales publishes a new book. There's no charge and no obligation.

https://books2read.com/r/B-A-YWMZ-ZIQRD

Connecting independent readers to independent writers.

About the Author

Semi-retired after a lifetime of fiscal debauchery, celeste de sales finds herself in the rather tenuous position of adding to her retirement by writing light romances.

Read more at celestedesales.com.

Milton Keynes UK
Ingram Content Group UK Ltd.
UKHW021554230824
447235UK00011B/371